S0-CFI-879

ACCLAIM FOR KELLY IRVIN

"Kelly Irvin's *Through the Autumn Air* is a poignant journey of friendship and second chances that will illustrate for readers that God blesses us with a true love for all seasons."

—AMY CLIPSTON, BESTSELLING AUTHOR
OF *ROOM ON THE PORCH SWING*

"Irvin's fun story is simple (like Mary Katherine, who finds 'every day is a blessing and an adventure') but very satisfying."

—PUBLISHERS WEEKLY ON *THROUGH THE AUTUMN AIR*

"With a lovely setting, this is a story of hope in the face of trouble and has an endearing heroine, and other relatable characters that readers will empathize with."

—PARKERSBURG NEWS & SENTINEL
ON *MOUNTAINS OF GRACE*

"Irvin (*Beneath the Summer Sun*) puts a new spin on the age-old problem of bad things happening to good people in this excellent Amish inspirational . . . Fans of both Amish and inspirational Christian fiction will enjoy this heart-pounding tale of the pain of loss and the joys of love."

—PUBLISHERS WEEKLY ON *MOUNTAINS OF GRACE*

"This second entry (after *Upon a Spring Breeze*) in Irvin's seasonal series diverges from the typical Amish coming-of-age tale with its focus on more mature protagonists who acutely feel their sense of loss. Fans of the genre seeking a broader variety of stories may find this new offering from a Carol Award winner more relatable than the usual fare."

—*LIBRARY JOURNAL* ON *BENEATH THE SUMMER SUN*

"Jennie's story will speak to any woman who has dealt with the horror of abuse and the emotional aftermath it carries, as well as readers who have questioned how God can allow such terrible things to happen. The choice Jennie makes to take a chance on love again and to open her heart to God after all she has suffered is brave and hopeful, leaving readers on an uplifting note."

—*RT BOOK REVIEWS*, 4-STAR REVIEW,
ON *BENEATH THE SUMMER SUN*

"Kelly Irvin's *Mountains of Grace* offers a beautiful and emotional journey into the Amish community. Readers will be captivated by a heartwarming tale of forgiveness and finding a renewed faith in God. The story will capture the hearts of those who love the Plain culture and an endearing romance. Once you open this book, you'll be hooked until the last page."

—AMY CLIPSTON, BESTSELLING AUTHOR
OF *ROOM ON THE PORCH SWING*

"A moving and compelling tale about the power of grace and forgiveness that reminds us how we become strongest in our most broken moments."

—*LIBRARY JOURNAL* FOR *UPON A SPRING BREEZE*

"Irvin's novel is an engaging story about despair, postnatal depression, God's grace, and second chances."

—*CBA CHRISTIAN MARKET* FOR *UPON A SPRING BREEZE*

"A warm-hearted novel that is more than a romance, with lovable characters, including two innocent children caught in the red tape of government and two people willing to risk breaking both the Englisch and Amish law to help in whatever way they can. There are subplots that focus on the struggles of undocumented immigrants."

—*RT Book Reviews*, 4-star review
of *The Saddle Maker's Son*

"Irvin has given her audience a continuation of *The Beekeeper's Son* with complicated young characters who must define themselves."

—*RT Book Reviews*, 4-star review of *The Bishop's Son*

"Once I started reading *The Bishop's Son*, it was difficult for me to put it down! This story of struggle, faith, and hope will draw you in to the final page . . . I have read countless stories of Amish men or women doubting their faith. I have never read a storyline quite like this one though. It was narrated with such heart. I was fully invested in Jesse's struggle. No doubt, what Jesse felt is often what modern-day Amish men and women must feel when they are at a crossroads in their faith. The story was brilliantly told and the struggle felt very real."

—*Destination Amish*

"The awesome power of faith and family over personal desire dominates this beautifully woven masterpiece."

—*Publishers Weekly*, STARRED
review of *The Beekeeper's Son*

"Storyteller extraordinaire Kelly Irvin's tale of the Amish of Bee County will intrigue readers, who will want to eavesdrop on the lives of these characters on a regular basis."

—*RT Reviews*, 4 ½ stars review
of *The Beekeeper's Son*

"Something new and delightful in the Amish fiction genre, this story is set in the barren, dusty landscape of Bee County, TX . . . Irvin writes with great insight into the range and depth of human emotion. Her characters are believable and well developed, and her storytelling skills are superb. Recommend to readers who are looking for something a little different in Amish fiction."

—*CBA Retailers + Resources*
for *The Beekeeper's Son*

"*The Beekeeper's Son* is so well crafted. Each character is richly layered. I found myself deeply invested in the lives of both the King and Lantz families. I struggled as they struggled, laughed as they laughed—and even cried as they cried . . . This is one of the best novels I have read in the last six months. It's a refreshing read and worth every penny. *The Beekeeper's Son* is a keeper for your bookshelf!"

—*Destination Amish*

"Kelly Irvin's *The Beekeeper's Son* is a beautiful story of faith, hope, and second chances. Her characters are so real that they feel like old friends. Once you open the book, you won't put it down until you've reached the last page."

—*Amy Clipston*, bestselling author
of *Room on the Porch Swing*

"*The Beekeeper's Son* is a perfect depiction of how God makes all things beautiful in His way. Rich with vivid descriptions and characters you can immediately relate to, Kelly Irvin's book is a must-read for Amish fans."

—RUTH REID, BESTSELLING AUTHOR OF *A MIRACLE OF HOPE*

"Kelly Irvin writes a moving tale that is sure to delight all fans of Amish fiction. Highly recommended."

—KATHLEEN FULLER, AUTHOR OF THE HEARTS OF MIDDLEFIELD AND MIDDLEFIELD FAMILY NOVELS

Through the
Autumn Air

OTHER BOOKS BY KELLY IRVIN

AMISH OF BIG SKY COUNTRY NOVELS

Mountains of Grace

A Long Bridge Home

Peace in the Valley

EVERY AMISH SEASON NOVELS

Upon A Spring Breeze

Beneath the Summer Sun

Through the Autumn Air

With Winter's First Frost

THE AMISH OF BEE COUNTY NOVELS

The Beekeeper's Son

The Bishop's Son

The Saddle Maker's Son

STORIES

A Christmas Visitor included
in *An Amish Winter*

Sweeter than Honey included
in *An Amish Market*

Snow Angels included in *An
Amish Christmas Love*

One Sweet Kiss included in *An Amish Summer*

The Midwife's Dream included
in *An Amish Heirloom*

Mended Hearts included in *An Amish Reunion*

Cakes and Kisses included in *An
Amish Christmas Bakery*

Candlelight Sweethearts included
in *An Amish Picnic*

ROMANTIC SUSPENSE

Tell Her No Lies

Over the Line

Closer Than She Knows
Her Every Move (available February 2021)

THROUGH THE
AUTUMN AIR

AN EVERY AMISH SEASON NOVEL

Kelly Irvin

ZONDERVAN

Through the Autumn Air

Copyright © 2018 by Kelly Irvin

This title is also available as a Zondervan e-book.

Requests for information should be addressed to:
Zondervan, *3900 Sparks Dr. SE, Grand Rapids, Michigan 49546*

ISBN 978-0-310-34814-6 (trade paper)
ISBN 978-0-310-34818-4 (ebook)
ISBN 978-0-310-36017-9 (audio)
ISBN 978-0-310-36216-6 (mass market)

Library of Congress Cataloging-in-Publication Data
CIP data available upon request.

All Scripture quotations, unless otherwise indicated, are taken from
The Holy Bible, *New International Version*®, NIV®. Copyright © 1973,
1978, 1984, 2011 by Biblica, Inc.™ Used by permission. All rights reserved
worldwide. www.zondervan.com. The "NIV" and "New International
Version" are trademarks registered in the United States Patent and
Trademark Office by Biblica, Inc.™

Any internet addresses (websites, blogs, etc.) and telephone numbers in this
book are offered as a resource. They are not intended in any way to be or
imply an endorsement by Zondervan, nor does Zondervan vouch for the
content of these sites and numbers for the life of this book.

All rights reserved. No part of this publication may be reproduced, stored in
a retrieval system, or transmitted in any form or by any means—electronic,
mechanical, photocopy, recording, or any other—except for brief quotations
in printed reviews, without the prior permission of the publisher.

Publisher's Note: This novel is a work of fiction. Names, characters, places,
and incidents are either products of the author's imagination or used
fictitiously. All characters are fictional, and any similarity to people living
or dead is purely coincidental.

Printed in the United States of America

20 21 22 23 24 25 / CWM / 20 19 18 17 16 15 14 13 12 11 10 9 8 7 6 5 4 3 2 1

Dedicated to my mother, Janice Elliott Lyne.
You were a stay-at-home mom before it was called that.
You know how to feed a family of seven with
fifty recipes featuring hamburger, twenty-five
recipes that start with Jell-O, and fifteen recipes
for disguising eggplant. Love always.

Praise be to the God and Father of our Lord Jesus Christ, the Father of compassion and the God of all comfort, who comforts us in all our troubles, so that we can comfort those in any trouble with the comfort we ourselves receive from God. For just as we share abundantly in the sufferings of Christ, so also our comfort abounds through Christ.

2 CORINTHIANS 1:3–5

Now instead, you ought to forgive and comfort him, so that he will not be overwhelmed by excessive sorrow.

2 CORINTHIANS 2:7

Deutsch Vocabulary*

ach: oh
aenti: aunt
bopli, boplin: baby, babies
bruder: brother
daed: father
danki: thank you
dawdy haus: grandparents' house
dochder: daughter
doplisch: clumsy
eck: married couple's corner table at wedding reception
Englisch, Englischer: English or non-Amish
fraa: wife
Gelassenheit: yielding to God's will; forsaking all selfishness
Gmay: church district
Gott: God
groossdaadi: grandpa
groossmammi: grandma
guder mariye: good morning
gut: good
hund: dog
jah: yes
kaffi: coffee

kapp: head covering worn by Amish women
kinner: children
lieb: love
mann: husband
mudder: mother
nee: no
Ordnung: written and unwritten rules in an Amish
    district
rumspringa: period of running around
schweschder: sister
suh: son
wunderbarr: wonderful

*The German dialect spoken by the Amish is not a written language and varies depending on the location and origin of the settlement. These spellings are approximations. Most Amish children learn English after they start school. They also learn high German, which is used in their Sunday services.

Jamesport, Missouri, Featured Families

The Ropps:

Mary Katherine (widow,
  husband was Moses)

Thomas and Joanna–six
  children

Dylan and Samantha–four
  children

Dinah and Nathan Plank–
  four children

Mary and Robert Shrock–four
  children

Elijah and Nyla–three children

Ellen and Luke Hostetler–three
  children

Josiah and Hannah–two
  children

Angus and Rebecca–one child

Beulah and Jacob Burkholder

Barbara and Joseph Beachy

The Millers:

Ezekiel (widower, wife was
  Lucy)

Leah and William Gingerich–
  Kenneth, 7; Caleb, 3; and
  Liliana, 18 months

Carlene and Samuel Raber–
  three children

John and Nora Miller–two
  children

Andrew and Emma Miller–
  one child

The Kauffmans:

Laura (widow, husband was Eli)

Children all grown

The Grabers:

Leo and Jennie

Matthew Troyer

Celia Troyer

Micah Troyer

Cynthia Troyer

Mark Troyer

Elizabeth Troyer

Francis Troyer

Aidan and Bess Graber

Joshua Weaver

Leyla Graber

The Weavers:

Solomon (minister) and Diana

Elijah

Luke and Jane–William

Ruth and Dan Byler

Sophie and Obediah Stultz–
Esther, Lewis, Martin, and
Angela

Hazel and Issac Plank–Rachel,
Sarah, Levi, Gracie, Jonah

Other Families:

Freeman (bishop) and Dorothy
Borntrager

Cyrus (deacon) and Josephina
Beachy–Iris, Joseph, Rueben,
Samuel, Carl, Louella, Abigail

CHAPTER 1

At what point did a person realize that the special moments in life streak by in a flash, distilled into memories before they could be truly lived? Mary Katherine Ropp stood motionless in the middle of her kitchen, a platter holding a two-layer German chocolate cake covered in whipped cream cheese frosting nestled in her hands.

The other women bustled in and out, serving two hundred wedding guests seated at tables set up in all the other rooms and spilling out across the broad expanse of the front yard. Serving spoons clinked on bowls. Pots banged. The fire in the wood-burning stove sizzled. Mary Katherine closed her eyes and inhaled the mingled scents of roasted chicken and dressing, gravy, coleslaw, freshly baked cookies, cakes, and bread.

Like every mother, she'd imagined her daughter Barbara's wedding day since the night of her birth, nineteen years earlier. She imagined the blue dress Barbara would don. The crispness of her white *kapp*. The way her eyes would tear up when the bishop took her hand and put it in her husband's for the final blessing.

A lump lodged in Mary Katherine's throat. She breathed and wiped at her eyes. *Oh, Moses, if only you could see this. Your youngest daughter is a bride today. She's only a passable cook, she hates to sew, and she never knows when to stop talking, but Joseph loves her anyway.*

I'm here, Fraa. I see her. She sounds a lot like the girl I married. Gott has blessed us.

Mary Katherine sighed at the imagined deep, always amused voice in her ear. Of course he was here. Even after seven years of widowhood, she could depend on Moses to be at her side. He would never forsake her.

She needed to write these thoughts down. Her notebook lay on the counter, splotches of lemonade and chocolate frosting on the outside. She took two steps toward it.

"What are you doing, *Mudder*?" Beulah's voice sounded irked—which was nothing new.

Mary Katherine turned to find daughter number four standing in the doorway. Her hands were full of dirty dishes and her face beet red with exertion. "You're in my way, and Thomas is looking for you."

"Just taking a second to breathe." Mary Katherine cleared her throat and edged away from the counter. Her habit of taking notes in the middle of life's events baffled some of her loved ones. "Your *bruder* will have to wait until after the wedding to boss me around."

As her oldest son, Thomas considered himself the head of the house, even if he hadn't lived in Mary Katherine's house in many years. When it came to bossiness, he was much more like her than his easygoing father. Her other sons, being more like Moses, let him do the bossing. For the most part.

"You know he only wants what's best." With her slightly rounded body, sandy-blonde hair, and blue eyes, Beulah was the spitting image of Mary Katherine when she was younger. "You're always tired. If you moved into the *dawdy haus*, you'd have him and Joanna nearby. Do you really want to be alone in this big house? You know you don't."

Everyone seemed to know what she wanted and what she needed, except Mary Katherine. If she was tired, it was only because of the wedding preparations, not because she needed to be put out to pasture at the mere age of sixty. During the two weeks since the wedding announcement for Barbara and Joseph Beachy at the church service, she had worked nonstop. Writing wedding invitations, cleaning and scrubbing the entire house, borrowing extra tables and chairs, stoves and refrigerators, pots and pans, buying groceries and baked goods they didn't have time to make from scratch. Lining up the cooks and the servers. Praying that September's fall weather would hold, allowing them to serve people outdoors.

Plain weddings were simple, without adornment, but the receptions were mammoth in the sheer amount of food needed to serve all the guests who'd come to Jamesport, Missouri, from Ohio, Indiana, and as far away as Texas. It might make a much younger woman tired, but Mary Katherine only felt invigorated.

That was her story and she was sticking to it. "I'm fine. Take this cake out to the tables outside."

"Fraidy cat!" Beulah deposited the dirty dishes on the counter but made no move to take the cake. "You can't hide from him forever."

"Who are you hiding from?" Laura Kauffman trudged through the door with empty serving dishes in both hands. She might be seventy-two and a little hard of hearing in one ear, but she had avoided the pasture as well. She served as not only a good friend but an excellent example of how to live and grow after losing a husband. "Dottie? Why would you be hiding from Dottie? She's looking for you."

Dottie Manchester, the Jamesport Branch Library's only librarian and Mary Katherine's closest *Englisch* friend, meant well, but she had a one-track mind and a penchant for taking the long road to make a short point. As much as Mary Katherine enjoyed a good chat, she didn't have time right now. "I've got a lot on my plate at the moment."

Beulah snorted and Laura chuckled.

"So to speak. You could eat the cake instead of serving it." That bit of wisdom came from Jennie Graber, who stood at the sink washing dishes in an enormous plastic tub. She, too, had been a widow until she remarried a few months earlier. That she was exceedingly happy was apparent in the smile on her heart-shaped face and the sparkle in her pale-blue eyes. "You should pay attention. There might be someone else looking for you. Weddings make minds turn to romance."

The women giggled in a chorus that made them sound like young girls at their first singing, not mature women from every stage of life—from just married to a widowed great-grandmother. Mary Katherine couldn't help herself. She rolled her eyes. "The last thing an old Plain woman thinks about is romance."

Not so. If memories of Moses' sweet kisses rushing through her like a warm summer breeze could be called romantic, she was guilty. But she would never admit such foolishness, not even to her dearest friends.

"Speak for yourself." Laura plucked a roll from an overflowing basket with knuckles swollen with arthritis. "Besides, I think I spied a certain old Plain man staring at you during the service."

"You're talking about Ezekiel, aren't you?" Jennie was eager for her friends to find marital bliss again. "He did look distracted during Solomon's message."

"You're dreaming. Ezekiel thinks of nothing but his *kinner* and his restaurant." Hoping her own distraction during the minister's message hadn't shown as well, Mary Katherine wiped tiny drops of sweat from her warm forehead with the back of her sleeve. Ezekiel had been a widower for about ten years. He was a kind man with a generous laugh. He always refilled her tea glass when she ate at the Purple Martin Café and always asked about her day—but then, he did that with everyone he served. "Anyway, I have too much to do to worry about such silliness."

A smirk on her face, Beulah swiped a dollop of frosting from Mary Katherine's cake and stuck it in her mouth. She smacked her lips. "If you think marriage consists only of silliness, you've been a widow far too long!"

This from her own daughter. Another round of giggles rippled through the kitchen.

"I reckon I'm better off out there than I am in here." Mary Katherine headed for the door, dodging Beulah's outstretched fingers. "I'll deliver the cake myself. I'll be back. In one minute. In one piece."

God willing.

She strode through the doorway and into the fray. The front room was filled wall to wall with tables covered with white tablecloths and chairs occupied by friends and family—some she hadn't seen in years. No time to visit now. She edged through, cake platter held high.

"Mary Kay! Mary Kay!" Dottie's high voice carried over the dozens of conversations that created a low-pitched, continuous roar. She squeezed through the narrow aisle between tables, her husband, Walt, right behind her. His portly figure struggled with the tight fit much more than Dottie's skinny frame. "Congratulations, my friend. You did it! You married off number ten. You're done."

"Yep, thanks for inviting us. It's a joy to watch all your kids get married. You must be relieved to marry off the last one." Walt laughed and his belly—which reflected his love for his wife's pecan pie—shook. "And you know they'll stay married. Not like us Englisch folks with a 50 percent divorce rate."

They were the only Englischers invited to those weddings. Their friendship stretched back years to the first time Mary Katherine ventured into the library to do research on covered wagons on the Oregon Trail.

Dottie had helped her find sources and quickly. A mother with ten children waiting at home didn't have time to dally. Dottie approached research like she did everything else—full steam ahead. A friendship had blossomed.

"*Danki.* Right now, I'm up to my kapp in food."

"Joseph and Barbara look so happy. I always cry at weddings." Dottie dabbed at her smooth pink cheeks with an embroidered hankie. "They're a perfect couple."

At times Mary Katherine had despaired that any man in his right mind would consider Barbara a good catch. It would take another man like Moses, and those were few and far between. Finally, Joseph had accepted the challenge. Love truly was blind. An occasion to be celebrated to be sure. A strange void bloomed in Mary Katherine's midsection, like a hole that seemed to grow deeper and darker as the day progressed. Forcing a smile, she shifted the platter to one hand and waved. "I don't know about perfect, but they'll do."

Dottie wore a flowing, dark-purple broomstick skirt and a white, long-sleeved, Western-style blouse with pearl snap buttons. It matched Walt's purple Western shirt with its white piping. He wore blue jeans pressed with a seam down the middle and black cowboy boots. Why a librarian and an accountant chose to dress like cowboys remained a mystery to Mary Katherine.

"I need to talk to you. Bob Sampson put his building on Grant Street up for sale yesterday." Dottie's voice rose with uncontained excitement. Her turquoise chandelier earrings shook. "It would be perfect for our bookstore. He's including the furniture—a bunch of wooden shelves and tables and that wooden counter he had by the front door."

Our bookstore. The words had a sweet ring to them—sweet and bitter like life itself. "I told you, I'm not able to commit to another store yet."

It had only been a year since Amish Treasures caught fire right before local businessman Lazarus Dudley took over its lease. Jennie and Leo Graber wanted her to help with their newly opened Combination Store. Everyone wanted something from her. Cake held high, she dodged a gaggle of toddlers and zigzagged around two teenagers who stopped to talk in the middle of the aisle.

Dottie and Walt stuck to her like bubble gum on the sole of her favorite sneaker. "I love the idea of a bookstore, don't get me wrong, and working with you would be wonderful. It's just not possible right now."

Maybe ever. It had taken years to save the money to join three other families in opening Amish Treasures. Their investment went up in smoke and flame six months later. She didn't have the funds to share in ownership of the Combination Store, but she could contribute goods for sale there as a start. It was finding the time to sew that was the problem.

"It would be more than wonderful." One hand patting the jewel-encrusted comb that held back her shoulder-length silver hair, Dottie took Walt's hand as if to anchor her to the floor in her euphoria. The two wore matching plain silver wedding bands. "I mean, me with you. I have savings. Tourists and local folks alike will flock to a store with Amish fiction, romances, mysteries, and travel books and cookbooks and cards and such. We'll earn back our investment in no time. I have a business plan. A good one."

They'd said the same thing about Amish Treasures.

"It's a good investment." Walt removed his black cowboy hat, revealing his shiny, perfectly round, bald pate. "I've run the numbers several times. The square footage is perfect for a bookstore, and Bill's asking price is decent. Not a steal, by any means, but fair."

A bookstore was more problematic than a craft store. Tourists loved Amish quilts and toys and jams and jellies. They came to Jamesport seeking Amish-made products. People didn't read as much as they used to. Plain folks didn't often read the fiction written by Englisch authors about them. It was hard to believe readers found their simple lives that interesting. "Can we talk about this later?"

"Meet us there Saturday afternoon to see the space." Dottie stopped short of saying "pretty please with sugar on top," but her thrust-out lower lip and puppy-dog eyes said it for her. "Just look at it, okay? For me?"

"I have a quilting frolic Saturday. When does Bill need an answer?"

"He says he has a couple of other offers. He'll wait one week for us, but then he'll have to consider them."

"It can't hurt to look at the space, but not Saturday morning." It couldn't hurt, could it?

"You'll come with us, won't you, Walt, after your appointments?"

"Anything for you, sweets."

"We're set, then." Dottie stretched on tiptoe and

gave her husband a big smooch on the cheek, leaving pink lipstick behind. "You can skip out of your quilting frolic by two. We'll see you at three."

"I want some more chicken and stuffing." Walt swiped at his cheek with an abashed look on his face. "I think the wife needs another plate—she's gotten so skinny she might blow away. She worries too much about her girlish figure. The more of her I see, the better I like it, personally."

"Oh, you." Dottie blushed as she turned back to Mary Katherine. "We'll talk to you later. If you need any help cleaning up, let me know. I'll drag Walt over here."

"We have it covered. I'll talk to you later, though."

"*Jah*, you will, because right now you need to talk to me." Thomas, who looked so like his mountain of a father, Moses, blocked the doorway. He kept his voice low as he glanced around, but his scowl said he meant business. At thirty-six and the father of six himself, he took his role as head of the house seriously. "Have you started packing yet?"

"Let's get another plate." Still hand in hand, Dottie and Walt melted into the crowd. Dottie knew all about this skirmish, and she also would surmise that Mary Katherine wouldn't want an audience. She would be right.

Mary Katherine stepped closer to her son. "*Nee.*"

"Mudder," he grumbled, but at least he didn't raise his voice. "We've talked about this."

He talked about it. "*Suh.*"

"Don't get your dander up with me." Shaking his

head so hard his blond beard swayed, Thomas sighed. "You cannot live alone in this house. It's not right. It's time you moved into the dawdy haus at my place. The kinner love having their *groossmammi* around, and you know Joanna likes your company."

It would also open up her house for son number two, Dylan, and his wife, Samantha, and their four children, and Samantha's parents, who lived with them. They needed a bigger place. Besides, Dylan worked the farm. It would save him time and effort to live on the homestead. It all made sense, but her heart simply refused to acquiesce. The empty nest loomed in front of Mary Katherine yet again. Besides, Thomas's wife, Joanna—she'd never told a soul this—rubbed her the wrong way more often than not. Mary Katherine didn't want to live with her. She had ten children. Did it have to be Thomas? Not something a mother said aloud.

She tightened her grip on the cake platter and lowered her head, preparing to bulldoze her way past her son. "I've lived in our house my entire adult life."

"You lived here with *Daed*." Thomas had his father's deep voice, his blond hair and blue eyes, but his personality was all Mary Katherine's. Stubborn as the flu. "But that time has passed. You can tell your stories to the kinner like you did us when we were little."

His smile said he remembered story time sitting on his daed's lap in the rocking chair next to the fireplace with the same tenderness she did. It seemed eons ago, but at the same time, only yesterday.

"We'll talk about this later." She edged forward. Thomas's expression turned stony. His feet were planted, his arms crossed. Mary Katherine stared back at him, refusing to waver. "This isn't the time or the place. You don't want to spoil your *schweschder's* wedding, do you?"

"I don't think that's possible." His scowl deepened. Mary Katherine tugged at his arm and tried to squeeze past him. They did a two-step dance through the door and onto the porch. Thomas leaned into her. "Mudder, this conversation isn't over."

She kept moving. Thomas took her arm. She tried to shrug him off. At that moment he must've realized how this looked to their guests because his stance shifted and he let go of her. She stumbled forward, gaining momentum fast. The cake flew from her hands.

"Nee, nee!" She flailed, trying to regain her grip, then fell into the open space. In that split second she caught the look of surprise on Ezekiel Miller's face. He had one boot on the top porch step, the other in midair.

His eyes, the color of caramel candy, widened behind black-rimmed glasses. His mouth dropped open. His arms came up. The cake hit him square in the face and slopped down his long, brown beard spun through with silver threads.

Mary Katherine toppled into his open arms. They teetered on the steps for a split second. White frosting glopped onto the front of his pale-green shirt. The dark chocolate of the cake clung to the frosting. Its silky texture slid across her cheeks. She tasted the sweetness of powdered sugar and butter, then chocolate—until that moment her favorite.

Together, they tumbled down the steps and landed in the grass. Stunned, Mary Katherine gasped for breath and coughed. Cake spewed from her mouth. Into Ezekiel's face. His good black hat tumbled back, revealing a bald pate fringed by dark, curly hair with those same silver highlights.

She lay on top of his sprawling body.

CHAPTER 2

God had a sense of humor, no doubt about it. Ezekiel Miller stared into wide eyes only inches from his face. They held horror and a smidgeon of something else. Laughter. Mary Katherine had a sense of humor. How did a person get through this life without one? Her white kapp tilted to one side, revealing hair more silver than the sandy brown he remembered from childhood. A breeze ruffled it. She smelled of roasted chicken and dill pickles. And chocolate cake. The sun created a halo around her head. That did not make her an angel. Never mind that this was the closest he'd been to a woman in ten years.

Chuckling, Ezekiel wiped cake mixed with slobber from his cheek. "I usually just get my own piece of cake."

Mary Katherine's thin eyebrows popped up. "Maybe you'd rather have strawberry. Or we have a nice vanilla cake in the kitchen."

"I like them all. I have a bit of a sweet tooth."

Their gazes held for a second.

Mary Katherine smiled. Her bottom teeth were slightly crooked, but the smile transformed her face, taking Ezekiel back to when they were mere children, sitting in the classroom. Mary Katherine always smiled when she wrote her English essays. He could never understand that. Who smiled while laboring over a writing assignment in a difficult language? She did have a nice way about her, even if it disappeared when she opened her mouth on the playground and bossed everyone around. Including his future wife, Lucy, whose sweet self never seemed to mind.

In those days he hadn't liked being bossed around by a girl. Now, truth be told, he wouldn't mind a little sass to brighten his evenings.

Ignoring the pain in his bony behind, he rolled and gently set her to one side in the grass. He picked up her glasses, handed them to her, and then scrambled to his feet. Light-headed, he swayed for a second. That happened a lot lately—a fact he chose to ignore. Simply the product of turning sixty in August. Gritting his teeth, he shook it off.

Hands reached out to help him. Murmured concerns mixed with snickers from the teenagers in the crush of people who'd raced to help them after their fall. Let them have their fun. Ezekiel held out his hand to Mary Katherine. With great dignity she took it and he pulled her to her feet.

She stood almost a foot shorter than he did. Her body was round and curvy under her rumpled, frosting-and-leaves-decorated dress. Despite her age—late fifties he reckoned—her fair skin looked soft and smooth with only a few sun lines around those expressive blue eyes that seemed bigger behind her brown-rimmed glasses and laugh lines around full lips. At the moment her cheeks were radish red and decorated with sticky frosting. She stared up at him, those lips pressed together as if suppressing a laugh.

He swallowed his own laughter. The bishop wouldn't find their antics funny, unplanned or not. "Are you all right?"

"Fine. I'm not usually so *doplisch*." She raised her hands as if to wipe away the cake that clung to him. Her fingers came within inches of his beard, then retreated to her own stained apron. "I was talking with my suh instead of watching where I was going."

Arguing with him, if Ezekiel's ears had heard correctly. As the father of four and grandfather of nine, he recognized the tone even if he didn't catch the content.

Ezekiel had had plenty of chances to observe Mary Katherine since those schoolyard days. A person couldn't help but know everyone's business in the *Gmay*, what with the frolics and church services. Every time he saw her, she was on a mission to get something done. It was her nature. She had a penchant for charging about as if the seas would part for her. The church elders didn't always look kindly on that in a woman. She hadn't remarried after Moses died. They didn't like that either.

Ezekiel understood, if they didn't. It had been ten years since his Lucy passed, and he hadn't hankered to remarry. She had been his partner in life. It was that simple and that complete. No other could fill her shoes. Some days, his heart still ached for her in the quiet of dawn and the dusk right before sunset.

Mary Katherine looked nothing like his petite,

dark-haired Lucy. She said little, letting her work speak for her. If he asked for her opinion, she was quick to offer it, but she always deferred to his wishes in the end. God had given this woman in front of him an extra dollop of gumption.

"Are *you* all right?" Mary Katherine stared at him, her expression quizzical. "Did you hit your head?"

"The shirt will wash." He sucked in air, willing the rushing sound in his ears to subside, and hitched up pants that seemed to hang from his suspenders more than they used to. "The pants too. No harm done."

"Mudder, you're a mess." Thomas Ropp hastened toward them. He loomed over his mother and glowered at Ezekiel as if he'd been at fault in the mishap. He put his hand on his mother's arm. "Go to the kitchen. Beulah will clean you up."

"I'm not a child," Mary Katherine whispered, but she ducked her head, looking for a brief second like a penitent little girl. "No harm done."

"No harm done?" Thomas leaned closer to her, but his hissed whisper carried. "You landed on top of a *man* on the ground in broad daylight."

Mary Katherine lifted her chin. She had a look in her eyes that didn't bode well for her eldest son. "Aren't you helping grill the meat? I'm sure you're needed in the back."

She turned to Ezekiel and smiled. "If you want to come to the kitchen, you can wash up there."

Cool as ice cream in winter. Her gaze met his head-on. Despite being disheveled, sticky, and covered with frosting, she didn't hesitate. He'd known Mary

Katherine since she was knee high to her daddy's britches, but he'd never seen her look quite so pretty, all rumpled and covered with cake. He shooed away the thought. *You must've hit your head, old man.* "I think I'd better." He held up his hands. "Although I'm tempted to make a meal of this cake. It really is tasty."

"We can do better than that." She turned and made a path through the crowd. Bishop Freeman's wife, Dorothy; Ezekiel's oldest daughter, Leah; Deacon Cyrus; Solomon, who served as minister to their burgeoning Gmay; and a dozen others lingered, talking among themselves. News of the incident would spread through the entire wedding in a matter of minutes. Mary Katherine surely knew that, but she held her head high. "We have half a dozen cakes in the kitchen, five kinds of cookies, and several pies. They won't be mixed with grass and dirt."

Or beard. "My favorite dinner—dessert."

"Me too."

Smiling, he followed her through the living room. She really could part the seas.

In the kitchen she pointed to a tub of soapy water on the counter. "You first."

"Mudder, Thomas told me what happened. Are you hurt?" Mary Katherine's newlywed daughter, Barbara, roared into the kitchen and skidded to a stop, her question delivered in a screech. Behind her, full tilt, came her entourage of sisters, Beulah, Ellen, Mary, and Dinah. "You're a mess."

The same could be said for the bride. Her kapp was askew and she had what appeared to be grease stains on her blue dress. She looked exactly like her mother had thirty-seven years ago when she married Moses Ropp, if Ezekiel's memory served. Even then Mary Katherine had been a force to be reckoned with.

Mary Katherine seemed unfazed by her daughter's precipitous entry or her accusing tone. "I had a little accident. You need to get back to the *eck*. Joseph will be looking for you."

"He's busy roughhousing with the boys. They're ribbing him hard. They're being so silly."

"You have no business in the kitchen." Mary Katherine fixed her other daughters with a glare that would send children of any age ducking for cover. "The rest of you are supposed to be serving. Ellen, we need more clean silverware. Go on, go. I'm making a plate for Ezekiel while he gets cleaned up."

"But Mudder—"

"Go."

The women scattered except for Barbara, the bride, apparently as stubborn as her mother. She headed to the stove.

Rubbing at the frosting with a wet washrag only served to make a bigger mess. Ezekiel shoved his hands in the warm water and wrung out the rag a second time. No luck. His shirt had blotches top to bottom.

"Let me try." Mary Katherine commandeered the rag. Her head bent, expression intent, she scrubbed hard. Ezekiel propped himself against the counter to keep from stumbling back. She glanced up, her face reddened, and she took a wide step back. "That's a little better."

"Here's your food." Barbara had taken it upon herself to fix the plate. She frowned as she shoved it between them. The frown deepened as she glanced at her mother, and then him. "You should be able to get a seat at a table. The first round has finished."

"He can sit right here at the prep table. You go sit with your husband."

With one last glance at Ezekiel, Barbara flounced out. Ezekiel sat. It felt good to get off shaky legs. He tried to remember if he'd eaten breakfast before the service. No. He'd overslept—something he never did. Inhaling the scent of chicken, green beans and bacon, a vinegary coleslaw, barbecue baked beans, and dill pickles, he picked up his fork. The roasted chicken was tender and juicy, the gravy savory, mashed potatoes creamy. He dug in and ate with a gusto he rarely felt.

Owning and working daily in a restaurant had stolen some of his love of food. That and the sheer lack of time. He started work at the Purple Martin Café before sunrise and finished the last scrap of paperwork and cleaning well after sunset six days a week. He fell into bed at night, his head still whirling with all the balls he had to keep in the air—the staff, the bills, the produce and staples that had to be bought, the endless cleaning, the health code, keeping the books. Restaurants were labor-intensive, massive undertakings.

"This is *gut*." He waved his fork toward the plate. "Did you make all of this?"

Her nose wrinkled, Mary Katherine scrubbed her dress with such force it was a wonder she didn't tear the fabric. She pushed her glasses up her nose with the back of her wrist. "With help."

"You are a gut cook." Plain women learned to cook as little girls. Ezekiel had learned that lesson in the ten years since he opened his family restaurant. "Every dish is gut."

"I appreciate your opinion." She stopped scrubbing long enough to offer him a smile. She seemed to have a good supply of them. That was something *he* appreciated in women—in people in general. His customers ran the gamut from appreciative to cranky to downright obnoxious. "I reckon most Plain women can cook."

"Some better than others."

"You'd know gut food when you taste it." She stopped and looked up at him, her gaze keen with interest. "You also know everything that's going on. Tell me. What do you know about the break-ins?"

Ezekiel let his fork drop to his plate. "You want to talk about that now, at your daughter's wedding?"

"What else would you expect from the district's scribe?"

"You're also more curious than ten cats. They should rename *The Budget* to *The Gossip*."

She tossed the washrag in a tub of soapy water and plucked a notebook from between a stack of dirty plates and a skillet. A blob of grease decorated the cover. "You spend your day at the roots of our grapevine." She pulled a stubby pencil from behind her ear. "Someone stole a crib quilt heirloom from Bess's house last week. She's heartbroken. And it's not the first time. What is Freeman doing about it? Have they talked to the sheriff?"

"It's the third burglary in the last month. Every time it's something of no material value but of importance to the family." Ezekiel had been invited to sit with Freeman, Cyrus, and Solomon, the church elders, while they struggled with how to address the problem. No one wanted the Englisch sheriff messing in their business. Even if it was his job. Yet the safety of their families was of great importance. "It's a mystery we haven't been able to unravel. Why steal from us? We don't have any computers or cameras or TVs. Because the value is so small, they'd rather keep it within the Gmay."

Mary Katherine's harrumph said more than a hundred words.

"You don't think that's a gut plan?"

"We don't care about material things, but neither do we appreciate someone breaking one of the Ten Commandments in our homes." Her blue eyes snapped with electricity. Her cheeks were pink. She was so alive.

Ezekiel forced his gaze to his plate. He had no business cataloging Mary Katherine's fine physical qualities. Still, some things simply could not be ignored. Even by a tired old man.

Her energy flowed around him. Ezekiel inhaled it and the exhaustion lifted. It was the food, not Mary Katherine. He simply needed to eat. An idea flitted by. He chewed a succulent piece of chicken and snatched the thought back for deeper scrutiny. "You cooked at the bed-and-breakfast a while back, didn't you?"

"I did. Are you changing the subject?"

"I am. We should leave the thefts to Freeman and

the others. They know best."

She rolled her eyes like a teenager. "Fine. I'll pester Thomas some more."

"I have no doubt you will. You're worse than a mosquito at a summer picnic. Did you enjoy cooking at the B and B?"

"It didn't matter whether I enjoyed it. At the time I was needed."

If the grapevine had the story correctly, Mary Katherine had taken the job to shepherd her friend and new widow Bess Graber through a dark time.

Bess had remarried and no longer needed her older friend's mentorship.

"We need a cook at the Purple Martin." That was an understatement. Keeping staff at the restaurant was one of the many thorns in his side. They'd been through three different cooks in a month's time. One Plain and two Englisch. Didn't seem to matter which. No one could keep up with the pace needed. One had simply been a bad cook. Another cried and ran out of the kitchen never to return when he suggested she needed to add more salt to the potatoes. Every time one of them quit, he had to take on more work. "It doesn't pay much and it's hard work, but if you like to cook, it's a gut job."

She sighed and nestled the notebook back in its hidey-hole. The pencil returned to its spot behind her ear. "I'm not looking to work in a restaurant."

"I figured since Amish Treasures closed, you might need another way to earn a dollar." The fire at Mary Katherine's store and Lazarus Dudley's greedy property grab had been the talk around many of the tables in Ezekiel's restaurant the entire month of July. "We sure could use a good cook. We've been having trouble keeping them since my daughters married."

It was good that Leah and Carlene had started families of their own, but he missed seeing their faces in the kitchen every day. Taking over the restaurant from another Plain family after Lucy died had allowed him to make a living after he sold his floundering farm and still spend each day with his children. The Purple Martin kept his family together. Customers loved Leah's chicken-fried steak and gravy. Carlene's buttermilk pie garnered raves as well. But once they'd started families of their own, continuing to work was out of the question. His sons had no interest in running a restaurant.

His children had grown up and become good men and women. Ezekiel was blessed. Yet he was left with a *what-now* feeling that pressed on his chest until he couldn't breathe.

Had the Purple Martin outlived its purpose? Was it worth the exhaustion that weighed him down each night as he stumbled to bed? The aching back and legs? The numbers that swam in front of his eyes when he did the books and paid the bills?

The cinnamon-laden scent of apple pie baking in the wood-burning stove flirted with his nose, enticing with it a memory of Lucy standing in front of him at the kitchen table, serving him a slice of pie. Her presence was so real he felt the soft skin of her hand on his and saw the curve of her lips as she smiled and leaned into him, the way she always did when he returned from a day in the fields.

"I have plenty to do."

The sharp edge of Mary Katherine's tone tumbled him back to the present day.

She was the Gmay's *Budget* scribe. She had at least twenty-eight or twenty-nine grandchildren—a person lost track after a while. She belonged to a letter-writing circle. She was first with cards for card showers. She never missed a work frolic or hesitated to help a sick friend. Ezekiel knew these things because he listened and he watched. Taking his time, he took another bite of mashed potatoes and gravy, savored their peppery flavor and creamy texture. "Maybe so, but give it some thought."

Mary Katherine had turned to discuss the dearth of clean silverware with Laura Kauffman, so she didn't hear. Or pretended not to.

He burped softly and scraped the plate clean. Mary Katherine might be used to getting her own way, but so was he.

She turned toward him. "I'll take that plate—and the fork."

He stood. "Come by the restaurant when you're ready to talk about the job."

"I don't—"

"I know." He tipped his hat. "But you will."

On that optimistic note, he dodged Laura and headed for the door before Mary Katherine could say no again.

CHAPTER 3

Some experts say the older a person gets, the less sleep she needs. Mary Katherine flopped onto her back and stared at her old buddy darkness. Apparently, they knew what they were talking about. Despite spending the entire day cleaning up after the wedding, she couldn't sleep. Every muscle and bone yearned for it, but her brain refused to give them what they so desired.

It might be because she was alone in this house for the first time in thirty-six years. Barbara and Joseph were spending the night at Joseph's sister's, the first of many post-wedding family visits before they moved into the house they'd built on his father's property. Mary Katherine rolled back on her side and stuck her clasped hands under the pillow where it was cooler.

Maybe it was the knowledge that she was alone in the house and someone was making a habit of breaking into Plain homes and stealing precious mementos. The hair on her arms prickled. Her ears strained to hear any tiny noise. Was that a thump? The power of suggestion. She peered into the darkness. *Stop it. Close your eyes.*

She forced them closed. *Go to sleep.*

Her mind refused to cooperate. Maybe it was her

rancor at Thomas's latest lecture regarding the cake incident that kept her awake. He'd been embarrassed in front of the others. That gave her no pleasure. It had been an accident. Ezekiel's offer of a job roosted in her brain right next to the lecture. She didn't want to stand on her feet eight hours a day five or six days a week. Did she? She liked to cook. Cooking for ten children gave her joy. When they gathered for the holidays with all twenty-seven grandkids spilling out into the yard and running from corral to barn to pond and back, she reveled in their appetites and their appreciation for the food she and the other women cooked.

The money would allow her to rebuild her nest egg. Which meant she could take Dottie up on her offer to partner in a bookstore. She loved reading as much as she loved cooking. She loved books and libraries and stories. She loved words.

A path to her desire. A plan for the years that may or may not stretch in front of her as a widow with no husband for whom to keep house and cook. A place where she belonged. A place where people saw her as a vigorous, alive woman whose work still had value. Not as a widowed grandmother who needed tending as much as the kinner. It might be her desire, but was it God's plan?

The question squeezed onto the roost in her brain next to the others. Freeman and the other elders likely would see her working at the restaurant as a better place for a widow woman such as herself. Not going off on her own with an Englischer to open a shop that would sell all sorts of worldly books.

But working at the restaurant would put her in close proximity to Ezekiel. Ezekiel with the warm, pensive eyes and time-weathered face. She snorted aloud. The power of suggestion. The girls had planted that seed with their silly chatter after the wedding.

What would it be like to have a man around again? She rolled over on her back and stared into the darkness. A man not Moses. She would never know another person the way she knew Moses. The way a woman knew a man who was the father of their ten children. Through croup, measles, the flu, through broken bones and hurt feelings, through endless *rumspringas* and the joy of weddings and the birth of grandchildren. Joys now missed by Moses.

The house creaked and groaned in the September wind as if feeling her pain. Despite the cool air wafting through the open windows, heat raced through her like a flash fire. Irritated down to the last fuzzy gray strand of hair on her head, she ripped off the thin cotton sheet and sat up. Getting old was not for the faint of heart—especially for women.

Of course, she knew nothing about what men suffered as they aged. Moses had left her before she had a chance to find out. Before he had a chance to know himself. That could be seen as a blessing—for him, not her.

"You are a crotchety old woman tonight." His deep voice, with its ever-present hint of laughter, bellowed in her ear. *"Are you planning a pity party for one?"*

"No, I'm not. If you must know, I have a story percolating. I plan to finish it."

Moses didn't have a literary bone in his mammoth body with its size 14 feet and hands like bushel baskets. But he seemed to take true pleasure in settling into the rocking chair by the fireplace, arms around a child on each knee, to listen to the story she'd composed that day while kneading the bread and weeding the garden. His blond beard bobbing, he rocked, he nodded, and sometimes he chuckled. When she stumbled over her own words, unable to read her hasty scribbles, he chipped in with a suggestion. His ideas were always good.

"Gott gave you a gift, Fraa. He truly did." He'd uttered that same sentence after every story, raising his voice over the children's clamor for more.

Every time, she reveled in the sweetness of those words of affirmation coming from the only man she'd ever loved. Would ever love.

The first time he'd said those words—long before they were married—she knew he was the one. He didn't call her lazy or a dreamer the way her mother had. Her mother couldn't understand her daughter's penchant for living in a make-believe world. She'd tried hard to squeeze it out of Mary Katherine. To her everlasting disappointment, she couldn't.

No use agitating over the past. God was good. Period. End of story. She'd been telling herself that for seven years.

"Might as well make use of the time." She fought with her sweaty nightgown, tangled around her thighs and knees, and stood. Her knees creaked and her back complained. "Just never you mind. You'll be fine once we get going again."

Fanning herself with one hand, she trudged barefoot to the small, square pine table pushed up against the window that faced her front yard. If it could talk, it would groan under the weight of copies of *The Budget*, notebooks, half a dozen books she intended to read, and stacks of cards for the card showers. She had a notebook for her *Budget* articles, another for short stories, and one for poems, as well as the one with the pink cover, which she reserved for ideas. Her idea book— ideas for stories, ideas for business, ideas for life. She kept a similar set on the table in the kitchen. The less wear and tear on her knees from the stairs the better.

Propped in the windowsill was her ledger for household accounts. The one for *Amish Treasures* lay on the floor under the table. Ignoring that irksome memory that smoldered in the corner of her mind, she lit the kerosene lamp. The pungent odor stung her nose. She plopped into the mismatched straight-back chair, put on her glasses, and grabbed the pen that waited patiently for her next thought. Her spiral notebook lay open to a page half filled with her haphazard scrawl.

She perused her article in *The Budget* with its list of all the out-of-town visitors who came for the wedding. Added the Borntragers from Bee County, Texas. Done. Tomorrow she'd take it to Dottie to be faxed from the library. Her hand moved to the notebook with her latest work in progress.

"Fine, Sophie, tell me what you've been doing since we last talked." She wiggled in her seat and closed her eyes for a second. "The chuck wagon's axle broke. The wagon toppled over and sent you flying onto the hard, rocky ground. Goodness. Did you lose the food supply?"

Delighted with this new hardship, Mary Katherine opened her eyes. The pen flew across the page. She loved getting lost in the story. Sophie had her hands full, posing as a man to be a cowboy-cook on a cattle drive. It was the only way women could work a cattle drive on the Chisholm Trail in the 1880s. The only way to have the adventure of making the nine-hundred-mile trek from Fort Worth to Dodge City with three thousand head of cattle.

Wrinkling her nose, she stopped and stared out the window. She could see nothing. An adventure would be nice. What a fanciful thought. A woman with ten children and twenty-seven grandchildren didn't have adventures. "I'm not that old."

Old enough to know better.

The sound of something—a plate or a bowl crashing to the floor—broke the peaceful silence.

The pen slipped from her hand. She froze.

Thump, thump.

Vermin, mostly likely. A skunk or a possum or even a raccoon. They were famous for finding their way into homes and scavenging for food. It would make a big mess in her kitchen.

Or an intruder intent on stealing something no one else would miss, except her.

Mary Katherine popped from her chair and raced to the far wall where Moses' hunting rifle rested high on a rack, its home for the last thirty-odd years. Moses wanted to make sure little hands couldn't reach it. She stood on tiptoe and stretched until her fingers reached the stock. It was covered with dust.

She'd never shot a gun of any kind.

"There's a first time for everything."

Funny, Moses.

"Best check to see if it's loaded."

As if she wouldn't know to do that. Men were so bossy. Thankfully it was. If there were cartridges in the house now, it was news to her.

If she could reach the broom in the kitchen, she would simply sweep the critter out of the house. It likely would be more scared of her than she was of it.

Let it be a critter, Gott. Please let it be a critter. Not a two-legged vermin.

She slapped her kapp on her head despite the fact that her hair hung down her back below her waist. Even if it was vermin of the four-legged variety, it didn't need to see her uncovered head. It wouldn't be right. A skunk or a possum wouldn't mind her ankle-length nightgown.

She scurried from the safety of the lit room and down the dark hall to the top of the stairs. Her eyes adjusted after a long, breathless moment.

Dish clinked against dish. A sound that could only be the door opening and closing on her propane-driven refrigerator echoed in the empty night air.

Not a four-legged vermin, then.

The two-legged variety had decided to make himself at home in her kitchen.

CHAPTER 4

Mary Katherine tightened her grip on the rifle. She eased down the stairs, avoiding the spot that squeaked on the fifth step. At the bottom she sucked in a breath. The oxygen made her light-headed.

One. Two. Three. Go.

A thin, weak light seeped from the kitchen. She stormed in. "Whoever you are, you weren't invited."

A man stood in the middle of her kitchen, a large sandwich made with her homemade sourdough bread and ham in one hand. A large flashlight had been set up so its light shone on the ceiling. The sandwich dropped. His hands shot into the air.

He chewed and swallowed, his Adam's apple bobbing.

At least he had the good manners not to talk with his mouth full.

"Now look what you made me do." His blue eyes sad, he frowned and gazed at the floor. "That was a good sandwich. Homemade bread."

"I'm glad you like the bread. I made it." Her voice sounded cool as a December morning, much to Mary Katherine's delight. "I always have more than enough to share, but people usually ask first."

"I was hungry. I planned to leave an IOU. As soon as I get a job, I'll reimburse you."

As if that explained it all.

She let the rifle barrel shift so it was aimed at the wood floor. "At least pick up after yourself."

As if the mess on her kitchen floor topped the list of her problems.

Without a word, he squatted and reassembled the sandwich. In the meantime Mary Katherine edged toward the lantern on the table. She lit it with surprisingly steady hands. She needed plenty of light to examine her intruder.

The nails on his bony fingers were jagged but clean. His scarred deck shoes squeaked. He wore no socks. The knobby bone of his ankle stuck out, a detail that somehow made him seem less scary. He did wear a baggy black T-shirt and faded blue jeans with white strings across holes in the knees. His sandy-brown hair sprinkled with gray was cut in an old-fashioned military flattop that thinned noticeably toward the back. Salt-and-pepper stubble darkened his chin. Lines around his blue eyes and mouth told her he was no spring chicken. Not as old as she was, but old enough to know better. His eyes were red rimmed.

"Did you break into my house to steal something?"

"Only food." His gaze stayed on the sandwich. "Just a sandwich, I promise."

Food had not been the object of the other break-ins. This man was hungry. Mary Katherine had food to spare. "Whatever made you think it was all right to come in my house in the middle of the night to steal a sandwich?"

"You left the door unlocked." He rose, the bread and ham cradled in his hands. A smear of mustard decorated the spot on the floor where the sandwich had landed. "That seemed an invitation."

In the thirty-seven years she'd lived in the house with her family, they'd never locked the door. They had nothing to steal and not much to fear in this rural community. "Not if your mother taught you any kind of manners."

"That's true. My mother would be horrified. Be assured she taught me better."

Mary Katherine waited for him to elaborate. His gaze unfocused, he stared into space. The weight of the rifle increased with each passing second. "What's your name?"

He jumped as if aware of her presence for the first time. "Burke McMillan."

"I'm Mary Katherine. I'd say help yourself to some food, but you already did."

"It's not like a man takes joy in stealing food." His voice dropped lower yet. "I'm sorry I scared you."

"Takes more than a man with a ham sandwich to scare me."

"Hence the rifle."

What kind of burglar used the word *hence*? "I could've shot you, you know."

"I read that you were pacifists." He shrugged. "I assumed there weren't any guns in the house."

"You figured wrong. My husband liked to hunt. Most Plain men do. Throw that sandwich away. My floor is clean, but I don't expect you to eat from it." She settled the rifle in the corner and padded to the counter. He was right in one respect. Plain folks didn't shoot people. "Sit. I'll make you some eggs, bacon, and toast."

"I may be hungry, but I promise you, I don't eat from even the most sparkling floor."

He had a way of talking that was delightful. A person should not be delighted by a burglar. "I didn't mean to insult you. Sit. I'll fix you breakfast."

"I don't want you to go to any trouble." Disbelief dusted his words. "You really should follow your first inclination and send me packing."

"You break into my house in the middle of the night and you don't want to cause me any trouble?"

"There are degrees of trouble, I suppose."

"Why did you decide to raid the refrigerator in *my* house?"

"I thought you'd be asleep by now. I'd be in and out without disturbing you. I didn't count on being so clumsy. I'm not usually. But I don't usually break into houses either."

Concern sent a chill up Mary Katherine's spine. He'd been watching her. On the other hand, if he'd intended to hurt her, he would've headed for the stairs, not the kitchen. Or maybe he needed to fortify himself first. She shivered and picked up the knife lying on the cutting board next to the hunk of ham. "I really should call for help."

The sheriff? Would Freeman and the elders want her to involve the Englisch police in this? Probably not.

"I suppose you could run out to the phone shack." He edged toward the door and picked up a faded blue duffel bag that gaped open. "You can put down the knife. I mean you no harm. If I did, I would've whipped up the stairs instead of heading for the kitchen."

A mind reader?

"Also, I understand you are a forgiving lot. I'm hoping you'll forgive me my trespasses, so to speak."

The words of the Lord's Prayer echoed in her head. She'd recited them every day of her life. Freeman and the others would have to forgive her. The mother in her had to feed the man. "Maybe you needed to eat first to get your strength up."

Burke chuckled. "You're one cool customer, Mary Katherine Ropp."

"How do you know my last name?"

"It's on the mailbox down the road."

"Have you been watching me?"

"Not just you. That would be creepy. I'm a student of human nature." His arms tightened around the duffel bag. "I've been . . . looking for something. I was wandering around lost and found Jamesport. You Amish folks interest me so I've been hanging around taking notes. Observing. Thinking."

A notetaker like her. "Writing an article or a book, then?"

"No. Just following bread crumbs, hoping they lead me somewhere."

"Where?"

"Anywhere that isn't lost." He shifted and took another step toward the door. A slim paperback with a bookmark stuck near the back toppled from the bag. Burke scooped it up. "Your house probably isn't it, though."

"You read books?" A person who packed books at the expense of socks couldn't be all bad. "What are you reading?"

"*The Odyssey*. By Homer. It's really a poem, not a book."

"What's it about?"

"A man who's on a long trip trying to get home."

Mary Katherine pulled ham and a chunk of cheddar cheese from the refrigerator. "I'll make you a sandwich." She itched to look at his book. "You eat and then you go."

"Yes, ma'am."

"No need to ma'am me."

Burke cleared his throat. "I thought maybe I could do some work for you. Like a farmhand."

"You break into my house and you expect me to give you a job?" She laid the sandwich on a white ceramic plate and added a pickle. It didn't seem enough for a hungry man. She rummaged in the refrigerator, extracted a plastic container of macaroni salad left over from the wedding, and added a scoop to the plate. She carried his dinner to the table along with a paper napkin. Or was it a breakfast of sorts? The night had taken on a surreal feel. Maybe she was sleepwalking—and talking. "I don't work the land. One of my sons does. We really can't afford to hire workers."

"I understand." He took a huge bite of the sandwich, chewed, and swallowed, quickly working his way through one half and then the other. Still standing by the counter and the knife, she watched and waited. He glanced her way. "I could take it to go if you'd rather I get out of your hair more quickly."

Mary Katherine's hand went to her head. Heat burned her cheeks. She'd forgotten the state of her hair and her dress. Or lack thereof. "That's for the best, I reckon."

The macaroni salad and the pickle went the way of the sandwich. It was a wonder he didn't choke. He wiped his mouth with the napkin, folded it in half, and dropped it on the plate. He stood and picked up the plate.

"Do you have a place to go?"

"I do."

"I don't believe you." Why she cared wasn't clear. "You're welcome to bunk in the barn for the night."

Thin gray eyebrows rose and fell over his sharp blue eyes. "That's probably not a great idea."

"Are you dangerous?"

"Not to others."

"Then the offer stands. You'll find some old horse blankets on the shelf. Throw them on a pile of hay in the empty stall."

He moved past her, ignoring her outstretched hand, heading to the counter where he dropped the napkin in the trash pail and placed the plate in the tub of water in the sink. "That's very kind of you." He washed the plate and laid it on the towel on the counter. "I'll see myself out. I'll be gone in the morning."

"Or you could apply for a job at the Purple Martin Café if you're not too proud."

"They have an opening?" He dried his hands on his jeans. "I'd work for food at this point—which would work out well at a restaurant."

"I know the owner." Ezekiel needed a cook, not a dishwasher. He would have to take both Mary Katherine and this man. A package deal. "I have a quilt frolic in the morning and then something I have to do after that. Meet me at the porch around suppertime. We'll drive into town."

"I'll be here." Burke nodded. "You're a kind person, Mrs. Ropp."

"It's Mary Kay to my friends."

"Are we friends?"

"That remains to be seen."

He slipped through the back door and was gone.

Mary Katherine stood in the middle of the kitchen for a long moment. She sucked in a deep breath and went to get the mop. No way she would sleep now.

She had a new project.

CHAPTER 5

If Dottie's reaction was any indication, Mary Katherine might have a spot of trouble on her hands when it came to her new project by the name of Burke McMillan. In the light of day, she could see why. "Yes, I let him spend the night in the barn."

For one moment Dottie seemed to lose her single-minded focus on the store space she'd insisted Mary Katherine see without delay. The airy room, flooded with late-afternoon sunlight through the floor-to-ceiling windows, was meant to be a bookstore. Even through bleary, sleep-deprived eyes, Mary Katherine could see that. She stood in the middle of the room and turned so she could examine every nook and cranny. The walnut shelving was perfect. The counter would have to be moved to one side, but that presented no problem.

Her expression expectant, Dottie smoothed her hand over the polished wood of a shelf. She wore her librarian uniform—white blouse, blue A-line skirt, sensible low-heeled slip-on shoes. Her hair was caught back with rhinestone combs, and silver-and-turquoise earrings shaped like leaves dangled from her ears, her only nod to her love of Western fashion.

"He broke into your house and you offered him a place to sleep." Dottie looked around as if Burke might lurk in some dark corner of the big, empty room. "Walt would have a fit if I did that."

Moses would have done the same as Mary Katherine, but he would've been there to make sure she and the children stayed safe.

Walt was in the back room looking over the electrical wiring and plumbing with Jim Tompkins and Jerry Rivers, electrician and plumber respectively. Walt might not know anything about such things, but he knew people who did. He did their taxes.

"When you say it like that, it sounds crazy."

"It is crazy. He could be a hatchet-wielding serial killer who breaks into houses and kills women and then eats their flesh and buries their bones in their own backyards. You could be gone, and no one would know what happened to you."

"There was no hatchet, Dottie. I had the gun."

Dottie, who loved to binge-watch *NCIS* and *Bones*, should write suspense novels. She loved to regale Mary Katherine with her TV "stories" after she watched them. Like story hour for adults. Her friend had an imagination and she was surprisingly bloodthirsty.

Mary Katherine moved to the counter. It was a lovely varnished oak, polished to a high sheen. It had some gouges, some scars, but the back side had dozens of shelves and compartments for storage. "He ate a ham-and-cheese sandwich, macaroni salad, and a pickle. That doesn't seem like something a cannibal would do. Besides, he had a book."

"He had a book. Which one?"

Like any book lover, Dottie knew the important questions. "Something called *The Odyssey*."

"A serial killer who likes the classics. Maybe that's his calling card. Maybe he likes to lull his victims into trusting him before he pounces." Dottie arched her back like a cat and thrust both hands, fingers curled, in the air. "Then he reads to them while their last breaths fade away. Did you tell your quilting peeps about this nocturnal visitor?"

Far too bloodthirsty. "I did not."

"Because you know they wouldn't approve, and with good reason. What if he was one of those burglars breaking in to steal you blind?"

"They're not stealing us blind. They take two or three possessions of no material value. And they've never hurt anyone."

"Yet. No one has caught them in the act."

"They don't steal food. The man was eating a ham sandwich."

"You caught him before he had a chance to steal anything else. Laura and the others will have a fit when they find out. Not to mention that bishop of yours."

They would find out soon enough. Mary Katherine hunched her shoulders and brushed the thought aside. Time to change the subject. "Do you think Bill really has other offers, or is that just a negotiating ploy to get us to bite?"

"I heard the Johnsons were thinking about opening a smelly store. You know, homemade candles, sachets, potpourri, incense." The question took Dottie's mind off Mary Katherine's thief-slash-alleged serial killer for a second. "Just what we need, more smelly stuff in Jamesport."

Mary Katherine tried to fend off the onslaught of mental images. Books here. Books there. Books everywhere. Even her own books. Pride and vanity, twin sins, popped up their nasty heads. "It's a wonderful space. Perfect, really."

"That's what Walt says and he doesn't even read books. And you know him—if it doesn't have numbers in it, he's not interested. I can see a few small love seats, some benches, places for people to sit and read." Dottie threw her arms out in a flourish. "We could stick a Keurig on the counter and bottled water. Serve cookies. Over there we can create a children's area and have story time. You'd be so great at reading stories to the kiddos."

"You too."

Dottie's cheeks flushed. "I practice with our grandkids every chance I get."

Dottie and Walt's two daughters lived in Texas. Their son had moved to California to make animated movies, according to Dottie. Mary Katherine didn't really know what that meant, but it seemed Chad was good at it. Between the three of them, they had produced six grandkids. They didn't get to see them as much as Dottie liked. Their plan was to buy an RV when they retired and roam the country spoiling grandkids. Only five more years to go. Mary Katherine counted it a blessing that most Plain kids settled close to home.

"How are those grandkids?"

"Brian and Kayla are great. Michelle just got braces and hates them. Josh grew a foot this summer. Brooklyn and Olivia are going to a Mother's Day Out program."

She rambled on and Mary Katherine let her. She knew how it felt to have grandchildren who filled up every corner of your heart. "You'd better visit your daughters at Thanksgiving and Chad at Christmas."

"That's the plan. But right now my concern is getting this bookstore off the ground."

Mary Katherine leaned her elbows against the counter, rested her chin on her palms, and contemplated the ceiling fans. They made a slight *thump-thump* when the blades revolved, creating a lovely breeze that dispelled the stuffy air that had greeted them when they opened the door. Probably needed oiling or tightening. What did she know about these things? What would Freeman say? And Cyrus? And Thomas? Her oldest son had definite ideas about her retirement years, as he called them. "I don't know if I can swing it."

"If anyone can, you can." Dottie trotted across the room, then propped herself against the counter, mimicking Mary Katherine's pose. "You can sell the idea to the others."

"I don't know. A bookstore isn't like Amish Treasures. It's a bigger risk." She chewed her lower lip. Thomas would go whichever way Freeman and Cyrus went. "People come here to buy Amish trinkets."

"They'll buy Amish romances too. Count on it." Dottie patted Mary Katherine's shoulder. "Talk to your folks. If it's about going into business with an

Englisch woman, let me know. I'll come talk to them some more."

"I don't think that's it." They would think being a cook at the restaurant more suitable. Thomas would think staying home and embroidering tablecloths for the Combination Store and playing with the grandchildren more suitable. Everyone had an opinion on her future. "Let me see what I can do. Right now, I have to go. I'm taking Burke to the Purple Martin for supper. I want to see if Ezekiel will give him a job."

"You left the serial killer at your house?"

"Not inside the house and he's not a serial killer."

"What serial killer?" Walt tromped into the room, his cowboy boots clacking on the wood floor, Jim and Jerry right behind him. Walt had a cobweb on his cowboy hat, a gray Stetson this time. "You're dating a serial killer and didn't tell us, Mary Kay?"

The other men guffawed. The idea of an old Amish lady dating a serial killer probably did sound preposterous. "He's a homeless man who needs a job, that's all. How does the wiring look?" After the fire that destroyed Amish Treasures and the antique store next door, Mary Katherine wasn't taking any chances. "Would we need to do repairs or ask Bob to do them— or reduce his asking price?"

"Wiring is good." Jim had a gravelly smoker's voice to match the stench of cigarettes that followed him around.

"So's the plumbing. Solid," Jerry chimed in. He sounded almost sad. No work here for him. "You're good to go."

No stumbling blocks there. Pleasure mingled with disappointment that no excuse presented itself in the building itself. "I still need to mull this over. We shouldn't jump into something just because Bob is in a hurry to sell."

"Agreed." Walt pursed his lips and crossed his arms over his rotund body. "That's what I always say. Proceed with caution. Invest with care."

"That's because you're an old fuddy-duddy." Dottie patted his arm. Her tinkly laughter softened the words. "Both of you are. I'll talk to Bob. Ask him to hold off on selling to anyone else. We might be able to get an option on it."

"Don't do anything that will cost you money if we decide not to go forward. Unless you can approach someone else to join you. Like Zoe. Zoe would be perfect."

Zoe was the volunteer who watched the library when Dottie had an appointment—like today.

"Zoe is sweet, but she did her time as an ER nurse in the hospital in Chillicothe. Her husband wants her at home now. He barely lets her volunteer at the library. I need someone who can take the reins when Walt and I have our RV adventures."

"Sounds like Zoe listens to her husband a lot better than you do." Walt's grin said he wasn't complaining.

Dottie laughed with him and spun like a ballerina across the room with amazing agility for a woman of her age. Walt clapped. His buddies joined in. She bowed deeply. "We should have some background music. Jazz or classical." She sounded breathless, but she was smiling. "Walt and I have got this covered. You just worry about getting rid of your serial killer."

"See you later."

If the serial killer didn't get Mary Katherine first.

CHAPTER 6

What on earth had she been thinking? Mary Katherine halted the buggy in front of the Purple Martin Café, with its lovely wooden sign featuring its namesake painted by Mahon Kurtz, local farmer and artist. Mary Katherine made no move to get down. What seemed to make perfect sense in the middle of the night appeared much more like the indigestion-induced musings of a sleep-deprived old woman in the early evening sunlight the following day. If this were a story, Dottie's flight-of-fancy serial killer would be waiting around the corner ready to muffle the victim's bloodcurdling scream. And Mary Katherine was the would-be victim. Burke McMillan sat unmoving next to her, as he had done throughout the thirty-minute ride into town.

Her attempts at conversation with the man who'd broken into her house to make a ham sandwich had been met with brief but not unfriendly responses, which told her little about her new acquaintance. He hailed from a place he vaguely referred to as the East Coast. He sounded educated. He'd worked a variety of jobs. He had no family here. So why had he come to

Jamesport? His response was a shrug and something to the effect that he decided he needed a change and found himself hitchhiking this direction. A lost man, a writer following bread crumbs.

Hitchhiking. Who would pick up a man who looked like a scarecrow and smelled like he hadn't had a bath in a month? She'd kept that thought to herself. No sense insulting a person when he was down.

Why her house? Her ham and bread? Her mustard? She knew no more than she had the previous night.

"Are we going in, or are we going to sit here and enjoy the last vestiges of light before the sun sets?" Burke raised his head to the sky and closed his eyes. "Not that it doesn't feel good. A person has to enjoy it while he can."

Why did a man who looked and smelled like this one use such highfalutin vocabulary? Not that she didn't like it. The writer in her couldn't help it. He was a thinking person too. The puzzle pieces didn't fit. He'd been ensconced in the hickory rocker on her front porch, the dirty duffel bag at his feet, when she returned early from Josephina's frolic. He was so engrossed in reading a tattered paperback called *The Hitchhiker's Guide to the Galaxy* that he didn't look up until she called his name. Then he simply removed skinny reading glasses, tucked the book in his bag, and came aboard without speaking. He was a much thinner man so she couldn't offer him the one set of Moses' clothes she'd saved as a memento of her husband. Surely Ezekiel would see past a little dirt to a man who needed a job and was willing to work.

Where would he stay when winter came with its snow and cold? Not in her barn. They needed to get in there and get him a job. A job would give him the money to rent a motel room, at the least. "Did it occur to you that you might want to get cleaned up before asking a restaurant owner for a job?"

"I thought about it." He leaned forward, elbows on his knees, head down. "But you didn't offer to let me back in your house, so I figured I'd better let well enough alone."

Mary Katherine gave herself a mental slap on the head. Of course, he had no place to get cleaned up. Which begged the question, where had he spent the day? "I'm sorry. I should've—"

"You're not responsible for me being a ne'er-do-well." He raised his head and stared at the restaurant. "It'll be fine."

It would be what it would be. "Let's go, shall we?"

Telling herself to ignore the large number of buggies interspersed with half a dozen cars parked in front of the long rectangular building with dark faux wood siding, she strode to the squeaky-clean glass double doors and tugged one open. The place would be busy on a Saturday night. No matter.

Walking into the Purple Martin Café was like walking into her mother's kitchen on a fall night. The flood of warmth, the mingled aromas of chicken frying, bread baking, and peach pies cooling on a table next to an open window, and the lively chatter of her sisters fixing food for people they loved. The Purple Martin smelled like love. It sounded like family. It felt like home. Ezekiel Miller had discovered the secret to a good restaurant wasn't just the food. She paused, inhaled, and immediately felt lighter for a few seconds.

All eight of the stools at the front counter were full. Almost all the picnic tables and the booths that ran along the wall to her left were occupied. They always were on Saturday night. Several people looked up when she stepped inside, Burke close behind. A person would think they had never seen a homeless man with a Plain woman. She and Burke made an odd couple. Not a couple. Her face heated at the thought. *Don't be ridiculous.*

She waded into the crowd, then stopped to greet her sister Willa, who sat in a red Naugahyde booth with her daughter, Amelia, and two grandsons who were using salt and pepper shakers as imaginary horses galloping across the gray Formica–topped table. Willa gave Burke the up-and-down once-over and went back to her pot roast. Having grown up with Mary Katherine, she could be counted on for a lack of surprise and for minding her own business. Amelia opened her mouth, but upon seeing the firm shake of her mother's head, closed it.

Thomas sat at a far corner table covered with a red-checked tablecloth. His wife and four youngest children sat with him.

Fortunately for Mary Katherine, the wrestling-slash-basketball-slash-track team from Tri-County High School, along with their parents and the coaches, had commandeered four tables and shoved them together for a team dinner of some sort. When a high school had only seventy-some students, everyone went out for all the sports. Their presence made a perfect wedge between Mary Katherine and her son. And a perfect excuse for not squeezing through to say hello. The exuberant conversation of the athletes, filled with the requisite hoots, hollers, and fist bumps between intermittent selfies with phones and double thumb tapping on screens that could only mean the photos were winging their way to kids all over Jamesport, ensured that Thomas would never notice her.

Coach Larry "The Claw" Wilson nodded as she passed. A former football player and wrestler, he coached all the sports and taught math at the high school. His wife, Phoebe, had frequented Amish Treasures and dragged him along occasionally. More often, their daughter, Nicole, who waitressed here at the Purple Martin, got roped into accompanying her mother. It seemed mean—or at the very least oblivious—to have an athletic dinner where their daughter worked and might have to serve her classmates.

Phoebe grinned and waved with more enthusiasm. She would want to talk quilt patterns and when Mary Katherine would have her wares at the Combination Store. Mary Katherine waved but veered in the opposite direction. "Keep moving. Keep moving."

Burke edged closer and raised his voice to be heard over the rambunctious high school kids. He smelled of barn—manure and straw, both of which clung to his jeans and ragged tennis shoes. "Who are you avoiding?"

"My son."

Thankful Thomas seemed engrossed in his food and conversation with Joanna, Mary Katherine headed toward the kitchen in the back. She hadn't expected Thomas to be here. He was a frugal man who didn't set much store by eating in restaurants. Joanna must've pleaded exhaustion after the cooking she'd done for the wedding. Thomas had a soft spot for his wife, even after seventeen years of marriage. He also had a soft spot for Ezekiel's traditional meatloaf served with baked potato, buttery corn, and huge slabs of home-made sourdough bread.

Ezekiel had a reputation for serving all his Plain dishes at reasonable—some might even say cheap—prices. He didn't gouge the tourists, nor proclaim his menu as the be-all and end-all of Amish foods. Food was food. His menu varied depending on the season, with fall full of warm comfort foods that heralded the beginning of cooler weather in the Midwest. Pot roast with mushroom gravy, baked pork chops, fried chicken, chicken pot pie, chicken dumplings. Soups, like Mary Katherine's favorite, with ham hock and navy beans, would come later when winter presented its snowy self.

"I don't want to cause you trouble." Burke squeezed between a table full of Bylers and another that surely held tourists. They made it obvious with their loud ex-clamations over their server Anna's dress and kapp and requests for "selfies" with her. "We can do this some other time."

"It's okay. I just need to find Ezekiel."

"Mary Kay, over here, over here!"

She turned toward the familiar high-pitched voice. Dottie and Walt sat at a table for four near the kitchen doors. Dottie half rose from her chair and waved. Mary Kay sighed and shook her head. Dottie couldn't help herself. She had to see the serial killer. "Come on."

She threaded her way toward the table, then stopped to let Nicole pass with huge trays hoisted over her shoulders. The look on her face as she trudged toward the tables where her classmates waited confirmed Mary Katherine's earlier thought. Bringing the kids here and then sitting in her area added insult to injury. She might be a cheerleader for the boys' teams and member of both the girls' basketball and softball teams, but tonight she was the server. "How are you doing, Nicole?"

She shook her head. Her long ponytail of ebony hair shook with it. "No time to talk." One tray, laden with heavy, steaming plates of chicken-fried steak, hamburgers, and fried chicken with all the trimmings, wavered. "Busy tonight."

The boy who bused the tables, Tony Perez, followed her with a foldout table to set the trays on. "Make way, Miz Ropp, make way," he hollered. He seemed to labor under the illusion that all people over the age of forty were going deaf. As if she could miss the gangly six-footer whose weight couldn't seem to catch up with his height. He was so lean a good northerly wind would blow him south to Texas. His jet-black hair, parted in the middle, was caught back in a ponytail almost as long as Nicole's. "I don't want Nicole to drop all that food."

"Come on, Mary Kay, we saved you and your guest a spot." Dottie's voice carried over the clatter of plates and spoons. "Don't dawdle."

Feeling like the rope in a game of tug-of-war, Mary Katherine squeezed past Tony and made it to Dottie and Walt's table. "I've never seen such a crowd off-season."

"It's a testament to the fact that the locals like this place." Walt patted his lips with his paper napkin. "You can't beat Ezekiel's chicken-fried steak or his pork chops."

"We moved from our usual spot because the coach's kids were making so much racket over there." Dottie sank into her chair with a *tut-tut* of disapproval. "Why didn't they take them to a pizza place in Gallatin? They're way too rowdy for this place, and you know The Claw is missing his beer. Phoebe probably has a flask of wine in her purse."

"Dottie! We don't gossip." Walt feigned disapproval as he dumped a packet of artificial sweetener in his iced tea. "Leastways not in public."

"It's true. When they come to our card games, she can barely stagger to the car after."

"I'm surprised to see you here." Mary Katherine tried to guide the conversation back to safe waters with quick introductions. "I thought you were dieting this week."

"We were. Dottie suddenly had a hankering for Ezekiel's chicken-fried steak. Surprised me. She's had me on this low-fat, low-taste diet for months. Doc says my blood pressure and my cholesterol are too high." Walt shook Burke's hand. "We saved you a seat. The fried chicken is so good it reminds me of my mother's."

"Is there something wrong with my fried chicken?" Dottie's lower lip protruded.

"Only that you refuse to make it for me."

"That's because I love you and I want you around forever."

Mary Katherine exchanged glances with Burke. Her friends' obvious love affair after forty years was a thing of beauty. It could also make a person a little sad and a little jealous if a person were small. Mary Katherine tried hard not to be small. "Actually, we want to talk to Ezekiel before we eat."

"I'd like to clean up a little first." Burke smiled at Dottie. "But it was nice to meet you."

Mary Katherine pointed out the back hallway that led to the restrooms beside another door marked EMPLOYEES ONLY that led to Ezekiel's office. She sank into the chair closest to Dottie. "What are you doing here? Checking up on me?"

"He looks like Kevin Costner." Dottie threw her hand against her forehead and pretended to swoon. "The older Kevin, not the young one. He definitely doesn't look like a serial killer."

"Who's Kevin Costner?" And what did a serial killer look like?

Walt voiced that question aloud and then added, "You know, *Field of Dreams*, *For Love of the Game*, *Bull Durham*—the baseball trilogy. I like his older movies better than his new ones."

Mary Katherine didn't know about the movies, but she nodded. "An actor."

"Not just any actor." Dottie waved her fork. Drops of gravy splattered on the tablecloth. "Sexy. Cute. Sweet. Funny. He's the kind of guy who makes you drool in your popcorn and Milk Duds. He's aged really well, if you ask me."

"Nobody asked you." Walt scraped the last of the gravy off his plate. "I think I've aged pretty well too."

"You have, sweetie, you have." Dottie blew him a kiss. He grinned and dug into the few kernels that remained of his creamed corn. "Thomas is here."

"I know." Mary Katherine nodded.

"You should talk to him about the building."

One thing at a time. "I will, but not tonight."

"Are you worried about how he'll take to Burke?"

That would be an understatement. She'd like to avoid the moment for as long as possible. She craned her head, looking for Ezekiel. She needed to get this over with and get out. The object of her search, with a pie in each hand, backed through the kitchen's swinging double doors. He didn't look up.

Burke arrived at the table. He looked marginally better with a clean face, but his dirty T-shirt and bedraggled jeans didn't bode well for a job interview. It couldn't be helped. "Let's go." She pushed off the table with both hands and nodded at Dottie. "We'll talk to you later."

"You bet your bottom dollar." Dottie offered her hand to Burke, who took it with solemnity worthy of a subject bowing to his queen. "I'll look forward to talking to you too, Burke. I want to know all about you."

"Yes, ma'am."

"Lovely manners too."

Mary Katherine scowled at her friend, who finally let Burke's hand drop and picked up her fork. "Come back for dessert."

"We'll see." Mary Katherine focused on her mission to convince Ezekiel to hire Burke while making no promises of her own.

Ezekiel slid the pies on the counter and turned to a battery-operated calculator. An old-fashioned cash register took up a chunk of space next to it, along with a pile of oversized laminated menus. Dark circles hung beneath his eyes, and his clothes looked as if they'd been made for a larger man. A rotund lady in green sweatpants and matching sweatshirt asked him a question.

His deep voice carried over the steady hum of conversation. "I am glad you liked the sugar cream pie." He pointed his thumb down toward the glass display case that ran the length of the wooden counter. "They come with the recipe."

"So you won't give me the recipe unless I buy the pie?" The lady ran her chubby fingers through flyaway hair the color of cinnamon-drop candy. "What would it cost to get you to come to my house in St. Louis to bake one for me?"

Despite exhaustion apparent in the way his shoulders slumped, Ezekiel chuckled. He had a nice smile. For the briefest of moments, Mary Katherine's mind veered off track, remembering how solid his muscles had been when they fell together in the grass. He smelled like soap and peppermint. He smelled good.

Heat rushed through her. *You've cracked your gourd, old woman.*

"*Or you're alive.*" Moses' laugh tickled her ear.
You hush.

Ezekiel's gaze meandered over the woman's shoulder and collided with Mary Katherine's. He smiled again, this time with more feeling. "I have my hands full running the restaurant. I reckon your best bet is to buy a pie."

Mary Katherine pointed toward the wide-open double doors behind Ezekiel that led to the kitchen. His hands busy boxing up the pie his customer had settled upon, Ezekiel nodded without missing a beat.

"They're really busy here." Burke followed her into the kitchen, then backstepped and threw himself up against the wall to allow two more waitresses—Miriam and Anna—room to pass with trays loaded down with plates of steaming food. He straightened, a smile stretching across his face. His upper teeth were even, but the bottom row could only be described as snaggled. "No wonder they need a dishwasher."

They had a busboy and two commercial-size dishwashers. She wasn't sure they did.

"Mary Kay! I'm so happy to see you." Daphne, sister-in-law to Thomas's wife, untied an apron spattered with grease and flour. "Ezekiel said you'd be taking over the cooking. Not a minute too soon. My plantar fascia is killing me. Doc says I need to stay off my feet for a while." She tossed the apron into an overflowing basket in the corner and pushed through the swinging doors before Mary Katherine could respond.

"You didn't mention you work here." Burke crossed his arms over his chest. A tattoo of a ruby-throated hummingbird fluttered on his forearm. "What's the owner like?"

"I don't work here. Ezekiel is just overly optimistic or he overestimates his powers of persuasion. For someone who is stalking me, you seem to be short on information."

"I wasn't stalking you. I'm observant."

"Where was Daphne headed?" Ezekiel stuck his head through the swinging doors. "I've got a line at the register and half a dozen orders up on the wire."

Mary Katherine wrestled with the angel on her shoulder who whispered in her ear, *He needs help. Get a clean apron and get to work.* "She said her feet hurt. She thought I was here to spell her."

"Well? Are you?"

She wanted to start her workday smelling fresh ink and paper, not bacon frying and toast browning. "I brought you someone to wash dishes." He would get over the disappointment. "This is Burke McMillan."

"Tony Perez takes care of that on Saturdays." Ezekiel took a breath. She could almost see him counting to ten. "What I need is a cook. Daphne has health problems and she can't be on her feet all the time."

"I can cook." Burke plopped his duffel bag in the corner and held up both hands. "Where do I wash up?"

Ezekiel moved inside, letting the doors swing shut. "Who are you?"

"I was a short-order cook at a truck stop for a stretch. Before that I managed a Mexican fast-food joint." His expression earnest, he introduced himself again and stuck out his hand. Ezekiel shook it. Burke smiled. "You need a cook. I need a job."

A strange résumé that didn't seem to fit the man who

stood in front of them. Where had Burke McMillan come from, and what was he doing in Jamesport?

His face puzzled, Ezekiel's gaze meandered from Burke to Mary Katherine. He looked worn and frazzled. She studied the corn on the cob steaming on the stove. Something smelled a little burnt. The potatoes. The silence stretched. "You'll not take me up on my offer, then?"

"Nee. I can't." The entreaty in his voice made her want to change her response. If she started working here, she would never have her dream. She was getting too old to keep postponing it. "I'm sorry. I've got my hands full. Really I do."

"I understand." Ezekiel's tone held disappointment and resignation. "I think."

Nicole peeked through the big window next to the doors. She pinned two more tickets on the wire that stretched across it. "Meatloaf plate and a fried chicken plate." She stuck her pen behind her ear. "They're getting restless out there." Her head disappeared.

Scrubbing at his face with his sleeve, Ezekiel returned his gaze to Burke. A second passed. Then another. "Let's call it a practice run. Put on a clean shirt. There's a stack by the sink in the back. While you're there, wash up good. Take a bath in the hand sanitizer if necessary."

Burke nodded, his expression somber. "Thank you, boss. I appreciate the opportunity."

"Call me Ezekiel."

Burke whirled and disappeared into the back.

Ezekiel pushed through the swinging doors. He held

them open for a second and looked back. "Thomas is making his way over here. Any idea what he wants?"

"Maybe he just wants to say hello before he pays his bill."

"He looks grim. Like someone died." Ezekiel shook his head. "I reckon you did something that got on your suh's last nerve."

"I haven't done a thing."

"You brought me a stray man."

"You needed a cook. He needed a job. Two problems, one stone."

"If he's a bad cook, you'll have to take his place."

"It's a deal."

"Mudder, I know you're back there. Phoebe told me." Thomas's deep voice, so like Moses', carried. "So did Willa. I need to talk to you."

Ezekiel stepped aside. "After you."

Feeling like a prisoner walking the plank, she lifted her chin, dusted off her dignity, and slipped past him.

She was almost certain she heard a soft chuckle behind her back.

CHAPTER 7

The silent treatment. Mary Katherine followed her normally talkative son through the restaurant doors. He said nothing, but the set of his shoulders shouted irritation. He stomped ahead toward his buggy at the far end of a string of them parked in front of the Purple Martin.

She picked up her pace. No need to have him accuse her of dawdling. The sole of her sneaker stuck to the sidewalk. Pink bubble gum. She yanked her foot up. The shoe stayed on the sidewalk. She hopped on one foot.

An Englisch boy dressed in a Tri-County High School Mustangs T-shirt and sweats danced around her, his gaze on the phone in his hand. He was followed by a girl in virtually the same outfit—except her T-shirt fit much tighter and the phone was wrapped in a glittery pink case. Members of Coach Wilson's team.

"Sorry!" He squeezed past her, the hand with the phone held up high as if he might get her germs if he passed too closely. "You're holding up traffic."

"Yeah, you're holding up traffic." The girl tossed her long ponytail over her shoulder with a flick of her head.

She snapped her bubble gum and smiled. "We're sneaking out, so we're in a hurry. We've got stuff to do."

The boy looked back. "Shut up, Kerri."

"Don't tell me to shut up, Jason."

He scowled. She scurried after him.

Mary Katherine hopped backward. "Sorry. Gum on my shoe."

"Hate it when that happens." The girl's voice floated over the rumble of a diesel pickup truck.

"Me too." Mary Katherine said it more to herself than anyone else. She hated it when a lot of things happened. She plopped onto the bench in front of the restaurant and extricated the blob from her shoe with the tips of her fingernails.

The kids ducked into a pickup truck the color of rust parked a half foot from the curb. It sputtered to life and sped away with tires squealing, leaving Mary Katherine in a cloud of stinky oil and gas fumes.

"Mudder!" Thomas stood next to his horse, his scowl evident for miles. "Mudder, come on."

She attempted to toss the bubble gum in the brown trash can that sat near the door. It stuck to her hand. She pulled. The blob stretched in long strings that dangled from her fingernails. She blew out air so hard it made the tiny wisps of hair on her forehead tickle her skin. "What is everyone's rush tonight?"

Thomas waited for her to climb into the buggy, then stomped around to the other side. "Why didn't Dottie mention you were here?" He pulled out onto the road. Even the *clip-clop* of the horse's hooves had an accusatory ring. "You can't tell me she didn't know.

She made it a point to say hello to Joanna and then avoided me."

"She was probably in a hurry to get home to finish her John Sandford book. She told me she's three-quarters of the way through his last Prey book and it's so suspenseful it keeps her up at night."

"Mudder!"

"Why are you dragging me out of the restaurant? Why did you leave your fraa and kinner to take me home? I have my own buggy."

"I didn't leave them. Joanna is taking your buggy to our house. We'll switch back later."

Mary Katherine sideswiped Thomas with a glance. His face could only be described as gloomy. Dusk took over for the sun. The air began to cool. Still, it remained decidedly warm in the buggy. "Why? What is the problem, Suh?"

"What is the problem?" His pitch and volume climbed simultaneously. "Cyrus sent Joseph to find me. He and Freeman and Solomon are at your house. They wanted to know where you are."

The deacon, the bishop, and the minister. A fierce threesome. "They're at my house?" Now her voice squeaked. "What do they want?"

Thomas glowered at her. "What do you think?" The grapevine was more of a raging grass fire in this Gmay. "Where is this man who spent the night in your barn?"

"That was him at the restaurant."

"You spent the day with him?"

"Nee, I met him at the house—on the porch, earlier."

"At the house? What were you thinking?"

"That I'd help him get a job."

Thomas groaned. "A nice thought, but not one you should take upon yourself. You should've talked to me or Dylan. Any of your suhs. This isn't one of your make-believe stories where you get to give the hero a happily-ever-after ending."

Her characters didn't always get happily ever afters. Her stories reflected life as it was, but Mary Katherine didn't argue. She would only dig the hole deeper, so she settled back in her seat and glued her gaze to the passing landscape in the deepening dusk.

The remainder of the drive passed in strained silence. They drove up to the house and parked in full view of Cyrus, Freeman, and Solomon seated on her porch. She took a breath and lifted her chin as she followed Thomas up the steps. The three men sat in lawn chairs side by side, looking like triplets with their long white beards, thick black-rimmed bifocals, black hats, and blank expressions.

One of them had added two more lawn chairs from the side of the house, making a long, narrow semicircle on her pristine, freshly painted porch framed by shrubs and tall sunflowers that drooped. Freeman waved in the direction of the first chair and Thomas plopped into it without a word. He was probably tuckered out from chewing her out up one side and down the other.

Endeavoring to arrange her face in some semblance of obedient humility, she eased into her chair with all the grace she could muster after a long day. The chair's woven nylon seat groaned under her weight. Heat warmed her cheeks.

"That breeze sure feels good. It was a long, hot summer." Somehow speaking first made her feel as if she'd taken the reins in the conversation. Which was, of course, the exact opposite of what she should do. So much for humility. She tucked her hands together in her lap and locked gazes with Freeman. "Thomas said you wanted to see me."

"I'm sure you can figure out why." Freeman tugged his glasses from his face and wiped the lenses on his cotton shirt. He looked no less fierce with his piercing pale-blue eyes, shaded by jutting white eyebrows, unmasked. "You've had an eventful week."

"The wedding went well. It's a blessing to have all my children married. I'm thankful for all the help from everyone."

Freeman and Cyrus exchanged glances. They let her words hang in the air as she had often done with her children when they failed to admit to a wrongdoing in hopes of avoiding punishment.

"Mudder—"

"Let me." Freeman interrupted Thomas with one hand lifted, palm out. "Tell us about the burglar who spent the night in your house."

"He wasn't a burglar. He didn't steal anything. And it was the barn, not the house."

"Mary Katherine."

The use of her full name in that tone that reminded her of her parents so many years ago told Mary Katherine she'd gone far enough. She inhaled the scent of fresh-cut grass and men who worked hard. No point in dillydallying any longer. She told the story without faltering, without leaving out a detail. Thomas squirmed in his chair, his face getting redder with each new revelation. Freeman's only reaction was an occasional sniff. Cyrus stroked his silver beard. Solomon's skinny white eyebrows roamed higher and higher over wide blue eyes.

After she finished, Freeman wiped his nose with a huge bandanna for a full five seconds before nodding. "This Burke McMillan, where is he from?"

"I don't know."

"What is he doing in Jamesport?"

"Now he's working at the Purple Martin Café."

"You're a grown mother with ten kinner. I'm certain you know it doesn't pay to be lippy about this situation."

"It's not my intent to be lippy." She did know. Humility and obedience. *Gott, does that mean I cannot be treated as a grown woman who raised ten kinner? Is this some sort of lesson in breaking my pride?* Of course it was. As well it should be. She took a deep breath and let it out. "I only wanted to help a stranger in need."

"Your intentions were gut, I'll give you that." Freeman leaned back in his chair and steepled his fingers over his paunch—which seemed to have grown over the last several months. "We should all help those in need."

If only he would stop there, but Mary Katherine knew he wouldn't.

"You're alone in this house now. I shouldn't have to spell this out for you, but I will. A woman alone with a man—not your suh or your *mann*—and an Englischer at that. An Englisch stranger. You should've gone to the phone shack and called me or Cyrus. Immediately."

She couldn't argue with any of those statements—though she really wanted to. *Gott, help me be more obedient. Please.* She ducked her head, breathed, and nodded. She'd handled the situation badly, but how could they know what it was like? They hadn't been there, in her shoes, at that moment when a decision had to be made.

"Freeman and I have discussed this with Thomas." Cyrus spoke for the first time. For a big man, he had a small, quiet voice, so unlike Freeman's sonorous bass. "We're concerned for you."

"Thomas tells me he intends for you to move in with him and his fraa," Solomon added. "He also says you have argued with him. I—we—find that odd. Most groossmammis want to spend all the time they can with their grands. Your suh Dylan already has his in-laws with him—both of them. It's a happy arrangement for them all."

He left the thought hanging, as if waiting for an explanation. How could she explain that she'd lived in her house her entire adult life? She'd lived there with Moses. It was the last place she'd seen her husband alive.

She could visit, but it wouldn't be the same.

"You have nothing to say for yourself?" Freeman's tone held exasperation mixed with a touch of tenderness. The tone a father used with a child. "Surely you have an explanation for your reluctance."

"Dottie would like for me to open a bookstore with her." Mary Katherine draped sweetness and concili- ation over her words. "She has a spot picked out on

Grant Street. It would keep me well occupied and provide a source of income. I would hardly be home alone at all."

Except at night.

"You wouldn't need an income if you moved in with Thomas. Dylan will have more room for his growing family. Joanna will have help. No worries about break-ins."

"Or falling when no one is around." Cyrus and Freeman spent so much time together, they finished each other's sentences like an old married couple. "That's a concern, as you can imagine."

"I didn't fall. I tripped over Thomas." She covered her mouth with her hand, wishing she could take back the words. Better not to argue. She knew that. If Moses were here, he'd cover it for her. Then grin. "I'll be more careful. I'd like to have a little more time in our home. Moses' and my home."

"You've had several years." Freeman's features softened. "It's not an easy thing to get over. I understand that. But Gott's will is never to be questioned."

He still had his wife. Sweet Josephina. He couldn't understand. Not really. "I know that."

He allowed his fingers to intertwine and rest on his belly. "I'm concerned over starting a business with an Englisch woman. Especially after the disaster at Amish Treasures."

Cyrus's chuckle was more of a sigh. "This is what happens when a woman doesn't have a mann to take care of."

That she should still want a life and reason to arise

each morning seemed to surprise and disconcert them. "Books are good."

"There are plenty at Dottie's library, and they're free." Cyrus's tone spoke of a certainty that money could be spent in better ways. "I'm sure she can find other friends willing to go in with her."

Englisch friends. He didn't say it, but that's what he meant.

"Leo and Jennie could use some help at the Combination Store. I've heard they invited you to go in with them. Consider it." Freeman stood as if to punctuate the statement. Cyrus and Solomon rose together. Thomas followed suit. "Strongly. They are working to make a go of it. This is a gut thing, especially for Leo. You are better with people. They need you."

He said "better with people" as if it weren't the best quality to have. Mingling with the world instead of keeping to herself. Bookstores with Englisch women. Mary Katherine remained in her chair. Disappointment tangled with relief. They hadn't made her move. Not yet. But no bookstore. As usual she couldn't leave well enough alone. "Ezekiel also asked me to cook at the restaurant."

Freeman put both hands on the porch railing and leaned over it, his head craned as if he were searching the dusk. "Ezekiel needed a cook. Now he has one. This Burke fellow."

"He needs more than one."

Freeman straightened and faced her. "We'll talk with Ezekiel tomorrow after church. We need to know more about this man."

Working at the Combination Store would help her earn the money to buy into the bookstore. With time. "I'd like to work there to earn back the money I lost when Amish Treasures burned down."

He nodded at Cyrus and Thomas. "It's late. Church tomorrow."

A self-satisfied grin on his face, Thomas hopped from his seat and bounded down the steps. "We can trade buggies at church."

Mary Katherine knew it was a woman's lot to have men in charge. It had never seemed onerous—until now.

CHAPTER 8

The bolt made a beautiful clicking sound when it slid into the lock. It signaled the end of another day at the Purple Martin Café. Rubbing his neck with one hand, Ezekiel flipped the sign that hung on the door to CLOSED with the other. His back hurt and his legs ached. His head throbbed, but he couldn't complain. Customers had flowed through the restaurant in a steady stream. His costs would be covered and payroll secured. In the restaurant business, that was success. That was more important than the toll it took on his body to plow through these long days on his feet. Mary Katherine's stray man could cook. Who knew where Burke McMillan came from or how he arrived in Jamesport, but he had been a blessing this Saturday night.

Unfortunately, Mary Katherine had left the café with Thomas and hadn't returned. That left Ezekiel with no opportunity to serve her a piece of banana cream pie, her favorite, according to her daughter Beulah, who nattered about everything under the sun when she stopped in for lunch on her grocery-shopping days. According to Beulah, Mary Katherine had a sweet tooth to match his. She'd looked nervous as a cat in a rainstorm as she walked away with Thomas.

At this point it was hard to say if she would be back on Monday. Whether Thomas objected more to his mother working in the restaurant or to her gallivanting around the countryside with a strange man was also open to question. In all fairness, if she were his mother, Ezekiel would object to the strange man in her house too.

He would try to ferret out the answers after church in the morning. He turned to survey the dining area. Miriam and Anna were in back, emptying the high-powered commercial dishwashers. Nicole trudged from table to table, replacing dirty tablecloths with clean ones. She picked up a pile of linens that reached above eye level and stumbled toward the last row of tables.

"Careful there. Let me help you."

Nicole pushed down the load with one hand so he could see both of her pale-gray eyes. "That's okay. I've got it."

"You must be raring to get out of here." Ezekiel had tried a few times to carry on a conversation with his newest waitress, but she didn't have much to say. He'd hired her on Anna's recommendation. He wasn't sure how Freeman's granddaughter knew her, but they seemed to get along well. "It's Saturday night. Your friends are probably waiting."

"Not really." She stopped at the last table and dumped her load in a chair while she grabbed the dirty tablecloth. "I'm just going home. Daddy will be watching game videos and Mom will be reading one of her Amish romances."

"She reads Amish romances?"

"I know, right?" Nicole added clean tablecloths to the last two tables with admirable efficiency. For a teenager, she didn't seem to mind manual labor. She picked up her load again. "She lives in the middle of a bunch of Amish people, and she still wants to read fake stories about them."

"No harm in it, I guess."

She snorted and headed toward the kitchen doors and the back room that held a commercial-size washer and dryer. "Anyway, I can stay until the tablecloths are dry and fold them, if you want."

"No, no need. I don't want you staying out that late. Do you have a ride home?"

"It's only eight blocks."

"Still."

"I can give you a ride." Tony Perez bounded across the room with all the energy and enthusiasm of an overgrown puppy. He'd removed his apron to reveal a black T-shirt that featured a band Ezekiel didn't recognize. His jeans had holes in both knees, but his black Nikes looked new. "My car is running again. At least it was when I drove it over here."

The pause that followed lasted long enough to be awkward. Ezekiel cleared his throat. Tony's expectant look faded. "Or whatever. A girl like you probably has plans."

Her face scarlet, Nicole made a beeline between them. She glanced at Tony, then away. "My friend Kaitlyn and her boyfriend are picking me up."

"Oh, yeah, that's good. Whatever."

"Maybe next time." Nicole's words came out in a stutter. "You know, next week or something."

"Oh, yeah, next time. For sure." Grinning, Tony saluted Ezekiel. "I'm done, Mr. E. I'm out of here."

"Careful out there."

"Always."

The door closed harder than necessary. The bell tinkled until the desire to silence it grew fierce.

Andrew marched out of the men's restroom, bucket in one hand, mop in the other. He had stopped by, as he did most nights, to help clean the tables, mop the floors, and restock the salt and pepper shakers, along with other condiments. He looked up and waved. He'd been married almost a year, but that didn't stop him from helping out. Summoning a smile, Ezekiel waved back. Andrew also would take out the trash. He was a good man and a good son. "I'll be back to help in a minute."

"We've got it." Andrew settled the mop on the floor next to the closest table. "You deal with the food and the receipts. You don't want me doing either."

True. His sons had no interest or aptitude for the restaurant business. Only a desire to please Ezekiel, something that always touched his heart, even if he didn't have the words to tell them that. He headed for the kitchen.

"Daed, wait."

He turned to find Andrew leaning on the mop, his expression hesitant. "Got a minute?"

"Sure, always." Ezekiel moved toward the counter. "The *kaffi* is probably still warm, if you have a hankering—"

"Nee, I just wanted to talk to you." He twirled the mop around with one hand. Then he looked back as if to see if Nicole was within earshot. "About a couple of things."

"I still have the paperwork to do. We're shorthanded—"

"I know. Just for a minute." Andrew plopped down on a stool and leaned the broom against the counter. "John said you offered Mary Kay a job."

"She couldn't stay tonight, so this man Burke McMillan did a trial run."

"And Mary Kay?"

"Why do you want to know?"

Andrew's face turned beet red. His gaze shifted to the ceiling.

"Do you want that kaffi?" Taking pity on him, Ezekiel turned and strode to the line of coffeepots and tea pitchers situated on tables along the wall behind the counter. "Is black okay?"

"Black is fine."

When Ezekiel turned around with two mugs of lukewarm coffee, Andrew took a mug and cupped it in his hands as if to warm them. He didn't meet Ezekiel's gaze.

"What's on your mind, Suh?"

"We were just talking about how you never remarried."

"It's hard for an old dog to learn new tricks."

"It's not gut for you to be alone."

"I'm fine."

Andrew sipped the coffee, swallowed, and set the mug down. "Just because you're old doesn't mean you can't learn new tricks. It's harder, but it can be done."

"Whatever you're trying to say, spit it out. I'm growing roots standing here."

"Mary Kay."

He got that part. "Jah?"

"Are you . . . I mean . . . am I . . . I don't want to . . ." He sputtered to a stop, his expression so grim a person might think he had a terminal disease. "She fell on you at the wedding. You ate in the kitchen. We thought maybe . . . there was an interest."

"I had cake all over my clothes." At the time it had made perfect sense. It still did. He paused, the cup halfway to his lips. The memory of Mary Katherine's weight pressed against him again for a split second. He'd forgotten how it felt to be that close to a woman. Soft. She felt soft. And she smelled sweet. Like cake, naturally. She smelled good.

"Mudder has been gone a long time." Andrew studied the dregs in his mug, his expression somewhere between morose and downright sad. "I reckon she wouldn't mind if you didn't spend your last years alone."

Ezekiel forced himself back to the present. "I'm not dying yet. I'm not that old."

"You don't look so gut. You've lost weight."

"I could stand to lose a few more pounds. I've gone soft through the middle eating my own cooking."

"Daed!"

"Your mudder was it for me." The words didn't do justice to the void where Ezekiel's heart had once been, but he had no flowery sentences to describe his love for his wife. Besides, it was private—not even his sons had a right to those feelings. "I'm gut on my own.

You and your bruder and your schweschders have gut fraas and manns. You have your kinner. That makes me happy."

"We don't want you to be alone." Andrew slid the mug toward Ezekiel. "Other widows and widowers have married again. They found someone new."

"It's not that easy. At least it isn't for me." Ezekiel stared into his mug. If he drank coffee now, he'd be up all night. He pushed it away. "Besides, I'm not alone. I have the bunch of you and your kinner, plus a lot of customers."

Love between a man and a woman was a special creature. That it could happen more than once in a lifetime seemed incredible. That it happened once was hard enough to believe. "Are you taking out the trash or what?"

Andrew ducked his head. "I don't like sticking my nose in your business—"

"Then don't. Cleaning up around here is all the help I need from you."

Andrew slipped from the stool and grabbed the broom. "Sorry."

He was halfway across the room before Ezekiel managed to clear the lump in his throat enough to speak. "Suh."

Andrew looked back. Ezekiel summoned a smile. "No need to be sorry. I *lieb* you too."

It shouldn't be that hard for a man to express his love for his children. Lucy had taught him that. Most Plain folks didn't hold much store in that sort of thing, but Lucy did.

Andrew smiled and nodded. "I'll take out the trash after I finish mopping the floors."

Ezekiel heaved a sigh of relief. He didn't like dredging up this stuff. What possessed his children to do it for him? Better to let it lie. A man couldn't expect lightning to strike in the same place twice. He'd seen it happen with others, but maybe they settled for something less, something better than being alone. He had no intention of settling. God had taken his wife. He got the message loud and clear. His was not to be the life of those around him. He was a widower.

The word cut his throat like slivers of glass when he swallowed.

He didn't understand it. God's plan. He shouldn't expect to understand it. All these years and he still wanted an answer. *Why, Gott?*

He let his gaze follow his son and the girls as they worked, but his mind captured Andrew's words and spun a story against his will, no matter how entrenched in widowerhood he intended to be. The images were vibrant, clear as the sky on a spring morning, and inescapable. Instead of leaving at the end of the day, Mary Katherine came home with him. Their voices and their laughter echoed in the evening air as they shared the buggy ride back to their home. They shared their impressions of the day and the customers who ate at their tables. She chuckled at his grumpiness. He pretended to be hurt. She coaxed him from his mood. At home she lit the lamp and plopped into the rocking chair to do her darning for a half hour before bed. He made a produce list and soaked his feet in Epsom salts. She smiled at him from her seat. He smiled back through tired, bleary eyes. She looked pretty.

Lucy had rocked all four of their children in that rocking chair. The story in Ezekiel's head screeched to a halt. An uncomfortable, sick feeling rocked his stomach. The kind of guilty feeling a child experienced when he stole a piece of candy at the grocery store and got away with it. The candy tasted vile and a dry throat made it impossible to swallow. "Nee," he whispered to himself. He needed to keep his mind on the restaurant and not fanciful dreams. "You can't teach an old dog new tricks."

Gritting his teeth, Ezekiel shoved through the kitchen doors. Burke stood at the grill, a drumstick midway to his mouth. His cheeks bulged and his lips shone with grease. "Sorry." The food in his mouth mangled the word. He lowered the drumstick. "Hungry."

"You never took a break." Regret blossomed in Ezekiel. "You never ate, did you?"

Burke chewed and swallowed. He wiped his fingers and face with his apron. "I didn't know if we were allowed to eat. Everyone was busy, and no one said anything."

The man's arms were bony, his chin sharp, cheeks sunken. Ezekiel grabbed a pan that still held a few meager slices of meatloaf surrounded by congealed grease. He held it out. "That's my fault. Eat. Warm it up first. Employees are allowed one free meal per shift."

"I'm full. Thank you."

Ezekiel doubted that, but he didn't press. He would send a bag home with the man.

"If you plan to work here, you'll need to fill out paperwork. We'll have to give the government its due. I'm careful to follow all the rules." He let his gaze sweep the kitchen. Burke had made great headway in cleaning up. The only tasks Ezekiel had left were tallying the day's receipts and making a list of produce and meat that needed to be purchased Monday morning. "I have everything in the office. We haven't even talked about your salary."

"We can do it Monday if you're bushed." Burke covered the meatloaf with foil and slid the pan in the refrigerator. His movements were quick and efficient, despite the long hours he'd worked. "I'm not done cleaning."

"I have to take care of receipts in the office anyway. You finish here, and I'll be back."

He plowed through the receipts and stowed the money in the safe as usual. Then made a list for the next day. He'd bought too much hamburger and not enough chicken the previous trip to the store. Even after all these years, predicting the quantity was impossible. Fortunately, it froze, unlike the limp lettuce and overripe tomatoes that had to be tossed. Forty-five minutes later he strolled back through the restaurant, employee application and the other routine paperwork in hand. The lights were off. Andrew and the others had finished their work and left.

The quiet soothed him. The paperwork did not. It was his least favorite part of being an employer, but he kept up with it—that and the finicky Health Department rules. He didn't want those spot inspections to trip him up. Which was why the state of the kitchen perked him up. The sinks, the stoves, the grill, the floor—everything shone from the obvious application of elbow grease.

Burke rinsed out a washrag and laid it flat on the edge of the huge stainless-steel sinks before he turned to face Ezekiel. "I think that's it."

"Good job. Everything looks real nice. Here's the application. I'll need a photocopy of your driver's license and your social security card after you get it filled out. They have a machine over at the post office. I think it's fifteen cents a copy. You can bring them later, when you get a chance. Just fill out the application."

Burke took off his apron and stuck it in the overflowing basket. He didn't reach for the papers. "I should get out of your way."

"Take it with you then."

His gaze averted, Burke sidestepped Ezekiel and pushed through the double doors.

Ezekiel followed. "Is there some reason you don't want to do the paperwork?"

Or couldn't. Maybe he couldn't read. Or he was afraid of that part of the application that asked about felony convictions. Ezekiel had seen it all in ten years. "I've had convicts work here before. As long as you're on the straight and narrow now, we're fine." He hesitated. Sometimes the not-being-able-to-read scenario was a more tender subject than being a criminal. "If you need help filling out the application—"

"I have a college education, including a master's and a doctorate. I've read *Don Quixote*—in Spanish."

Something sparked in Burke's eyes, but whatever it was faded just as quickly. "And I'm not a convict. I've nothing to hide."

Ezekiel had only a vague idea as to whom Don Quixote might be, but the point was well taken. "Gut. We'll get this squared away on Monday. Mary Kay never came back. You'll need a ride." Ezekiel laid the papers on the counter, within Burke's reach. "All I can offer is a buggy, but it's better than walking."

"I'm fine. It's close."

"I haven't seen you around here. Are you new to Jamesport?"

"Yes."

"Where do you live?"

The answer was long in coming. "Out Mary Katherine's direction."

"That's too far to walk. Let me give you a ride."

"I don't want to inconvenience you."

"It's not. It's a nice, cool fall night. It'll feel good after being inside all day. I guess you have a car to get you back here on Monday."

"No." Burke ran his fingers through the sparse light-brown hair on top of his head. "Look, this isn't going to work. I didn't think it through. I don't like lying to people. Sorry." He picked up a scruffy duffel bag and edged toward the door.

"You don't live out by Mary Kay, do you?"

"I don't live anywhere to speak of."

Which made it hard to put an address on an application or a W-4.

"Then I guess you're coming home with me."

CHAPTER 9

The house fit Ezekiel like his favorite boots. Just the right amount of room without pinching or rubbing. But it seemed a little snug for two. He shut the door behind Burke and moved to the oak table that separated the kitchen from the front room. He lit a propane lamp next to the table. The flame flared and the wick glowed. The familiar, homey scents of phosphorus and propane mingled. The light created shadows on the wall that, on most nights, served as his only company. He pointed to the short hallway that held his bedroom and the spare. "Your room is the first door." He gestured in the other direction. "There's the kitchen and the front room. That's pretty much it."

"It's plenty."

Ezekiel tried to see his living quarters through a stranger's eyes. *Sparse* might be the best word. Two chairs by the fireplace, an end table overflowing with his books, his Bible, and the restaurant ledger. A small kitchen table with four chairs—in case the grands came for a sandwich. A calendar on one wall. That was about it. He chuckled. "It is. House for one."

"You don't live with your family?" Burke's curious glance landed on Ezekiel. "Neither does Mary Katherine. I thought all Amish people lived with family."

"They're right there." He jerked his head in the general direction of the house that Leah and William shared. "This is called the dawdy haus. Usually a husband and his fraa—his wife—live in it together when they get older. My daughter and her husband live in the bigger house with their three kinner—children."

"Why don't you live with them?" Burke still stood in the middle of the room. He shifted his bag from one hand to the other. "The grandkids get on your nerves?"

"Not at all. It's a long story. I like kids."

"Me too."

Something in Burke's tone spoke of another long story that would not be shared.

"I usually fix myself a hot chocolate or tea." Ezekiel moved into the kitchen and set the kettle on the propane stove burner. "It helps me sleep."

Helped him put off that moment when he climbed into bed, pulled up around his neck the Flying Cardinals patchwork quilt Lucy made the winter Leah was born twenty-six years ago, and listened to the absolute silence in his tiny home. It took them years to have babies. They'd thought they might never. Then they'd lost two before they were born. Then Leah. Like a miracle. And Carlene, John, and Andrew in rapid succession. Miracle upon miracle. Noise. So much happy racket. These days, not even a dog's restless panting broke the silence. He often thought of getting a dog, but he never did. Dogs had short lives. A person got attached, only to have a dog die of old age or get hit by a car.

He didn't need any more death for company.

"You don't have to do this."

He swiveled to look at his guest. "Do what?"

"Bring a strange man into your house and feel obligated to make conversation."

Ezekiel tore open a packet of instant hot chocolate. The sweet scent filled his nostrils. The image of Lucy standing at the kitchen counter making cocoa floated in front of him. If she were here now, she'd scold him for using an instant mix. 'Course, she wouldn't allow it in her house to begin with. "I don't mind company. Besides, you don't look all that strange to me."

A snorting sound told him what Burke thought of that comment. "Hot chocolate sounds good. There's a chill in the air tonight."

"Yep, fall is definitely here."

The weather always served as a no-fail topic of conversation.

It took a few minutes to heat the water. Ezekiel dumped in some extra marshmallows without asking. By that time, Burke had settled into a chair by the empty fireplace, his long legs sprawled in front of him, the duffel bag at his feet, hands in his lap, eyelids half closed. He sat up and Ezekiel handed him the mug. He lowered himself into the rocking chair he usually avoided—because it squeaked, but also because Lucy had rocked their children to sleep in it.

The silence had a peace to it, just as it had on the buggy ride home. Burke apparently was one of those rare people who didn't feel a need to fill it with idle conversation.

They slurped, a companionable sound to Ezekiel's way of thinking.

His mind wandered. Tomorrow was Sunday and church. The thought didn't arouse a great sense of joy. Still, if he couldn't be a joyful believer, he could be an obedient one. He always had supper with the family at the big house. Burke could join them, unless he had something better to do. Monday, Ezekiel would rise before dawn to start cooking. Anybody who worked at his restaurant needed to be clean and neat, but especially clean.

"I hope you have some more clothes in that bag." Ezekiel figured a direct approach was best. "If you take those pants and that shirt up to the house tomorrow, Leah will wash them for you on Monday. I usually give workers at least two shirts so they can rotate. You can buy more if you want, later on."

"My complete wardrobe is in that bag." Burke nudged it with his ragged sneaker. "I can do my own laundry, though."

"Just a thought."

More silence. Ezekiel finished his hot chocolate and stood. "If you need another blanket, there's a stack on the shelf at the other end of the hall."

"Mary Katherine is a nice lady."

Mary Katherine again. Ezekiel sat back down. "She is."

"Why was her son so mad? Was it about me?"

"I don't know. With Thomas, it's always something.

He has a need to be in control. He's young. He still hasn't learned that we don't control life." God did, whether a person liked it or not. "How did you meet Mary Kay?"

"I broke into her house last night." His face flushed. "I don't make a habit of it. I told the truth when I said I'm not a criminal. I was starving. I planned to leave an IOU."

Leave it to Mary Katherine to take a burglar and find him a job. The woman had a backbone made of pure Christian concrete. "You were in her house at night alone with her?"

That explained the grievous expression on her son's face this evening. The district was small and the grapevine merciless.

"Just long enough for her to make me a sandwich and send me to sleep in the barn—which was her idea. Today I waited outside the house on the porch for her to pick me up and bring me to the restaurant. That was also her idea."

"I reckon word got around. It's likely Freeman, Cyrus, or Solomon heard and told the others."

"Who are they?"

"They make and enforce the rules." It was a simplification, but it was late and Burke was an outsider. He didn't need to know the finer details.

"She was nothing but kind."

"You put her in an awkward position."

"And she got in trouble because of me?"

"Not because of you exactly." Ezekiel had little trouble imagining the conversation. Mary Katherine, as outspoken as she was, surely knew when to close her mouth and listen. He swallowed a snort of his own. "I imagine the bishop had something to say about her being a woman living alone and not exercising good judgment in her old age."

"She's not old. It's my fault. What will happen to her?"

"They only have her best interests at heart. They would like to see her either move in with one of her sons or remarry. Either way, she's taken care of."

"She's a grown woman. Isn't it up to her what she does?"

"Plain families are close knit. We take care of our young and our old. We take care of each other."

Burke didn't look convinced.

"I should get to bed. I have church services in the morning." Ezekiel upended the cup to capture the marshmallows he'd saved for last. They were his favorite part. Certainly better than church. He hadn't looked forward to church in a long time. A thought he didn't share with anyone—least of all an Englisch stranger. "You headed to your church in the morning? I can loan you a horse."

The Englischers at the local churches wouldn't find it too odd if one of their kind showed up on a horse. Not in these parts.

"I don't ride." Burke shifted in his chair and winced as if his legs hurt. "Why did you call the restaurant the Purple Martin Café?"

A diversion from the church question, or did Burke really want to know? It wasn't Ezekiel's business if the man chose to sleep in on Sunday morning. He sat back down. "My fraa liked birds."

"Your fraa?"

"My wife. Lucy." He stood again and went to the kitchen where he rinsed the cup and set it in the drain, ready for his morning coffee.

Ezekiel's hand hovered over the towel as he stared out the window over the sink. An inky, starless night stared back at him. A chunk of silver moon played hide-and-seek between clouds. Tree boughs dipped and swayed in the breeze. Lucy had made him build birdhouses and place them in their old yard in specific spots so she could see them through the kitchen windows while she and the girls cooked and washed dishes.

The birds were migrating now. He'd seen an oriole earlier in the day. That would've made Lucy happy.

How many times at supper had he sat at the kitchen table in their old house and watched her watch the birds? Her delight at the first sighting of a purple martin in the spring had tickled him. *"Oh, look, look, they're here. They've arrived. That means there'll be babies before we know it. Winter's over. I'm so glad. My bones are tired of the cold. Aren't they pretty?"*

He would nod and tease her that she was more excited over those birds than she was her own babies. Which was impossible. The woman lived for those babies. She'd waited so long, and she wanted more. So did he. "A dozen," she said. "Why not two dozen?" he asked. "Gott willing," she said.

He hadn't been.

Ezekiel grabbed the towel and rubbed his hands as

if he could rub away the memories that always seemed to crowd him at night. The memories and the doubts. A Plain man should have no doubts. No questions. Accept God's will and God's plan. That's what Freeman would say, if Ezekiel asked. Which, of course, he wouldn't. Doubts in a man his age were an ugly thing.

"My wife liked to feed the seagulls at the beach." Burke washed his cup and settled it onto the rack next to Ezekiel's. "I always considered them flying scavengers."

"I've never been to the beach." Ezekiel always intended to go someday, but now it didn't seem likely. He moved to extinguish the lamp. Time to sleep. "Where is your wife now?"

"Dead."

The darkness caused the word to linger, quivering, much longer than a single syllable should.

"I'm sorry. It's a hard road."

One with which Ezekiel was exceedingly familiar. One he walked every day, wandering, seeking the end, the destination, the finality. Ten years and he still wandered.

"I got the hummingbird tattoo when my daughter was born." Burke's voice sounded hoarse and disembodied in the sudden dark. "She was two months premature and a tiny little thing. Her arms flailed, and her legs kicked. She reminded me of a hummingbird."

"They are one of Gott's special creations." Babies and hummingbirds. "It's gut you've got her, then."

"She died of leukemia when she was nine. My wife died the next year."

When God said there would be troubles in this world, He meant it. He also said He had overcome those troubles. Ezekiel didn't offer those words, intended by some to be words of comfort. He'd been on the receiving end, and he knew how little they assuaged the grief. Not even time seemed to help.

Some days, nothing helped.

He said, instead, the only hopeful words that came to mind. "See you in the morning."

He waited in the dark.

His visitor's voice carried from down the hallway, softer, less raspy. "See you in the morning."

CHAPTER 10

The elbow jab came at just the right moment. Mary Katherine could always count on Laura to keep her on track. She settled to her knees on the hard-packed earth in Cyrus's barn for the final prayer. Not getting a wink of sleep the second night in a row didn't help, but that wasn't the only problem. A story niggled at her brain, and her fingers itched to write it down. God would smite her if Freeman didn't. Inhaling the calming smells of hay, dirt, and manure, she closed her eyes and summoned the words. *Humility. Obedience. Surrender all.*

Cyrus's words washed over her. She wanted to surrender all. Really, she did. So why did she struggle to be obedient? She wanted her house. She wanted to work, surrounded by books, talking about books, and writing all day long. Not in a restaurant, surrounded by food, talking about food, all day long. She loved cooking, but it didn't call to her the way books did.

"Mary Kay."

Laura's whisper and the sound of people scrambling to their feet brought her back to the barn. *Lord, have mercy on my wayward soul. Your will, not mine.* She stuck her hand on the pine bench in front of her and struggled to stand. Her knees ached. Her back joined in.

"Whatever is on your mind?" Laura managed to get to her feet a second before Mary Katherine. "You're a hundred miles away, if not a thousand, this morning."

Mary Katherine had filled her friend in on the discussion with Freeman, Cyrus, and Solomon on the ride to the service. They'd made it a habit of coming together since their children's buggies had become full of grandchildren and, in Laura's case, great-grandchildren. "I was praying."

"If I know you, and I do, you were praying to get your way." Laura's chuckle was dry but still sweet. "You know what it says in Proverbs."

"'You can make many plans, but the Lord's purpose will prevail.'"

They chanted the words together.

Beulah and Barbara, ahead of them in the crowd surging toward the doors and a beautiful fall day, looked back at the same time. Barbara rolled her eyes. "What are you two cooking up now?"

"Nothing, *dochder.*" How could she? The elders—and her sons—had spoken. "We're only commiserating over the aches and pains of getting old."

"Speak for yourself." Laura picked up her pace and reached the wide-open doors first. "I'm a spring chicken. Squawk, squawk."

The other women laughed and scattered so Laura, who had delivered both of them, could take the lead in the procession to Josephina Beachy's kitchen and preparations for the after-church meal.

Trailing behind a few steps, Mary Katherine tugged off her glasses and wiped tears of laughter from her eyes. Laura had an endless ability to make her laugh. For that, Mary Katherine thanked God.

"Everything turned out all right, then?"

Mary Katherine squinted into the sudden bright sunshine. Without her glasses she couldn't see her hand in front of her face. "Ezekiel?"

"Forgotten running into me already?"

Beset by sudden nerves, Mary Katherine juggled her glasses in an attempt to lift them to her face. They slipped from her fingers. She dove for them. The sudden bang of her head against something equally solid and the immediate pain that followed told her in no uncertain terms that Ezekiel had done the same.

"Ouch!" She straightened and rubbed her forehead. The blurry image of the top of his head gave way to the glasses stuck in front of her nose. She grabbed them from his outstretched hand and returned them to their rightful place. "Sorry."

The sight of Ezekiel rubbing his forehead came into focus. He was hurt and trying not to show it. "It's all right. You wear glasses for a reason, I reckon."

"I do."

He studied his church boots. Mary Katherine did the same, wondering what he saw there that held his fascination. Her own black shoes were covered with a fine coat of dust. "I have to get to the kitchen. I told Josephina I'd help serve the apple cider. They pressed it fresh yesterday. You should have some. It's very tasty."

Why was she blathering on like this?

Ezekiel shoved his black hat back on his head. He smiled. A tired smile but still a smile. He always looked tired. Even at church. "I enjoyed your *Budget* report, but I'm not sure Sarah is so pleased with you telling the world about her adventure in the canoe."

Sarah's canoe got stuck in the creek on a family canoe trip. She stepped out and ended up in mud so deep she couldn't get out. She pulled one foot out, and the other went in deeper.

"I had her mann's permission." Mary Katherine grinned at the memory. "He told me the whole story. He was still laughing. It struck her so funny she couldn't get out for laughing so much. Jason and her suhs had to pull her out."

"So your article said." He studied something beyond her shoulder. "I wanted to tell you Burke worked out really well last night. He's a gut cook. Hard worker."

"I thought he might be."

"Based on how he broke into your house?"

"He told you?"

"He also said he doesn't make a habit of it."

"But you're wondering if a burglar might also be a liar." He shouldn't judge a man by one error. Especially a hungry man who knew no one. "I agree he made a mistake—a big mistake—but I forgive him. As we're called to do."

"Forgiveness is one thing. Inviting the wolf into the herd of sheep is another."

"I don't think he's your average burglar." Sweat trickled down her forehead. The fall breeze didn't help one iota. "He didn't steal anything. He has a good vocabulary."

"That makes perfect sense."

Now he was making fun of her. "You want to turn away a man who has no place to go? Who you just said was a good cook? You need a cook, and sometimes beggars can't be choosers—"

"Whoa, whoa!" He put up both hands. "I agree. That's why I'm hiring him. That's why I took him home with me last night. That's why he's still asleep in the back bedroom—leastways he was when I left for church."

"Oh. Oh." Mary Katherine fluttered her fingers and landed them on her kapp string.

A cluster of boys, including three of her grands, rushed past them, already tossing a weathered football back and forth. Mary Katherine instinctively ducked. Little Thaddeus waved and ran on. The extra time didn't help her draw any conclusions. "Well, why didn't you say so?"

"You didn't give me a chance." His smile was rueful. "You tend to pop off before you have the whole story, just like you did in school."

"I did not." She stopped. She couldn't remember that far back, but Ezekiel could? "You're making that up."

"You think you'll take me up on my offer?"

"It's still open? You're hiring Burke."

"For the evening shift. I'm still short on the day shift. It seems like I'm always short in some position. I can never keep a full staff."

"Mary Kay."

Freeman's bass carried over the chatter of the small groups gathered across Cyrus's front yard. Cyrus followed, Solomon behind him. Not again. Their serious expressions said their talk the previous evening was about to have a part two.

Several folks glanced their way, Thomas among them. He broke away from his conversation with Aidan Graber and started their direction.

Her son the busybody. *"Wonder where he got that?"* Moses' snort resounded in Mary Katherine's ears. "I have to go."

"I think I may be part of this conversation."

"Why?"

"Just a feeling."

"You, too, Ezekiel." Freeman pointed toward the barn. "Let's have a talk."

Ezekiel was way too smart for his britches.

. . .

From Mary Katherine's smile to Freeman's frown, Ezekiel had whiplash. Getting his mind off that smile and onto the bishop's concerns would be a challenge. Better to keep his gaze on his feet so he didn't stumble in front of Mary Katherine, her oldest son, and the church elders.

Cyrus shut the doors behind them, blocking out the raucous laughter of the younger ones and the rumble of conversation among the older ones. Freeman settled onto the front bench. Thomas took a spot across from him. Mary Katherine looked flummoxed for a moment. During church, the women sat on one side, the men on the other. Ezekiel nodded toward a spot next to Thomas. She shrugged, shot him a grateful smile, and sat. He chose to stand. Three hours of sitting on a hard bench took its toll on his sciatica.

"We'll make this quick. Everyone is hungry." Freeman patted his ever-expanding paunch. "Not that I couldn't live off the fat of the land for a while."

Cyrus and Solomon chuckled. Mary Katherine stared at her hands.

Freeman's gaze landed on Ezekiel. "You hired this Burke McMillan?"

It sounded more like an accusation than a question. "I'm trying. He hasn't filled out the paperwork yet. I'm hoping he will."

Freeman's eyebrows arched.

"There are still some matters to be resolved."

"Such as?"

Ezekiel had hoped to avoid diving into the details. No matter. "He doesn't seem to have a home address."

"Where is he staying?"

"With me." His gaze traveled to Mary Katherine, despite his best intentions not to look at her. "For now."

Mary Katherine smiled. "That's—"

"What do you know about this man?" Thomas interrupted.

"He has no family. He's a widower." Who'd suffered the loss of a child. Children were gifts from God and He often took them home for reasons parents couldn't fathom. Just as He took wives and husbands when He deemed it their time. That didn't make it any easier for the poor souls who lived it. Certainly not the trite words of comfort that seemed to come so easily to a person's lips. "He knows his way around a kitchen. He's a decent cook."

"So you don't know any more than Mudder did when she let a would-be burglar sleep in her barn?"

"Enough that I let him sleep in my house." Ezekiel drew on the reserve of patience he had cultivated during many years of being the only parent to four children. "I'm still here, so I reckon he's not to be feared."

"We want to discuss whether you still need Mary Kay at the restaurant." Cyrus intervened. "She's needed at the Combination Store. They're working hard to get a foothold with the tourists, while the restaurant is well established. We also want to talk about whether we can trust this stranger in our midst."

"I can see the reason in that." Ezekiel could also see the determined set of Mary Katherine's mouth and the way the lines deepened around her eyes. She reminded him of a beautiful purple martin he'd discovered one day, its leg caught in a fence's barbed wire. The bird must've known it did no good to struggle, but it couldn't help itself. Ezekiel was positive he received a look of thanks before the purple martin fluttered away in a rush of ecstatic winged flight after he freed it. "One cook can't cover all the day shifts. She could be a great help."

"I don't want Mudder working with this McMillan." Thomas rose and began to pace. "He was watching her house."

Mary Katherine's hand went to her mouth, then dropped. "Not just my house. He was observing the Plain ways. He's a student of life. He wanted a sandwich." Her lips pressed together. She heaved a breath. "He was polite. He washed his plate when he was done."

Ezekiel kept his smile to himself. She truly couldn't contain herself.

"He preyed on an elderly woman living alone." Neither could Thomas. He was digging himself a hole with his mother and didn't seem to realize it. "He duped you into helping him."

"I'm not elderly. Or a fool." She rose and stepped into her son's path. "I managed to raise you, didn't I? Although I sometimes wonder if I covered the respect for parents mentioned in Scripture often enough."

"I lost my daed early." Thomas ducked his head. His Adam's apple bobbed. "I'd rather not lose my mudder too."

The heart of the matter. Not an easy thing for a man to admit in front of others. He was the eldest son, and he spoke for the family in his father's absence. His wishes carried a great deal of weight. Mary Kay wouldn't be happy about it, but Thomas was right.

"Gott's will be done." Solomon offered this advice. Good advice, to be sure. "We're only passing through this world."

Wise words that didn't help as much as they should.

"If it is of such concern for Thomas, then I think it's best that Mary Kay work with Leo and Jennie." Ezekiel peeked at Mary Katherine. Her lips pressed together. She probably feared her response would leap out and smack him in the head. It couldn't be allowed to matter. "She has a lot to offer them with her experience at Amish Treasures. I'll find my cook elsewhere."

Mary Katherine glowered at him. He responded with his best apologetic smile. He understood too well Thomas's fear of losing another loved one. He'd spent years fussing over his kinner, fearing Gott would decide their days were finished as well.

"That sounds like a plan." Freeman glanced from Thomas to Mary Katherine, his eyes bright behind his glasses. "Can the two of you agree to such a plan?"

"It's a gut plan. As far as this man Burke goes, I still think it's best not to have a stranger in our midst." Thomas had inherited a fair share of his mother's stubbornness. "Our kinner eat at that restaurant."

"I'm inviting him up to the house for supper tonight with all my grands." A wave of dizziness swept over Ezekiel. The muted light of the barn darkened for a few sickening seconds. He took a breath, then another. The swaying stopped. "Leah said something about hamburger macaroni and cheese casserole."

"Are you feeling all right?" Cyrus cocked his head, his expression quizzical. "You look as white as a sheet."

Ezekiel teetered to a bench and sat. "I'm fine."

"Are you sure?"

"I think I forgot to eat breakfast." Unless coffee and a hard, leftover chocolate chip cookie counted. Burke had still been asleep when Ezekiel awoke, and he saw no reason to dirty dishes for one. He planted both hands on his knees and squeezed. *Breathe.* The air cleared, but he felt cold. "I'm just hungry."

"I ate a big breakfast and I'm still famished." Freeman nodded at Cyrus, who headed to the doors. "Having a fraa does make a big difference, though."

That statement tripped and fell flat on the ground somewhere in the six or eight feet that separated Ezekiel and Mary Katherine. He no longer felt cold. Instead, heat curled around his neck, and he was sixteen all over again, stomping up the steps to his first singing. He hazarded a glance at Mary Katherine. She looked about as comfortable as a cat who suddenly woke up in a pit bull's pen.

"You're doing too much at the restaurant. You need to get more rest."

"Don't worry. I'll find someone. If all else fails, Carlene will come back for a few weeks until I can get someone."

"Fine." She hesitated. "I'm glad you gave him a job. He needed it."

"He's a gut cook. A gut call on your part."

"Gott's timing." Cyrus threw in the comment.

Mary Katherine nodded. Ezekiel forced himself to do the same.

"I'll come up to the house for supper tonight to meet Burke." Freeman seemed to have no appreciation for the unsettling nature of his remark. Or that he'd just invited himself to supper. "I'd like to draw my own conclusions."

"I'll let Leah and William know."

The others trooped toward the doors. Ezekiel remained seated, watching them go, hoping they would simply file out.

Mary Katherine looked back. "Are you coming?"

Leave it to her. Ezekiel managed a smile. "I have a pebble in my boot or a twig. I'm right behind you."

She nodded and disappeared through the door.

It was a small white lie, but still a lie in the very place where they'd just worshipped the Lord. Not that he'd done a good job of it. He'd spent the last ten years coming to church services hoping to find an answer to a question he couldn't even begin to frame aloud.

He didn't even dare think it. How dare he question God's will?

The thought made him queasy. Or maybe it was his empty stomach.

He leaned over and put his head down. They didn't need to know he was afraid to get up in front of them for fear he'd keel over.

CHAPTER 11

A ramp fashioned from unfinished wood kept the steps company in front of Leah and William's house. Burke's pause in front of it told Ezekiel the other man was contemplating the need for such a contraption. He trudged up the incline, feeling every move in his back and hips. Despite being a day of rest, the Sunday had been long. He'd come home from church to find Burke planted in the same chair as the previous night, tiny glasses perched on his nose, reading a ragged paperback entitled *On the Road* by Jack Kerouac. He agreed to the invitation to supper after a long, pondering moment.

The rest of the afternoon had passed in more companionable silence with Burke reading his novel and Ezekiel his stack of *Budget* newspapers. He'd gotten behind. He heard most of the local news at the Purple Martin, but he liked to see what Mary Katherine contributed, as well as keeping up with all his family and friends across Amish country.

"My grandson uses crutches to get around."

Burke tromped up the ramp, his arms swinging as if to gain momentum. His flattop was covered by a scruffy New York Yankees ball cap. "None of my business."

"Kenneth was born too early and he came out the wrong way. It did something to his brain. When he was about three, we noticed something was wrong with the way he walked. On tippy toes and holding on to stuff. His calves were stiff as boards. It has a fancy name. I had my daughter write it down for me. Spastic diplegia cerebral palsy."

His pronunciation no doubt left a lot to be desired, but Burke nodded. "If he has cerebral palsy and he's able to walk under his own speed, he's doing well."

"He thinks so. He walks like his legs are scissors, but he's still all over the place all day long. He plays volleyball using just one crutch, and the cousins run him back and forth in a wheelbarrow so he can shoot baskets during their basketball games."

"Kids are way more resilient than adults."

"And kinder sometimes."

"My girl came two months early, but it didn't affect her development." Burke didn't elaborate.

It wasn't any of Ezekiel's business either, so he opened the door and motioned the other man in. Together they traipsed through the front room to the kitchen. The scent of potatoes and onions frying mingled with the sweeter aroma of fresh-baked bread.

"Groossdaadi." Kenneth waved from his seat on the bench. His metal crutches lay on either side of him. He grinned, as usual, his blue eyes bright with anticipation behind black-rimmed glasses that made them huge. Boo, his mutt and constant companion, settled to one side, panting, his tongue hanging out of his mouth as if he'd been running instead of following

the boy around all day. Kenneth's delighted shout lightened Ezekiel's load. "Who did you bring? He looks like a hobo."

How did this child know what a hobo was?

"Burke is not a hobo." Ezekiel scrubbed the boy's silky, fine blond hair with his water-chapped fingers and added a quick buss on the head for good measure. "He's a guest in your daed's house."

"Groossdaadi is right. Little boys should keep their mouths zipped shut." Leah set a huge dish full of macaroni and cheese–hamburger casserole on a pot holder in the middle of a pine table flanked with long benches and fixed her son with a stern stare. "Let your groossdaadi introduce our guest."

Burke removed his cap, slid onto the end of the bench closest to the boy, and introduced himself. "I like your dog." He patted Boo's gray head.

If he didn't know better, Ezekiel would have thought the mangy old mutt smiled.

"He's a handsome fellow," Burke said.

That was a matter of opinion. The dog, who might be part bulldog and part dachshund, was fat. He slobbered. He'd been known to snore. Ezekiel grunted and sat on the other side. "About as handsome as I am."

Kenneth roared as if this were the funniest thing ever. "He's a dog. He looks like a dog." Made sense. "Do you have a dog?"

Before Burke could answer, William strode into the kitchen, Freeman behind him. More introductions. Freeman and Burke eyed each other like two bulls sharing a pasture. Freeman nodded and plopped onto the bench next to Ezekiel. "Good to meet you. Mary Kay told me about you."

Burke nodded. "She is a kind woman."

"A kind woman who has shown a lack of good sense recently."

Burke's eyebrows rose and fell. He smoothed Boo's gray fur. The dog's mouth opened in a wide smile that revealed a set of yellow teeth. "I could see how a person might think that."

"We should pray before the food gets cold."

They prayed silently. Freeman punctuated it with an amen. They passed heavy dishes of fried potatoes, green beans, sliced tomatoes, and corn on the cob. They buttered rolls and sipped lukewarm water. Kenneth never stopped talking. "Where did you come from, Burke? Do you have a family? Are you going to come to supper again? Do you have a dog?"

"Kenneth, mind your manners and eat." William plopped a piece of corn on the boy's plate. He gave Freeman a nervous glance. It wasn't every day the bishop ate at their house. Freeman had his mouth full, corn in one hand and roll in the other. "It's not a child's place to ask an adult questions like that."

"It's all right." Burke laid his roll on his plate and picked up his fork. "Children are far more honest than adults, in my experience. It's an attribute I value."

"So do I." Ezekiel passed the green beans to Leah. She accepted with a bashful smile. She wasn't much of a talker, but she was a good cook and a good mother. "So is being nice."

"I'm nice." Kenneth gripped a corncob. He had more

butter on his fingers than the corn. He chewed and grinned, kernels stuck between his teeth. "I give Liliana my cows. And Caleb plays with my horses."

"Wooden cows and horses." Leah handed him a napkin. "Hush, little one. Wipe your face and let the men talk."

Liliana, Kenneth's youngest sister, banged her fork on her wooden high chair as if agreeing. Caleb, a shy three-year-old, was busy stacking his green beans and tomatoes with his fat fingers. Leah shook her head and removed Liliana's fork with a gentle tug. "Sorry, she's a rambunctious little girl."

Burke handed his roll to Kenneth. "You're a growing boy. Have my roll."

"Aren't you hungry?"

"I'm full."

"He shared his roll," Kenneth crowed. "I like him."

"I like you too." Burke pushed his green beans around on his plate. "You're a good boy."

"You've been out of work for a while then?" Freeman manhandled a fork in one hand and a knife in the other. He speared a green bean and let it hover in the air while he posed the question. "Whereabouts did you work before?"

Burke leaned back in his chair. "For a while. Here and there."

Freeman's gaze hardened. "You'll have to be more specific when you fill out the job application at the Purple Martin."

"It's all right—"

"Nee, it's not." Freeman shook his fork at Ezekiel. "My youngest granddaughter is a waitress at the Purple

Martin. Your grands help out. We need to know who we invite into the midst of our kinner."

He was right, but that was no reason to treat a man like a criminal. Ezekiel shot Burke an apologetic look. Burke shrugged. He laid his napkin next to his plate. "I'm from back east, Virginia. Not originally, but that's where my last real address was."

"Where?"

"Norfolk. I was a Navy chaplain."

"You're a man of religion?"

"Worse than a criminal, you've let a preacher into your midst." Burke's smile held no mirth. "I'm not sure I'd go so far as to call myself a man of religion these days."

"What denomination?"

"Presbyterian. But chaplains have to be able to accept all faiths and minister to those who have beliefs different from their own." Burke plucked another roll from the basket and began to tear it into small pieces he tossed one by one onto his plate, still full of macaroni and vegetables. "I did that for eight years, then I resigned my commission. You don't have to worry. I won't try to convert your little ones."

"What qualifies a man to be a chaplain? Is it like a preacher who goes to seminary?"

"A graduate degree in theology. Officers' school. A willingness to be deployed and not carry a gun."

That was a lot of book learning. Ezekiel couldn't help himself. He jumped into the conversation, which was more like an interrogation. "You joined the military, but you didn't bear arms?"

An oxymoron if Ezekiel ever heard of one.

"I'm not a fan of guns."

"But you were in the military."

"Because I wanted to minister to men and women who were serving our country and putting their lives on the line for us."

"It must have been a rewarding occupation," Freeman interjected with a grim glance at Ezekiel. "I doubt it was easy to get this commission you had. Why stop?"

It wasn't Freeman's business—it wasn't anyone's business. Ezekiel stuck an entire tomato slice in his mouth to keep from speaking again.

"That's a story for another time." Burke pushed his plate away. His tone was firm, his expression neutral. His gaze met Freeman's. "Someday."

His forehead wrinkled, Freeman shook his shaggy head. "Where did you lose yourself?"

"Who says I did?"

"You're here."

This was far too much for the supper table. They would all end up with indigestion. Ezekiel searched for a way to break tension so tangible he had trouble swallowing. Or maybe it was the size of the tomato grown in Leah's garden. "The casserole is gut, Leah. I might have to use that recipe at the restaurant."

Kenneth coughed. He inhaled and coughed harder. His face turned red and his hands flailed.

Burke shot from the bench. He slapped the boy's back. His cough was gut wrenching. Burke held his glass of water to the boy's lips. "Can you take a sip?"

Kenneth obliged. He coughed a few more times, then belched so loud Liliana and Caleb giggled.

"Better?"

"Went down the wrong pipe, that's all." Kenneth shrugged. "I think I'm done eating. Can I go outside? I want to check on my frog out by the creek. He's my pet, but Mudder says he has no business being in the house. I think he'd like my room."

The boy's enthusiasm and his desire to have the men take his side made Ezekiel stifle a smile. "Won't Boo eat it?"

"Nee, he's not fast enough."

Ezekiel could see that. The dog was a tad on the tubby side. "Still, a creek seems like a gut home for a frog. He's probably pretty set in his ways."

"I'll go with you." Leah stood and squeezed past Liliana's chair. "The grass is high down by the creek and the path is rocky."

"Maybe Burke would like to meet Kenneth's friend." Ezekiel wanted Burke out of Freeman's reach for now. He'd shared all he needed to share. "You have all these dishes to do."

"He doesn't need to be waited on hand and foot." William cocked his head toward the kitchen. "I know you made a pie for dessert, Fraa. Don't you want some, Suh?"

"Nee." Boo at his side, Kenneth tucked his crutches under his arm and swung toward the door. "It'll be too dark soon."

"Would you mind my company?" Burke dropped his napkin by his plate. "I ate too much. I sure could use a walk."

"Do you like frogs?"

"I sure do. Used to have a frog named Hopalong when I was a kid."

"You did?" Kenneth took in this bit of information with an enthralled look. "My frog's name is Nate."

"Good name."

"We'll be back, Mudder."

Leah nodded, but her fingers tugged at a strand of her blonde hair as her gaze followed Kenneth, who was shuffling out the back door.

"They'll be fine," Ezekiel assured her, although no words had been spoken. "It's a short walk."

"He's fallen twice in the last week. He skinned his nose the second time. It swelled up so much I thought it was broken. We're blessed he didn't break his glasses. We've already replaced them once. He's so rambunctious."

"He's a boy. All boys fall down."

She ducked her head and began clearing the table. Freeman applied a toothpick to his teeth. Ezekiel exchanged looks with his son-in-law.

"A chaplain." Freeman dropped the toothpick on his plate. "For the Navy."

A religious man in the military.

Ezekiel had a hard time fitting those two pieces together in the same puzzle. Plain folks didn't believe in bearing arms or going to war.

A religious man should accept that God was good and His plan was meant to prosper, not harm him. Freeman couldn't know how hard it was to walk that walk. He hadn't lost his wife. "His fraa and dochder both died. It might be he lost his way for a time."

"He should know Gott took them home when He saw fit."

"I'm sure he does." Ezekiel bit his tongue. This fact did not make the grief any less potent. Or the sudden fits of anger. After ten years, his still kept him up at night. "Maybe hard work and a few people he can call friends are the prescriptions he needs to be cured of his melancholy."

Freeman wrinkled his nose. He tapped his fork and then his knife in an absentminded, off-kilter rhythm. "You're right."

Ezekiel nearly fell out of his chair. William smothered a grin behind his hand.

"How is Kenneth doing aside from the falling down?" Freeman seemed unaware of their reaction. "He's a cheerful boy."

William's smile disappeared. He took a long sip of water and wiped his mouth with his napkin. "He is cheerful. He doesn't complain about the physical therapy. He doesn't complain about his muscles hurting. The doctor has suggested we take him to Kansas City. They may do an operation to help him walk better. We're still praying about it. He sees the other boys hunting and driving the wagons in the fields and he keeps smiling. He tries hard to do for himself when he can."

"His attitude is gut." Ezekiel rescued his son-in-law. Leah and William tried hard to be good examples for their three children. They tried to be cheerful believers, but their oldest boy's cerebral palsy broke their hearts. "He keeps me company at the restaurant some days. The customers get a kick out of his jokes."

Kenneth was blessed to have no learning problems. He had seizures but was a bright boy who kept up in school.

"A special gift from Gott." Freeman nodded. He smiled at Leah, who placed a saucer of pecan pie and a cup of kaffi in front of him. "You're blessed."

"We are." Her thin shoulders bent, she took his dirty plate and disappeared into the kitchen.

"How did Burke's dochder die?"

"Leukemia."

Freeman squinted as if looking at something beyond the house's walls. "Hmm. And his fraa?"

"He didn't say."

"Hmm."

Whatever wheels were turning in the bishop's head, he apparently decided not to share. Instead, he dug into the pecan pie without another word.

In the absence of a statement to the contrary, Ezekiel decided this meant he had a new cook. One who had some unique qualifications and who needed more than a job. Burke needed mending. Mary Katherine had seen this. She brought Burke to Ezekiel for a reason.

He excused himself and went in search of his new project.

CHAPTER 12

The Combination Store's goods spilled out onto the grounds with the Grabers' latest venture—gazebos and fort playscapes that took up a chunk of land that had been mowed for that purpose. Mary Katherine admired Jennie's arrangement of pumpkins, mums, and gourds around wooden house facades on the porch. Very nice. Homey. She pushed through the door and inhaled the smell of wood shavings, scented soaps, and aromatic candles. A bell tinkled. Laura and Jennie, who stood behind the counter, turned to look, then waved wildly as if they hadn't seen her in a month of Sundays.

"You're here. I'm so glad." Arms outstretched, Jennie trotted around the counter and met Mary Katherine halfway with an enthusiastic hug. Her mauve dress was perfectly pressed and her white kapp crisp with only a few tendrils of her graying sandy-blonde hair showing. She looked younger than her thirty-eight years and seven children should allow. "I hope you're happy to be working here. I know you wanted to do other things."

"I guess Freeman stopped by—or Cyrus—with the news. I'm happy to help out. It's for the best. You've done a gut job of arranging things." She smiled at Laura over their friend's shoulder. "What are you doing here, Laura?"

"Helping out." Laura pointed at the canned goods lining the shelves in the middle of the room. Pickles, tomatoes, green beans, peaches, cherries, and more, all neatly displayed in careful rows. "I might not be able to wield a needle with my fat fingers anymore, but I still can pickle with the best of them. And those are my fry pies over there."

Even at seventy-plus years of age, Laura could still do most things with the best of them. Her arthritis pained her too much for sewing, but her baking skills hadn't suffered in the least.

"The store looks beautiful." Mary Katherine took a moment to let her gaze roam the expanse of goods. Everything imaginable. A true combination store. Leo had remodeled part of the barn and moved his tools into his new shop, giving them this space with its windows and light for their new store. Hickory rocking chairs, an oak desk, coatracks, dressers, and cradles filled the area to her left, with wood shelves and shadow boxes hanging on the walls, all samples of Leo's exquisite handiwork.

Shelves on the other side held Jennie's work, including embroidered tablecloths, knitted sweaters, and crocheted pot holders. They displayed full-size quilts made by other members of the community, as well as Iris Kurtz's crib quilts on a series of dowels under the windows. Her husband Mahon's framed drawings hung on one wall. Jennie's jams and canned vegetables took up more space by the door. Everything neat and tidy in its place. The sight reminded Mary Katherine so much of Amish Treasures, her heart lurched and then settled back into a more sedate rhythm.

"It's a labor of love." Jennie squeezed Mary Katherine's arm. "I know it's not your dream. It's strange how things work out. You encouraged me to work at Amish Treasures. You got Leo and me started. I'm so thankful for what you've done for us."

"Gott's plan. We're silly if we think we know what it is." The words stuck in Mary Katherine's throat. She loved her friend and she was thrilled for Jennie's newfound happiness. She'd played only a small role in it. God did the heavy lifting. "Things will work out in the end. I need to learn to be patient."

Not her strong suit.

"They will. I know they will." Jennie glowed. There was no other word for it. "Gott is gut."

"He is indeed. We simply have to get out of His way." Mary Katherine followed Jennie back behind the counter and settled her bag on top. "I've come for my schedule and I brought my contribution to the sewn goods. Some dresser scarves and some cute little girl sweaters in pink that I knitted."

"Those will go fast." Jennie touched one of the sweaters that lay on top of the pile. Her smile disappeared. She sighed. "So sweet."

Mary Katherine patted her arm. "Another thing that must be left up to Gott." Jennie wanted to share more with her new husband. A baby. It was written all over her face. At thirty-eight it was possible, but with each passing month, it seemed less probable. "How are the kinner doing with you working here now?"

"Celia and Cynthia have it covered." The doorbell dinged and Jennie moved that direction, still talking over her shoulder. "And now that you're working, I'll be able to spend more time at home with Elizabeth and Francis."

Soaking up the sweet moments of motherhood that might not come again.

Jennie greeted the customer, a tourist from the looks of her clothes, without missing a beat.

"She's gotten over her shyness, hasn't she?" An abusive first marriage had left Mary Katherine's friend with a dearth of self-confidence. Life with Leo had changed that. "I'm so happy for her. And for Leo."

"She's a different person. She loves her life." Laura's gaze followed their friend. "I pray Gott's will on the other thing." It was delicate. They didn't talk about it. "Have you spoken to Bess?"

"Nee, not since the break-in at their house. How's she doing?"

"Still a little shaken. To come home and find that someone has pawed through your things would be enough to shake anyone." Laura's expression became grim. "Aidan is her protector, though. She needn't worry. Her mann will take care of her and little Joshua."

"A crib quilt. Who would take such a sweet little memento?" The tumbling blocks quilt had been made by Bess's great-grandmother. "Why pick on us?"

"I don't know." Laura shook her head. "We'll leave that to Freeman, Cyrus, and Solomon." Her words hung in the air. "I know this wasn't your first choice. You wanted the bookstore, didn't you?"

"I did, and I hate to let Dottie down." Mary Katherine tried to keep the disappointment from her voice but failed. "I haven't told her yet. I know life isn't fair. It seems as if we should do what we feel called to do."

"Called to do? That sounds awfully grandiose." Laura tempered the criticism with a gentle smile. "It's a bookstore, not a church. And we don't get called to anything. Only Gott knows His plan."

"I know. But sometimes He gives us gifts. Don't you think He expects us to use them? I just want to use my gift of writing and the love He gave me for books."

"I'm going to take our visitor out to the barn so she can see Leo working on a double rocker." Jennie interrupted as she walked by with the customer, a dark-haired woman dressed in paisley-print leggings and a lilac smock. "She's a newlywed. Like me."

That explained everything. She wanted to sit in the rocker with her new husband. Eventually there would be babies to rock.

Laura watched them go, then turned back to Mary Katherine. "He also gave you the gift of kinner and a whole herd of grands."

"I know."

"Next you'll stamp your foot." Less gentleness in that prediction, but still Laura smiled. "I think I know this story. Widowed groossmammi doesn't like bishop's instructions. Feels sorry for herself. Runs away from home in a snit. You're blessed that Thomas didn't get his way. You get to stay in your home, even though it would be more sensible to let Dylan and Samantha move in with her folks."

"You've forgotten what it feels like, then?" Mary Katherine's temper ran away from her. If anyone knew what this felt like, Laura did. "To leave the home you made with your mann?"

"Don't get your dander up with me. I haven't forgotten what it feels like to wake up on Christmas morning and realize my mann has died on Christmas Eve, in our new home, our dawdy haus, next to me." Laura didn't raise her voice. Her playful tone didn't change. But her green eyes misted. "I may be old, but I'm not senile."

"I'm sorry. That was small-minded and mean of me." Mary Katherine swallowed the lump in her throat. She rushed to close the space between them, reaching to give Laura a hug. "You're a better person than I am. I don't know why I find it so hard to let go. It's just a house. A bunch of Sheetrock and wood and old furniture."

"It's not the material things you're hanging on to. It's the memories." Laura's return hug enveloped Mary Katherine in forgiveness. "You don't have to give it up yet, but it will be easier if you make the decision to do it—for everyone. Then Thomas won't have to feel bad about making you do something he knows you don't want to do."

Laura pulled a clipboard from a shelf under the counter and handed it to Mary Katherine. Clipped to it was the schedule for the next week. Mary Katherine accepted it with what she hoped was a willing smile. "Is that how you felt when you moved into the dawdy haus?"

"Last Tuesday I held my latest great-great-grandchild in my arms only ten minutes after she was born." Laura's delight at the memory made her look younger. Her eyes shone behind silver-rimmed glasses that matched her thick iron-gray hair. "Samuel and Victoria named her Rachel. She has a full head of brown hair and cheeks that remind me of Eli."

"A sweet memory." It didn't seem to bother Laura that she no longer delivered babies. Nothing seemed to faze her, in fact. Mary Katherine longed to be as resilient. "How many does that make now?"

Laura grinned and tapped her fingers in the palm of one hand as if counting. "Four. That's four great-great-grands, twenty-eight great-grands, fifty-two grands, and nine kinner. We have to put some of them in the barn and out in the pasture when we all get together for a meal." Her smile faded. "Only Luke is gone now."

Laura had lost her oldest son to a heart attack like the one that took his father. No self-pity marred her words. "He and Eli must have so much to talk about, should their paths cross in heaven."

"Gott willing."

"Amen. I treasure every memory. You should too."

"I do. I will."

"Make some new ones." Laura's expression could only be described as sly. "What did Ezekiel want at church yesterday?"

Not a memory Mary Katherine intended to share. "Never you mind."

"He's a gut man."

"Everyone keeps saying that. Is that all it takes? There were several gut men my age when I married Moses. They didn't seek me out. They didn't look at me the way he did. I didn't think about them morning, noon, and night. Moses was a gut man, but to me he was—"

"The One."

"Jah. Do you think it's possible to have that again?"

"Look at Jennie. Look at Bess."

"They're younger."

"Our bodies are old. I'll give you that." Laura smoothed her gnarled fingers over the slick varnished pine, her expression absent. "But my heart still feels young. Doesn't yours? If you looked in a mirror right now, wouldn't you be surprised to see those wrinkles and that gray hair? I look in the store windows when I'm walking in town, and then I look around, wondering who that old woman is reflected in the glass." She chuckled. "Maybe I *am* getting senile."

"You're not." Mary Katherine had experienced that exact phenomenon only the week before. She'd been looking in storefronts and daydreaming like a foolish girl about the bookstore she and Dottie would open. "I looked at Moses and I knew he was The One. I haven't ever felt that for anyone else. Maybe my ticker is broken."

"Or maybe you just haven't opened yourself up to the possibility that another man could be The One."

"What if my brain has latched onto another dream, one that doesn't involve being a fraa again?" If she could ask anyone this question, it was Laura. "What if there is something else that calls to me more strongly?"

"Dottie's bookstore?"

"Our bookstore."

"What does Freeman say about that?"

"He says I should work here."

"Freeman has the best interests of the Gmay and each one of us at heart." Laura stopped. Her bushy gray eyebrows lifted. "And Thomas fears for your well-being and your common sense."

"Not you too." Was there no loyalty among friends?

"I would've smacked your serial killer upside the head with a skillet."

"You would not. We don't believe in violence. 'Love thy neighbor.'"

"Thy neighbor doesn't steal from you in the middle of the night." Laura frowned. "Except for the ones who keep taking quilts and Bibles and our kinner's favorite toys."

"Burke didn't steal anything from me. He was hungry."

"I would have fed him too." Laura's frown faded. "We're women. That's what we do. Freeman knows that."

"What did he expect me to do? Run to the phone shack and call him while the man ate? The sheriff?"

"Freeman knows you did what you thought best. He wouldn't want you to call the sheriff. But he surely expected you to be the one to let him know—when you could. If you're not going to remarry, he wants you to be closer to family. Like Thomas."

"Freeman isn't making me move. He's letting me

work here, even though I would rather work in the bookstore. I don't see the harm in selling books."

"It's not the books that worry him. We can sell books here. Pick out a space." Laura waved her hand toward a small opening between a shelf filled with candles and another that featured handmade toys. "Leo will make some more shelves and we'll buy some books. Those Amish romances the Englisch like. Books aren't bad. Leastways not the kind you and Dottie would sell, but it's not about the books."

Freeman measured every request, every change in the *Ordnung* against the yardstick of how it would affect the Gmay's ability to remain true to the fundamental tenet that they must keep themselves apart from the world. They could never do anything that would allow worldly ways to creep into their community. Mary Katherine agreed with this concept. She simply wanted to make room for the little slice of heaven on earth represented by rooms filled with books. Stories. The written word. A silly dream for a silly woman.

"I will always put faith and family first." She straightened and fixed a smile on her face. "Always. If that means being open to a new start with a new mann, so be it. We'll find one for you too."

"You are a goose." Laura cackled, her ample bosom heaving with laughter. "No one followed me into the kitchen after the wedding and complimented my cooking by offering me a job."

"Ezekiel just needed a cook." He had been nice about her clumsiness, though. And a little sweet. She was the one getting senile. Instead of thinking about herself, she should be thinking of her friend. What men Laura's age might come calling on her? The oldest single man was Zechariah Stutzman, a curmudgeonly widower who'd as soon bite a person's head off as look at him. No way Laura would put up with that. No one else came to mind. "You never know."

"You never know. That's the challenge and the beauty of Gott's plan." Laura stood with one hand on her hip, her laughter replaced by a grunt of pain. "Let's get your things on the shelves."

"Work is the best medicine."

"And we'll have fun working together." Laura's hug was as encompassing as the first. "You can put the story of your serial killer in your *Budget* report, along with your new employment at the Graber Handcrafted Furniture and Homemade Goods Combination Store."

With all the excitement she had missed a *Budget* deadline. That never happened.

The doorbell tinkled. Laura went to greet a group of older ladies who filled the store with high-pitched chatter and laughter.

Mary Katherine couldn't talk about her serial killer in *The Budget*. It didn't seem right. Instead, her mind returned to the story she was writing about a grown woman who disguised herself as a man and ran away from home in a snit to be a cook on a cattle drive. While she wrote in her head, she measured a space in the corner.

For the books.

CHAPTER 13

Daviess County sheriff's deputies made a habit of stopping by the Purple Martin for pie and coffee. Ezekiel moved to get Deputy Dan Rogers Jr. his usual cup of coffee, black, and a double slice of apple pie. The deputy plopped onto a stool at the counter about a half hour after the noon rush ended. He looked tired and an awful lot like his dad, Dan Sr., who had been a deputy, too, before he retired.

"Nice fall weather." Ezekiel set the pie in front of him. "Are they keeping you busy over there in Gallatin?"

Gallatin, a town of about ten thousand, was the county seat about ten miles from Jamesport. Dan removed his brown wide-brimmed hat, revealing a smoothly shaved head. He was a polite man who kept his uniform with its long-sleeved tan shirt and dark-brown pants clean and wrinkle free. He wore the uniform and his gold badge with the five-point star in the middle with pride. He slapped the hat on the counter and picked up his fork. "Actually, they're keeping me busy over here in your neck of the woods."

Jamesport made its name as a farming community and home to a tourist industry driven by the desire of Englisch folks to see how the Amish lived their lives.

Daviess County had its share of meth labs and domestic violence, but Jamesport didn't head the crime blotter in the *Tri-County Weekly* or the Gallatin *North Missourian*. It could only be one thing. "More burglaries?"

Frowning, Dan blew on his coffee, took a swig, and swallowed. "Yep. Four in the last two weeks. Sheriff Dawson put me on the case."

Uneasiness stole over Ezekiel. He moved down the counter and refilled Larry Mitcham's coffee cup and set the pot back on its burner. The other pot was low, so he started a new one, his hands moving in the usual ritual of fresh water, new filter, coffee with no thought required.

"That's why I stopped by to talk to you."

Dan's bass followed Ezekiel to the cash register where he rang up Jeff Carver's cheeseburger and made change from his twenty-dollar bill. A wave of dizziness swept over Ezekiel. He slapped the twenty under the lever and shut the drawer. His stomach rumbled. He'd skipped breakfast again.

"I heard you have a new cook."

"I do. Two of them." Ezekiel teetered toward Dan's end of the counter. Anna and Miriam had the three tables with customers covered. His other cook, Martha, was in the kitchen finishing up her shift. No sense in avoiding this conversation. "What does that have to do with the break-ins?"

"I stopped by Freeman's to tell him I'd be talking to a few of y'all."

Law enforcement in these parts dealt with the Plain community enough to know how to ease into these things. That Freeman would share information about Burke with Dan was surprising. They tried to keep contact with the sheriff's deputies in their professional capacity to a minimum.

By the same token, they had nothing to hide. "Freeman mentioned my new cook?"

"He said the guy broke into Mary Katherine Ropp's house." Dan tugged a small notebook from his shirt pocket and consulted it. "Burke McMillan is the name."

"He didn't steal anything."

"Mrs. Ropp is one lucky lady. Most burglars would do bodily harm if confronted by a woman like that."

"She had a rifle."

"Was he armed?"

"No. And all he wanted was something to eat. He was hungry."

"That's what he said when caught in the act." Dan's tone chided Ezekiel for his naïveté. "Who knows what he would've taken if given the opportunity."

The object of their conversation shoved through the restaurant door.

"Mary Katherine, what are you doing here?"

"I stopped by the Combination Store and asked her to come over after she got off her shift." Dan twirled around on his stool and saluted her. "Thanks for coming."

"You didn't give me a choice." She strode over to the counter. Her face was damp and pink from the afternoon sun. Her lavender dress brought out the blue in her eyes behind her glasses. She looked good, as usual. "I don't know why you're involved. I didn't call the sheriff's office to make a report. I'm not filing charges."

Dan repeated what he'd told Ezekiel. "McMillan may be involved in all these burglaries. If that's the case, I need to put a stop to him."

"He didn't take anything from my house. All he wanted was food." Mary Katherine plopped on the stool next to Dan. "He was hungry. He's a religious man."

And outspoken as usual.

"Breaking into a widow's house in the middle of the night is a strange thing for a religious man to do." Dan clicked the cap of his pen with his thumb in an irritating rhythm. "I want you both to tell me everything you know about him."

"Now's not really a good time." Ezekiel cocked his head toward the kitchen. "I need to help get ready for the next rush."

"I have plenty of time. And I'd really like a tall glass of iced tea, if you've got it." Mary Katherine sent the stool spinning around like a little girl on a carnival ride, then stopped facing Ezekiel. "I know he's well spoken and he knows his way around a kitchen. He cleans up after himself. He's from back east somewhere."

"He is—was—a Navy chaplain," Ezekiel interjected as he settled the glass of tea in front of her. She smiled her thanks. He found it hard to look away. Her fingers brushed his. The lines across her forehead puckered. He looked down. He had failed to let go of the glass. He whipped his hand down to his side. "He has a good heart. Leah's suh Kenneth took to him right away. So did his *hund*."

Why defend the man? Because Ezekiel needed a cook? No, because Burke was a kindred spirit, lost in a world filled with couples still united in holy matrimony in a way neither of them likely could ever be again.

"You figured all that out after two days?" Dan grimaced, his gaze fixed on his notebook as if trying to decipher his own writing. "How do you know he's told you the truth about any of this?"

"Check him out."

"I will. Where do I find him?"

"Here. This afternoon. After two." Ezekiel started toward the cash register. He'd left Dan's bill next to it.

The deputies never accepted his offer of a free piece of pie. The wall on the other side of the counter wavered. The coffeepots and tea pitchers shimmered. His legs stopped working. He raised his hand to his head. At least, he thought he did. His fingers grappled with air.

"Ezekiel, are you all right?"

The words floated through a dark haze. Was that Mary Kay or Dan? The floor smacked him in the nose with a right hook worthy of a heavyweight champion.

. . .

It happened fast and slow all at the same time. Mary Katherine beat Deputy Rogers to Ezekiel's prone body lying facedown on the floor behind the counter. Her own body responded before her mind comprehended that his staggering dance had ended in complete collapse. The sudden strange silence in the restaurant registered as she knelt and touched his cheek. Several customers crowded the narrow space, buzzing with concern and curiosity. His cheek was damp with sweat.

His skin was a pasty white. "Everybody back up. Someone call 911." The calm in her voice surprised her. Her insides quivered like jelly. "He may be having a heart attack."

"Nee. No ambulance," Ezekiel grunted. His legs moved. His hand went to his head. "Nee. My heart is broken, but I'm fine."

"Ezekiel—"

"I'm fine." He rolled over and sat up. His nose had turned a fiery red from smacking the floor. "Did I say something about my heart? It's fine. I'm fine."

The customers began to drift back to their tables, their conversations a low murmur. Mary Katherine nodded at Anna, who grabbed Miriam's arm, and the two waitresses disappeared into the kitchen to keep the food coming. Ezekiel would hate a scene, and he wouldn't want the customers' meals interrupted—especially by his own health.

"You passed out." Deputy Rogers squatted next to Ezekiel. "That's not fine. Has this happened before? We need to get you to a doctor."

"Whoa, whoa. Give a man a minute." Ezekiel rubbed his eyes with the heels of his palms. His fingers shook. "Give a man a minute."

"Get him a glass of water." Deputy Rogers peered at Ezekiel's forehead, covered by thick salt-and-pepper hair. "Did you hit your head?"

Mary Katherine rushed to get the water and scurried back. "*Has* this happened before?"

"You two are like angry hornets buzzing around me." Ezekiel shoved Dan's hand away and ignored the glass Mary Katherine thrust at him. "A man can't think with all that buzzing. I'm fine."

"You're not fine." She settled the glass on the floor next to him. "We're taking you to the clinic."

"Nee."

"Jah."

"Yep." Deputy Rogers took Ezekiel's arm. "Grab the other one, Mary Kay. Help him into a chair."

Together they guided him to the closest chair. She set the glass of water on the table in front of him. "Take a sip and I'll tell the girls to keep an eye on things until we get back. Anna's perfectly capable of running the register. Burke will be here to start his shift within the hour."

"We don't have to go." He leaned forward, hands on his knees, and sucked in deep breaths. "I forgot to eat breakfast. A couple of scrambled eggs and toast, I'm right as rain."

She ignored his protest. A few minutes later they were in Deputy Rogers's patrol car headed for the clinic. Mary Katherine had never been in a law enforcement car. Neither had Ezekiel, she was sure. At least Deputy Rogers didn't turn on the siren, although he did make the tires squeal in his haste to pull away from the curb in front of the restaurant. The businesses whizzed by outside her window, but she could still see the blurred outlines of people who stopped to stare.

"I don't want this." Ezekiel squirmed in the seat next to her. "It's just a bill to pay."

"The Gmay can help with that."

"It's a waste of money." He craned his head to scowl at her. "There're plenty of home remedies available."

"If you knew what was wrong, which you don't. You remind me of Moses. He was always cranky as a bear with a thorn in his behind every time he was sick."

"I'm not cranky."

"As a bear."

"You two sound like an old married couple." Deputy Rogers chuckled, his blue eyes glancing at them in the rearview mirror. "If you wanted to spend time with the lady, there are easier ways."

The heat wave that rolled over Mary Katherine rivaled the worst night sweats she'd experienced during her change of life. She stared out the window, afraid to look at Ezekiel. What a ridiculous statement.

Ezekiel cleared his throat. The chuckle that followed was weak, but clearly a chuckle.

She ventured a glance. He winked at her.

He winked.

She nearly broke her neck in her haste to return to looking out the window. Goose bumps rippled across her arms and her neck. From the car's air conditioner, for sure. Not from that ridiculous wink.

She was cornered in a car with two silly men.

That's all, Moses, just silliness.

"Ezekiel is sitting in the backseat of a police car. He just passed out in front of you. He probably doesn't know how to act. Just like you. He's embarrassed. Be nice."

Compassion and plain old common sense were two of Moses' best qualities. She missed that about him. She missed everything about him.

Her mind's eye replayed the memory of Ezekiel's collapse. Had her heart stopped beating? "You need to take care of yourself." Notwithstanding the wink, she considered Ezekiel a friend, a member of her community, a member of her church family. "I don't care to have anyone else keel over and die in front of me."

He cleared his throat. "I'm sorry to have scared you like that."

"Don't do it again."

"Don't get out until I open your door to help you." Deputy Rogers shoved the gear in park and slid from the seat. Mary Katherine did the same.

Of course, Ezekiel opened his own door, but she and Deputy Rogers managed to shepherd him into the clinic. She explained the situation to the receptionist and seconds later, Ezekiel, looking every bit as hangdog as her children when they got in trouble at school, disappeared into the back.

Mary Katherine settled into a plush green chair while the deputy spoke to someone on his cell phone. The call lasted a long time. At least it seemed that way to her. She spent as little time on the phone as possible.

Finally, he stuck the phone in his pocket and ambled her direction. "You really let this man Burke McMillan stay in your barn after he broke into your house?"

The deputy had a one-track mind. "I did. He needed a place to sleep and I had one."

"What if he'd come back in and stabbed you in your sleep?" He eased into the chair next to her. "Or worse."

"If he'd been going to do that, he'd have done it to start with."

"That's one scenario." He leaned back and clasped his hands over his flat belly, his gun holster nestled against his leg. "The other one is that he's a con man insinuating himself into a trusting, kind community so he can take advantage of its members."

"Advantage how? We don't have money or jewels or much of anything worth stealing."

"I don't know yet. The most valuable thing you have is your land, your farms. Your stores."

Burke didn't seem much interested in material possessions. He hitchhiked across the country with a duffel bag containing all his earthly possessions. "You haven't even met the man."

"He broke into your house."

"Not an auspicious beginning."

"Nice word. Auspicious."

"You think because we're not educated, we can't learn big words?"

"I never said that." He pulled his hat down over his eyes as if he planned to take a nap. "I had my guy look up Mr. McMillan. He is who he says he is. A Navy chaplain, retired. His daughter died of leukemia. Then his wife committed suicide."

Mary Katherine closed her eyes and examined the inside of the lids. Burke McMillan's hurt and his pain and his suffering welled up inside her as if it were her own. The mystery of his desolate stoicism had been solved. "That doesn't make him a criminal or a con man. Far from it."

"Maybe not, but it could make him unhinged. His family hasn't heard from him in more than two years. What has he been doing? How has he been surviving?"

"He's hurting and trying to heal."

"How does he support himself?"

"Not very well from the looks of it."

"By stealing."

"Prove it."

"I will."

They lapsed into silence, much to Mary Katherine's relief. She smiled at the frazzled-looking mom with two little ones who took turns coughing, that terrible, loose, croupy cough she remembered so well. Her gaze wandered to the *Highlights* magazines on the table. She loved those stories.

The door swung open. Cyrus Beachy strode in, his mammoth body blocking the sun that streamed through the doorway. His silhouette told her nothing of his expression. He made a beeline for her.

"How is he?" The deacon's voice was low, his tone neutral, the question directed at Deputy Rogers. "We were told he fell or fainted."

"Both." Deputy Rogers stood and shook Cyrus's hand.

"Gott's provision that you were there to help." Cyrus nodded at Mary Katherine. "I have my buggy out front. I'll take Mary Katherine to hers and get Ezekiel when he's ready."

In other words, *Go about your business.*

"It's likely I'll need to talk to Mrs. Ropp again." Deputy Rogers slapped his hat on his head. "I'll run by the restaurant later today to talk to Mr. McMillan."

It wasn't a threat. Was it?

CHAPTER 14

F inally."

"Barbara!" Mary Katherine slammed the door behind her and turned to face her youngest daughter. "You scared me."

Barbara let the curtain on the front room window drop. She marched to the sofa and plopped down, her arms crossed over her chest. "Where have you been?"

Helping at the restaurant. She'd convinced Cyrus that someone was needed to oversee the operation in Ezekiel's absence. Burke was too new and the waitresses, however experienced, too young to have the entire weight on their shoulders. Mary Katherine ran the cash register and took care of to-go orders while visiting with customers and making sure the tables got properly bused. It had been busy but enjoyable. "Ezekiel passed out at the restaurant today. I helped out while he was at the doctor."

Barbara wanted all the details, which took a few minutes to impart. Mary Katherine eased into the rocking chair and rubbed her aching knees. Her feet hurt worse. Standing during her shift at the store followed by more standing at the restaurant had taken its toll. She left out the reason for Deputy Rogers's visit to the restaurant and Burke's story.

And the wink. Ezekiel's wink. What did that mean? She kept shoving the question into the corner the entire ride home, but like a recalcitrant child, it refused to stay there. Cyrus had returned after taking Ezekiel home from the clinic. The doctor's diagnosis was diabetes. Not the kind that required the shots. Who knew there was such a thing? Either way, a serious condition that would require changes in Ezekiel's life. He needed someone to take charge of his meals.

He needed a wife.

Most men did. Even when they didn't have diabetes. Even the ones who owned restaurants. Especially the ones who owned restaurants. They didn't have time to eat properly. Mary Katherine forced herself to concentrate. Her newlywed daughter sat in her front room when she should be home getting ready for bed. "What are you doing here? Where's Joseph?"

"He went to pick up some feed at his daed's. They must've gotten to talking or something." Barbara straightened her kapp, then plucked at a loose thread on her apron. "He knows I planned to come visit."

Rubbing her aching back, Mary Katherine rose and trudged to the sofa. Her feet longed to soak in Epsom salts and water. She sat next to her daughter. "It's late for a visit."

"Yet you're just getting home."

"I'm not a newlywed."

"Maybe you should be." Barbara scowled. Sarcasm soaked her words. She looked just like the woman

Mary Katherine used to see reflected in the store windows. Before the gray hair and wrinkles came for a visit and stayed. "You act like you want to be."

"Excuse me?"

"Everyone saw the way you fell all over Ezekiel at the wedding. It was embarrassing."

"It was an accident."

"Now word is you jumped at the chance to ride in a police car with him." Barbara shook her finger at Mary Katherine the way her mother used to do. Somehow roles had been reversed. "Everyone is talking."

"It was a sheriff's car and Ezekiel was sick. I was helping out a member of our community. Stop turning this around on me. How is married life?"

"Everyone's always so happy to get married." Barbara's tone deflated. "At least they always seem to be happy."

"I should hope so. They want to spend the rest of their lives with the people they love."

"It hasn't been easy. But that's beside the point. It doesn't help that we're all concerned about you."

"Don't blame it on me, Dochder." Putting two lives together as one took some doing. A little scooching this way, a little scrunching that way. "No one said it was easy. You don't hightail it for home when things get rough. You and Joseph are in it for the long haul. Remember your vows. Remember your wedding day."

"It was fine while we were doing the visiting."

Others did the cooking and cleaning. Newlyweds helped out, but mostly they visited. "And now that you're in your new home?"

"It turns out, I'm not gut at it."

Mary Katherine scratched an itchy spot on the back of her dishwater-dry hand, contemplating. This was treacherous territory. Not much got said in Plain homes about certain topics. "Not gut at what, exactly? Your cooking is fine. Your sewing—"

"Not gut at anything." The girl wailed.

"Some things take time." The heat that roared across Mary Katherine's face could've burnt the pasture grasses to a crisp. "If the mann is patient, you'll relax and it won't be so uncomfortable."

"Mudder!" Barbara jumped to her feet and began to pace. "Not that. I can't believe you even said that. That's, that's, that's—"

"*Ach*, then tell me what ails you, child." Another thought occurred to Mary Katherine. She couldn't contain a smile. "Are you in a family way? Already? Nee, you couldn't know that fast, but you could—"

"Nee, not that I know of. It's not that. I'm no gut at being in the house all day by myself. My garden is fine, but the house is messy and my bread dough didn't rise and the kaffi tasted like brown water and I burned his shirt because I left the iron on the stove too long."

Not gut at it. Our girl isn't gut at it.

"*You told me she wouldn't be.*"

Not a good cook, not much of a sewer. Given to bouts of independence.

"*Like you.*"

Leave it to Moses to draw the line between those two points. "These are things you can learn to do better. Slow down. It's not a race. Finish one task. Move to the next."

"Joseph has no patience. I put sugar instead of salt in the spaghetti sauce. It was awful. He asked me what I do all day. He said I needed to pay attention. He treated me like a little girl."

"He's trying to help. He's your mann. You have to respect his wishes."

"He's a know-it-all. He's bossy."

"He's the mann."

"Mudder!"

"Dochder, a fraa's place is in the home, taking care of her mann and her kinner. You'll have *boplin* soon and you'll feel so happy, you'll forget all about how hard it was at the beginning. That's a promise."

"He says I'm just like you."

Her vices coming home to roost. "He should be more respectful of his elders."

"I'm beginning to think I need to come home and keep an eye on my elders."

"Very funny, child."

A rap at the door made them both jump.

"Oops." Barbara scowled. "I may have stayed too late."

"You said he was fine with you coming over here."

"I may have stretched the truth a bit. He'd been gone so long, I got bored and came over. I left a note."

Shaking her head, Mary Katherine stalked to the door and opened it. A scowl on his face that matched the one on his new wife's, Joseph stood on the porch, arms crossed over his broad chest. "I'm looking for my fraa."

"Come on in."

"We're just talking. I lost track of the time." Barbara

hopped up and scurried toward the door. "I didn't mean to worry you."

"It's too late for talking." Joseph stomped across the living room, his boots leaving bits of grass and leaves on the wooden floor. "You shouldn't be traipsing around the countryside by yourself."

"It's not that late."

"You always have to argue, don't you?" He muttered something Mary Katherine couldn't hear, but most likely along the lines of "like your mudder." "You waited until I went to Daed's and then sneaked out of the house like a girl on her rumspringa."

"Nee. I left a note."

"Let's go."

"I'll be by for a visit soon." Mary Katherine patted Barbara's shoulder as she passed. "We can start a new quilt. We'll have the next frolic at your house."

"That would be gut." Joseph spoke first. "Keep you both occupied."

"I'm plenty busy—"

"He means me," Barbara interrupted. She gave Mary Katherine a familiar look. *Hush. Don't stir the pot.*

The same look Mary Katherine used to give the children when they tangled with Moses.

"Have a gut evening." She closed the door behind them and leaned against it. How times had changed. Now her children thought they needed to stick their noses in her business. Even her youngest daughter, who had her own row to hoe.

The perils of being an old widow woman with ten children. At least they didn't live in a shoe.

CHAPTER 15

Ezekiel was famous for his sweet tooth. Stealing cookies. Taking the last piece of pumpkin pie. Dessert for breakfast. His children loved it. Not anymore. Ezekiel smacked a rock with his boot, sending it flying down the dirt road. He kicked another one for good measure. The sun had disappeared behind the horizon. He should be sleeping. He should be at the restaurant cleaning up after the supper rush. The doctor had nixed that idea. Take a break, she said, eat some protein and some fruit. Drink plenty of fluids. That's what she called water. Rest. Get back in the saddle tomorrow.

A soft breeze cooled his face. He felt like a kid again, being told what he could and couldn't eat. The dizziness, the constant thirst, the frequent trips to the bathroom. It all came down to one thing. Diabetes. No shots, not yet, not ever if he took care of himself and ate right.

Eat right. Cut down on refined sugar. How was that different from plain old sugar? Exercise. The doctor had a whole list of things she wanted him to do, starting with using a whatchamacallit that measured his blood sugar—excuse me, his blood glucose—before every meal. Keeping track of what he ate to balance out the proteins and starches. No more chocolate pudding cake. No more whoopie pies. No more of Mary Katherine's three-layer German chocolate cake. No more ice cream. What was this world coming to when a man couldn't eat a bowl of ice cream before bed?

No more cocoa. Unless it was sugar free. Also known as taste free.

He owned a restaurant and spent six days a week working around food.

"Stop whining. Big bopli."

A group of toads croaked in a gravelly concert. Joining his pity party. A dragonfly whizzed past him, headed toward the creek. No one disagreed with him.

He kept walking. Walking counted as exercise, while standing on his feet at the restaurant did not. No meandering she said. A brisk walk. He picked up his pace, nearing the intersection where the dirt road met the highway. He would have to turn back soon. How much exercise did it take to work off a peanut butter and jam sandwich and an apple?

Peanut butter was good protein, but it had sugar in it. Who knew? Strawberry jam had a lot of sugar in it. No one would know but him. And his blood glucose. "Our little secret."

He snorted to himself. Acting like a spoiled brat, not a grown man.

A car whizzed by on the highway. Another one. Then a truck. He started to do an about-face and then stopped. A dusty green minivan pulled over on the shoulder of the road and stopped. Burke got out, shut the door, leaned in the open window to say something, and then started down the road.

"Hey." He waved. "Fancy meeting you here."

"You hitched a ride?" Ezekiel waited for Burke to catch up to him. "I thought you would bring my buggy home."

"I don't drive buggies." His stride matched Ezekiel's. "Besides, John brought Andrew into town to drive it home."

No one had bothered to tell him that. His son had insisted he go straight to the dawdy haus and "rest." "And nobody gave a thought to how you would get here?"

"I'm used to getting around on my own. So what did the doctor say?"

"Nothing worth repeating."

"Come on. Anna said you passed out. Must've been something."

"I got the diabetes. Not the shot kind."

"Still, no fun. My dad had diabetes. My mom learned to make a lot of desserts with artificial sweeteners. He said you couldn't tell the difference. Cookies and pudding. He even bought candy that was sugar free."

"I can't wait."

Burke chuckled. "At least it isn't your heart. Or cancer."

Or leukemia.

"Do you have brothers and sisters?"

"Only child."

"Aunts and uncles?"

"On my dad's side. Nobody I'm close to."

The wanderer had no real family, it seemed. "That's hard for me to imagine."

"I got all the presents on Christmas morning and all the eggs on Easter." Burke's chuckle sounded grim. "It had its moments."

Lonely moments. "It's a wonder you didn't turn into a spoiled brat."

"Who said I didn't? My parents took good care of me. They brought me up right." His tone was lighter. "Deputy Rogers came to see me this afternoon."

"He told me he would." Ezekiel veered off onto the well-worn path that would take them to the creek. He glanced back. "If you're tired, go on up to the house. I've been told to exercise."

"It feels good to be outside after being in the kitchen all day." Burke kept pace. "After a while, food doesn't smell that good."

"And it's greasy and hot and noisy."

"Pretty much." Burke snatched up a tall, spindly blade of browning grass between two fingers. "Don't you want to know what Deputy Doolittle said? Or asked me?"

"I think you mean Deputy Rogers."

"Sorry. No disrespect intended."

"I know you haven't been running around the countryside burglarizing folks' homes."

"Only the one. If Mary Katherine hadn't given me a place to stay that night and helped me find a job, I might've done more."

"But you didn't."

"Deputy Doolittle—Rogers—told me not to leave

town. He took my fingerprints. I let him. He's not going to find them anywhere they shouldn't be. Except on the mustard jar at Mary Katherine's."

"She didn't mind sharing the mustard."

"You're kind people." His tone carried a touch of accusation. "I can see the face of Christ in you."

"That's mighty grandiose. We would never be so vain or prideful." Ezekiel swatted away a horsefly that buzzed his head. "Plain folks show what we believe by our example."

Burke's steps slowed. "You don't sound all that convinced."

"We're not given a choice in the matter." Plain folks took their lumps and kept walking. "Gott has a plan for us. We don't always like it, but He knows what's best for us."

"You sound bitter."

"Don't mean to."

"Come on. You lost your wife." Burke's voice held a tiny quiver when he reached the word *wife*. "You have a right to your feelings."

The pot calling the kettle black. "From what Deputy Rogers said, you've had some severe heartaches yourself."

"I wish he wouldn't have told you how my wife died." Anger replaced the quiver and Burke's voice grew stronger. "I hate that pity look people get. Like the one you have right now."

"It isn't pity. I just recognize that some folks got it worse than others."

"It doesn't serve a purpose to compare degrees or

levels of loss." Burke waved his way through a swarm of gnats. "Spit it out, my friend."

Were they friends? They'd only known each other for a short time. The man worked in Ezekiel's restaurant and slept in a bedroom down the hall. By the same token, one day he'd move on down the road, gone forever. What did it hurt for Ezekiel to give voice to his thoughts? Maybe then they would leave him alone. "Most days I struggle to hold on to my belief in the Father and the Son."

"I get that." Burke's voice softened to a hoarse whisper. "But it tends to make a man lonelier. I know that for a fact."

"My wife was standing at the counter cooking supper. One minute she's peeling potatoes." Keeping his gaze on the trail in front of him, Ezekiel wound his way past a cluster of oversized black-eyed Susans and purple coneheads. "The next, she's on the floor, dead of an aneurysm. But yours chose to end her life. She chose to leave you alone. I could understand if that shook your faith."

"You think my pain is worse because my wife chose to take her own life?"

"I don't know." Ezekiel halted, unable to go forward, but he kept his back to the other man. He couldn't let him see his face. "She left you behind to find your way on your own. That must hurt."

"I was alone in a burnt no-man's-land where nothing would ever grow again. I've come to see that she felt the same way. I failed her. I failed to see her need because I was so wrapped up in mine. She needed me, and I was too selfish to look up in time to see it." Burke stepped in front of Ezekiel, then turned and faced him. "Having been in that place, I recognize it when I see it in someone else."

Unable to bear the agonizing pain that had aged Burke a hundred years, Ezekiel brushed past him. "We believe people have a certain number of days that God has given them on this earth." He'd said these words many times, to his own children who lost their mother. "When their time is done, He takes them home."

"I understand how pompous and cliché those words can sound when a person is in excruciating pain." Burke chuckled, no mirth in the sound. "I was a chaplain. I helped men and women deal with their pain all the time. I look back and wonder why they didn't kick me out of their houses. Or beat me senseless."

Ezekiel had been on the receiving end of a bunch of words like that. "You did your best. You tried. That's something."

"I quit and ran away."

"It's not for us to have the answers, only to trust and obey."

"Yet you can't seem to do it and you feel exceedingly guilty for it." Burke flung the blade of grass into the dirt. "I believe God knows and He understands. He, too, suffered a terrible loss."

"I reckon He's getting impatient. I can't seem to get over it in my heart, as much as my head says it believes that God knows what He's doing. I say the words, but I can't bring myself to mean them."

"It'll take whatever time it takes. We don't grieve on a timeline. He knows that."

Ezekiel inhaled the cool, humid air. His throat ached with the effort to keep his voice level. "How do you know?"

"Because He's done it with me."

"I don't see you running back to Virginia to your chaplain job."

"That part of my life is over. I come seeking a new start." Burke raised his head to the heavens. "I just don't know exactly where or doing what. I cut myself loose from my old life without any thought for where to go from there. I just know I'm supposed to be here now."

"Sticking your nose in other people's business?"

Burke shrugged. "Once a chaplain, always a chaplain."

"I don't want to talk about this anymore."

"Give Him a chance. He'll shine a light in your life, and you'll follow it and find the path again."

"I'm trying to find God." The lump grew. Ezekiel cleared his throat. "He's hidden Himself from me. If He doesn't show up soon, I'll give up."

"Don't do that. Think of your children. Your grandchildren. You've been given great blessings."

"And you have none. How can you be so forgiving of God?"

God would strike him down. The flash of lightning would burn the grass and the flowers and destroy all life around him. The words had been stuck in his throat for ten years, bottled up by his upbringing and his fear of reaching that point of no return.

"Feel better?"

"What?"

"You've been needing to say those words for a long time." Burke man-patted his back. "You've torn the Band-Aid off the wound. Now it can heal."

"You didn't answer my question. How did you forgive God?"

"Who says I did?"

"So it's good enough for me, but not you?"

"God found me wanting, not the other way around." Burke raised his face to the sky again as if seeking evidence of the divine. "I blew it. I don't deserve His mercy or His grace."

"None of us do. That's why it's called grace."

Burke snorted. "See. I knew you would get there before me. You're a good man."

Not that good.

"You don't believe me. Look at the people He's placed in your life. Look at Mary Katherine."

What did Mary Katherine have to do with anything? Mary Katherine with her sweet smell and quick smile. Mary Katherine, who made heavenly pies and wrote stories.

Pretty wrapping around a gift of agony down the road? A person couldn't know the future.

A ferocious bark filled the sudden silence. Followed by the dog's high-pitched whining. More barking.

Burke cocked his head. "Is that Boo?"

Ezekiel pushed past him. "Kenneth."

Boo's barking grew louder. Ezekiel raced down the path toward the pond. His boots smacked in the mud. Low-hanging branches and bushes whipped in his face. Time whistled in his ears, passing but not passing. The pounding of his heart filled his head, so loud it muffled any thought but getting to his grandchild. The sound of panting told him Burke kept pace.

Kenneth lay facedown in the mud, water lapping at his blond hair at the overflowing creek's edge. One crutch floated in the creek, the other lay just beyond his reach.

"Lord, have mercy."

Ezekiel dropped to his knees. "Kenneth! Kenneth?"

He rolled over and sighed. His face covered with mud and leaves. His glasses were lopsided and smudged but unbroken. His skin was ruddy and bruised looking. Angry red scratches marred his cheeks. Ezekiel wiped at the mud. "Talk to me, child."

His small, dirty hands grasped at Ezekiel's shirtsleeve. "I fell."

"I see that." Ezekiel's heart flopped back into his chest and beat again. "Are you hurt?"

"My nose hurts."

Kenneth's red nose matched Ezekiel's. He touched it with one finger. Kenneth winced and yelped. Boo whined. "It's okay, hund. He's okay. I reckon. Gut hund, gut hund."

"He is a good friend to have." Still panting, Burke stood, bent over, and put both hands on his knees. "I'm too old to be running around like that." He straightened and ruffled the dog's fur. "A man could use a friend like you, buddy."

"What are you doing down here by yourself?" Ezekiel didn't know whether to hug Kenneth or take him to the woodshed. "Your mudder will have your hide when she finds out."

"I wanted to say good night to Nate, my frog. Mudder was cleaning up the kitchen. I decided not to wait." Kenneth didn't sound too scared of Leah. "I reached down to pick him up. The mud sucked up my crutches. Boom, over I went."

Ezekiel pulled him into his lap and hugged him tight against his chest. "Don't ever do that again. There's a reason you're not supposed to be down here alone."

"I can do stuff on my own. I'm not a baby." Kenneth grimaced and tugged free of the hug. "I just got down, and I couldn't get myself back up."

"Everybody needs help sometimes." Ezekiel glanced at Burke, who shrugged and smiled. "It doesn't make you a baby."

"No one thinks I can help myself ever." His scowl made him look just like his mother at that age. "Are you going to tell Daed and Mudder?"

"I think they'll notice your nose, the scratches, and the mud all over your clothes." Ezekiel brushed at the mess, but it only made it worse. He didn't want to imagine the look on his daughter's face when she found out what Kenneth had done. She would be on fire with indignation, like Lucy had been the time Leah at age four tried to light the stove. "They'll probably want you to see your doctor tomorrow, just to be on the safe side."

"Nee, I'm fine." Kenneth's sigh was rueful. "Doctors don't do nothing to help. They just poke and prod and give me more icky pills to take."

Ezekiel tended to agree, but Leah would have *his* hide if he said as much. "Do as your daed tells you."

"I always do."

Ezekiel let his *harrumph* talk for him.

"Boo's a good hund, isn't he?" Kenneth hugged the dog, who lathered the boy with slobbery kisses. That was one way to clean off the mud. "He's like a big brother, isn't he?"

"Something like that."

"Do you see Nate anywhere?" Kenneth sounded almost as anxious about the frog as he was about his fall. "I hope I didn't scare him so bad he decided to move to a new creek."

Burke surveyed the scene. "I don't see him, but he probably called it a night."

"This is the only creek within hopping range. We'll come look for him tomorrow." Ezekiel stood and lifted Kenneth to his feet. The child didn't weigh much more than a sack of potatoes. He handed him one crutch and then the other. The boy swayed but didn't go down. "I better never catch you down here alone again."

"You won't. I promise."

The water lapped against the shore in a soothing rhythm. Night sounds overtook them. An owl hooted. Dragonflies buzzed. The frogs took up their songs again. Burke turned and faced the water. "Sometimes the reason to go on living smacks us in the face."

"Oftentimes." Ezekiel put his hand on Kenneth's shoulder. They began the slow march home. It was tough going on crutches in the soft dirt and mud. "Blessings are everywhere. The trick is to recognize them."

They started to gain headway toward the path. Boo trotted ahead, his pink tongue lolling to one side of his mouth.

"I think you need a dog." Burke fell into step next to Ezekiel. He began to whistle off-key a tune that sounded a little like "Yankee Doodle Dandy." "A big one."

"What are you talking about?"

Burke didn't answer. His whistle faded away and he began to hum "Amazing Grace."

CHAPTER 16

The battery-operated lights shone on a figure walking along the highway's shoulder. Mary Katherine peered at the figure. Man or woman? Or a delusion brought on by the exhaustion of another day filled with working in the store? And not thinking about Ezekiel and his sugar levels and his winks. They'd done an inventory afterward and she'd had supper with the Grabers. A nice meal cooked by Jennie's girls. But time had gotten away from her. Dark came early now.

She shivered in the cool October north wind and peered into the dusk. Maybe she needed a new prescription for her glasses. A woman—no, a girl—stumbled to a halt, her hand to her forehead as if shielding her eyes.

"Whoa, whoa." Mary Katherine slowed the buggy. She pulled over to the shoulder and stopped. It was a girl. "Hi there, do you need a ride?"

"Mrs. Ropp?"

"Nicole?"

Coach Wilson's daughter and Ezekiel's server wore her purple Mustangs cheerleading outfit and no coat. She had to be chilled in that skimpy outfit. "What are you doing out here all alone in the middle of the night on the side of the road?"

The girl threw her arms up in the air as if to surrender. Sobs blotted out the sound of frogs and crickets and distant highway traffic.

"Ach, honey, it's okay. You're fine."

Whatever it was, it would be okay. At that age everything seemed bigger than it was. Mary Katherine snatched a blanket from the buggy's backseat, climbed down, and went to Nicole. She wrapped the blanket around the girl's shaking body. Nicole's braids were a mess and her shoes dirty. She had a scrape on one knee, but her uniform was as clean as could be expected after a basketball game. She didn't look seriously hurt. Not physically. "Come on, I'll give you a ride home. It's not a zippy taxi service, but we'll get there eventually."

Nicole hiccupped another sob in response, but she crawled into the buggy without argument.

Mary Katherine settled next to her and clucked at Samson. "Tell me what happened." The girl didn't have her own car. It had to have been a spat with a boyfriend. No boy worth a lick left a girl on the side of the road, no matter what the argument had been. "It'll make you feel better."

"It's nothing."

Mary Katherine dug around in her bag with her free hand and offered a tissue to Nicole. "It can't be nothing or you wouldn't be out here all alone."

More sobs.

"I promise I won't tell anyone."

"I can't." Nicole swiped at her face and heaved a dramatic sigh. "Especially you."

"Why especially me?"

She groaned. "Forget I said that. Please."

The entreaty in her voice made Mary Katherine glance her way. Thick, woolen clouds clothed the stars and moon. Nicole's features were hidden in darkness. "It's forgotten." Mary Katherine snapped the reins and Samson picked up his pace. "But it's important for kiddos to know they can tell adults just about anything. If something bad happened to you out here, if someone did something bad to you, you should find an adult to tell. Just because I'm an Amish woman doesn't mean you can't tell me."

It was true they didn't like to get involved in Englisch tussles, and they certainly avoided law enforcement issues whenever possible. But children who needed help needed help. Period.

Freeman and the others would agree on this one.

"It's nothing like that."

"You didn't just wake up and find yourself out here on a dark country road on a school night."

"Sometimes after the ball games we don't go straight home." She wiggled on the buggy seat. "Some of us get together."

"Even the coach's daughter."

"He won't notice." Bitterness replaced the earlier fear. "He never does."

"I know your daddy. I imagine he pays attention to everything."

"He has a busload of players to think about."

"You play sports."

"I'm not that good. I play because everyone does." The resignation that filled her voice mingled with sadness too great for a girl her age. "It's a small school. I'd rather be reading a book."

"Like your mom."

She'd stopped crying and her breathing was lighter, calmer.

"So you don't go home after the ball games. Where do you go?"

"Here or there. No place in particular."

"Keggers?"

"Mrs. Ropp! What do you know about keggers?"

"I have ten children. Sometimes Amish kids veer off the road for a bit." Mary Katherine leaned over and sniffed. "You don't smell like beer."

"I don't drink. It stinks. It's gross. I have school tomorrow."

"But you went."

"They invited me. Usually they don't."

"Because you're the coach's daughter."

"Yep."

"They dumped you on the road because you wouldn't drink?"

"No. No. Look, I can't tell you. Don't worry about it."

She couldn't tell Mary Katherine. Especially Mary Katherine. Why especially? "Okay. Let's get you home and to bed."

They crawled into town at the usual buggy speed—snail's pace. Nicole sank into her blanket. Occasionally she sighed, then wiggled. A cell phone appeared in her hand. She thumbed a message, then stuck it in her pocket. It chirped like a cricket. It came out again. She thumbed some more.

"How hard is it to become Amish?"

The question seemed to emanate from nothing and everything the girl hadn't said. "That's a long conversation, and I'm probably not the best one to explain it. Do you think you want to be Amish?"

"It seems easier."

Nicole worked hard waitressing at the Purple Martin, but she likely gave no thought to what it was like to cook, clean, and do laundry for ten children with no electricity, no dryer, no microwave. How would she survive without a cell phone, a hair dryer, and two hundred cable channels? Without internet? Mary Katherine smiled in the darkness. "*Easy* is a relative term."

"I know it's not easy, like you work hard and you don't have cars or electricity. I mean you're nice to each other. You have big families and you're never, you know, alone."

An unexpected knot formed in Mary Katherine's throat. Her arms ached to dispense a medicinal hug. "We have our moments. We're not always nice. But we try. We make mistakes and get mad like everybody else."

"You're always nice."

"I try."

"I can't believe you have ten kids. That's a ton. I don't even have one brother or sister. My mom couldn't have any more. I always wanted a sister."

"I have four. And four brothers."

"With you that makes a baseball team."

"True. But I liked volleyball better."

"I guess I wouldn't want to be Amish, but someday I'm having at least four kids. I won't let my baby be an only child."

"It's not the worst thing in the world. Parents lavish their love on their only child."

"And want them to be everything they wanted to be but weren't." Bitterness laced the words. "My dad wanted a boy."

"But he loves his girl."

"I suppose."

Her phone chirped again. She studied the screen and sniffed. Thumbs engaged in rapid-fire typing. This time, she didn't resume the conversation but sank back in the blanket, her head turned toward the countryside she couldn't see in the dark.

Mary Katherine held her peace, but her imagination wrote half a dozen scenarios, each wilder than the next about the girl's countryside adventure. Nicole wasn't getting attention at home so she sought it elsewhere? Not uncommon. Mary Katherine had ten children, but she never worried about giving them enough attention. They had each other, and they spent hours together as a family, every night before bed and on Sundays. Life on the Farm, Dutch Blitz, checkers, chess, puzzles, story time, volleyball, baseball, fishing, birding, camping, wagon rides with their pony. Free time was family time. Work was family time.

What couldn't Nicole tell her? A simple kegger wouldn't cause her such distress. Why couldn't she tell Mary Katherine? Because it was a bigger crime than underage drinking? Drugs? More than taking drugs? Making drugs? A meth lab?

"What do you think of Tony?"

"Tony?" It took Mary Katherine a few seconds to place the name. "The busboy?"

"My dad says he looks like a girl with his long hair." She wiped her phone's screen with her sleeve. "I don't think he looks like a girl at all. I think my dad says that because Tony doesn't play sports. He doesn't play sports because he has to work a lot to help his family."

"That's a good thing, helping his family." Mary Katherine's knowledge of Tony was limited to the fact that he had pretty hair for a boy and he seemed to think she was hard of hearing. "Amish boys work a lot. They play basketball, but only for fun. That doesn't make them like girls."

"That's what I said. The boys on the team make fun of Tony's car because it's old and rusty. They have big diesel pickup trucks."

"We don't measure anything by the size of cars."

"That's what I'm saying. I like the Amish."

"Me too."

Nicole laughed. She sounded less like a weary old woman and more like the sixteen-year-old girl she was.

It sounded as if she might like Tony too. Mary Katherine smiled to herself. Young love was so hard to decipher. Come to think of it, so was old love. Or love at all.

Lights blazed in every window of the Wilsons' two-story redbrick house. Coach Wilson stood on the front porch, a cell phone to his ear. Mary Katherine reined in her imagination and the buggy. She pulled into a wide cement driveway that held an enormous silver diesel pickup.

Wilson put the phone to his chest and turned toward the open door. "She's here, Phoebe. She's here," he bellowed. "Where in the . . . ?"

He clamped his mouth shut, stomped down the steps, and marched across the grass to the driveway. The white picket gate had been left open as if in anticipation of their arrival. After a fierce glare filled with a mix of parental fear, angst, and anger, he opened his mouth again. "Are you all right? What happened? Where have you been? I was ready to call the sheriff's office and the state police, the National Guard, you name it."

"I'm cold. I'm tired." Nicole's glance directed at Mary Katherine was filled with misery. "Can I get my punishment in the morning?"

"No explanation? Are you kidding me—?"

"Larry." Phoebe's voice held a measure of warning. She stood at the porch railing, hands on the belt of her pink paisley-print housecoat. "Let's bring it inside. No need to wake the neighbors."

Scowling, Coach Wilson snorted and kicked at the ground with a scuffed cowboy boot. "Get in the house."

"Thanks for the ride, Mrs. Ropp." Her voice trembled. "You're always so nice to me."

Like she somehow didn't deserve the kindness. "Anytime. I mean that."

Nicole unwrapped the blanket, dragged herself from the buggy, and trudged toward her father. Coach Wilson's hand went out when she passed him. Nicole dodged it and kept going. On the porch she paused long enough to accept an embrace from her mother, who followed her inside and shut the door.

Coach Wilson's cell phone played a country music song Mary Katherine recognized. He glanced at it and grimaced. With a growl he stuck it in the pocket of his purple Mustangs windbreaker emblazoned with COACH on the left pocket. "How did she end up with you?"

"I found her out on the road." Mary Katherine described the location and circumstances. "She looked half frozen and very upset, so I offered her a ride."

"Did she tell you what she was doing out there?"

"She wouldn't say."

"I'm better with boys, and all God gave me was one girl."

A blessing. Ask couples with no children at all. Mary Katherine bit her lip to keep from opening her mouth.

Coach Wilson ran stubby fingers through thinning gray hair. "I don't know what's gotten into her. She's never done this kind of thing before."

He couldn't be that naive. Surely he asked himself what the players on his teams did after the games. Hadn't he heard from the other parents? "Maybe she'll tell you. She hardly knows me."

He growled deep in his throat. "That'll be a first."

One by one, lights extinguished in the Wilson house. "I'm sure she'll talk to her mother. I should go. I didn't even say thank you."

"No need."

"She's grounded until forever."

"I'm sure you'll do what's best."

He slammed the fence gate again and paused on the other side. "Be careful driving home. If it weren't for the horse, I'd offer to take you in the truck. It's cold and dark out there."

"I don't mind." She pulled out of the driveway. At the corner she looked back. Coach Wilson stood on the porch, his cell phone to his ear, gesticulating with his free hand.

Parenting was hard, whether a person had one child or ten.

CHAPTER 17

The boys were up to something. Ezekiel was sure of it. They never came to the produce auction with him. They had work to do on the farm. Even in October. Still, they'd insisted on coming with him, claiming he needed help picking up the boxes. Diabetes did not make him weak. Shaking his head, he squeezed past the owner of the local grocery store, a farmer's market coordinator from Gallatin, and a bunch of women who wanted to can peaches. An Englisch couple took photos with their phones as their kids tried to climb on a 1,072-pound pumpkin on display. The buzz of conversations reached a crescendo and echoed against the gargantuan shed's tin roof. Several days a week, the auction teemed with folks waiting for the auctioneer to turn on the microphone and blare that singsong voice of his.

His sons followed along behind him like faithful puppies past rows and rows of enormous boxes of pumpkins, multicolored gourds with wrinkles like fat tumors, flats of tomatoes, and boxes of potatoes, peaches, onions, and cantaloupe. Both had an air of something to be said about them. Finally, he veered between the wooden columns into the late-afternoon sunshine. He halted between two flatbed trailers filled with clay pots of mums, their yellow, burnt orange, red, white, and mauve blooms arranged in brilliant stripes against a blue autumn sky.

"What?" Ezekiel faced his two sons and crossed his arms over his chest. It was like seeing double. Himself at twenty-four and twenty-two. Before the top of his head became smooth as an egg. No glasses. Smooth, tanned skin. Brown eyes. Nose on the long side. John had Lucy's smile and her chin. Andrew, her cheeks and dimples. But mostly they looked like him, which made life easier. "Tell me whatever it is and get it over with."

Andrew shifted from one boot to the other and looked at his big brother. John hooked one hand around a suspender and rubbed his nose with the other. "You should sell the restaurant. Shut it down and sell it."

"Excuse me?" He squinted as if seeing them better in the bright sun would make him understand their intent. They suddenly spoke Greek or Chinese. Or both. "What are you talking about?"

"Carlene and Leah agree. As the men in the family, they thought we should tell you, even though they're older."

"Oh, they did, did they?" He tugged at his beard and turned his back on them. "I have to get the produce and get back to the restaurant. We're out of potatoes and they have a good price on the onions. I want a bushel of peaches. Burke says he makes a pretty gut pie. I believe him. He's a fine cook."

"Daed, wait!"

"Nee, you wait." He whirled around. Then stopped. Deep breath. *In and out.* No sense in making a scene in front of neighbors and friends—or strangers, for that matter. "I opened that restaurant ten years ago as a way to earn a living and keep this family together. It has done that. It's a place where our kind go and get a meal and see friends, talk to neighbors. The food's decent. There's no reason to close it."

A family in another Gmay decided to sell the restaurant only months after Lucy's death. It had been a godsend. They simply wanted someone to take over the payments so they could move to another state. His heart wasn't in farming anymore. The decision had been made in a heartbeat. The money from the sale of the farm had provided the seed money for his new venture. His new life.

"It served its purpose. We all liked working there when we were younger." Andrew jumped in when John seemed to waver. "Now you're working yourself into the ground for no reason. Running a restaurant is a young man's business."

"I'm not dying."

"We know that." John gritted his teeth. His pulse jumped along his jawline. He took a breath. "It's in Gott's hands. We know that, but we figure He took Mudder early. We'd like you to stay a little longer."

The slightest quaver in his voice sent Ezekiel ricocheting backward in time to a thirteen-year-old who tried so hard not to cry as he crouched next to his mother's body, calling for her, calling her to come back. He'd come into the kitchen to see if supper was ready.

A hungry, growing boy who played practical jokes on his sisters and wanted to fish every chance he got. He'd changed that day. They all had.

"You're right. It's in Gott's hands." Ezekiel softened his tone. "In the meantime, stop worrying. The doctor says my ticker's fine. Nothing else is wrong with me. If I eat right and keep my weight down, I'll be around a while longer."

"At least think about it."

"Nothing to think about."

"Daed!"

"You want to do something to help? Tell Leah and Carlene to make extra pies and bring them over when they can. Your fraas could do the same with cookies and cakes. It'll take a little of the load off me and the cooks."

"We'll do that. They can do that." John's jaw jutted, his smile grim. "But it's not necessary. You're getting up there. What, sixty-five—?"

"Sixty. Young. Way too young to sit around and twiddle my thumbs."

"You can farm with us." John threw out both hands as if encompassing the countryside where the crops would grow. "Nobody said anything about twiddling thumbs. You liked farming. You only stopped because you couldn't make a living."

He had liked it once. When Lucy met him at the kitchen door after a hard day in the fields. "If it was hard then, it's ten times harder now." Ezekiel chucked John on the shoulder in a gentle gesture. "The big super farms have taken over. You're hanging in there, but I see the restaurant as a fallback. We'll have it if you can't make a go of it. We can all work there, together again."

"It's not likely that will happen."

"People always have to eat."

"They can't always afford to eat out."

Andrew watched the argument like a man watching a volleyball game, his head moving side to side with his gaze.

"I'm your daed. You don't tell me what to do."

"Nee, we don't." John cleared his throat. "Just think about it."

"Let's get those potatoes." He jerked his thumb toward the building. "And pumpkins. I reckon Burke can make pumpkin pies. Nothing says fall like pumpkin pie."

"I could make some pumpkin pies."

He turned at the sound of the familiar voice.

"Mary Kay, I figured you'd be working at the Combination Store today."

The words came out crankier than he'd intended.

Her smile died. Her eyebrows rose. "I wanted to see how you're feeling." She held two pots of mums, one burnt orange and one red, in her arms. Her blue eyes were made bluer by her mauve dress and her now scarlet cheeks. "Carlene told me about the diabetes."

"He's too stubborn to take care of himself." John threw that in. Andrew's head bobbed in agreement. "Don't be giving him any of that pie. He'll probably eat it. Take it to the restaurant."

"Like I can't eat all the pie and cake and cookies I

want at the restaurant?" Ezekiel turned his best scowl on his sons. "Go. Bid on the potatoes, onions, tomatoes, zucchini, cantaloupe, and peaches. And grab a box of gourds and some mums. Miriam can make something pretty to sit by the front door. But don't overdo the tomatoes and cantaloupes. I don't want them to spoil—"

"We know what to do."

They stomped away, two angry peas in a too-tight pod.

"Grumpy seems to run in the family today." Mary Katherine nudged aside a few pots and set her mums on the flatbed. She dusted dirt from her hands, her expression pensive. "Are you upset because I can't cook at the restaurant?"

"I reckon I had a hand in that. You're not mad at me for siding with the elders?"

"You did what you thought was right." Her tone could cut a tree stump in half. "I'm sorry about the diabetes."

"Nothing to be done about it. No sense fussing."

"Why are you so grumpy?"

She didn't beat around the bush. "My suhs want me to sell the restaurant. They say it has served its purpose. I should come farm with them."

"Funny how kinner start to think they know more than their parents."

"Funny like finding a rattlesnake under the pillow on your favorite chair." He tried for a chuckle. It sounded halfhearted. "They always think they know more than their parents. It's just that when they get older, they feel free to say so."

She smiled. The morning sun beamed down on them, warmer than it was a second before. Her smile stirred something inside him that had been dormant for years. It was a summer evening sitting in a lawn chair on the riverbank, pole in hand, hook and line in the water. It didn't matter if he caught anything. It only mattered that the sun shone, and the wispy clouds floated on a breeze scented with mud and honeysuckle. Life was simple. The smile was lazy.

He blinked. "Are you buying produce for the store?"

"Nee. Thomas and Dylan are selling produce. I came along for the ride."

"It would've been nice to work together." Nice. She would think him forward. He hadn't thought those words until he said them. They served no purpose.

She ducked her head like a teenager. Her smile deepened. "Did you ever get the chocolate off your shirt?"

Her thoughts had gone back to Barbara's wedding day too. That encounter in front of God and everyone. The sun shone even hotter. "Carlene did. Sure is hot for fall."

The auctioneer's singsong voice boomed. First up, tomatoes.

"Sure is." She picked up the pots. "Thomas will be looking for me." She paused at the opening to the shed. "How's Burke?"

"Still waiting for the other shoe to drop."

"Me too." She chuckled, winked, and disappeared into the crowd.

Ezekiel looked around. No one else had noticed. He shook his head and chuckled. Mary Katherine had winked at him. Reminding him of that wink in Dan Rogers's car. What had he been thinking? Nothing. He'd been delirious. Diabetes would do that to a person.

So what was Mary Katherine's excuse?

CHAPTER 18

The aroma of frying meat, bell peppers, and onions wafting from Leah's open kitchen window teased Ezekiel's nose. His stomach rumbling, he picked up his pace toward the back door of his daughter's house. It smelled like chili, venison chili, his favorite. It was an excellent choice for a cold fall Sunday evening. His daughter was a good cook, like her mother. The thought of Lucy floated in the air, then dissipated like an iridescent bubble embraced by the breeze.

His head cocked, Ezekiel halted on the steps. The vague feeling that he'd forgotten something tugged at him. His hand went to his chest. To his heart. The long-standing ache that had accompanied him for the past ten years felt different. More of a gentle, almost nostalgic hug.

Did that mean he could retire and sell the restaurant? Retire and do what? Fish. Play volleyball with the grandchildren. Good pastimes, both, but not enough to fill endless days between now and when God called him home. Diabetes did not mean he was on his deathbed. Even if giving up strawberry-rhubarb pie made him want to wail.

A shabby blue-and-black motorcycle sat next to the steps. It leaned precariously on a kickstand. He stopped. None of their Englisch friends drove motorcycles. The machines usually drove around buggies with careless abandon and frightened the horses with their noisy engines.

Laughter—the high, breathless giggles of a child and the deeper guffaw of a man—spilled through the screen door. Kenneth. And Burke.

Ezekiel shoved through the screen door, steeling himself against the desire to swipe a cookie for himself. "Hey, Leah, whose motorcycle?"

No Leah. Burke stood at the woodstove, a stained apron wrapped around his waist and a wooden ladle in his hand. A huge cast-iron pot sat on the burner. Its contents sizzled and crackled. Kenneth sat on the counter, his legs dangling, feet bare. They both looked up and grinned.

"Mine." Burke sounded rather surprised at the fact. "Can you believe it?"

"No."

"It's like a mechanical horse, Groossdaadi. Mudder says I can't ride on it." Kenneth's face turned woebegone. "Not even with Burke. Not even with a helmet."

"Your mudder's right. Plain people don't ride motorcycles any more than we drive cars." Motorcycles were dangerous and annoying. "Where did you get it?"

"A guy advertised it on Craigslist. I can't keep mooching rides."

"You'll end up roadkill. Especially when winter comes and the roads get icy."

"It came with a helmet. Two wheels are cheaper than four." Burke's abashed look reminded Ezekiel of his boys when they put their money together to buy a two-seater for courting. "It was all I could afford. Besides, I like the idea of wind in my face, the open road ahead of me."

"More like bugs in your teeth and rain on your head."

"Spoilsport. Look at it this way. Your cook will be more available and less of a burden." Burke slurped soup from a wooden spoon, closed his eyes, and hooted. "Now that's a spicy chili."

"You are not a burden." More of a friend. Surprising as it was. Ezekiel glanced around. No Leah in sight. "What are you two doing in the kitchen making chili?"

"I'm teaching Kenneth to make my world-famous chili." Burke waved the ladle with an extravagant flourish. "My recipe was handed down from my grandmother. It has a secret ingredient that I may or may not share with Kenneth. This recipe won the chili cook-off at my dad's church three years running."

"We're also making corn bread. Mudder said it was okay." Kenneth broke off a chunk of peanut butter cookie and tucked it in his mouth. He swung his feet, which were exceedingly dirty. "Even though she says Plain men don't cook much. Just for weddings and such."

"Again, she's right." Ezekiel poured himself a glass of water from the pitcher sitting on the counter. He leaned against the cabinets so he could watch the proceedings. "Unless you own a restaurant like I do."

"How did you learn to cook, Groossdaadi?"

"Yeah, Groossdaadi, how did you learn to cook?" Burke grinned. "And how come you haven't imparted that skill to Kenneth?"

"I learned because I wanted to earn a living for my family after your groossmammi died. I taught myself. Mostly trial and error. I remembered what I'd seen Groossmammi Lucy do. I threw more than a few of my creations in the trash."

"Why didn't you ask Mudder to show you?"

"She was young and she didn't know yet. Groossmammi didn't have time to teach her everything before she had to go."

Again, no razor-sharp pain. Only a nostalgic feeling that ached with the perfectness of the memories. Lucy pulling a tray of gingersnaps from the oven. Lucy kneading bread dough with a steady shove, shove, turn, fold, shove, shove. Lucy chopping the vegetables for stew with an amazing rapid-fire accuracy. "It never hurts to know how to do something, whether everyone is doing it or not."

Burke ladled a spoonful of soup from the huge cast-iron pot and offered it to Kenneth. His forehead furrowed, expression serious, Kenneth sipped and frowned. "More salt. More chili powder."

"You like it spicy." Burke's vigorous nod said he did too. "You want to try it, Ezekiel?"

He sipped. "I agree. Maybe some cayenne and oregano. I always use a little oregano."

"Yeah! Cayenne. You like it spicy too."

"Of course. Who doesn't?"

Burke dumped a generous amount of chili powder

into his concoction, followed by some cayenne pepper and oregano. The lines around his mouth and eyes disappeared. His movements were measured, relaxed. He set the oregano aside and grabbed the salt. His gaze connected with Ezekiel's. He shrugged. His eyebrows rose and fell. "It seemed like a good day for chili."

"Do you put beans in your chili?"

"No way."

"What kind of meat?"

"Today it's venison—cut in cubes, not ground—because that's what's available. Leah was kind enough to give me a big jar of it. It's still strange to me to think that meat would be canned."

"It's gut."

"So she says. Kenneth is my new language teacher. Did I ever tell you I speak four languages? Spanish, Italian, French, and English. I figured I should learn another one while I'm here."

"Jah, he knows *jah*, *gut*, *Gott*, *bopli*, *mudder*, *daed*, and *hund*." Kenneth shoved his glasses up his nose and nodded. "Now we have to put them in sentences."

"But first we need to start on the corn bread." Burke put his hands around Kenneth's waist and gently settled the boy's feet on the floor. He handed him his crutches. "Can you get the cornmeal? I'll get the bowl."

His face determined, Kenneth ambled toward the long shelves that lined the opposite wall. His legs scissored, knees bent in, toes out, in the gait he'd employed since he was old enough to drag himself through the house.

Burke pulled a mixing bowl from an upper cabinet

and set it on the table. "I caught him headed out to the creek again." His voice was low. He glanced toward Kenneth, who balanced on his crutches and examined the contents of his mudder's pantry. "He said he was thinking about going fishing."

"What's wrong with that child? Does he want a whipping if his daed catches him out there alone?"

"He heard Leah and William talking this morning. They've decided to take him back to the specialist to see about some surgery."

"They were hoping not to do that." Leah hadn't said anything, but her silence wasn't surprising. She was the quiet one, the most likely to suffer in silence. "He's fallen a lot lately."

"This is what I know how to do, so I suggested it. I hope I didn't act out of turn. Leah seemed surprised, but she didn't object."

"She probably was surprised. She's not used to men cooking in her kitchen. She would never admit it, but I know she has a hard time figuring out what to do with Kenneth. She wants to give him leeway to be a boy, but she doesn't want him to kill himself either."

The minute the words were out of his mouth, Ezekiel wanted them back.

"You got the cornmeal, Kenneth?" Burke turned his back and went to the propane refrigerator. "I've got the eggs and the milk."

"Got it."

"Okay, we also need flour, sugar, baking powder, and salt. You'll do the measuring while I grease the muffin tins."

Kenneth hooted as he turned back to the pantry shelves. "I know how many teaspoons in a tablespoon."

It couldn't be unsaid. "I'll be looking forward to supper." Ezekiel patted Kenneth's shoulder as the boy walked by. "Should I run into town and get a fire extinguisher in case the chili's so hot it starts a fire?"

"Nee. We'll throw some cornmeal on it." Kenneth chortled. "Or a bucket of water."

Ezekiel found Leah in the front room sitting at the treadle sewing machine. Caleb played with wooden blocks at her feet while Liliana slept in a nearby playpen. Leah stopped pumping, lifted the lever, and snipped the thread. "I think Kenneth grew a foot this summer. All his pants are too short." She maneuvered the material to start a new seam and dropped the lever. "How are yours?"

Ezekiel made a show of looking at his pants. "I think I'm getting shorter, not taller. The stoop of old age."

"Are they doing all right in there? No fires?"

"Kenneth has a new friend."

"I know. The other day I found them playing baseball using a beach ball and Kenneth's crutch as a bat."

"Burke has a bit of kinner in him, it seems."

"A bit?" She smiled and sighed, which made her look even more like her mother when she'd been Leah's age. "Gott's timing, it seems."

Ezekiel picked up Caleb and swung him up in the air. The boy giggled.

"Careful, his tummy has been upset. He might throw up on you."

He eased him back on the floor. "Better play down here."

He strode over to the playpen where Liliana slept, her dark-brown curls covering her chubby face. She also was a picture of her mother at that age. He brushed back her hair with one finger, careful not to wake her. "Gott's timing for Kenneth or for Burke?"

"Both. It seems as if Kenneth is gut for Burke."

God's plan was always bigger and better. Ezekiel had made Burke his project, when the true healing balm for the loss of his child was a little boy on crutches. "That's what I think. And Burke for the boy. I know cooking isn't what most boys are doing on Sunday afternoon, but Kenneth isn't most boys."

She nodded, but worry creased lines on her forehead. "Kenneth talks about him all the time. Burke this and Burke that. Burke is a decent man, a gut man, but he's not from around here. What happens when he leaves?"

"It's not as if Kenneth doesn't have playmates here. The kinner include him."

"He's started turning down invitations to play. He's started sitting on the sidelines. It's like he knows he slows them down."

"Maybe it's a phase."

"Maybe. What's going to happen to him when he's older? How will he be a mann and take care of a family?"

"Are you borrowing trouble from the future?"

"I suppose I am."

Kenneth's high-pitched giggles floated in the air like musical notes. "There are many occupations a man can do with his hands that don't involve his feet." Ezekiel savored the sound of his grandson's happiness. "For now, enjoy this moment. Leave the rest to Gott."

"If anyone knows that, you do." She plucked a loose thread from the material and laid it aside. "You set the example for us."

His picture of the past ten years was different. A grim, tight-lipped effort to appear content in his fate. "You turned out all right."

She chuckled. "High praise."

"I hope you have some of those indigestion tablets."

"The chili?"

"It seems we like it spicy."

"Like life?"

"Like life." He went to the window and stared out at the yard. Dark, puffy clouds lumbered across the sky. The sun hid behind them, taking with it his light mood. "You agree with Andrew and John that I should retire."

The *thump-thump* of the sewing machine treadle began again. He turned. Her head was bent over the material. Her hands guided it along a neat, even hem. Her gaze lifted. The machine stopped. "They asked my opinion."

"And what did you say?"

"Gott's will be done."

"We always say that. We mean it. But it doesn't tell me what you think."

"It's not my place."

"I'm asking you for your opinion, Leah."

Her gaze went to Caleb, busy building a tower of

blocks. He had the hiccups. Every time he hiccupped, he giggled. "I think ornery bulls don't always know what's best for them. Working yourself into the ground all these years won't make you forget. You haven't forgotten yet."

"I enjoy work."

"You use it as an excuse to not think. To not feel. That's why you never remarried. You're the only one."

"Not true. Zechariah is a widower."

"His fraa died last year. And Zechariah is seventy-some years old. Not a lot of choices. You have choices."

Like Mary Katherine. None of this was his children's business. "You can't just replace a fraa like your mudder."

"She would want you to be happy."

"What do you know about what she would want? You were a little girl when she died."

"Exactly. A little girl who needed a mudder."

"You had *aentis* and a groossmammi."

"And I was fine. I am fine. Andrew and John want you to be around a while longer. I'm not so concerned with how long you're around as I am about the quality of that time. To be with someone who cares for you and for whom you care is what makes life on this earth bearable. That and the possibility of eternal life with Gott."

Leah was far smarter than her brothers. But he wouldn't tell them that. Or her. "I'm content. I have my kinner and your kinner. Life is gut."

"You may fool others. But not me."

"I'm not trying to fool anyone."

"Maybe you should talk to Freeman."

"Maybe you should hush."

"You asked for my opinion."

"I lost my head there for a minute."

"It's your heart that is lost, Daed."

The sadness in her words curled around his heart. It ached with a loss that was old and refined by time and tears. He had no words that could assuage. He dropped a kiss on her kapp. "I'll see if William needs any help with the chores."

"You know what they say."

"What's that?"

"You can run, but you can't hide." She smiled and cast her gaze on her babies. "None of us can."

CHAPTER 19

The door didn't budge. Mary Katherine turned the knob and pushed. Nothing. "Silly woman." She'd started locking the door after Burke's foray into her kitchen. She set her bag of groceries on the porch and pulled the key from the flower box where she'd planted the mums she'd purchased at the produce auction the previous week. The door opened. Feeling pleasantly tired after a long day at the store and a quick stop at the grocery store for coffee and a few other staples, she trudged inside. Keeping busy kept her mind off the niggling thoughts in the back of her head. The bookstore. Ezekiel. His wink. Her wink. She wasn't a teenager.

Something had possessed her. What, she had no idea.

"You're living."

Ach, Moses, I've been living for almost sixty years.

"Except for the part where you've been pretending to talk to your dead mann."

"Bah humbug." Humming "How Great Thou Art" to drown out his voice, she kicked off her sneakers and padded barefoot into the kitchen. A nice, hot cup of chamomile tea and she would start a vegetable stew for supper. Maybe make a pecan pie. What did a woman living alone want with a whole pie? She could take the rest to the store for the customers. Some gingersnaps too. Fill up the rest of her day and evening.

Halfway across the floor to the prep table, a stabbing pain shot through her right foot. Something sharp gouged her sole. "Ach, ouch." She hopped on the other foot and managed to set the pots on the table before collapsing in the closest chair.

She tugged her foot up onto her knee and examined her injury. A jagged piece of glass protruded from the pad just below her big toe. "Ach." She plucked the offending glass from her foot and stared at it. "Ow. Where did you come from?"

A quick appraisal of the kitchen floor brought her back to her feet. Glass lay strewn from the midway point all the way to the back door. Someone had shattered the window. The back door stood open.

Her lungs fought to do their job. Adrenaline kicked in, a heady rush that made her dizzy. What if her intruder was still in the house? She surveyed her kitchen. A cast-iron skillet or a butcher knife? Or a pie? Could she entice them with food the way she had Burke? She had no desire to smack someone with a skillet. Or shed blood. She owned nothing of value. She could run out the back door. Dodging jagged pieces of glass and the less-easy-to-see slivers?

Likely they were long gone. The house had an empty feel. Like it always did when she came home at the end of the day.

Breathe. Breathe. She snatched a napkin from a pile on the table and hobbled back to the living room. "Anyone here? Hello, is someone here?" No answer. Somehow it didn't seem likely a burglar would announce himself. Or herself. "It's me, Mary Katherine. Help yourself and go about your business. I'll sit right here by the fireplace until you leave."

She grabbed her shoes and plopped into the rocking chair. If she had to make a run for it, she preferred to do so properly shod.

"*Get out of there, Mary Kay.*"

I'm not leaving my own house.

"*Then go get my rifle.*"

They probably ran out while I was in the kitchen.

"*Or they're hiding in the closet, waiting to jump out when you walk by.*"

You're no help at all.

"*Go for help.*"

She swallowed. Her throat was drier than a stale saltine cracker. "I'm leaving now." She tucked the napkin around her bleeding sole, tugged on her shoes, and went to the bottom of the staircase. "Just close the door on your way out, if you don't mind."

Her voice sounded far too timid. "Even if you do mind."

Ignoring the stab of pain in her foot, she trotted double time out to the phone shack. The tiny building with its two windows, one chair, and rickety old table steamed with heat and humidity. The light on the ancient cassette recorder blinked red. She ignored it and punched in 911. The dispatcher had a kind, calm bass. Mary Katherine explained and hung up.

Now what? It would take one of the deputies a good bit to get to her place. She sat in the oak chair Moses had made for that purpose.

The light was still blinking.

She punched the button.

The voice, though slow and scratchy on the old tape that had been rewound too many times, clearly belonged to Dottie. Her southern twang had deepened, a sure sign of agitation. *"Mary Kay, I need you. Please come. As soon as you get this. I know it might be a while, but come."*

She strung out *a while* for three long seconds, like any transplant from Texas would. The recording ended with a sigh and hiss. It could have been a sob.

"What is it, Dottie? What's wrong?" Mary Katherine spoke to the machine. She knew it wouldn't speak back. She wasn't an idiot.

She had to go to Dottie.

But the sheriff's deputy was on the way. She'd dialed 911. She couldn't leave. They would think she'd been kidnapped or Dottie's serial killer had chopped her up and buried her in the backyard.

They didn't know about the serial killer. Thank goodness.

She slammed the phone shack door and raced across the yard—or her version of what racing would look like if she wasn't a sixty-year-old mother of ten who rarely walked faster than a trot and had a cut on her foot. In the house she snatched a pen from the desk in the front room and scribbled a note. *Gone to Dottie Manchester's house. My friend needs me. Mess in kitchen. I'll be back when I can. Mary K.*

The police would be aggravated with her. So be it.

She lifted her skirt and ran. She was getting better at it.

CHAPTER 20

M ary Katherine rarely wished for a car to whisk her across the country. Traveling by buggy offered time to enjoy the countryside and muse on new twists and turns for her stories. Not today. It took more than thirty minutes to drive the buggy into town. By the time she arrived, a long, black funeral home hearse, waxed to a sparkle in the afternoon sun, was parked in front of Dottie's two-story wood-frame house with its black wrought-iron fence. Next to it was a gray Suburban. No ambulance. No fire truck. Firefighters were the first responders for Daviess County Fire and Rescue. She knew that from her experience with the fire at Amish Treasures.

Dread, black and heavy, weighted down her shoulders. Legs like lead, she climbed down from the buggy, trudged across the grass, and headed through the gate. A knot of anxiety twisted in the pit of her stomach. Dottie had planted rosebushes on trellises along the porch. The lavish red, pink, and yellow flowers were fading into fall, withered from a long summer. Dying.

Mary Katherine paused at the open screen door. Voices murmured inside. Gut-wrenching sobs drowned them out. "No, no, don't take him. Not yet. I'm not ready yet."

"Oh, Dottie." Fierce memories burst from behind barricades to the dark corners of her brain. The world disappeared, the future disappeared, in that moment when a person realized the love of her life had gone on ahead without her. Surviving for the next second, let alone the next day, didn't seem possible. The goal became to draw a single breath. If that worked, a person endeavored to draw the next one and then one more. The bright colors of laughter and joy snuck away, leaving behind a grimy world filled with shadowy gray if-onlys and whys.

"You have to go in."

I know. I'm gathering my courage.

"She needs you."

I know.

"You've been where she's been right now. Gott has sent you to comfort her."

I don't know if I can, Moses.

"You can. You're uniquely suited. Gott knows what He's doing."

She dug a tissue from her canvas bag, wiped her nose, took a breath, and slipped through the door.

Dottie knelt on the carpet in the living room next to Walt, who lay on his back, eyes closed, mouth slack. His shirt was torn open, revealing thick gray hair on a chest dotted with white patches the paramedics had left. Mary Katherine fastened her gaze on his face. Desperate to look away, she found her gaze locked on the purple-gray loose skin of his jowls. The cowboy with the belly laugh had slipped away. A shell of a body remained, his features cold and blank.

Don't look. Focus on Dottie. Dottie needs you.

She swallowed the bitterness in the back of her throat. Her stomach heaved. She sucked in air and ripped her gaze from Walt. He didn't need her anymore. He rested in eternity.

Joe Elliott, the Daviess County coroner, stood next to her, a clipboard in his hand, scribbling furiously on form after form. Christopher Johnson and Lee McKee from the funeral home attempted to cover up Walt with a white sheet so they could load him on the gurney.

Dottie swatted Christopher's hand. "You can't have him. Not yet. He needs a fresh shirt. Look what they did to his shirt. It was brand new from Ray's Western Wear."

She looked up at Mary Katherine, her expression imploring. Her face was blotchy with tears and her nose running. She hiccuped another sob. "He would be so embarrassed for anyone to see him like this. Tell them."

"Dottie, honey, it's okay." Mary Katherine knelt and wrapped her arm around her friend. Dottie's thin body shook. Mary Katherine hugged her close. "They'll take him over to the funeral home and get him fixed up. You can pick out another nice shirt, his favorite one, and a pair of those Levi's he likes. We'll take them over later. He's already wearing his favorite boots."

"He likes the ostrich-skin boots better for dress-up."

"Then we'll take those too."

"Oh, Mary Kay." She rested her forehead on Mary Katherine's shoulder. Her sobs poured out, the tears wetting Mary Katherine's dress. "This can't be happening. It can't."

But it was. The unreality of it would last for a few hours, maybe a day, then the numbness would set in. Followed by an anger that threatened to set the world on fire. Mary Katherine nodded at Christopher. He and Lee heaved Walt's body onto the gurney as gently as they could under the circumstances. He was a big man, big in body, big in heart and soul. To think he was gone didn't seem possible. They grunted a little. Mary Katherine smoothed Dottie's hair, keeping her head turned away from seeing her husband's undignified progress onto the gurney.

They covered him gently with a blanket as if he might get cold. Moses died in summer. They still covered him with a blanket. Mary Katherine shivered. She looked away and her gaze connected with Joe's. He shook his head and gave her a ghost of a smile. He was a muscular, fit man with rimless glasses and thinning silver hair. He looked like a runner. He'd likely done this hundreds of times in his career as a doctor who also served as the county's coroner. "Natural causes. Cardiac arrest. I gave Walt's doctor a call. He's had heart disease, hypertension, the works, for years." He started to say something else, but his gaze swung to Dottie. The wrinkles in his forehead knotted. "I'm sorry for your loss."

"Come see us when you're ready to make arrangements." Christopher's voice was gruff. He'd done this hundreds of times too, but nothing in his tone suggested it had become rote. "There's no rush since you two already picked out your caskets and paid for our services. We'll have everything ready for you. We're so very sorry for your loss, Mrs. Manchester."

Mary Katherine helped Dottie to her feet.

"Thank you." Dottie's voice quavered. She lifted the blanket and patted Walt's face, then kissed his cheek hard once, then again more gently. "Take care of him for me."

"We will, ma'am. I promise."

Her knees buckled. Mary Katherine grabbed her around the waist and guided her to the La-Z-Boy recliner that sat next to an enormous chocolate-brown sectional couch. They were situated facing a big-screen TV that took up most of the far wall. The Manchesters were famous for their football game parties and movie parties and cribbage parties. All those friends would need to be called.

Dottie sank into the chair. She looked two sizes smaller than she had the day before. Hands in her lap, Mary Katherine sat on the edge of the couch. They itched to do something, anything, that would keep her from having to look at the face of her own grief after all these years. "Let me make you a cup of tea. It'll calm your nerves."

"No, it won't. But thank you." Dottie tugged at her silver hair with trembling hands. It stood out in ratted tangles around her head. "It's a nightmare. I'll wake up and it'll be over. Won't it?" She stared at Mary Katherine as if she didn't recognize her. "I'd just walked into the house after work. I always come in the back door through the kitchen because it's closest to the garage door. Binkie was barking—one of the paramedics locked him in the guest bedroom, poor thing is probably beside himself—Cleo kept wrapping herself around my feet so I couldn't make my way across the room."

Mary Katherine nodded. She didn't need to know all this, but Dottie needed to tell the story the way she needed to tell it. Cleo, a Siamese with burnished cream-colored fur and sapphire eyes, sashayed across the room and leaped into Dottie's lap. Likely she was better medicine for what ailed Dottie than a cup of tea.

"I yelled out to Walt. He called me earlier complaining of indigestion and a headache, so I knew he was home. Besides, I pulled into the garage next to his truck like I always do."

"And he didn't answer you?"

"No, he did. He was in the living room. The TV was on. He was watching a rerun of *American Pickers*. He loves that show." She chuckled for a second. The sound petered out and her watery smile faded as the realization that he would never watch his program again raged in her face. She swallowed. "I came on in, ready to scold him for eating a steak last night and french fries and a big bowl of ice cream. He had a little helping of broccoli like that was supposed to make it all okay. Then he wouldn't go for a walk with me. He said he was too full."

She stared into space, her hands sliding through Cleo's fur. The cat's purr reverberated in the split second of silence. "I came into the room." Her voice broke. She swallowed again. Tears teetered in her eyes, then slid down her cheeks, leaving tracks in her powdery foundation. "He got up to give me a squeeze the way he always does. He looked at me kind of funny. His hand went to his shoulder. He took a few steps. Then he sank to his knees." Her hands covered her eyes as if she could block out the memory. Cleo meowed, at her owner's distress or because she demanded more petting.

Dottie's hands resumed smoothing the cat's fur. "I ran to him. He panted. It hurt. He looked at me like he wanted me to explain what was happening. Then he keeled over. He stopped breathing."

She bit her lower lip and shook her head. "He wasn't breathing. I called 911 and started CPR." Her hands moved from Cleo to her shoulders and rubbed. "I pushed on his heart just like I learned over at the community center. Over and over. My arms hurt from doing it so long." Her head drooped. She sobbed. Yowling, Cleo leaped from her lap and scurried under the couch.

Mary Katherine covered the space between the chair and the couch in two long strides. "You did everything you could. You did everything right." She pulled Dottie into a hug. The woman's head rested on her shoulder. Her entire body shook with the force of her sobs. "There was nothing more you could do."

"I couldn't save him."

"You couldn't. It was his time to go." Mary Katherine closed her eyes. Those words hadn't helped her after Moses died. They wouldn't help Dottie now.

Moses had been gone by the time she went into the bedroom to see why he hadn't come out for breakfast. His skin was cool. When she shook his arm, his head lolled to one side. The teasing words calling him a lazy old man had died on her lips. She climbed into bed next to him under the covers, thinking she could somehow warm him. She said his name over and over again, determined to call him back by sheer force of will.

He never answered.

Dottie's head jerked up. Horror etched lines in her tear-streaked face. "How will I tell the kids? Mary Kay, how will I tell them?"

"Gently." The same way she'd told each of her children. Angus, Beulah, and Barbara were at home that morning. She told them first. Angus went to fetch Cyrus, who told Freeman. With the men's help, she told the others. The simple truth. God had taken Moses home. "Call your sister first. She can come up from Oklahoma to help you."

Dottie nodded. "Walt's brother and his parents. They're eighty-five and eighty-six. They're in Lampasas, Texas."

"Maybe your daughters can stop and pick them up."

Dottie's unfocused gaze skipped around the room. "He wanted a church service with all the trimmings. Singing and praising God that brother Walter has gone to the Lord. That's the way the Baptists do it. We wrote it all out last year. I never thought we'd need those papers so soon."

"No one does."

Dottie threw her arms around Mary Katherine in a stranglehold hug. "I'm so sorry for what you went through. I saw it. How you suffered after Moses died. I thought that would never happen to me. I don't know why. It's ridiculous. Of course it could happen to me. It just did."

"We don't like to think about it." Mary Katherine loosened Dottie's grip. "Let me start some tea. We'll make a list of who needs to be notified and what needs to be done. After you've had your tea, you can call the kids."

"You'll stay with me while I do it?"

"Absolutely." She helped Dottie to her feet. "You can count on me."

CHAPTER 21

The soft whine was the first clue something had changed. Ezekiel stood on the pieced rug inside his front door and listened. The whine faded away. He waited. Paws made a *clickety-clack* sound on the wooden floor. An animal had somehow weaseled its way into his home. Raccoon? No, something heavier. Bobcat. He swallowed a snort. That would be quite a shock for both of them. He edged toward the living room. A butterscotch, midsized dog loped down the hallway. Its tail whipped, its big ears flopped, its tongue hung from its mouth, slobber trailing in the air.

Its *yip-yip* held a note of joy at Ezekiel's arrival even though they'd never met before. The dog seemed to have little control over its oversized paws as it skidded and landed at Ezekiel's feet. He leaned over and addressed the stranger directly. "How did you get in here?"

The dog barked and jumped up on Ezekiel, paws reaching to his waist, nearly knocking him back. It was a he. Still a puppy despite his size. His fur smelled as if he'd rolled in roadkill. His breath stank even worse. "Down, down."

He dropped into a sitting position, but his snout still smiled. Drool dripped on the floor. "So you're smart. Gut boy. That doesn't mean you can stay."

"Oh good, you met the dog." Burke came through the door behind Ezekiel. He wore a gray, long-sleeved T-shirt, baggy blue jeans, a New York Yankees baseball cap, and his usual ragged tennis shoes. Apparently he'd used his paycheck to buy himself some warmer clothes at the Walmart in Chillicothe. "I wanted to introduce you, but you got home earlier than I expected."

Ezekiel moved out of his way. The dog followed. "Andrew came in. He insisted on taking over my shift. What is this dog doing in here?"

"You needed a dog. I thought I saw a fishing pole around here." Burke strode past Ezekiel and headed toward the hall. The dog stayed with Ezekiel. "Kenneth and I are going fishing. Want to come?"

"He stinks. What makes you think I need a dog?"

"He smells like dog, but you can give him a bath later. It's too quiet around here at night."

"I like quiet. Why don't you have a dog?"

"It's too hard to travel with a dog." Burke tugged two fishing poles from the storage closet at the end of the hall and returned. A satisfied grin stretched across his grizzled face. "Come on, let's go fishing."

Ezekiel took the pole. Force of habit. He never turned down the opportunity to fish. "Wouldn't early morning be better?"

"Not for channel catfish." A note of mock horror resonated in Burke's voice. "Besides, it's not about the fish."

"Does Leah know? Kenneth isn't allowed to go to the creek anymore without one of them."

"I asked. She gave her blessing. I guess my lesson in fine cuisine convinced her."

The chili had been a three-indigestion-tablet delight.

"He's on his way down." Burke headed for the door. "Bring your dog."

"You brought him home." Ezekiel followed him out to the porch. "He isn't my dog."

"He is now." Burke snagged a tub of night crawlers from the porch. "Who could reject a face like that?"

"He's a little dopey looking."

"He's a puppy. He has to grow into his feet. What are you gonna name him?"

"Nothing. He's not my dog. Where did he come from?"

Burke waved to Kenneth, who swung along on his crutches, Boo keeping pace at his side. "Hurry. Daylight's burning!"

"Keep your pants on, boy." Burke strode across the yard, headed for the road. "I think Mike is a good name. I went into town this afternoon to Teeter's Outdoor Supply to get the worms, and Mike was hanging around outside. The guy there, what's his name, said he'd been hanging around for days. No collar. Friendly as all get-out."

"His name's not Mike."

"What then?"

"He must be really fast."

"I drove slow."

Ezekiel studied the animal lollygagging its way

across the yard. Boo circled and sniffed. The dog did the same, nose to nose. Boo barked. The dog responded. Then the two of them took off toward the path that led to the creek. Kenneth followed. "Come on, Groossdaadi."

"Coming. He looks like Sonny to me."

"Sunny like the sunshine or Sonny like Andrew, your son?"

Not like a son, for sure. "The first one."

Burke grinned and took off after Kenneth. "Wait up. You'll take a spill on those rocks."

Ezekiel shook his head. Burke had him now. He'd named the dog. "Doesn't mean nothing."

"He's a fine example of canine diversity."

"Can't you just speak English?"

"From a guy who speaks Pennsylvania Dutch most of the time, that's rich."

"You like to show off your education."

"You like to pretend you're superior because you don't have any."

"Not so."

They went back and forth as they headed to the creek. Kenneth got in on the discussion with names like Butch and Smiley and Caramel. Ezekiel held out for Sunny. Even if he wasn't his dog.

He settled onto the bank, the grass making a soft pillow under his behind, and threaded a worm on his hook. He preferred bobbers, but he could deal with live bait too. Burke helped Kenneth get situated, then took a spot between the two of them.

"It's a good thing you got off early today." He cast

his line with a nice flip of his wrist. "You've been out of sorts since your visit to the doctor."

"Sorry about that." Ezekiel kept his gaze on the tiny ripples on the water and the turtle that sunned himself on a rock across the way. His face heated more than the late-afternoon sun warranted. "Doctor says my body's all out of whack. I have to get used to not eating sugar. It makes me cranky."

"No more hot chocolate before bed."

"Nope. Doctor suggested hot tea. Who wants tea without honey? That's like mashed potatoes without gravy."

"Cupcakes without frosting."

"Hamburgers without fries."

"You need a woman to take care of you." Burke's remark came out of left field.

"No more than you." Instead of letting it go, Ezekiel had to let his nose get out of joint and into someone else's business. "Forget I said that. We didn't choose our lots."

Burke reeled his line in. "I don't deserve another woman." His tone held no self-pity, only certainty. "You do and there is one right down the road waiting."

"God gives us what we need, not what we deserve." Ezekiel was thankful for that. Otherwise, he would be destitute by the side of the road. "For a chaplain you don't know much."

"This is about you, not me." Burke settled his ball-cap visor farther down his forehead. It shaded his eyes and hid his expression. "You like her."

"Who?"

"Don't play dumb. Mary Katherine."

"What makes you say that?"

"You have this lovelorn look on your face right now. Just thinking about her makes you all warm and fuzzy."

"Does not."

They sat in silence for a few minutes, watching Sunny chase butterflies and dragonflies. The dog's tongue hung out his smiling snout the entire time. Boo, being older and wiser, curled up at Kenneth's feet.

"It's not treason to get on with your life."

"Says the man who dumped his entire life and ran away."

"I know. It's easier to fix other people's lives than our own."

"Mine don't need fixing. I'm fine where I am."

"Not sleeping. Working six days a week. Still sick at heart over your wife's death."

Getting better. One second after another. It wasn't anybody's business. "Like I said, look who's talking."

"You guys are scaring away the fish with all that jabbering." Kenneth could've been his uncle Andrew at seven and fishing at their old watering hole back in the day when Lucy would be waiting to fry the fish with cottage fries and hush puppies. "We won't catch a thing if you keep it up."

"Sorry, we'll keep it down." Burke's voice dropped to a low, hoarse pitch. "Do you know who the biblical man Ezekiel was?"

"Only that he was a prophet in the Old Testament. They called him the watchman." His mudder had told

Ezekiel about his name. She said she liked the sound of it. "That's about it. We don't do a lot of Bible study."

"Ezekiel was an obedient man." Burke's line went taut. He hooted and reeled it in. Nothing. The night crawler was gone. He sighed. "Some days the fish are smarter than the fisherman—except for the Fisherman, of course."

He slid another worm on his hook and let it sail. "God told Ezekiel he would take away with one blow his dearest treasure, his wife. He wasn't to show any sorrow. Do not weep. No tears. Groan quietly, but do not mourn for the dead. Sound familiar?"

"We don't make a big show of our grieving."

"I'll wager you never showed it at all. You put on a strong front because that's what's expected, and you wanted to set a good example for your children."

Indeed. It was the Plain way. "Something wrong with that?"

"Do you know what the stages of grief are?" Burke's voice had taken on a teacher-like quality. "Psychologically speaking."

"No, but I reckon the chaplain will tell me."

"Denial, anger, bargaining, depression, and acceptance. You're stuck in depression."

"I'm fine. You're the one who's stuck."

"I don't believe that just because Ezekiel wasn't allowed to show his grief to the Israelites, that he didn't actually feel it. I think he went in a cave somewhere and pounded on the walls where no one could see him."

"Maybe."

"You feel guilty for having feelings for Mary Katherine.

You shouldn't. If God gives you a second chance at what you had with your wife, you should jump all over it."

"Would you?"

"It's different."

"It's not."

"I'm not mad at God. I'm not mad at Dee Dee. Not really." Burke plucked at sprigs of dried, brown grass. "I'm mad at myself. I should've helped her, but I didn't. The chaplain who was too wrapped up in himself to help his own wife."

"You're only human."

Sunny romped in front of them, chasing a sparrow, who cheeped, dipped within inches of the dog's nose, then soared away. "Sunny, leave the birds alone." The dog skidded to a stop on the edge of the water, turned, and raced right at Ezekiel in a flurry of happiness. His muddy paws left prints on Ezekiel's blue shirt. He licked at his face with a rough tongue, leaving a trail of slobber in his wake. His exertion made him stink even more. "Jah, jah, you can stop now."

Burke and Kenneth roared. "He likes you," Kenneth shouted.

Burke laughed so hard he threw himself back on the grass and gasped. "No, he loves you."

Ezekiel wiped at the slobber with the back of his sleeve and shook his finger at Sunny. "Hey, we just met."

"Love at first sight."

Maybe so, but the dog took off, this time in pursuit of an orange-and-black butterfly.

"Short attention span." Burke's grin faded. "You're not getting out of this conversation so easily."

"There is no conversation. It's over."

"Why can't you take a chance?"

"Not mine to take."

"Why not?"

"You're like a little kid with all these questions."

"Nothing else to think about when I'm cooking that food at your restaurant."

"You're mighty nosy."

"You're mighty stupid."

Now this stranger from back east was making Ezekiel mad. "Excuse me?"

"Life is short. If anybody knows that, it's us."

Sunny took a flying leap in pursuit of a turtle on a log. He landed in the water with a splash that rained down on all three of his human friends and a perturbed canine companion. They stood as the dog splashed and barked. Ezekiel took a few steps down the embankment. "Surely the thing can swim."

"He's not a thing, Groossdaadi." Kenneth had both hands on his crutches as if he planned to launch himself into the water. "Help him."

"You stay put." Ezekiel waded into the water, boots and all, and hollered at the dog. "Come on in, you silly goose."

"He's not a goose, Groossdaadi." Kenneth sounded disgusted. "You'll hurt his feelings."

Burke laughed. Ezekiel couldn't help it. He laughed too. "Come on, Sunny, leave the turtle alone. Let's go, buddy."

With a woof the dog paddled toward him. He gulped water, sputtered, woofed some more. Together they trudged ashore. Sunny immediately shook himself. Water drops sprayed everywhere. "Ach!" Ezekiel threw his arm up to protect his glasses, but it was too late. He was wet from head to toe now.

And his pole was floating away in the creek.

"Now neither one of you will need a bath." Burke laughed so hard he sputtered. "You look like a ragamuffin."

"What's a ragamuffin?" Kenneth wiped water from his face. "What about me?"

"I don't know," Ezekiel admitted, "but surely you're one too."

Kenneth giggled and Ezekiel joined in. "I don't think we're catching any fish now."

"I told Mudder we'd bring home fish for supper." Kenneth's glee disappeared. "She'll be so disappointed."

"But not surprised." Ezekiel shrugged. "We'll try again on Saturday, how about that?"

Kenneth nodded. "I like Sunny. He's funny."

"Funny Sunny. You're a poet and didn't know it." Burke got sillier by the second. He had a way about him. He cheered up others. A good trait in a chaplain. And it covered his own despair.

Ezekiel fished his pole out of the water. "You take Kenneth up to the house. I'll take care of the poles."

"You don't want to come with us?"

"I have to walk my dog."

"Do Amish men walk dogs?"

"No. Not usually. But my doctor says I need to walk. If I'm walking, so is my dog."

"I'm really happy you're taking this so well." Burke

slapped him on the back. "I knew you and Sunny were made for each other."

Ezekiel responded with a *harrumph*. Sunny barked.

Burke laughed all the way up the trail and out of sight.

Ezekiel didn't need a dog, but maybe the dog needed him. Did Mary Katherine like dogs? He'd never seen her with one. Maybe she needed one.

Ezekiel groaned. Just because a stranger from back east thought he should have a dog or court a woman who may or may not like him, didn't make it right. Mary Katherine's life was complicated enough for a Plain woman. So was his.

He wasn't mad. Not at God. Maybe at himself. Like Burke.

The watchman. Burke's name should've been Ezekiel.

He slowed his pace and meandered along the path, staring at the weeds. Burke was right about one thing. Life was short.

Sunny barked at a passing sparrow. "She's out of your reach, dog."

Ezekiel squared his shoulders and headed home. It remained to be seen if a certain Plain woman was out of his reach.

CHAPTER 22

Time to face the music. Mary Katherine would rather face music than the grim looks on the faces that confronted her in her own living room. That's what happened when a person left her front door standing wide open. People wandered in. All five of her sons, Thomas, Dylan, Elijah, Josiah, and Angus, stood around the fireplace, looking like versions of their father at different ages. Cyrus. Freeman. Solomon. The church elders. Deputy Rogers sat in a rocking chair, a fancy-looking camera resting in his lap.

And Barbara. Her youngest daughter. Again. Exhaustion swept through Mary Katherine. She'd sat with Dottie deep into the night, making lists, helping her find telephone numbers, and holding her hand while she made the calls. Her cribbage friends had shown up, Zoe from the library, people from her church. The house began to fill up fast, but Dottie begged her to stay. So Mary Katherine made coffee and tea and set out plates of store-bought cookies and Dottie's famous banana bread. Dug out more boxes of tissues from the pantry. Washed cups and saucers. Nodded when necessary. Hugged frequently.

Finally, Dottie insisted Mary Katherine spend the

night in the guest bedroom. She took off her shoes and lay on top of the comforter, listening to the murmur of conversations, Binkie's anxious barks, and the squeak of the box springs. The murmurs reminded her of the night Moses died. Her ten children under the same roof again, talking in whispers by the fireplace. Comforting each other. Sometimes laughing at the good times of the past. The occasional sob. Her long-established defenses against such memories thinned and collapsed, allowing a flood of other memories. Knowing sleep wouldn't come, she did the only thing she could. She prayed for Dottie and her family. That God would ease their pain and suffering.

Now morning had arrived and facts had to be faced. She'd run out on her own home.

From the looks on the faces that confronted her now in her own home, she might want to pray for God to ease her own suffering. "Make yourselves at home. I'll brew some coffee." She dropped her bag on the desk and started for the kitchen. "Or would anyone rather have tea? It's nippy today."

"You called 911 and told the dispatcher someone broke into your house." Deputy Rogers laid the camera on the table next to his chair. He leaned forward and put his elbows on his knees. He needed a shave. "When I got here yesterday, the door was standing wide open, but no one was here. Not a burglar or you. If it weren't for your note, we would've had a missing persons alert and a massive search going on."

"I meant to call your office, but I completely forgot. Walt was still on the floor when I got there. And Dottie was a mess." The break-in, as crazy as it might sound to a law enforcement officer, had been the last thing on her mind. "Besides, like you said, I left a note."

"I knew where you were because Ezekiel saw the coroner's SUV in front of Dottie's house," Thomas jumped in. "He told Angus when he went into the Purple Martin to pick up a pie for supper last night. Angus came by to tell me. Then Dan came by the house to tell me about your call. You can't have a break-in and not tell me." He glanced at Freeman as if looking for confirmation. Freeman tugged on his beard. His eyebrows disappeared under the brim of his hat. "Or the bishop, for that matter. You can't not tell anyone."

"Or one of us," Dylan interjected. "Any one of your five suhs."

"Jah," the others chorused.

"Or me." Barbara sounded less certain. She lifted her chin at her brothers' frowns. "I would ask Joseph if it was okay."

"Why are you here, anyway?" Thomas scowled at Barbara. "You couldn't have known."

"I came to talk—"

"Let's not get sidetracked." Freeman put a finger to his lips to shush them, then turned his stare to Mary Katherine. His frown deepened. "Well?"

"Dottie needed me." That explanation was more than sufficient. "Whoever broke in was gone."

"How do you know? You needed to wait outside for a deputy to search the house to make sure no one was hiding in here, waiting for you." Deputy Rogers's fierce gaze shot daggers at her. "You needed to walk through the house to see what was missing. I reckon it wasn't just a ham sandwich with mustard this time."

Mary Katherine looked around the front room. The mantel clock that belonged to her groossmammi was gone. A chess set Moses' daed carved from walnut was missing from the spot where he'd left it. The cherry-wood box Angus gave her for Christmas one year was also gone. She kept her cash earnings from craft days in it. Mentally she calculated the loss. Maybe three hundred dollars.

The sentimental value of these material things was greater. She would miss cradling the king or the queen or the bishop when she dusted, knowing Moses' hands had done the same. She would miss winding the clock and thinking about how her groossdaadi gave it to Groossmammi for her seventieth birthday the year she died.

Mary Katherine pulled out the chair from the desk, turned it around, and plopped into it. Her legs didn't want to hold her anymore. She listed the missing items from the front room. "I suppose there could be more from the other rooms, but nothing of any greater value. Material possessions don't mean a lot to us. Community is more important."

"She's right."

At Cyrus's pronouncement, Mary Katherine's mouth opened of its own accord. She took a second to regroup. "I am?"

"We help those in need. Dottie is a friend in need." Cyrus gave Freeman a sideswipe glance. The bishop's forehead wrinkled, but he nodded. "The timing was bad, but that wasn't your doing. Walt Manchester was a gut man. We are sorry for her loss."

"The dollar value isn't great." Thomas contemplated the ceiling as if he might find patience there. "Why would anyone go to the trouble to break into a Plain house to steal these things? We don't have TVs or cameras or computers or fancy painkiller prescriptions. Nothing they can sell to get money to buy drugs."

"It's hard to say." Deputy Rogers scratched his chin. "We've had similar break-ins at other Plain farms in other church districts. Same deal. In and out. Minor stuff taken. So far nobody's been hurt. The last couple of times they've ripped off some food too." He fixed Mary Katherine with an accusing stare.

She bristled. "You're not still thinking about Burke, are you?"

"Lucky for him, he was working when this burglary occurred. But I'm still running down a timeline for the others."

"He has a job now. A paycheck. He has no reason to run around breaking into houses and eating ham sandwiches."

"Maybe he has a fetish."

"A what?"

"You know, he gets his kicks sneaking into houses and checking out the ladies' drawers. I don't know." Deputy Rogers pursed his lips and dug in his heels. "I'm not ruling out anything."

They didn't have a lot of crime in Daviess County. Crimes that targeted Amish families even less. It was creepy.

"I don't have drawers." Mary Katherine crossed her legs at her ankles and examined her hands in her lap. "And Burke McMillan doesn't have this whatchacallit."

"I am trying to confirm the facts, that's all."

"In any case, it's best that you gather your things." Freeman's tone held a hint of regret. "Thomas will take you to his house. You can't stay here alone."

"Until the burglars are caught." Trying to hang on to some sliver of optimism, she made it a statement rather than a question. "I'll just need a few things."

"It's time to make a permanent move." Steel replaced the softer regret. "Thomas and your other suhs can pack the rest later when you decide what you need and what you can leave for Dylan and his fraa."

"If you don't want to live with Thomas, you can come stay with me." Barbara slipped over to Mary Katherine's chair and patted her shoulder. "Joseph wouldn't mind. He'd be grateful for me to have company."

A newlywed who wanted his mother-in-law underfoot. Something was amiss at the Beachy house. The joy of a not-so-distant wedding day dissipated. All her children were married, but this one not so happily.

"Or with me and Hannah," Josiah piped up.

"Why not my house?" Elijah said.

Six of her kids spoke at the same time. Argued, rather. Freeman whistled. "Enough."

They subsided and all but Barbara had the good grace to look abashed.

"You have a small house, Barbara. Just right for your needs, but not more at this time." Freeman smiled at her. He swiveled and stared at the men. "Thomas has

the most kinner, therefore the most need for help. He
has a dawdy haus. It needs some fixing up, but it'll do.
Mary Kay can stay at the house until it's ready. Joanna
will welcome the company and the help."

It seemed unlikely that Joanna would welcome Mary
Katherine's company. She always seemed peeved whenever Mary Katherine came around. Like she didn't need
a mother-in-law intruding in the home she'd made for
her husband. It didn't matter—Freeman had spoken. "I
should cover that window in the back door." She stood.
"I think I have a piece of plywood in the barn."

"That's fine." Deputy Rogers picked up the camera.
"I've taken photos of the back door and dusted for
prints. That's about all I can do. We don't have any fancy
crime-scene investigators in our little office."

Sounded pretty fancy to Mary Katherine, but she
had no experience with this sort of thing. Nor did she
want any.

"I'll take care of the door. Mudder, you go pack.
Enough for a week. We'll get the rest later." Thomas
shot from his chair and headed for the front door. "The
rest of you can go. No point in everyone missing a
whole day of work."

Before he could open the door, a sharp rap sounded.
He tugged it open.

Ezekiel stood on the porch, fisted hand raised.

• • •

It wasn't the reception Ezekiel had expected. Or hoped
for. That's what he got for letting Burke get in his head.

Their discussion had echoed in his mind all week. Then he heard about the break-in. He lowered his hand and smiled at Thomas. Thomas's response was a puzzled smile in return. "Ezekiel. Why aren't you at the restaurant? Is something wrong? Freeman and Cyrus and Solomon are all here."

"Nee. It's fine. I'm fine. The restaurant is fine. Burke is getting everything ready to open." He peeked past Thomas. The three church elders were, indeed, standing in the front room. Along with all the other Ropp sons. And Barbara. And Dan Rogers. "I've shortened my hours recently. How is everyone?"

Nods all around. Some friendlier than others.

Dan slapped his hat on his head and bolted past the other men. "So you don't need me?"

"No."

"Good, I have work to do." He squeezed past Ezekiel and clomped down the steps. "If I think of anything else, I'll be back."

Plain folks didn't stand on ceremony. Ezekiel stepped inside and nodded at Cyrus, Freeman, and Solomon. The three men returned his nod in unison. "I heard about the break-in. I wanted to stop by to make sure all is well."

"Deputy Rogers will take care of it. No need for concern." Freeman nodded. "I also have work to do at home."

"Me too," Cyrus grunted. "I'll make the rounds, see if there've been any other break-ins."

They filed out, followed by four of the five Ropp sons. Her expression expectant, Barbara didn't move. Dylan looked back. "Get a move on. I'll follow you home."

"I thought I'd—"

"You won't. Go." Mary Katherine made swooshing motions with both hands. "Joseph will want his lunch."

Her expression morose, Barbara stepped out.

Only Thomas stayed behind. He pointedly turned his back on his mother. "I need to board up a door, Ezekiel. Help me carry in the plywood and I'll tell you the whole story."

Throughout all this Mary Katherine stood at the bottom of the stairs. Her cheeks were stained pink, but dark, puffy circles ringed her red-rimmed eyes. Her dress looked like she'd slept in it. Her kapp was limp and hair straggled down her neck and forehead. "Happy to help." He veered around Thomas and approached Mary Katherine. "Are you all right?"

She shrugged, her smile dim. "Long day yesterday. Long night last night. Very long. Now I'm to move in with Thomas and his fraa."

Ezekiel longed to comfort her. Thomas's presence kept him from saying more. "I'll help Thomas fix the door."

"I'll make kaffi."

He followed Thomas out to the barn. The other man did all the talking until he finished the story, surely with a few of his own flourishes. "And that's what happened." Thomas pulled a sheet of plywood about half the size of a door from a pile right inside the doors. "I'd say it was none of my business, but I am the oldest suh and Mudder's ability to make gut choices seems poor lately, so I'll ask. Why are you really here?"

"To make sure she's all right." Honesty was the best policy. Ezekiel hoisted his end of the plywood and they wrestled it through the barn doors. He didn't need Thomas's permission, but he, too, had been the oldest son. "Do you object?"

"Nee. Mudder has been a widow for a long time. If it's Gott's plan for her to marry again, so be it." Thomas jerked his head toward the house. "To be honest, it's tiring to keep answering to Freeman for everything she does. I don't know why she can't be like other Plain women. She's young enough to marry again. Instead, she has all these delusions of grandeur with bookstores and businesses. Her writing is fine and all, but she doesn't seem to find it enough. Nothing is enough."

Maybe because she had a void in her life. A longing that couldn't be filled by stories and business. She was looking for fulfillment in the wrong places. As Ezekiel did with the Purple Martin. "So you'd like for her to be someone else's problem."

"She's my mudder. I wouldn't put it that way."

"How would you put it?"

"I don't want her to have to make a kneeling confession in front of everyone, especially at her age." He stomped up the steps and maneuvered the sheet of wood through the door. Ezekiel hustled to keep up. "I want her to live a godly life and be happy. She should be able to do both."

"She has a gut heart. She raised ten kinner. She was a gut fraa and mudder."

"I know that. I just don't understand her. She needs to—"

"Be quiet and be still."

"Exactly."

Ezekiel stifled his chuckle at the image of Mary Katherine attempting to be quiet and still. Thomas would need to hog-tie her and slap a piece of tape over her pretty mouth. If Thomas really expected that of his mother, he was in for a long, painful wait. "I'll see what I can do to help."

"Much appreciated."

Thomas couldn't know that Ezekiel liked Mary Katherine's flights of fancy and her chatter and her dreams. He had no intention of changing her.

CHAPTER 23

Englisch funerals were different from Plain ones. Lots of stories about how wonderful Walt had been. Great husband. Great friend. Great businessman. Volunteer of the year. Great father. Best granddad ever. Mary Katherine had expected that. The reception afterward was the same, though. Lots of casseroles and desserts brought by people who cared and didn't know what to say to the bereaved widow. All of Jamesport had turned out for Walt's funeral and then some. Family from Texas and California. The children and grandchildren. Little Olivia and Brooklyn looked like their grandmother with her blue eyes and sharp chin. The boys were all Walt. Tall in their black suits and cowboy boots.

Mary Katherine stayed close to Dottie, in case she needed her, but Dottie remained dry eyed and determined, patting shoulders, giving hugs, thanking folks for coming as if they needed her support and not the other way around. After a few hours, the crowd thinned. Mary Katherine found Dottie in the kitchen stretching plastic wrap over a half-eaten lasagna.

"This is going to spoil if I don't get it in the refrigerator." She fought with the wrap, which had become tangled. She tried to pick it apart. It got worse. She threw the box across the room. It hit the huge double-door stainless-steel refrigerator and landed with a smack on the rose-colored tile. "That stuff is more trouble than it's worth."

"Let me do that for you." Mary Katherine picked up the box and laid it on the wood-topped island covered with dishes. Orange Jell-O with fruit. Potato salad. Green bean casserole. Tuna casserole. Enchilada casserole. Chocolate-drizzled angel food cake. "You should rest. Take a nap. It's been a long day."

Dottie grabbed a dishrag. She swiped at a drop of coleslaw as if it offended her. "I'm not tired."

Mary Katherine tugged the rag from her hands. "I remember when Moses died, I fought sleep. I knew when I woke up, for a minute, I wouldn't remember. I'd think he was lying next to me in the bed. Then it would hit me and I would grieve all over again."

"I can't bear to go in the bedroom." Dottie's red-rimmed eyes welled with tears. She tore a tissue from the box on the counter. Some kind soul had positioned them throughout the house earlier in the day. "It smells like his Dry Idea deodorant and his Polo cologne. The shower in the master bathroom smells like Dial. It smells like him."

"I had mixed feelings about that." Moses didn't use cologne, but he had his own unique scent. "I wanted to wrap myself up in his shirts. I didn't want the smell to fade, but I knew it would. I had to pack up his stuff and give them to people who could use them. It was the hardest thing I've ever done. But it helped."

"I don't know why the smells are harder to bear than his clothes lying on the glider rocker by the window. Or the boots—ostrich, rattlesnake, red, black, brown—all those boots in rows in his closet."

"Smells evoke memories." The aroma of cinnamon rolls baking reminded her of Moses' kisses. He always kissed her, his lips sweet with frosting and cinnamon, after she made them because they were his favorite. "Sweet memories."

"I'm so mad at Walt." Her voice quavered. "I'm royally angry."

"I know." Mary Katherine squeezed her hand. "Believe me, I understand."

"I know you do." Dottie's lower lip trembled, but she managed a watery smile. "It hurts my heart to think of what you've been through. I thought I understood, but I didn't."

"I know it's hard to hear this, but little by little, day by day, it hurts less. It gets a tiny bit better until you realize you can go on." She didn't tell Dottie she still spoke to her dead husband. She didn't know of any other widows who did that. Fortunately, Dottie tended not to speak to Walt when she was mad at him. Childish and counterproductive though it was. "You're not the same as you were before, but you wouldn't want to be."

"He was supposed to retire in two years. We were supposed to buy an RV and travel around the country." Dottie made a fist of one hand with its fine wrinkles, age spots, and veins that bulged blue. She tapped the island with it lightly, but anger flashed in her eyes. "He was supposed to do the books for our store."

"It wasn't meant to be."

"If you give me that God-has-a-plan speech, I swear I'll dump this bowl of Jell-O on your head." She shook her fist at Mary Katherine. "His days were numbered, you'll say. God has plans to prosper, not harm you. Blah, blah, blah."

"Dottie." The words shocked Mary Katherine. Even though she'd had those same thoughts several years earlier, she'd never dared to share them with anyone. Not even Laura. What would Laura say in this situation? She always had the words. "You attend the Baptist church every Sunday. You never miss your Sunday school class. You said yourself you didn't know how folks get through life without Jesus. Don't you believe that?"

"Sure I do, but talking the talk is a heck of a lot easier than walking the walk." Dottie sank onto a swivel stool on the far side of the island. "Life was going along so perfectly. I praised God every day for my blessings. I know bad things happen, but I felt secure. Now I don't."

"So you believe in Him when things are good, but dump Him when something bad happens?"

"No, I suppose not. That doesn't mean I have to like this."

"Truth be told, I agree." Mary Katherine slipped around the table and rubbed Dottie's back. "If you can't sleep in your bed, try one of the guest bedrooms for a few nights. Sleep helps."

"The kids are sleeping in the guest bedrooms."

As if her words could conjure them up, Tanya and Miranda appeared at the kitchen door. "There you are."

Tanya, the older daughter, a honey-blonde beauty in a simple black frock that made her look even thinner than she was, took the lead. "You don't need to worry about this. We'll get it. You get some sleep. Tomorrow's another day."

Miranda sniffled and reached for a tissue. "Oh, honey." Dottie hopped up from her stool and rushed to her daughter. "It's okay to cry."

"I've cried buckets, Mommy. I can't stop." Miranda's strawberry-blonde hair was mussed. Her nose and her eyes were red. "I just can't believe it."

The three enveloped each other in a group hug. Mary Katherine edged toward the door. "I'll leave you alone. All of you could use some sleep."

"Mom will feel better when we get her situated in Dallas." Tanya wiggled from her mother's grasp and held out a hand to Mary Katherine. "Thank you for taking care of her until we got here."

Mary Katherine shook her hand. "No thanks necessary. Dallas?"

Dottie grabbed another tissue and mopped her face. "I can't stay here in this house. As soon as we get it packed up, I'm going back to Texas."

Mary Katherine searched for something to say. "A visit will do you good."

"I plan to sell the house."

"What about the bookstore?"

"I can't do it alone." She shrugged. "Not without you and Walt. It was simply pie in the sky."

Pie in the sky. Mary Katherine wanted a slice of that pie. Life without Dottie would go on, but it would

be poorer without her. All those afternoons comb-
ing through articles on the internet or ordering books
through the loan programs at the big city libraries.
And without the dream of spending their days in that
shared appreciation of a good book. Surrounded by
them, their lovely smell, the anticipation of reading all
those words. Her world continued to shrink. Loved one
after loved one disappeared. Swallowing the painful
lump in her throat, she forced a nod. "Take care. Don't
leave without saying good-bye."

"I wouldn't do that to you."

Mary Katherine climbed into her buggy and tried
to think. She should go to Thomas's, but the fourth cup
of coffee still buzzed through her veins. She wanted to
go home. To her home. Dylan's family hadn't moved in
yet, but that house would be filled with Moses' woody
scent tonight. Phantom scents. Like phantom limbs.
"Giddyap." She turned east, toward downtown. A buggy
ride in the dark on the highway wasn't a great idea. She
could take a leisurely path through town. Stretch it out
until her brain caught up with her weary body.

Funerals exhausted a person. Trying to keep a fa-
cade from crumbling wore a person out.

Dottie's pain looked so familiar.

*Gott, let her feel Your presence and know You are
with her. You hold her right hand. You are the Gott of
all comfort, even if she doesn't see that right now. Forgive her anger. I remember that anger. It burned like a
gasoline-fueled inferno in me for years. Let hers die to
embers that cool quickly. Heal her.*

Dallas would be a good place to do that, it seemed.

But memories could not be escaped. They followed a person around. They lived inside broken hearts. Sometimes they festered, keeping a heart from healing. Dottie would find that out. The desire to flee was understandable, but a person couldn't flee a loved one who never left her heart.

The horse stopped in front of the Purple Martin Café. She had no idea why or how she'd arrived at this spot.

Ezekiel stood on the sidewalk, locking the door. He turned. He looked tired, his skin sallow in the security lighting. His gloomy expression fled, replaced by a welcoming smile. "What are you doing out so late?"

She opened her mouth, expecting her impressions, her sadness, her rawness, to come pouring out. Nothing happened.

Ezekiel strode to the buggy and put his hand on the wheel. "Did you want to come in?"

"You're closed." She shouldn't go into the restaurant if no one else was there. "It's later than I realized."

"Everyone's gone." His other hand landed on the seat. "You've been to Walt's funeral, haven't you?"

"I went to Dottie's house to the reception . . . to help. It's chilly." For the first time she realized the night air held a chill. Dottie's house had been filled with warm bodies and grief that made the air heavy and hard to breathe. "It's almost as if winter isn't far off."

"Autumn air feels good to me. Fresh and sweet after the hot summer. It tells me change is coming. Change can be good. Come in and I'll make you some kaffi."

"No more kaffi. I won't sleep for a week."

"Chamomile tea then. With honey. For you. Just chamomile for me. Doctor's orders." His prattle made him seem nervous. Was he nervous? The thought made the hair prickle on Mary Katherine's arms. Her stomach flopped. Now she was nervous. He came around to her side and held up his hand. "I'll help you down."

"Are you sure? You're tired."

"I always have cocoa or tea at night."

His fingers were warm. She allowed him to help her get down. She fought the urge to hang on to his hand as they walked to the door.

Inside, he turned on the lights over the counter, leaving everything else off. He bustled around, letting water heat in one of the coffee carafes, pulling out the tea bags and some sliced lemons. She watched, lulled by the economy of his actions and the warmth of the room. His restaurant exuded comfort. That's why people liked it.

"Do you want a piece of toast or a cookie with that?" He set the mug of tea in front of her with a saucer of lemon slices and a plastic bear bottle of honey. "Tell me about the funeral. Tell me what's wrong."

"I can't look at another cookie." She picked up the honey bottle. "What makes you think something's wrong?"

"You're here." He slid onto the stool next to her. "I'm trying to imagine under what circumstances you would come here knowing we're closed or about to be closed. You should be on your way to Thomas's. He'll be looking for you."

"He won't look here." She managed a smile. Ezekiel

smiled back. His lips were full, his teeth even. Her gaze didn't seem to want to leave them. She jerked it away and studied the to-go dessert menu over the kitchen window. PECAN PIE $8.99. CHOCOLATE CRÈME MERINGUE PIE $9.99. Her gaze returned to Ezekiel's smile. Sweeter still. *Stop it.* "I didn't intend to come here."

"But you did." He creased a paper napkin into halves, then fourths. "And you winked at me at the produce auction."

"You winked at me in Deputy Rogers's car and you came to my house the other day."

"So there we have it."

What did they have?

"Seeing Walt there on the floor like that." She swallowed and pressed her hand to her mouth. *Breathe. Breathe.* "It was like seeing Moses all over again. All the memories came flooding back."

"So still. So without life."

"Jah."

"I kept calling Lucy's name. I was determined she would answer me. I couldn't fathom why she didn't answer me."

"She died in front of you. Moses was gone when I found him. Still, I tried to wake him. I called his name. I crawled under the covers . . . I don't know which is worse."

Her voice didn't want to work. The tiny crack in her composure grew like the cracks in the pasture during a drought that grew worse with each passing summer month. She fought to close the gap.

Ezekiel slipped from the stool and stepped into her

space. She closed her eyes, then opened them. His hand covered hers. Those warm fingers. He leaned closer. His beard brushed her cheek. She put her hands on his chest. Her breathing caught in her throat. He was so solid, so imposing. Her blood raced through her veins, but it wasn't the caffeine. "Ezekiel."

"I know." His lips brushed her forehead. "It's like we're traitors."

"Or adulterers." She leaned her forehead on his chest. His scarred heart lived there. It matched hers. A set. "It's confusing."

He backed away. She breathed again. He turned and propped both elbows on the counter, his expression pensive. "Others go on to marry again. Bess. Jennie."

He'd given this some thought. So had Mary Katherine. "I know. Even Jennie, who had such a wretched time with her first mann, was willing to take another chance."

"She fell in lieb again—despite her fears. That's something I don't expect to happen to me again. I had a happy marriage."

"Me too." Mary Katherine grabbed the spoon by her cup. She needed to do something, anything, to keep from touching him. She stirred so hard, tea sloshed over the cup's edge. "Maybe I'm here—we're here—now because we're lonely and we're tired and we know how short life is."

He straightened. "Is that what you think?"

"I still talk to my dead mann."

His eyebrows rose, but he didn't laugh or lean away as if he was dealing with a crazy woman. "Does he talk back?"

"Jah. I've never told anyone that, not in the seven years since he died."

I'm not crazy, am I? Moses?

No answer.

Am I a traitor? Am I an adulterer?

Silence.

"I lay in bed at night and imagine Lucy is there. I can hear her little woman snores." Ezekiel shook his head and laughed, a brusque, half-angry sound. "She steals the blankets and wiggles. I don't say anything because I don't really mind."

"Everyone has their way of getting through it." She wasn't the only crazy one. They had that in common. What else did they have in common, besides loneliness, bossy, caring children, and their community? "I know Moses isn't there. I know I'm not really talking to him. He's dead. He's gone forever. But I write stories and this is like another story in my head. What Moses would say if he were here with me now."

"He might be peeved that another man almost kissed you."

"I don't think so. He'd say I'm finally starting to live again."

Ezekiel smiled. She smiled back. His lips were so soft looking. She wanted to touch them. An old woman with a passel of children and grandchildren besotted by lips. Ridiculous.

He touched her lips with one finger. His hand dropped. "Sorry. I don't know what it is about you." He shook his head. "I've known you all my life."

"You never gave me a second thought."

"That's not true. I see you. I think of you. At least I have in the last few years. Before, Lucy was . . . my everything."

"Like Moses was for me."

"And then they were gone."

"I was trying to explain to Dottie today how we reconcile that with our faith." She squeezed fresh lemon into her tea. The light scent made her think of spring, fresh and clean. "We cling to the knowledge that Gott knows what He is doing even if we don't understand."

"We say the words until we can believe them." He spread his hands, palms down, on the counter's slick varnished wood. "Burke and I have been talking about that. I've been mad at Gott for a long time. I never told anyone that. He figured it out on his own."

"He recognizes the anger because he feels it himself. Dottie is angry too. I was never really angry, mostly bewildered." Mary Katherine touched the scar on the back of his middle finger. A mishap with a paring knife? "I have five sons who look like him. They walk like him. Talk like him. I go to family gatherings and I'm surrounded by him. Yet he's not there."

"I lost Gott for a while." His hand turned over and his fingers touched hers. "I felt like giving up."

"But you found Him again."

"I'm working on it. Burke is helping."

"The stranger from Virginia." She sighed. "The God of all comfort leads us through our struggles. We learn from our suffering and then we comfort others."

"Burke and me. You and Dottie. Me and you."

"I thought we were supposed to help Burke, not the other way around."

"Me too. My project."

"My project." How arrogant that must seem to God. *Sorry.* "Maybe his helping us helps him."

"I hope so. No matter how much advice he gives to others, he's still lost."

"And so are we." Her heart raised a fist and smacked it against her rib cage. At her age, it could be a heart attack. "After seven years, I still run my decisions by my husband. I tell him about my day and my joys and my concerns. About the grandbabies and the skinned knees and the sharp words."

"Because you haven't let him go. Like I haven't let Lucy go." Ezekiel dabbed at lemon juice with his napkin. His lips twisted in pain. "I don't talk to my wife, but Lucy is still present in everything I do. She's the reason I opened the restaurant. To keep our family together and strong."

"She was a sweet woman. She always will be."

"I know."

They were quiet for a few seconds.

"What now?" His tone was soft, the question barely a whisper. "My friend."

"It's as if you still have a fraa. I still have my Moses. So, for now, you get in your buggy and go home. I get in my buggy and go to Thomas's house."

He picked up his hat and let it drop on his head. "We have unfinished business. We both have to let go of the past before we can have a future. I'll follow you home."

"No need."

"What if those burglars break into Thomas's house?"

"They know there's nothing more to steal than there was at the old house."

"Maybe they were looking for you."

"I imagine Thomas sleeps with one eye open and his ears perked up, waiting for me to get home. So does Moses."

Ezekiel laughed, a deep, rich belly laugh. "Now you're scaring me."

She laughed with him. The hysteria of exhaustion tinged the sound. "Just a little joke. Let me wash out my cup."

"I've got it."

"You're tired. I don't want to make more work for you."

He stood and took her mug. "I'm right behind you."

Her limbs heavy with regret, she trudged to the door. The flowery aroma of chamomile with a hint of fresh lemon would remind her of Ezekiel from this night forward.

He made quick work of the cleanup, picked up the keys from the counter, and followed her through the door. Then he took her hand and led her to her buggy. For the first time in years, she felt enveloped in the care of another. She slowed her pace. The streetlight cast long shadows in the dusk. An old pickup truck putted past them, spewing gas and oil fumes. Ezekiel stopped on the driver's side but didn't let go of her hand.

"I'll need my hand back." She didn't try to remove it. "To drive."

He looked up the street, then down the street.

His gaze landed on her face. Wonder and trepidation mingled in his careworn features. He shook his head. "It's not a gut idea."

She waited. It was for him to decide.

He leaned over and kissed her, once, hard. She didn't have a chance to kiss him back. "Nee, not so fast." She stretched on tiptoes and did her own kissing.

His laugh was rueful. "Your kisses are so sweet."

"It's because it's been so long."

"Nee. They're simply sweet." He tested the theory with yet another kiss, this one longer, deeper. She slid her hands up his chest to his shoulders and held on for dear life. His hands found their way to her cheeks and caressed her skin. Shivers shot through her, followed by waves of heat. He rubbed his rough cheek against her. "Simply you."

The street seemed to grow uneven under her feet. Staggering, she turned to haul herself into the buggy. A strange euphoria fought with something akin to shame. Every nerve and every muscle tingled with aliveness, a feeling missing in her life for so many years she'd forgotten what it felt like. Kissing Ezekiel was new, unexplored territory. Soft lips, lined cheeks, a beard, a different country than the one she'd explored as a young newlywed who kissed her whiskerless husband on her wedding night. *Oh, Moses, I'm sorry.*

No answer.

She grabbed the reins. She shouldn't have come here. "Mary Kay?"

She allowed herself to look at Ezekiel one more time. He smoothed the folds of her dress, his hand near her knee. Another wave of heat, this one so intense it crackled like a wildfire kindled by lightning on a breathless summer night, raged through her. "If I should show up at your suh's house one evening, would you slip out to meet me?"

"Like teenagers on their rumspringa?" The words had a bitter taste to them, like grapefruit rind. "We're too old for this."

"Like two people trying to figure out what to do with the rest of their lives."

Would Moses be there with her if she went on a buggy ride with another man? Would he still speak to her? Could she live without hearing his voice every night before she went to bed?

Hope blossomed, a lovely sunflower that found light where before there had been none. Did she want to spend the rest of her life in the dark, lonely place or with someone willing to take the chance that new love could exist in the same place with a perfectly happy, perfectly too-short love?

Ezekiel smiled up at her, but his eyes were sad. "I know kisses don't mean lieb. But ours mean something."

"Give it time. Give me time."

"I have nothing but time."

No, he didn't. No one did. Walt's, Lucy's, and Moses' deaths proved that.

She clucked and snapped the reins. He stepped back as the buggy jolted forward. "See you soon."

"I hope so." She whispered the words. She didn't want him to hear them. They weren't a promise. They were the beginning of hope.

CHAPTER 24

The woody taste in Mary Katherine's mouth jerked her back to reality. Chewing on her pencil again. Wrinkling her nose, she pulled the orange number two from her lips. The eraser was wet and ragged, the metal edging around it bent, and the wood looked as if a mouth had been nibbling on it. The story had her stumped. If she revealed her heroine's gender too soon, the other cowboys would throw her off the cattle drive. She needed to make it to the end of the Chisholm Trail to Abilene where she would find love and a new life. How long could these silly men miss that their cook was, in fact, a young woman? Men tended to miss clues right in front of their noses in real life. Why not more so in fiction?

She raised her head and let the breeze from the living room's open windows cool her warm face. The curtains lifted and fell. An evening thunderstorm had cleared the humidity from the air and left a lovely evening behind. She stared into the darkness. What it must've been like on those cattle drives when it stormed. The thunder and lightning that she adored would've been close and scary. The cattle might've been spooked. The cowboys would've been soaked with no place to get out of the storm's fury. Mary Katherine bent over her paper. Somehow she could weave this thought into her story.

A dog began to bark. Remus, the stray who had decided to make Thomas's barn his home, sounded displeased.

Ezekiel? It was too soon. Only a week had gone by since her late-night visit to the restaurant. She needed time. She asked for time.

Memories of a sixteen-year-old girl anxious, yet petrified, to get to her first singing flooded her. Nerves fluttered in her belly. She wasn't ready.

"Jah, you are, Fraa."

Don't be silly, Moses.

"Leave the story. It'll be there when you return."

How can you encourage this?

"I know it will make you happy."

You make me happy.

"Made you happy, love. Go. Now."

"It's only a buggy ride." The memories from all those years she'd spent in her room listening to the sounds of her teenage children beginning their courting journeys, watching them learn of the delights of love, and then marrying, flooded her. "I promise to behave."

She said the words aloud.

"Like you did at the restaurant. He's The One, Kay."

Only Moses called her that. Kay.

The One. Surely Moses couldn't have been listening to her conversation with Laura. Because he was dead. Mary Katherine might be addled, but she wasn't crazy. Her conversations with her dead husband were a lovely figment of her writer's imagination. Born of terrible loneliness and the sense that they hadn't had the chance to finish their conversation before he was ripped from her life so suddenly.

What makes you think Ezekiel is The One?

"I saw the way you looked at each other the day of the wedding. When you fell all over each other. The sashay in your walk after that night at the restaurant."

Plain women don't sashay.

Had there been a look? She trotted out her memories from the wedding day. Ezekiel's scent. His warm brown eyes. The way his full lips turned up in amusement. The sturdiness of his body under hers. The way his hand gripped her arm and helped her up. Her heart tripped over itself.

You let your imagination run away with you.

A soft *rap-rap* sounded at the door.

Mary Katherine took a long breath and opened the door.

Ezekiel stood on the other side, his hand lifted as if to knock a second time. "I was hoping you would still be up."

"I'm up. Did you get caught in the storm?"

"I waited it out. Is everyone else asleep?" He pushed his black hat back on his head, his expression tentative. "I didn't have an invitation."

They were, for which Mary Katherine was deeply thankful. She didn't want Thomas's thoughts on this part of her life too. "You don't need an invitation."

"Gut to know."

The pause stretched. He studied his boots. She studied them with him.

"Can I come in or would you rather come out? It's nice out. A little nippy, though."

"Jah, jah. I'll come out." She started forward. The porch wood was cold and wet on her feet. Her bare feet. "I should put on shoes."

"You should. And a shawl. I'll wait right here."

She dropped one shoe. Her fingers fumbled with the laces. She couldn't get the knot out of the other one. Her skin felt damp under her arms. "I'm coming."

"There's no rush." His voice held a note of amusement. "Nobody knows I left the house. They won't miss me before morning."

She laughed. He'd meant for her to laugh. He wanted her to feel comfortable. The realization stilled her shaking hands. This was new for Ezekiel too. "You'd think we were on our rumspringa and my parents were sleeping upstairs."

"Instead of your suh and his fraa."

"Strange turn of events, isn't it?"

"Indeed it is."

Wrapping her shawl around her shoulders, she walked to the door without tripping over her own feet. He moved aside to let her pass. He wasn't much taller than her. Solid. Thick through the middle. Frayed around the edges. He didn't smell like farm the way Moses had. His scent reminded her of the barbecue pit behind the Purple Martin.

Ach, Moses, what am I doing?

No answer. Apparently, Moses drew the line at eaves-
dropping on her courting.

Her stomach flopped. "Do you want to sit on the
porch? I can get us some cold tea."

"Let's take a ride." He cocked his head toward the
buggy. "I'm feeling restless tonight."

She knew that feeling. "Shall we run away from home?"

He grinned, suddenly looking more carefree. "If we
do, we need to pack a knapsack with sandwiches and
whoopie pies. A person gets mighty hungry if he runs
too far."

"How do you know? Did you run away?"

"Nee. I threatened to once and my mudder packed
a bag for me. She put in an apple and two oranges and
some homemade cookies. For the road, she said."

"She sounds nice. I don't remember her."

"She was. She's been gone for twenty years. My daed
went a few months after her. He never got over it."

"Like you never got over Lucy?"

She shouldn't have said that.

"The Miller men are a faithful lot."

"Gut to know." She marched to the buggy and hauled
herself into it.

He settled in next to her and picked up the reins.
"How is it going, living with Thomas and Joanna?"

"It's an adjustment."

"That is a tactful way of putting it, I reckon."

"You reckon right." She plucked at her dress. "I miss
my house. This is Joanna's house."

"And she lets you know it. It's like you're a visitor all
the time."

"Exactly. She doesn't hide her feelings. She doesn't know how. At least you're with your daughter. She surely wants you around."

"I'm in the dawdy haus, but I eat most of my meals with Leah and William. I love my kinner, but I miss . . . the way it used to be."

"Not ready to let go of the memories yet."

He shook the reins and clucked softly. "I'm working on it."

"I guess it's hard for others to understand what it's like to lose someone. Some would say it's like losing an arm or a leg. To me, it's more like having your heart ripped out of your chest, cut in ragged pieces with a dull knife, and the smaller pieces stuffed back inside you. It still beats, but every second is painful."

"That's a gut description. I'm sorry it's an experience we have in common. I wouldn't wish it on my worst enemy."

They pulled onto the road that meandered across Thomas's property and linked it to the Beachys next door. The pause stretched and stretched. It sure didn't sound like either one of them was getting on with their life. It didn't sound as if either one of them had yielded to God's will and God's plan.

How could they be ready for each other? Love was more than the physical pleasure of warm kisses. They were both old enough to know that.

"What were you doing when I pulled up?"

"Writing."

He tugged on the reins and slowed the buggy. They turned onto a road that was little more than a wide path that led to a pond that had served as a swimming hole when she was a child. "Tell me about it. What's your story about?"

"You really want to know?"

"I wouldn't ask if I didn't."

"Most people get a nervous laugh when I tell them I write stories. They think it's silliness for a woman my age."

"Everyone should use their imagination at least once a day. Whoa, whoa." He slowed and brought the buggy to the edge of the pond. A full moon and a blanket of stars lent a glow to an otherwise dark night. "My daed was a big storyteller. He kept us tied up in knots with his stories every night in the winter when it was too cold to do anything but sit by the fireplace and play checkers. Far-fetched tall tales."

"Moses loved my stories."

"And you loved him for it."

"I did."

Everything came back to that first love she thought would be eternal. She breathed in the humid night air and listened to the frogs croak.

Ezekiel tied up the reins and leaned back in the seat. "It's okay. It doesn't hurt my feelings. I'm glad you had a gut lieb, a gut marriage. It means you understand when I say I stand at the kitchen sink and look out the window and see her hanging clothes on the line or weeding the garden."

"I see him working on the thresher or the tedder or playing volleyball with the kinner."

"What is the story about?"

She told him, slowly at first, then picking up steam as the story took shape and filled up her mind's eye. "She finally makes it to Abilene. She gets cleaned up. One of the cowboys sees her in town. He falls for her, not realizing she was the cook on his cattle drive. It makes for all sorts of lovely intrigue and romantic pratfalls."

"You do have a way with words."

"Comes from reading so much. Another thing most grown-ups around here can't understand."

"I find books are good company and a great way to escape on a long night." He sighed a sigh that was almost comical in length and depth. "A lot of cookbooks, though. Which makes me hungry so I eat a snack or two or three." He patted his belly. "I've been told by a lady doctor who studied all about such things that I should stop doing that now."

Since the diabetes. "It's a sad state of affairs when doctors tell us what and when we can eat."

"Exactly."

This time the silence was more companionable. An owl hooted. Crickets chirped. A fish splashed in the pond. Mary Katherine inhaled the scent of wet dirt, rotted plants, and fish. "It's peaceful, isn't it?"

"This is the most peaceful I've felt in a long time." Ezekiel's voice held the faintest of quivers. "I've been wrestling with my feelings for so long I don't know how to sit quietly and just be."

"I like sitting quietly and just being with you."

"Me too. You're different from most women I know. You find your way on your own. You think on things and figure them out with no help. You read." His rueful tone matched Mary Katherine's feelings. "You decided to fix Burke's life and you took action without leaning on anyone for help. You want to open a bookstore. You write stories."

Most folks didn't understand her predilection for fiction. Especially men. Except for Moses. *Ach, Moses, just because I'm in this buggy doesn't mean I don't miss you still. Where are you?*

No answer. Anxiety clutched at her chest like a child afraid of falling from her mother's arms. What was she doing on a buggy ride with this man who wasn't Moses?

Waiting for God to open a new door. Trusting in God to show her how to walk through it.

I'm sorry, Moses.

No answer. "How did you know about the bookstore?"

"Bob Sampson was talking about it to his wife while they were eating supper at the restaurant. Jim Tompkins and Jerry Rivers mentioned it over a piece of pie and coffee. Word gets around at the Purple Martin."

She had made herself stand out with her love of books, her writing, and her big plan to open a bookstore. That's what he was saying. No Plain person strove to stand out from the others. She swallowed a lump in her throat. Moses didn't see her writing that way and he wouldn't have seen the store that way, either. "Books give people joy. The store would be a way of spreading the joy. My dreams never got in the way of being Moses' fraa."

"They don't get in the way of working in the Combination Store now." He shoved his hat back and stared at the sky. "Telling stories that make people think is a gut thing. No matter what people say. They don't have enough work to do if they're talking about you."

He did know. He did understand. She breathed. The possibilities crowded her. Could he imagine a future with a woman who spent her days working in a bookstore and her nights writing stories? An odd future, for sure, for a Plain man.

He cleared his throat. "You don't think you could be happy cooking?"

Ezekiel's tone told her it wasn't an idle question. Mary Katherine's picture of the future crumbled and blew away, like dust being swept from an old house.

He was imagining a future with her that involved his restaurant. She fingered her kapp's strings and tried to see it with him. She could spend her days in the Purple Martin's kitchen, concocting dishes that folks enjoyed with their families. It would be hot work, but good because the days would be spent with Ezekiel. Books or kneading bread dough. Books or frying chicken. Books or baking pecan pie.

Dottie was leaving, taking with her any chance of a shared bookstore. The district's elders had directed her to work in the Combination Store. Now Ezekiel wanted to draw her into his dream, his restaurant.

Her own dream faded into the dark night.

"Your silence speaks for you."

"Nee, I was just . . . imagining."

"Me too."

"We were put on this earth to work. I know that." She hopped from the buggy and stood at the edge of the water. The sound of it lapping against the banks calmed her. The reflection of the moon rippled in the crisp breeze. She inhaled the night scents. Her shoulders relaxed. "I work as hard as the next woman."

"Harder." His footsteps sounded behind her. Goose bumps popped up on her arms as he drew closer. "No one would dispute that."

"I like hard work." She called herself a writer, yet she couldn't ferret out the words to explain the compulsion, the obsession, the neediness of her writing. "Writing is hard too. Not like physical work."

"I know in school it made my head hurt." She could feel his smile and hear it in his voice. "Not my favorite thing."

"That's just the physical act of shaping words. I'm talking about creating something out of nothing."

"Don't let Freeman hear you say that. He might take it like you're comparing yourself to Gott creating something from nothing. Do you think your stories come from Gott?"

"I don't presume to know. I hope and pray He is pleased with my meager efforts to make stories using a gift that surely came from Him."

Ezekiel's hand enveloped hers. He moved closer. "I've spent a lot of time thinking about that night at the restaurant."

"So have I."

"It's hard to know what it means. We've both been alone for a long time." He sighed, a mournful sound full of emotions she recognized, the same ones that battered her in the dark of most nights. "I feel like a blind man wandering around on a road I've never been on before. I'm not sure which way to go and I'm afraid of falling on my face."

"Maybe those feelings come from loneliness?"

"I don't know. What do you think?"

She shook her head. "I had this talk recently with Laura. She has this theory about The One."

"The one."

"With capital letters. With emphasis. *The One.*"

He chuckled, but his hand tightened on hers. "That sounds like Laura. She always has a theory."

"She's one who uses her imagination plenty. It's what makes her such a fun person to be around." Not many seventy-year-olds could be called fun. "My point being that I don't believe I would have those feelings if you weren't The One."

"I like this theory." He took a step closer still. "I think we need to test it to see if the feelings still hold."

He leaned into her. She met him halfway. More than halfway. His hand slid around the back of her neck and held her close when their lips met. Warm hands. Warm lips. Heat ran through her.

Not a hot flash. She giggled.

Ezekiel leaned back. His eyebrows tented. "I know I'm out of practice. Are my kisses that funny?"

"Nee, I'm light-headed." Downright woozy.

Ezekiel snorted. "I make you light-headed?"

"Lack of oxygen."

He laughed and pulled her back to him. His lips covered hers. They trailed across her cheeks to her neck, touched her nose and her forehead. Soft, glancing kisses. He leaned his forehead against hers and they breathed together. His warm breath touched her face. He smelled of soap and spearmint toothpaste. The same light breathlessness filled the air.

His beard tickled her cheek when he talked. "Did you ever think you'd feel this way again?"

"Never."

"We're not teenagers."

"Nee, but we know what we've been missing."

"I thought it was companionship."

"Is that not what this is?" His lips on hers muffled her response. His arms cradled her close. The kiss ended and she laid her head on his chest and listened to his heartbeat. Strong and healthy.

For now.

For how long?

He surely thought the same thing. His chest expanded against her cheek as he inhaled and then exhaled. "I know what you mean, though. This. . . . what we're doing here clouds our thoughts."

"You want a fraa to work with you in the restaurant."

"I do. The Purple Martin Café is more than a restaurant to me."

"You named it for Lucy's favorite bird."

"It kept me going. It kept my whole family going."

"I had kinner to raise and a farm and then Amish Treasures. Imaginary characters kept me company most nights."

"We had a season in our lives." Ezekiel put his arm around her shoulders. "Now the seasons are changing."

"I don't know if I can change that fast."

"It was a thought, that's all."

"It is it a onetime offer?"

"It's a standing offer."

Mary Katherine closed her eyes and listened to the night sounds. Autumn felt good after the heavy heat of summer. Change was good. Her throat ached with sudden tears. She swallowed against them. "Poor Dottie. She still has so far to go."

"She has you to help her." He didn't question her train of thought. "You're a gut friend."

"She says she's going to Dallas."

"Did you tell her you wanted her to stay?"

"That would be selfish of me. If she wants to be with her kinner, she should."

"It's hard to know what you want in the aftermath of a loss so sudden." The voice of experience. "You've had time to figure out what you want. If you'd rather work at the Combination Store or open a bookstore or just write stories, you should."

The church elders and her children thought otherwise. "Speaking of the Combination Store, I have to open tomorrow. Jennie's taking a hot lunch to the school and Laura is helping Iris teach a midwifery class. She can't get there until ten."

Without a word Ezekiel helped her into the buggy and hauled himself up on the driver's side. His horse nickered and headed toward the road with no encouragement. Likely he, too, was tired.

Old people weren't used to staying up late.

Or being in love.

At the door Ezekiel planted a chaste kiss on her

cheek and backed away. He clomped down the steps and across the yard as if a pack of wild boars chased him.

"Ezekiel."

He raised his hand and waved. Then he left.

"Be that way." He had his dream. She had hers. One of them would have to budge. *Gott, does it have to be me?*

Was she so selfish as to ask Ezekiel to do what she wouldn't?

She sighed, then closed the door and went to bed.

But not to sleep.

CHAPTER 25

Ezekiel's back, hips, and legs ached. Otherwise, he was as giddy as a teenager on his rumspringa and ready to go another round. The old man part of him tutted and shook his head. Mary Katherine wanted change, but not too much change. She liked his kisses, but not his plan for the future. He wanted change, but not too much change. He liked her kisses, but not her plan for the future. Stalemate.

He stifled a frustrated groan and tugged the door open. Exaggerated silence greeted him. The silliness distinctly like raging teenage-boy hormones disappeared, replaced by sudden uneasiness. He paused. No doggie snuffles and barks greeted him. No *clickety-clack* of doggie nails on the wood floor. No Sunny. It had only been three weeks and he already expected to be greeted at the door by a wandering mutt. And Burke, the wandering man, had a presence too. A kind of sharing of space that left the scent of restaurant and sweat. He inhaled. No stinky dog smells and no man smells.

Ezekiel sighed and started into the living room. He immediately stumbled over something. Arms flailing, he teetered, then fell. Rubbing his elbow and then his knee, he sat up and took stock. Nothing broken. He stuck his hand out and encountered solid wood, rungs. He followed the outlines. An overturned chair. He hadn't left it that way. Had Burke? "Burke, are you here?"

His voice petered out in the darkness.

When his eyes had adjusted and he could see shapes, he crawled over to the table and stood. He lit the lantern and held it up. The smell of kerosene and phosphorus, normally so homey, made his stomach pitch. That and the destruction that surrounded him. The other chairs around the table were overturned. His cookbooks were strewn across the living room floor.

Broken pieces of cups, plates, and glasses decorated the cabinets and the kitchen linoleum.

An intruder had soiled his small space. Anger skewered him. He sucked in a breath through gritted teeth. Material possessions weren't worthy of rage. The anger drained away.

Burke couldn't have done this. He wouldn't.

Where was he? He should be home by now. "Burke, are you here?"

Silence.

Ezekiel set a chair upright and used it to pull himself up. He tottered down the hall to the second bedroom. The bed was neatly made. Clothes hung on the hooks. But no Burke and no dog.

Ezekiel's legs shook. His hands trembled. He ran shaking fingers over his head. He breathed in and out. He would walk down to the phone shack and call the sheriff's office. They would want to know if anything was missing. Hard to say in this mess.

"Daed?" Leah's voice, high and tense, called from down the hallway. "I saw the light come on. Are you all right?"

He staggered back to the living room and plopped into the upright chair. "What are you doing out so late?"

"Kenneth's running a fever. He has strep throat. I keep getting up to check on him. Then I can't go back to sleep." She sidestepped a pile of cookbooks, turned upside down, their pages ripped and torn. "What happened in here?"

"It looks like someone decided to redecorate."

"It's not funny." Leah picked up one of the cookbooks. Its cover had been ripped off. A page featuring a photo of peach cobbler hung by one metal ring. "Were you here when this happened? Sleeping?"

Guilty pleasure coursed through Ezekiel. He stifled the thought as if she might read his mind. His daughter didn't need to know about the buggy ride with Mary Katherine. "I need to call the sheriff's office."

"Freeman first?"

"Jah, Freeman first."

"You sound funny." She cocked her head, her gaze worried. "Is it the diabetes?"

"I didn't eat any dessert today, if that's what you're asking. I reckon it's the shock of this mess."

"I'm just asking, that's all." She ran the words together as she laid the cookbook on the table. "Should I get you some juice?"

"We shouldn't touch anything until the sheriff's deputy gets here."

"Where's Burke?"

"I don't know."

"Shouldn't he be back from the restaurant by now?" She frowned in the flickering lantern light. "Do you think he did this?"

"Nee."

"Daed—"

"He didn't do this." Maybe it would be better if he had. Sunny would be with him, not in the hands of a thief and vandal. Ezekiel stood and trudged past her toward the door. "I'll call."

"I'll get William."

Within the hour Ezekiel's tiny home bulged at the seams with Dan Rogers, who'd been called in from home by dispatch, Freeman, with his mussed beard and sleepy eyes, and William, who stood by the fireplace, hands clasped, eyes closed, most likely praying.

Dan started off with the question that seemed to be on everyone's mind. "Where's Burke McMillan?"

"Last time I saw him was at work. He closed the restaurant for me tonight."

"He should be back by now."

"He should."

Dan's frown matched the one on Freeman's face. The bishop took off his glasses and rubbed his already red-rimmed eyes. They were all standing because Dan didn't want the crime scene, as he referred to it, messed up any more than it already had been. "Maybe you should go into town and make sure the restaurant hasn't been vandalized as well." Freeman gestured toward the door. "There's a lot more to destroy there. And it's a way of making a living for several people."

"It's my next stop." Dan snapped photo after photo with his fancy camera. The flash blinded Ezekiel each time. "After I document this scene."

It wasn't a scene. It was Ezekiel's home. He hadn't thought of the restaurant either. He didn't think that way. Besides, Burke worked hard at the Purple Martin. He wouldn't destroy the place that gave him a reprieve from his own thoughts. "This is more like the burglar who has been breaking into the other Plain homes."

"The burglar didn't vandalize the other places," Freeman pointed out. "The only damage at Mary Katherine's was the broken window in the back door."

"Or take a dog." Dan turned the camera toward the broken saucers on the kitchen floor. "You said Burke brought you the dog. Maybe he took him back."

"Why would he bite the hand that feeds him? That gives him a pillow to lay his head on?"

"We'd have to ask him that question." Dan let the camera, held by a strap around his neck, rest against his chest. His free hand gripped the gun on his hip for a second. His fierce expression spoke of what he thought of the situation. "Someone's targeting Amish folks and getting more violent about it."

"It's just property. Stuff." Ezekiel swept his arms through the air. "A broom and some trash bags and it'll be gone."

"It's against the law to come into a man's house and destroy his property, his stuff."

"I'm not saying I approve." Ezekiel shook his head, trying to find words the Englisch lawman would understand. "I'm not happy a stranger came into my home and did this. But no one was hurt. Dishes can be replaced. I'm not attached to these things. No real harm done."

"What about whatever was stolen? Are you attached to any of that stuff?"

Ezekiel hadn't thought about that either. He glanced around, trying to see beyond the intruder's handiwork to the way the rooms had looked before.

"The teakettle." William spoke for the first time. He pointed at the propane stove. "The one you like. It's always sitting on the stove."

No. Why would a burglar take a teakettle? Ezekiel brushed past his son-in-law to survey the kitchen. The green enamel teapot he used every night to heat water for his tea or his hot chocolate no longer rested on the propane stove. He surveyed the rest of the kitchen and its linoleum floor. Nothing.

"It's gone." He swallowed the ache in his throat. No one got upset about a kettle. Even if Lucy had bought it at the Fourth of July auction when she was expecting Leah. Not even if she used it every day after that until she passed away. William didn't know why his father-in-law liked it so much and Ezekiel didn't plan to tell him. "Why take a teakettle?"

"The burglar is collecting mementos. He's furnishing a house. He likes hot tea." Dan looked as baffled as Ezekiel felt. "I've never seen anything like it. What else?"

"The kitchen calendar. It had pictures of birds on it." Birds that also reminded him of Lucy. "I bought it at the Walmart in Chillicothe."

He picked his way through the kitchen to the drawers

that stood open. The woven loop pot holders the girls made with Lucy's help when they were six and four were also missing. "Pot holders." He stopped, afraid his voice would break.

"Ezekiel?"

William looked worried.

"Just pot holders the girls made." He cleared his throat. "Not worth two quarters."

"I have a fingerprint kit in my unit." Dan took a moment to look directly at Freeman. "I'd like to take all your fingerprints. That way I can eliminate them and see which ones don't belong here."

"We're not suspects, are we?" Freeman's tone was good-natured, much to Ezekiel's surprise. "And if the burglar wore gloves?"

"Then we won't know any more than we do now, which is par for the course with these break-ins. No one sees a thing because you folks have so little lighting or no lighting around your homes. You don't have alarm systems. You have regular schedules and do lots of visiting. Two of the burglaries occurred during church services."

"It's a mystery." Freeman smoothed his wild beard. "Why commit a crime that involves taking worthless things from Plain homes?"

"I don't know why they're picking on Amish folks. It's like a lukewarm hate crime." Dan snapped more photos. "Lukewarm but heating up with each successive break-in."

He glanced at Ezekiel. "That doesn't let your friend off the hook, either."

"He doesn't hate us. He likes us."

"We'll see." Dan headed for the door. "I'll get my fingerprint kit. After I take yours, I'm taking his."

A few minutes later, Dan called Ezekiel's name. Relieved at the thought of fresh air and escape from Freeman's piercing gaze, Ezekiel strode outside.

"I found some big oversized tire tracks out here." Dan held a high-powered flashlight in one hand. He pointed at two swaths of muddied, flattened grass that stretched from the dirt road to a spot next to Ezekiel's front door. "Didn't you notice this before?"

"It was dark."

Dan turned and followed the swaths out to the road, snapping photos as he went. The flashes lit up the starless night in startling bursts that made Ezekiel blink even though he knew they were coming.

"Burke doesn't have a car or a truck. He drives an old motorcycle." Ezekiel followed the deputy, using his light to make his way. "He couldn't have done this."

"Maybe tonight he brought a friend."

CHAPTER 26

The biggest difference between courting at sixteen and at sixty? Mary Katherine took a healthy swig of her coffee, laced with two tablespoons of sugar and three packets of nondairy creamer. The scalding liquid burned all the way down. A sixteen-year-old's body bounced back from lack of sleep more quickly.

She set the oversized mug on the counter and trudged to the Combination Store's door. She unlocked it, turned around the CLOSED sign to OPEN, and began rolling up the blinds. The morning sun's brilliance made her wince. After her buggy ride with Ezekiel, she'd tiptoed into her new bedroom and slipped into bed, but she hadn't slept. No matter what she did, she couldn't relax enough to fall asleep. Instead, she'd replayed the scene with Ezekiel in her head over and over like a sixteen-year-old. Thus the bleary eyes and faint headache that accompanied her to work this morning.

The door flew open and Bess trudged in, baby Leyla in her arms, a bulging canvas bag slung over her shoulder. Joshua toddled behind her. "You're here. Gut. I haven't seen you in forever."

"Let me at that bopli." Mary Katherine flew around

the counter and held out her arms. Now that Bess was married and mother of two, Mary Katherine didn't get to talk to her friend as often as she once had. Frolics and church services were too busy for real conversation. If no customers wandered in early, this might be it. "Look at her. She's grown. Her cheeks are so chubby. And look at you, Joshua. You're at least a head taller."

"I have two heads?" The three-year-old's eyes grew wide. He patted his brown hair, then held up one finger. "Nee. One head."

"You're right, my sweet." Mary Katherine giggled. "You're a smart boy."

"She looks like Aidan, don't you think?" Bess helped Joshua with his jacket and settled him on the floor with a plastic horse and two cows. "She has his gray eyes."

"She's a bit of you and a bit of him, I'd say." Mary Katherine eased into one of Leo's rocking chairs and cooed at Leyla. "How are you? Laura says you're still a little shaken over the break-in."

Bess dropped her bag on the counter and began pulling from it napkins and doilies embroidered with autumn leaves in oranges, reds, and browns. Her stitching was perfect. "I'm fine. Just perplexed, I reckon. Why would someone do such a thing?" She refolded the napkins and placed them in neat stacks on the counter. "That baby quilt has molasses stains on it. It's yellowed with age. It means nothing to anyone but me and my mudder."

"It's a mystery, isn't it?" Inhaling the soothing scent of baby, Mary Katherine began to rock. Leyla's eyes closed. Her tiny hands folded onto her chest. "Deputy Rogers is working on it. We have to trust he'll find the culprits."

"And my quilt." Bess sniffed. "I feel silly, being so attached to an old quilt. It's just a piece of material. I shouldn't care so much."

The wooden chess pieces once held in Moses' calloused fingers moved across a chessboard in Mary Katherine's mind. "It's not the material. It's the memories. It's family. It's babies. You wanted to give that quilt to Leyla someday. Your feelings are natural, and Gott understands."

"I hope so. I feel silly being so heartbroken over it." Bess turned, the stack of doilies in her hands. "You look sad yourself. And tired. Laura told me you lost some mementos too. I'm sorry you had to go through this."

"Like you said, they're only material things. I'll get over it."

"It's not the break-in. It's Ezekiel, isn't it?" Bess laid the doilies on a shelf next to a pile of dresser scarves and tablecloths. She clapped her hands like a little girl. "Did you take a buggy ride? Tell me all. For once, I want to be the first to know. You tell Laura everything."

"Laura has a big mouth."

"Laura knows how much Jennie and I want both of you to be as happy as we are."

"We're older. Set in our ways."

"Age has nothing to do with it. Solomon remarried and he's happy as a man can be."

Bess's first father-in-law lost his wife not long after Bess's first husband died in a buggy-truck accident. It had been a dark time for both of them. "Men are different. They are needier."

Was that what Ezekiel was? Needy? The image of his face before he bent to kiss her fluttered through her mind. Her face heated and her heart did its own fluttering. She kept her gaze on Leyla's exquisite nose.

"You're looking for excuses." Bess tutted as if she was disappointed. "Please don't. Life is too short, and things can change in an instant. No one knows that more than we do."

"I know I encouraged you to marry Aidan. You were meant for each other." Mary Katherine smoothed the blanket around her sleeping bundle of sweetness. "Now that it's a possibility for me, I keep wondering what I was thinking. You're exactly right. Things can change in the blink of an eye. I don't know if I'm up for that a second time."

Her bookstore would be simpler, easier. No worrying about a loved one slipping from her grasp again.

"It's worth it. So worth it." Bess caressed her baby's cheek. "I took a chance and look where I am now. What I have now. I hate to think of you sitting all alone in your dawdy haus and Ezekiel sitting all alone in his dawdy haus. It makes no sense if there's a spark between you two, and I know there is."

"Why? Because Laura said so? It's not a simple thing." Only because she wouldn't let it be. She was selfish to put her dreams ahead of Ezekiel's. But they both had a lifetime of experiences, and it would be hard to meld them into one life and one dream. "It's just taking time to get used to the idea."

"Time is the one thing we don't seem to have enough of. I need to pick up some flour and sugar at the grocery store and run by the hardware store for Aidan." Bess held out her arms and Mary Katherine reluctantly returned the baby. "Don't be a stranger. Come to supper one night. I want to hear all about Ezekiel. I bet he's a gut kisser."

"Bess Graber!"

The other woman's laughter made Joshua look up from his animals. He joined in, his chortles high and contagious.

"You are much too forward, you know."

"I know."

The doorbell dinged again. Their chat was at an end far too soon. Mary Katherine swiveled to greet their customer, but it was Laura who traipsed through the door.

"*Guder mariye*, my friends. What a beautiful day. I love the cool, crisp air and the breeze and the smell of fall in the air. Don't you?" She sailed toward them. "Bess, I'm so glad to see both of you! And these cuddly little snuggums! Wasn't that a great storm last night? Rinsed everything off. It feels so clean today, doesn't it?"

Mary Katherine stood. "What are you doing here so early?"

"Deborah Gingerich went into labor. Iris had to go deliver her bopli. She took Theresa and Esther with her." Chuckling, Laura set her canvas bag on the counter and swooped down to tickle Joshua, who ran shrieking toward the front door. "On-the-job training is better than a class any day."

Mary Katherine rubbed her forehead. Her friend was far too cheerful—and loud—for so early in the morning. "Iris must be eager to get them trained before her bopli comes."

"I have to go." Bess gave Laura a peck at the baby and then a quick hug. "Give Mary Kay a good talking-to. She was so sure about me and Aidan and Leo and Jennie, but now she's all cold feet and goose bumps."

"I'll do my best, but she's a stubborn old biddy." Chortling, Laura picked up Joshua's toys and dropped them in Bess's bag. "See you Sunday."

They were gone as quickly as they came.

"Don't look so sad. You'll see them again in a few days." Laura dug through her bag and produced a small bottle of aspirin. "You look like you could use this. In fact, you look like you put your clothes through the wringer with you still in them."

"Nice of you to notice. It was gut to see Bess. I never get to talk to her anymore." Mary Katherine accepted her friend's offering, but she laid the bottle on the counter. Aspirin on top of coffee would only compound her problems. "I didn't sleep well."

"Worried about Ezekiel?"

Heat singeing her cheeks, Mary Katherine strode away from the counter in a hurry. The shelves needed dusting. And the jars were a mess. She heaved a breath and schooled her voice in a matter-of-fact manner. "What makes you say that? And why did you tell Bess about him?"

"Bess guessed. I didn't have to tell her. You didn't hear what happened to Ezekiel last night?" Laura handed her rags and a can of Endust. "Someone broke into his house and tossed the place."

"Tossed the place?"

Laura read her share of mysteries now that her evenings were free of sudden baby appearances and she lived alone in her dawdy haus. "You know, messed everything up. Broke dishes. Knocked over chairs. At least that's what Leah told Carlene who told Theresa who told Iris who told me."

"Who would do such a thing? Was anything taken?"

"A teakettle."

"A teakettle."

"Jah."

The pain in Mary Katherine's temples intensified. Her stomach clenched. She set the can on the shelf and laid the rags next to it. "I should go . . ."

"Go where? To Ezekiel?"

"He might need help at the restaurant if he's stuck at home cleaning up."

"Carlene and Leah will clean his house."

"He likely didn't get any sleep. He probably isn't eating right, and his diabetes will be out of whack." Mary Katherine heaved a breath. "I could help out front while Burke cooks."

The front door opened, and their first customers of the day entered. A gray-haired woman dressed in a long-sleeved pink jogging suit entered, followed by a bald man in a similar suit, but his was gray. Either they were jogging by and decided to stop or the suits were keeping them warm this October morning.

Laura waved and nodded. "Burke didn't come home

last night." She spoke the words out of the side of her mouth like a kid trying not to be heard by the teacher during school. "And Ezekiel's dog is gone."

"Burke was at the restaurant, I reckon."

Laura harrumphed and trotted over to the couple. She urged them to sign the guest book Jennie had placed on a table by the entrance. They liked to keep track of how far folks came to shop and collect addresses to send sale flyers. She left them to their browsing and returned by the time Mary Katherine had given up pretending to dust.

"Or he came home and then left after he tossed the place."

"Tossed the place means looked for something."

"Oh. Well. Deputy Rogers is investigating this as a possible hate crime."

"Burke doesn't hate anyone. He's a former Navy chaplain."

"Whose life has been on a downward spiral."

Mary Katherine ducked behind the counter and picked up the lightweight blue shawl Beulah had knitted for her for Christmas the previous year. "Can you watch the store by yourself?"

"Are you going for Ezekiel or for Burke?"

Mary Katherine sat in Leo's lovely hickory rocker. Not something a saleslady should do. "Both."

Laura glanced at their customers. The woman held a colorful queen-size Double Ring Chain quilt to her cheek, a look of unadulterated love on her face. The man shook his head. "That thing costs more than my first car."

"I better see to our customers." Laura patted Mary Katherine's shoulder. "Do what you need to do, but pray first and remember that Gott is at work in this. You might not understand, but He knows what He's doing. All that's required of us is obedience to His will."

"I wish I knew what that was." Mary Katherine stood. She leaned closer to her friend—as if someone would overhear their conversation. "Ezekiel wants a fraa to share his life. That includes the restaurant."

Laura stopped. A smile blossomed across her face with its road map of wrinkles for every sad and happy moment in her long, sturdy life. "You talked?"

Heat as fierce as any that came from a wood-burning stove billowed through Mary Katherine. She opened her mouth, then clamped it shut.

"More than talked?" Laura crowed. She clapped. Their customers looked up from their argument over the merits of spending so much on a blanket—as the man put it. Laura waved. "If you need any help, let me know. Those quilts are hand-pieced and hand-quilted by women who live in this area. It takes months to finish one. They're sewn with love."

The man nodded, but he didn't look convinced. The woman's lower lip turned down and she gave him the puppy-dog look Mary Katherine had seen on the faces of so many women wanting to buy quilts in Amish Treasures.

"What did he say?" Laura grabbed Mary Katherine's arm and propelled her toward the door. "What did you say? When did this happen?"

"Last night." Mary Katherine answered the last

question first because it was the easiest. "It was gut. Really gut. Until we talked about the bookstore."

"Freeman says you should work here. Besides, Dottie's leaving." Laura might have her moments of sassiness, but she always came back to the practical bottom line. "Fraas do as their manns ask."

"I know." Mary Katherine did know, but the longing to spend her days buying and selling books held deep sway over her heart. More than her feelings for Ezekiel? "I know."

Two more customers came through the door. She should stay.

"Go to the restaurant. I can handle things here." Laura went to greet the two Englisch women, both with toddlers in tow. "It's not childbirth, for sure."

She chuckled all the way to the foyer.

Guilt assailed Mary Katherine. Laura was seventy years old and retired.

On the other hand, Mary Katherine had no doubt her friend would handle things. And handle them well. She scooped up her bag and headed for the door. Outside, the brisk breeze cleared the fog in her sleep-deprived head. She climbed into the buggy. A horn tooted, two insistent short toots followed by a longer one.

Dottie's elegant mauve sedan pulled into a parking space next to her. The passenger side window whirred its way down. Dottie leaned across the seat and waved. "I was hoping you would be here. Do you have a minute?"

"For you, always." Mary Katherine climbed back down, opened the car door, and slid onto the cool, brown leather seat. "I was going to come by the house later to-day. I want you to come out for supper before you leave town. Have you started packing? Do you need help?"

"Slow down the horses." Dottie grabbed a tissue from an economy-size box sitting on the seat between them. She wiped her already red, swollen nose. "Let me talk, will you?"

Mary Katherine's normally spiffily dressed friend looked like a dishrag. She wore a faded green-plaid shirt that was two sizes too big, baggy orange sweats, and pink fuzzy slippers. Her gray hair hung in clumps around her face, which bore no makeup. Her eyes were red with dark circles under them. "Of course, you first."

Dottie wadded up the tissue and tossed it in a growing pile on the seat. She sniffed and put both hands on the wheel. Her wedding ring, a chunk of diamond the size of a nickel, sparkled in the sun. She wore no other jewelry. She stared straight ahead.

"Dottie?"

"I don't think I can do it."

"Do what?"

The air in the car began to warm. The pause stretched. Tears trickled down Dottie's face, wetting her cheeks and sliding down her chin.

"Dottie, please, tell me what's going on." Mary Katherine slid closer and took her friend's hand. Dottie sniffed and let her head fall forward so her forehead rested on the wheel. Mary Katherine let go of her hand and patted her shoulder. "There will be rough days like this, but I promise you, it gets better."

"I can't sell the house. I can't leave it." Dottie closed

her eyes. "I can't leave him. How will I visit his grave if I move to Dallas? Who will put flowers on it and clean the headstone? What about his pickup truck? I can't sell his pickup truck."

"I understand. Completely."

"I know you do. That's why I had to talk to you." Dottie straightened. Her eyes opened. She grabbed Mary Katherine's hand. "We have to open the book-store. Walt loved the idea. He wanted me to be happy. He knew it was my dream and he wanted me to have it, even though he really only wanted to travel around in an RV, him driving and me in the passenger seat navigating. I don't know how to tell my kids I don't want to leave Jamesport."

"Walt will be with you no matter where you go."

"I know that. You knew Moses would always be with you, but you didn't want to leave your house either."

Letting the sun beating through the windshield warm her face, Mary Katherine folded her hands in her lap and stared at the store. Freeman had said no. Jennie and the others needed her here. Ezekiel wanted her at the restaurant. Ezekiel wanted a wife who wanted what he wanted. Dottie was offering her the chance to have her dream. But wanting her own dreams was tanta-mount to vanity. It was a far cry from *Gelassenheit*, the bending of her will to God's. It was selfish, not selfless. *Thy will be done.*

"I'm fine living with Thomas and his fraa. Moses is still with me—still in my heart. I work at the Combination Store and I'm fine. It's for the best. You'll get used to the idea, I promise."

"There's a difference between fine and happy." Dottie hiccupped a sob. "There's a difference between existing and living. I don't want to spend the rest of my life without Walt *and* just existing. I can't bear it."

She would bear it because she would have no choice. Mary Katherine didn't tell Dottie that. She couldn't tell her about Ezekiel, either. Not with Dottie's fresh, gaping wound where her heart once lived. Her friend wouldn't be able to imagine how love could tiptoe in when a woman least expected it and begin to mend that wound with tiny, perfect stitches. The mended heart was different—scarred, more mature, less trusting, but a heart primed for love nevertheless. "I wish I could say something to make you feel better. I know I can't. No one can. But I can promise that it won't always feel this way."

"I need to do something. I can't sit around the house and be sad all the time. It's killing me. I thought I would pack, but that's when I realized I can't let go of a single thing in that house. Every piece of furniture, every dish, every glass, every photo, even the TV remote, for goodness' sake—everything reminds me of him."

"Now is not the best time to make big decisions about your life. Give it some time."

Easy for Mary Katherine to say. Just as it had been easy for others to spout similar platitudes when Moses died. Few people could find the words that would serve as a life preserver for a person drowning in a flood of grief, no land in sight.

"The girls are upset with me. They think I should go with them. They're afraid I'll turn into a crazy cat lady living all alone in a little town where there's nothing to do and no one to talk to."

"We won't let that happen. You have friends here. You'll have your card games and the football game nights and church Bible studies." Dottie was one of the most social people Mary Katherine knew. "Tell them you realize you need time before you make any decisions about your life. They'll understand."

"There won't be any more card games or football nights. They're all couples. I'm not a couple anymore."

Plain women congregated together for frolics, while men did man things. Still, the conversations that swirled around Mary Katherine often filled her with a sense of sadness that she would not grow old with her husband, she would not share a cranky descent into achy joints and failing eyesight and thinning hair. She had been blessed by deep and steadfast friendships with Laura, Jennie, and Bess, who understood what it meant to be a wife without a husband in a tight-knit community where family was second only to faith.

"You may be surprised at the new friendships you'll forge. With time, you'll make new friends."

"The girls seem to think the loss of a husband turns a wife into a helpless old lady."

"You may be a lot of things, Dottie, but helpless is not one of them."

"What makes them think they're the boss of me?"

"I don't know, but my children think they're the boss of me." Mary Katherine chuckled. "Even Ezekiel's children have suggested to him what he should do. But it's different because he's a man. They'll abide by his wishes."

"Ezekiel? What does he have to do with any of this?"

Mary Katherine scolded her loose lips. "Just another example of a grown person who lost his loved one."

"It's different for men. I may be a woman, but I still have a mind of my own."

"So do Plain women, but we follow the dictates of Scripture. 'For the husband is the head of the wife, even as Christ is head of the church.'"

"Doesn't the Bible say children should respect their parents?"

"It does."

Dottie snatched another tissue and mopped her face. "Walt left me well taken care of. Life insurance out the kazoo. The house is paid for. The car is paid for." She wiggled in the seat so she half faced Mary Katherine. "I have the money to buy the building and fix it up. You could help me figure out what it should look like, stock it, and run it. No financial risk. What do you say?"

Mary Katherine looked away. She couldn't hold her friend's gaze. Ezekiel's words rang in her ears. He wanted a wife who would work with him in the restaurant. He wanted a partner. Plain men might be the head of the house, but they wanted partners in life. Someone with whom they could discuss decisions before making them. She'd experienced that special give-and-take with Moses. She wanted it again.

She also wanted her dream of a bookstore. A place where she could live and breathe books all day long. Write even. Between customers. Early in the morning. Over her midday meal.

Freeman hadn't said no. He'd said not now.

"I don't know if I can." She forced herself to meet Dottie's gaze. "I want to. I really do. But there are things going on."

Dottie gave her nose a good honk. "I'm doing it. Even if I have to do it alone. You're my best friend, Mary Kay. Don't make me do this alone too."

"I wish I could help. I really do. But it's not up to me. I know that's hard to understand."

"I've lived near an Amish community my entire life." Dottie tossed the tissue in the pile. "I understand. That doesn't mean I like it. I hope you'll understand when I move on without you."

Mary Katherine did understand. That didn't mean she had to like it.

CHAPTER 27

The sign in the window at the Purple Martin said OPEN. Relief swept through Ezekiel. He sucked in cool air. His chest felt tighter with each breath. Despite the cold, sweat dampened his shirt. William had insisted he sleep at the house. Sure he wouldn't sleep a wink, Ezekiel slid into the extra bed in Kenneth's room and passed out. The sun had been high in the sky when he finally dragged himself from a dreamless, deep slumber. Peeved that they let him sleep.

The world wouldn't end, William had said, if the restaurant didn't open right on time. No, but closed doors didn't pay the salaries of the people who depended on Ezekiel for a living. It took time to prepare for the lunch crowd.

No Sunny sitting on the porch, panting, tongue hanging out, greeted him. Which did nothing for his mood on the drive into town.

What kind of person took a man's dog?

The question nagged him as he stared at his restaurant. Just a dog. He should've known better than to get attached to a mangy old dog.

Not old and not mangy. Sunny was just a puppy.

Were they feeding him? Were they scratching that

spot behind his ears that he liked so much his tail thumped a hole in the rug and his smile grew so big he nearly choked himself?

He's just a dog.

A silver four-door car was parked at the curb in front of the restaurant. Should he be relieved or worried? Burke closed. He didn't open. Why would he be here now? Who else could it be? Besides Burke, only Andrew, John, and Ezekiel had keys. All the way into town he'd chastised himself for leaving the restaurant in the hands of a man he barely knew. According to Dan, the restaurant had been locked up tight when he checked the previous evening. Nothing had seemed out of place. His face haggard from lack of sleep, the deputy returned the restaurant key at midnight and urged Ezekiel to get some sleep.

A person could argue that the whereabouts of a man he barely knew was none of Ezekiel's business. On the other hand, he'd opened his home to Burke and given him a job. A hollow, ugly suspicion seemed determined to wriggle its way into his heart. He'd snapped the bolt on the door that led to all his feelings and his doubts and fears. He let the man in. Burke had no answers. He couldn't even fix his own life. Ezekiel wanted answers. To more than a break-in and a missing dog.

He didn't want a dog for this very reason. Sunny had snuck in right behind Burke.

The more Ezekiel stewed, the more he steamed. He drove around back and unhitched Swede. He left the horse in the enclosure he'd built for him right after he bought the building. His stomach roiled. A wave of light-headedness inundated him. He needed to eat. The doctor had been clear about that. How could a person eat in the midst of so much turmoil?

He barged through the back door, marched through his office, picking up speed, stomped through the kitchen, and hit the swinging doors at full velocity. They banged against the walls. The smell of coffee brewing and cinnamon rolls baking greeted him. Acid rose in his throat. He swallowed against the burning sensation. A woman's laugh sounded.

He halted.

Burke stood behind the counter, his back to Ezekiel. He had a dish towel slung over one shoulder and he wore a Purple Martin T-shirt with the restaurant's name emblazoned in black against the purple cotton material. A woman in a navy-blue sweatshirt that read GO NAVY in gold letters across her chest sat on one of the stools. Her deep-brown eyes filled with lively curiosity at the sight of Ezekiel.

Burke turned and held up an oversized coffee mug in a careful salute. "Hey, Ezekiel. I have the coffeepot fired up and cinnamon rolls in the oven. The lasagna is baking and all the vegetable and fruit prep has been done." He cocked his head toward the woman. "Meet Lieutenant Commander Carina Lopez. We knew each other in the Chaplain Corps in Norfolk. She helped with the prep."

Carina had silver hair cropped short and tawny-brown skin. She slid from the stool and held out her hand. "So you're Mac's boss." She grinned with a smile full of brilliant white teeth. She wore no makeup or jewelry and exuded health from the pink of her cheeks to the shine of her hair. "He's been bending my ear about you."

"Mac?"

"That's what we called him. When we weren't on duty. Then he was Lieutenant McMillan."

Courtesy required Ezekiel to move forward and shake her hand. He made quick work of it. "Good to meet you." Then he focused on Burke. "Where have you been?"

He sounded like his mother. From Burke's expression, his employee agreed with that assessment. "Around."

"Someone came into the house last night."

"While you were there?"

"While I was gone." He stuttered over the last word. While he was with Mary Katherine doing what Burke had urged him to do. Get on with his life. "Someone threw things around, tore things up. Stole a few things. And Sunny is gone."

"Sunny's gone?" Burke set his cup on the counter with a bang. His jaw jutted and a pulse beat in his temple. "They took our dog."

Our dog.

He started around the counter. Then stopped. His hands went to the towel on his shoulder. He whipped it from its perch and wiped his hands needlessly. "You thought I did it. You thought I messed up your house and stole from you."

"No. I did not."

"I can see it on your face."

"Mac—"

Burke held up his hand at Carina. "I told you I did things. Things I'm not proud of. I broke into a house when I first got here." Emotion deepened the lines around his eyes and mouth. Sadness mingled with a pinch of self-loathing Ezekiel recognized. "I was hungry. That's no excuse, I know. I didn't know these people—"

"You haven't been yourself for a long time." Carina patted the seat next to her. "Have a seat, Ezekiel. I got here about seven o'clock last night. Mac and I have been together ever since."

Ezekiel started forward. The words registered. He wavered. None of his business. He repeated the phrase a few times and worked to smooth his expression as he sat down an arm's length from her.

"No, no." Their laughter sounding of old friendship and easy camaraderie, Burke and Carina spoke in unison.

"She's an Episcopalian priest." Burke's tone said that explained everything. "We were friends in the Corps."

"Like a Catholic priest?" Ezekiel knew a little of that faith but nothing of Episcopalian practices. His face heated. His legs felt like boiled noodles. "Not that it's any of my business."

"We can marry." Carina chuckled. "But mostly, I'm married to my job. I came out here to make sure Mac was okay. I'm just doing a welfare check."

"An unneeded welfare check. We found a twenty-four-hour truck stop and diner on the highway." Burke's expression remained neutral, but his voice held a hint of something Ezekiel couldn't identify. Mixed feelings. "We talked all night."

"None of my business." Ezekiel wiggled on the stool. Carina came all the way from Virginia to Missouri to check on a friend. Ezekiel had intended to make Burke his project. He didn't even have to leave the house, and yet it seemed he had failed the man. "I only wondered because—"

"You were worried about me too." Burke's tone lightened a degree or two. "Sorry. I didn't mean to be so touchy. It's been a while since I slept."

"How did you know he was here?" Ezekiel turned to Carina.

"He sends me postcards now and then, but it had been a while." She frowned. Her forehead wrinkled. "You look a little pasty. Are you all right?"

"Did you eat breakfast? You didn't, did you?" Burke stuck a cup of coffee in front of Ezekiel. "I'll make you some eggs. An omelet with veggies. Some whole-wheat toast."

"I'll help." Carina popped off her seat. "I can handle toast. I could squeeze some fresh OJ."

"You're a terrible cook."

Carina's retort was lost in the shrill ding of the bell on the front door. Dan strode through it, letting in a rush of wind. He wrestled the door closed and then settled his hat back on his head. "I figured you were here already."

That was directed to Ezekiel. "Did you find out something?"

His gaze on Carina, Dan removed his hat again. "I don't believe I know you, ma'am."

Carina introduced herself.

"I'd like a word with you, Mr. McMillan."

"We can talk here. Carina is a friend."

"I need you to come over to Gallatin to our office."

Burke picked up a washrag and wiped off the counter, including the space under Ezekiel and Carina's coffee cups. "Am I under arrest?"

"Let's just say you're a person of interest." Dan rested his thumbs through his belt loops, fingers not far from the gun on his right hip. "Your fingerprints were all over two of the crime scenes."

"He's been staying at my house." Ezekiel lassoed his impatience. Dan was just as tired—or more tired—than the rest of them. "He admits to being in Mary Katherine's house."

"I wouldn't be doing my job if I didn't follow through on that coincidence, if it is a coincidence."

"I don't have a car, so you'll have to drive me." Stripping off his long white apron, still pristine in these early morning hours, Burke shot Ezekiel a penitent look. "Sorry, boss. I hate to leave you in the lurch this afternoon. Maybe Mary Katherine can help."

"She's working at the Combination Store this morning." Ezekiel stopped short of slapping his hand over his mouth. Barely. "That's what I heard, anyways. I'll figure something out."

Carina grabbed a black leather backpack purse from the counter and slung it over one shoulder. "I'll drive you, Mac, so you'll have a way back. Considering you had nothing to do with this, you'll be back in time for your shift."

Dan frowned. "Who are you again, exactly?"

"I'm his alibi for last night." She marched past Dan and pushed open the door. "Let's get a move on. Daylight's burning."

Had she been a chaplain or a drill sergeant? The two men hustled out the door behind her. The bell dinged. A sudden quiet ensued. Ezekiel breathed. His cook a person of interest in a slew of burglaries. This was indeed a twist in the life of a restaurant owner.

The bell dinged again.

"Did you forget something?"

"Nee. I saw Deputy Rogers drive off with Burke." Ezekiel whirled. Mary Katherine stood on the welcome rug. Concern etched her pretty face. "What's going on? Do we need to do something?"

Yes, they did, but for the life of him, Ezekiel couldn't figure out what it was.

CHAPTER 28

Out walked one cook. In walked another. Ezekiel tried to gather his thoughts. They ran amok in his brain. Mary Katherine had made it clear that she had no plans to work in a restaurant. "I could use your help." He peeked at her face. Pink and flustered. Pretty. "Dan took Burke in for questioning. I don't know when he'll be back. You're here. You could cook with me."

The emotion in her face fizzled, replaced with chagrin. Her eyes warned him. The next words out of her mouth would not be the right ones. She focused on the menu over his head. "I was on my way to see if you needed any help after the break-in at your house last night. Then Dottie stopped me in the store's parking lot. She was crying."

"She buried her husband a few weeks ago."

"She's decided to stay."

"I can't see how that's a bad thing."

"She's planning to buy Bob Sampson's building and turn it into a bookstore."

Air whooshed from his hope-filled balloon. The bookstore of Mary Katherine's dreams. "Are you planning to talk to Freeman about it?"

"Do you think I should?"

What was she really asking him? "Freeman wants you to help Leo and Jennie make the Combination Store a success." He scrambled for words to fit her needs, not his wants. "But he also recognizes the value of your friendship with this Englisch lady. He will balance your desires with what's best for the community."

"We don't need a bookstore."

"We might not like having tourists peeking into our lives, but we know they help us support our families. Another store—the right store—will help us provide, not hinder."

"So you don't think it's a bad idea?"

"I never said I did."

"You said . . ." She hesitated, a wary look on her face. "You said you could use help here. Your kinner would like to see you have help or retire."

"I wouldn't want help from a person who finds being here onerous."

"Who could find it onerous? The Purple Martin Café makes me feel at home the second I walk through the door." She rearranged the honey bear and a container of artificial sweetener packets. "It's just not what my heart wants."

"I understand that."

"That doesn't mean my heart doesn't want . . . other things."

"Like what?"

She sighed and switched the salt and pepper shakers with the catsup bottle. Her forehead wrinkled with worry, she shook her head. "So Burke won't be here to cook when you open?"

"I don't know. It depends on what he says in the interview, I reckon."

Her head bowed, Mary Katherine straightened a stack of laminated menus. "I can stay and cook."

"Your words say that, but your demeanor says something else." He grabbed an apron from the shelf behind the counter and tied it on. "Don't worry about it. I'll do the cooking. You go plead your case for the bookstore."

"Ezekiel, I'm sorry—"

"The thieves took Sunny."

She winced. "I know. I heard."

"He's just a dog."

"Animals can be better friends than people."

She had that right. A person couldn't depend on people much. "I have to get busy."

Her shoulders bent, she sighed. "Me too." She turned and trudged to the door. "Good-bye."

He backed away, unable to take his gaze from her retreating figure.

She let the door close gently behind her.

No way he would sell and retire. He needed the restaurant. He needed a place to go every day. Mary Katherine had her bookstore dream. He had his restaurant.

CHAPTER 29

A person couldn't hear the fiddle, banjo, mandolin, and harmonica of bluegrass music and not tap her toes. It was humanly impossible. Stenographer's notebook in hand, Mary Katherine paused in front of the grocery store sidewalk-turned-stage where Richard Baker and the Jamestown Buddies played to dozens of folks planted in folding chairs set up in rows on the street. She scribbled some quick notes for her next *Budget* report. Her memory wasn't as good as it used to be.

She loved Heritage Days, the last big outdoor crafts day of the year in Jamesport. The event also served the purpose of keeping her from her obsession over Ezekiel and their conversation at the beginning of the week. Right after her conversation with Dottie about the bookstore. Dueling dreams. No point in thinking about either one. No sense whatsoever. She had two choices. He'd made that clear. Not thinking about them.

"Jah, you are."

Hush, Moses. Aren't you supposed to be resting in peace?

"It's a little hard to do with all the racket in your head.

Go find Ezekiel. Tell him you'll cook with him. Tell him you're ready to start a new life with him."

What about the bookstore?

"There's still time."

Time like you had? Go away.

No answer this time. If he really went away, would she survive?

Mary Katherine raised her face to the sun. It would burn away the question. The forecast had been for rain. Instead the sun brightened the darkest corners of her mind. A brisk, cool wind ruffled the leaves in the elm and sycamore trees. Kids raced from booth to booth looking for fry pies and ice cream cones. The aroma of hamburgers cooking on a grill under a tent across the way made her mouth water.

She had half an hour before she had to report to Jennie's booth to sell jams, jellies, and canned goods. Leo had a booth for his small wood crafts—carved animals, toy trains, and blocks. They made good Christmas gifts for the grandkids. She needed a crib quilt from Iris's booth for her latest grand on the way. First, she would grab a burger.

"Haven't seen you in a while."

She swiveled in her chair at the sound of Burke's voice. He stood behind her. A silver-haired woman with brilliant white teeth, brown skin, and impossibly straight posture stood next to him. "It has been a while. I figured Deputy Rogers locked you up."

"To his great disappointment he had to let me go." Burke shrugged and nodded toward the woman. "I had an alibi he couldn't argue with. A lieutenant commander and Episcopalian priest. Meet Carina Lopez. She's been keeping me in line for the last week."

Carina held out her slim hand. Mary Katherine shifted her pencil and notebook to her left hand and shook. The woman's fingernails were cut blunt and covered with a sheen of clear fingernail polish. She wore tan slacks, a red blouse, and a blue corduroy jacket. Her handshake was firm, her smile generous. "I've heard a lot about you, and it's all good." Carina had to shout to be heard over the enthusiastic picking, strumming, and grinning on the makeshift stage. "Thanks for not blowing his head off with a shotgun, even if he deserved it."

"No one deserves that."

"I'm only kidding."

Mary Katherine hadn't heard a word about Carina. But she hadn't spoken to Ezekiel in five days. Or Burke. She dutifully helped Joanna with laundry, cooked, cleaned, and played with the kinner. They whipped the dawdy haus into shape and moved her into it. She filled three shifts at the Combination Store. She finished four more chapters in her story. She'd been plenty busy. "Are you enjoying your visit to Jamesport?"

"Very much. I've never spent this much time around Amish people before." Carina slipped her hands in her jacket pockets. "I know it's hard for you to understand, but I find the lifestyle intriguing. As a theologian, lifetime student, and a woman who is a feminist at the same time."

More words followed, but they were lost in the

raucous music. Mary Katherine cupped her hand to her ear. "I didn't quite get that."

"Doesn't matter." Burke rolled his eyes. His deep voice carried better. "She's getting all academic and philosophical on us. It's too nice a day for that."

"Are you still working at the restaurant?" Mary Katherine raised her voice to be heard over the band's rendition of "Just a Little Talk with Jesus."

"Yes."

No one spoke for a beat. Burke ducked his head. Mary Katherine studied Richard's banjo. He sure could play.

"I saw some beautiful beaded necklaces in that booth on the corner." Carina looked from Burke to Mary Katherine and back. "I want to get a couple as gifts for friends. Why don't I meet you at the burger tent?"

She pivoted and strode away without waiting for an answer. Burke cocked his head toward the yellow-and-white-striped tent. "Buy you a burger?"

Mary Katherine glanced around. She couldn't stroll down Main Street with an Englisch man. It wasn't done and she understood why. "I can buy my own."

"I owe you for a ham sandwich."

"It was on the house."

"So to speak. More like on the floor."

She laughed with him.

He studied the crowd. A boy on a scooter whizzed by. The *clip-clop* of a horse's hooves accompanied the squeak of wooden buggy wheels down the street. The crowd streamed around them in an ebb and flow of dozens of conversations and the mingled scents of cotton candy, popcorn, and funnel cakes. Burke seemed lost in thought. He looked like a different man. Still with the five o'clock shadow, but hair in a crew cut and neat, clean jeans, blue-plaid flannel shirt, and deck shoes made him look like a customer she might serve at the store. Not a guy who spent the night in her barn.

Still no socks.

"What if I said I'm headed over to the burger tent?" His grin made him look like a mischievous boy. "If I happen to run into you there, well, it'll be a nice surprise. Carina loves a good burger too."

They could run into each other twice in one day. It had been known to happen in a small town. She nodded. He smiled and slipped between dueling strollers.

After a few moments of labor over her notebook, Mary Katherine arose and followed at a decorous pace. Her stomach rumbled.

See there. It's hunger.

"And nosiness. You're a busybody who wants to know what the sheriff's deputy said and how Ezekiel is doing. And you like the idea of thumbing your nose at the others who have no idea what it's like to be alone at your age."

Moses!

"I call them as I see them."

I've never thumbed my nose at anyone in my life.

"Ahem."

Go away. She wasn't doing anything wrong. Carina would join them in a few minutes. They wouldn't be alone long. Burke was a man of God, after all.

Dorothy Borntrager and Josephina Beachy waved from the fry pie and whoopie pie booth. Ignoring the heat that scorched her face, she returned the wave and kept going.

Inside the tent Burke stood at the first table. Waiting. It was still early and most of the tables were empty. An Englisch couple with three noisy children took up a table in the back. Mavis and Aaron Yutzy sat across from each other at the other end. They waved. She waved back. They had moved to Jamesport in the last year and kept to themselves.

"What's up with you and Ezekiel? He's been crankier than a hound dog with a toothache." Burke didn't seem to notice her discomfort. Or he chose to ignore it. "You haven't been to the Purple Martin since the beginning of the week."

A nosy man of God who might be matchmaking. "I've been busy, what with helping my daughter-in-law and working at the store."

"So busy you don't have time to visit a friend who's just been diagnosed with a chronic disease and needs his friends around him?"

"Ezekiel has plenty of friends and family to help him out. I offered to cook. He turned me down."

"He did?" Burke sounded stunned.

"See, you don't know everything."

"Neither do you."

They both laughed. The Yutzys stared. The Englisch couple glanced their way and smiled.

"The hamburgers smell good. I'm hungry!" Mary Katherine turned her back on him with as much dignity as she could muster. She said hello to Abigail Plank, who stood behind the tables pushed together to make a long counter. On top were paper plates, condiments, napkins, and plastic silverware. An open cooler held lettuce, onions, tomatoes, and pickles. A second cooler held an assortment of pop. Abigail, who held a spatula in one hand, tugged at a screen she'd laid over the cooler to deter flies and any other bugs that decided to brave the flyswatter hanging from the side of the enormous cast-iron grill that filled the air with hickory-scented smoke.

Burke ordered two burgers with everything on them except onion, two bags of chips, and two individually wrapped brownies. All without consulting her. Abigail wrote it all on a ticket, added it up by hand, and offered the piece of paper to him. Her eyebrows remained hitched up and her lips turned down the entire time. The woman's mother and half a dozen older sisters would know by the end of day that Mary Katherine had been in the burger tent with the Englisch chaplain. Abigail would probably tell them she'd served as a chaperone.

"What kind of pop?"

"A bottle of water."

He paid, she thanked him, and they picked a spot downwind from the smoke and sat. She laid her notebook in front of her and fiddled with her pencil with both hands. "What did Deputy Rogers say about the break-ins? Anything new?"

"He said the break-ins are all at Amish homes. Only small items of little value are taken. Which we already knew." He gave her a rueful smile. "My fingerprints are at two of the homes."

"For reasons that have already been stated."

"Yep, and no suspects. No other fingerprints that are in the system. No witnesses. And no Sunny."

"It's sad that someone would take a man's dog."

"The deputy thinks Sunny ran off. We'd only had him a few weeks. Dan insists he probably went back to his old owner."

"But you don't believe that."

"Sunny adored Ezekiel. The man spoiled the mutt. He was already best buddies with Kenneth's dog, Boo. And he had good chow." He sighed. "I'm sorry I brought him home. Ezekiel didn't have a dog for a reason."

"He didn't want to get attached."

"Exactly."

"I wish we could figure out who's doing this."

"With all those big farms out there, it's a lot of territory for the deputy to cover." Burke snorted. "Especially when the deputy is mostly looking at me."

Deputy Rogers didn't have the good sense God gave him. "He really thinks you did it?"

"He doesn't want to think it's someone local. Easier to blame an outsider he knows burglarized an Amish home." Burke's face was full of regret. "I don't blame him. If it weren't for Carina, he would've thrown me in the slammer."

"Carina is nice."

"Carina saved my life." His fervent response matched the sudden spark of emotion in his face.

"And now she's here checking on you? Are you going back east with her?"

"I don't know. She wants me to." He snapped the

pop-top on his pop can, his forehead wrinkled in concentration. "I keep reminding her she's the one who encouraged me to leave Norfolk."

"To become homeless and hitchhike across the country." Mary Katherine added mustard and catsup to her hamburger even though she'd lost interest in eating it. "Interesting advice from a lady priest."

"She didn't intend for me to be homeless or hitchhike. She said I needed a fresh start." He sipped his pop and set the can on the table. "She probably meant teaching at a university or taking a post at a civilian church. Anyway, enough about me."

"I don't think so."

"Don't be a busybody. My chaplain skills must be rusty. I used to be able to steer these conversations better. I want to help you, not the other way around."

Another man calling her a busybody. "You think me and Ezekiel are your projects."

"You are."

"You're *our* project."

"I'm not anybody's project. Okay, maybe Kenneth's. That boy gives me hope for the world." He dribbled catsup and mustard over his hamburger and smooshed the bun down on the pile of lettuce, tomato, and pickle. "I'm fine."

His concentration on the burger could only mean one thing. "Is Carina a permanent fixture in your life?"

"You mean like a girlfriend-slash-fiancée?"

Mary Katherine had only known the man less than two months. The depth of her need for him to be happy caught her off guard. "Yes."

"Then no. I'm surprised you want to talk about this with me." He took a bite and chewed. Catsup decorated one corner of his mouth. He dabbed at his face with a paper napkin and swallowed. "Do Amish women talk to men about this stuff?"

"No."

"But you do."

"Moses always said I was incapable of keeping my nose in my own business." As recently as today he'd said it. Burke didn't need to know that. "Like you said, a busybody."

"No. A nurturer. In another life you might have been a minister or a psychologist or a social worker. You think you can fix people."

In another life? Burke had an active imagination too. "So do you."

"No. I just figure if I'm focused on others, I'm less likely to fixate on my own woes."

"Did you try to kill yourself after your wife died?" The question popped out. Embarrassment swirled around her. None of her business. Why ask him to tear open an old wound in the process of healing? "You don't have to answer that. Please don't answer that. I'm an idiotic old nosy busybody."

"No, you're not." He folded the remainder of his hamburger into its waxed paper. Sadness permeated his face. He looked older than she did. "The Bible is silent on whether suicide is a sin, but Scripture does say murder is a sin. Isn't killing yourself a form of murder? Only God should decide when it's time for us to go."

Maybe he needed to talk about it. "Does it worry you that you might not see her in heaven?"

"It worries me that I might not get to heaven."

Mary Katherine had that same thought in the dark of night. "Worry is a sin."

He sighed. "Worry is human." Burke plucked a pickle from the waxed paper and ate it plain, his pleasure in his puckered lips.

"Are you afraid to go back?"

He wrapped his napkin around the pop can, soaking up the condensation. "The worst thing that could ever happen to me happened. Then it happened again. I'm not afraid of anything anymore."

"I'm afraid of making the wrong choice." Here she sat in the middle of downtown Jamesport telling an Englisch man her deepest fear. No wonder her sons were concerned about her. Still, he was a preacher. A man who would go away as suddenly as he arrived. "I'm afraid I lack faith."

"I can understand that. Ezekiel is afraid of the same thing."

Mary Katherine dropped the remainder of her hamburger on the paper plate. "You're determined to work him into this conversation."

"Ezekiel is a good man. I'm determined for someone to be happy." Burke opened his bag of chips. It tore in two. Chips scattered across the table. He stared at them as if he couldn't fathom how it happened. "Suffice it to say I don't expect it for me."

Mary Katherine scooped up the chips, dropped them on his paper plate, and brushed the crumbs from the table. People didn't deserve happiness, but if it came their way, it was a blessing from God. "You can't foist happiness on others."

"I'm considering banging their heads together to knock some sense into them." His grin belied the words. "I know it's all about an attitude of gratitude and being thankful for what you do have. Every day I list my blessings. A roof over my head. A job at the Purple Martin. People like you and Ezekiel. I get it. The question is, do you? Do you see what God is giving you? It's right in front of your nose."

The tent flap opened and Carina stepped through. She carried two small brown paper sacks and a larger shopping bag. Smiling, she strode toward them. "I love this place. People are so kind." She slid onto the bench next to Burke and faced Mary Katherine. She handed him the large shopping bag. "I got you something, Mac."

"You shouldn't have." His tone was dry, but he seemed pleased. He pulled out a dark-blue, light-blue, and white block patchwork quilt the right size for a double bed.

"One of Jennie Graber's. Jacob's Ladder." Mary Katherine touched the block patchwork design. An odd gift for a woman to give to a man, but lovely all the same. "One of my favorites."

Burke scowled at Carina. "'He saw a stairway resting on the earth, with its top reaching to heaven, and the angels of God were ascending and descending on it. There above it stood the Lord.' Genesis 28:12."

"'Surely the Lord is in this place, and I was not aware of it.'" Carina continued to smile sweetly. Her gaze encompassed Mary Katherine, but her words were directed at Burke. "'He was afraid and said, "How awe-some is this place! This is none other than the house of God; this is the gate of heaven."'"

"Genesis 28:16–17." Burke's scowl deepened. "If you have something to say, say it."

"Stop pouting and get on with your life. God is with you. If He is for you, who could be against you?"

Mary Katherine eyed the table. She could duck for cover under it or make a run for the door.

"I'm done being a minister."

"You could have fooled me." Mary Katherine made the observation with one hand on the table in case she needed to slide under it. "You've been ministering to me and Ezekiel and Kenneth since you got here."

"That's different. It's called being a friend. I'm done with formal preaching. Who am I to guide a congrega-tion? I couldn't even save my own wife."

The depth of his despair showed in his face for a split second. He grabbed his pop and took a long swallow. The emotion disappeared behind the craggy moun-tains again.

"You're not responsible for your wife's actions. She is." Carina snatched one of Burke's chips and popped it in her mouth. The smile she directed at Mary Katherine was sad. "Men think they're superheroes, don't they?"

Ezekiel didn't aspire to be a superhero, but he did have a stubborn streak similar to Burke's.

He would say the same of her, no doubt. She picked up her trash. Time to run. "I have to get to Jennie's booth."

"Jennie is sweet. Her girls are precious."

The tent flap opened. Thomas and Joanna marched

through, their four youngest with them. Thomas's gaze immediately fell on her. His smile disappeared, replaced by that look like chronic acid indigestion.

"Oh boy." Burke followed her gaze. "Are you in trouble again?"

"Why should I be in trouble?"

"Leaving the cloister."

"I'm not in trouble." Mary Katherine dumped her trash in the rusted blue barrel. "It was good to meet you, Carina."

"See you when you get out of time-out."

Ignoring him, she went to the table where Joanna settled next to the children. "Having fun?"

Joanna's gaze went to Thomas. "The kinner loved the cake walk and the bouncy house."

Thomas settled their youngest, two-year-old Toby, on the bench. He patted the boy's blond head, but his gaze drilled Mary Katherine. "I thought you were working in Jennie's booth."

"I'm headed there now."

"You can't help yourself, can you?" His voice low, he jerked his head toward the table where Carina and Burke sat, still engaged in what appeared to be a heated argument. "You have to step outside the circle."

"I ate a hamburger with friends."

"He may be robbing Plain homes."

"He isn't."

Thomas glared. "Go to work, Mudder. Then come home. Straight home."

"Is Groossmammi in trouble?" Four-year-old Annie looked puzzled. "What did she do?"

"Hush and eat your hot dog." Joanna smoothed the little one's bun. "Don't interrupt when grown-ups are talking."

"I'm not in trouble." Mary Katherine held her son's gaze. "Not today." She wanted to stick her tongue out at Thomas. She refrained. Barely.

She took her time, stopping at the flap opening to look back. Carina leaned toward Burke, her expression intent, her hand on his. She wore no wedding ring.

Maybe Burke wasn't as done as he thought he was. Happiness might be right in front of his nose.

Could it be that it was in front of hers and she couldn't see it either?

CHAPTER 30

Ezekiel lifted two trays high over his head and squeezed past Miriam, who headed the other direction after delivering chicken dinners with all the trimmings to three couples seated by the windows. Pain rippled through his shoulders. His neck throbbed. The Purple Martin was packed to the rafters. Folks enjoying Heritage Days swarmed the restaurant for an Amish meal after making their purchases. It was a mixed blessing. Business was so good he was waiting tables with Miriam and Nicole. Anna would be in for the late shift, along with Burke.

The crowd didn't keep him from missing Mary Katherine. He missed her direct way of talking, the way she carried around a notebook everywhere and scribbled in it. He missed her nosiness and her abrupt smile. He missed kissing her. She'd hadn't graced the Purple Martin with her presence in almost a week. He shouldn't have pressed her to cook. He shouldn't expect her to give up her dream for his.

Since when did Plain women have dreams that didn't involve Plain men? What drew him to Mary

Katherine was that which kept him from having her. She was different.

He also missed Sunny. The slobbery mess of puppy bones and loose skin.

Not now. He was too busy to think about kisses or dogs.

The crash of china breaking followed by bellows of laughter stopped conversation around him. He eased around, trays still in the air, to see Nicole's miserable face as she squatted to pick up a pile of dirty dishes, some of them shattered, two tables over. The core of the boys' basketball team lounged around a table near the front. Two snapped photos with their smartphones, then proceeded with the thumb typing that meant the photo was about to fly off somewhere.

"You poor girl, Nicole." Bobby Davidson, captain of the basketball team and cleanup hitter for the school's baseball team, patted her dark head with a hand made to palm a basketball. "Maybe you can get a job making beds at the motel. You couldn't break anything there."

Nicole didn't answer. Her fair skin blanched whiter against almost-black hair. She kept picking up the pieces. Tony had called in sick, which meant the servers were doing double duty busing the dishes and cleaning the tables on one of the busiest days of fall. Unusual for him. Tony was as reliable as a Standardbred. Ezekiel slid two hot plates of french dip sandwiches and home fries, along with two plates of pork chops, mashed potatoes, gravy, and green beans onto the booth table. His customers agreed they needed nothing more at that moment, so Ezekiel went to help Nicole.

She rose as he approached. The shoulders of her painfully thin body were hunched. "I'm sorry, Mr. Miller."

"Accidents happen."

"Nicole is an accident waiting to happen." His arm, bicep bulging, propped on his buddy's chair, Bobby leaned back. He was a tall blond who favored jeans and camouflage jackets during hunting season. Today he wore sweats and a team jacket. "Coach says so. He said she was born with two left feet."

"Her feet are fine. You boys want dessert, or are you ready for your tickets?"

"I want pie. Can you bring me pie à la mode with a side of your sweet smile?" Mark Meade, a redheaded, oversized junior who did double duty as a basketball guard and a baseball catcher, swiped at Nicole with one meaty hand. "And fill up my tea glass again, will you? Thanks, babe."

Nicole jumped back. The tray hit the floor a second time. She burst into tears. "I'm so sorry, boss." She shot toward the kitchen.

Ezekiel knelt and picked up the dishes. He used the time to count to ten. Customers were customers, but that didn't give them the right to harass a young girl. He stood. "I'll be back with your pie."

"That's okay, Pops, let Nicole bring it." Bobby slapped Mark on the back and smirked. Mark shrugged, but a scarlet blush overtook his abundant freckles. "That's what you pay her for, isn't it?"

A strong urge to wipe the insolent grin off the boy's face by taking a hickory switch to his behind in the nearest woodshed blew through Ezekiel like a summer tornado. He gritted his teeth and counted to twenty. Then he set the tray on the table and settled into a chair across from Bobby and his laughing cohorts. "I know your dad. He and your mom eat here pretty regular." He picked up a nearly empty bottle of catsup and added it to the tray. "I know he taught you better than to be mean to girls. It's not a manly thing to do. You all are nearly men. Old enough where I come from to be treated like men. Men treat women with respect. Plus, I imagine Coach would have something to say about you treating his daughter this way."

"We're just teasing her." Bobby's sneer had lost some of its luster. Mark and his buddies, Trevor Watkins and Logan Reynolds, stared at the table, their hands messing with crumbs and splotches of pop. "We don't mean anything by it."

"Bottom line is that I reserve the right not to serve folks who misbehave in the Purple Martin. If you can't be polite to your server, then it's best that you find someplace else to get your hamburgers and pie."

He held the boy's gaze for a minute longer. Bobby didn't flinch. He was used to being a big fish in a little pond, All-state basketball, baseball, and track and field. Nothing that meant anything to Ezekiel, but the kids at the school seemed to idolize him. "I'll check on your desserts."

He headed back to the kitchen to find Nicole. She cut apple pie with shaking hands that threatened to spill blood.

"Let me do that. You get the ice cream." He took the

knife from her and made quick work of sliding pie onto the saucers while she went to the freezer. "What is going on with you and those boys? I've never seen you have trouble with them before."

A few jabs here and there about being the coach's daughter, but nothing as belittling as what he'd witnessed today. "It's nothing." Her gray eyes were red rimmed. "They just like to give me a hard time. My mom says it's their way of showing affection."

Phoebe Wilson had a strange notion of affection. But teenage boys were strange animals. "I don't think your dad would feel that way. Why don't you say something to him?"

"I'm not a tattletale. I'm a cheerleader. I spend a lot of time with these guys." Her face filled with grim determination. "You can't tell. He doesn't want anything interfering with their concentration."

"I won't tell, but I think you should. Regardless, I won't allow them to treat my servers like that. I let them know it. I'll take out the desserts."

"No, please don't do that. I promise not to break any more plates."

"I'm not worried about the plates." He exchanged glances with Esther, another new hire who now served as one of his early shift cooks. She shrugged and shook her head before going back to a basket of chicken crackling in the deep fryers. "I'm worried about a server being mistreated by my customers."

"It has nothing to do with you or the restaurant. They're just mad because I refused to do something they asked me to do." Her voice trailed away. She flinched and her lips formed a silent O. She rubbed her forehead. "Forget I said that."

The last words were stuttered.

Ezekiel's mouth went dry. His armpits began to sweat. He was not the person to have this conversation. Esther had the freezer door open and she was rummaging inside. He opened his mouth. Closed it. *Gott, are You really calling on me to have this conversation with an Englisch girl?*

He looked around. He was the only person available. "You shouldn't ever feel obligated or pressured . . . I'm sure your mother would tell you that you did the right thing. You know that, don't you?"

She backed away from the counter, the tray in front of her like a shield between them. "No, no, no, that's not what I meant at all." She grabbed the saucers and plopped them one by one on the tray. "I can't believe I, that you, I mean, that you think that they, that I . . . Never mind. Gross."

With a look on her face that Ezekiel had seen on deer fleeing hunters, she rushed through the swinging doors.

"You get her straightened out?" Esther slapped the freezer door shut, a bag of frozen home fries in one hand. "Poor thing is unhappier than a cat having a bath."

He didn't answer. Instead he grabbed a pitcher of iced tea and went to fill some glasses. After Nicole delivered the pie without incident, he made his way through the tables, dispensing tea as he went, until he reached the row one over from the athletes' table. They devoured the pie and ice cream while staring at phone screens. He turned his back and offered tea to Jon Peterson, an elderly patron who never turned down a refill—if only because it didn't cost him anything.

Ezekiel poured and listened, careful to keep his smile in place.

"She's gonna tell."

Mark Meade's voice.

"Is not. Nicole's not like that."

That was Bobby.

"We shouldn't have asked her. She's Coach's daughter."

One of the other boys. Ezekiel couldn't be sure which one without looking.

"Coach is the one who said we needed to have traditions." Bobby sounded less sure of himself. "We're just having fun."

"I don't think he was talking about this kind of tradition." Mark again, his tone full of sarcasm.

"How do you know? Remember the stories he told us on the bus?" Bobby's voice dropped and it became more difficult for Ezekiel to hear. He used his apron to wipe spilled water off a newly vacated table and moved closer. "He spent the night in jail for stealing the principal's car when he was in high school."

"He didn't tell us. He told Coach Reeves. He thought we were all asleep." One of the other boys.

"Naw. He knew. It's not like we stole a car. Not even close." Bobby again.

What *had* they stolen? Ezekiel moved to the next table, but the customer, an Englisch lady with a cranky toddler, waved him away and went back to the cell phone in her hand. Sports rivalries in the Englisch schools often led to mascots—including live animals—being stolen on the night before big games, but nothing had been in the local weekly this fall about such shenanigans.

He rounded the end of the row and moved back toward the boys. Bobby met his gaze. He leaned into Mark and his voice dropped to a whisper.

Ezekiel kept walking. "You boys want some more tea?"

"No, thanks. We're headed out." Bobby stood so quickly he knocked his chair back. He dug into his jeans pocket and pulled out a crumpled dollar bill. He threw it on the table. "Tell Nicole we were just giving her a hard time. We'll see her at the game tonight."

He sounded sorry. He looked sorry. Still, Ezekiel wasn't buying it. "I think she's aware of the hard time. Tell her yourself. You could do it now."

"I have to go home and get ready for the game." Bobby shrugged on his leather letter jacket and shoved blond bangs from his face. "I need to feed my dog too."

The other boys guffawed. A look of disbelief on his face, Mark elbowed Bobby. "Let's go. Coach'll be POed if we're late."

Ezekiel trained his gaze on the other boys. "Don't forget to tip your server."

The identical process of digging and producing crumpled bills followed. At least Nicole would get a semi-decent tip out of it.

They paraded from the restaurant in that typical muscle-bound gait employed by athletes who worked out seven days a week. Burke bustled in before the door could shut completely. He rubbed his hands together. "It's cold today."

"Come back in the kitchen. Hurry up."

"I'm coming, I'm coming. What's your hurry?" He glanced at the beat-up watch with a leather strap on his wrist. "It's two. I'm not late."

"No, you're not late. Wash up while I talk."

Nicole was in the kitchen. She'd removed her apron and had her time card in her hand. Ezekiel held out his hand for the apron. "Would you mind clearing the team's table before you head out? They're gone."

"Sure, Mr. Miller." Her smile wasn't convincing. "I just have to get moving. The cheerleaders are meeting before the game."

"They left you a nice tip."

"Thanks to you." This time the smile lit up her face. "You're a good boss."

"I try."

She pushed through the swinging doors.

"What was that all about?" Burke plunged his hands into hot water and began to scrub up like a surgeon.

Ezekiel talked fast. Nicole would be back any second.

"You think they were talking about the break-ins?" He dried his hands on a clean towel. "Some tradition."

"They looked really guilty when I came back with the tea."

"I don't know. I have more experience with the real world than you do." Burke pulled off a sweater, revealing a Purple Martin T-shirt. He hung the sweater from a hook next to the servers' jackets. "I hate to say it, but your first inclination with Nicole is more likely true. In this day and age, boys are looking to . . . I'm trying to think of the least offensive word—"

"I get the drift." Ezekiel scratched his cheek and contemplated such a world. His girls chose baptism and good men as their husbands. Blessings. The Englisch world often seemed a sad place for young people. "You could be right, but that comment about feeding the dog is bugging me."

"He wouldn't take somebody else's dog home. Wouldn't his parents ask where it came from?"

Ezekiel started to answer. Nicole pushed through the doors with the boys' dirty dessert dishes and tea glasses. He took the tray from her. "Go to your game. Enjoy it."

The girls' cheerleading outfits left little to the imagination. Another reason to be thankful his daughters freely and gladly chose the Plain way of life.

"I'll try." She pulled on her fleece-lined jean jacket and let down her ponytail. "Those guys aren't so bad. Really."

She slipped through the doors before he could respond.

"She was in tears a few minutes ago."

"Don't you remember the teenage years?"

"I do." Without a wife to lead the way. God had blessed him with sisters to help his daughters navigate those years. "I'd like to take a drive tomorrow. Past where those boys live. Some are in town, but at least three live on farms or have grandparents who do. Mark Meade's dad farms out west of town. So does Bobby Davidson's granddad."

"Do you plan to drive up to the house and ask them if their sons or grandsons are thieves? Or recently brought home a stray dog?"

"I'll just ask them if they've heard anything about the break-ins or seen anything or had anything stolen themselves. That should stir the pot."

Burke grabbed a paper towel and dried his hands. "Toward what end?"

"Maybe it'll scare them into stopping. That's all I really want."

"You don't want to tell Deputy Doolittle and let him handle it?"

"Tell him what? Some teenagers were giving a girl a hard time? They stole something from somewhere sometime? One had a dog to feed?"

Burke snatched the first order up on the wire and perused it. "I'm sure Carina would be happy to serve as taxi."

"After church and lunch. You're invited. Both of you. As always."

"Carina's going over to the Baptist church."

"And you?"

"We'll see."

Which meant no. "For a religious man, you're sure working hard to avoid the body of Christ."

"For a Plain man, you're sure working hard to stick your nose where it doesn't belong."

Freeman would probably agree. If Ezekiel wasn't careful, he might get it chopped off.

CHAPTER 31

No rest for the weary. Which was a good thing. It kept Mary Katherine's mind off her troubles. Her small, insignificant troubles. She clucked at the horse and the buggy picked up its pace. She needed more thread and material from the Sweet Notions store. Her to-do list included more pot holders, dresser scarves, and tablecloths for the Combination Store. If she could get several of each done over the next week, she'd be caught up and she would stay out of trouble.

She sang "In the Garden" as she rounded the corner onto Grant Street, to drown out the naysayers and make room for God in the day. Movement in front of Bob Sampson's vacant storefront caught her gaze. Two workers on ladders hoisted a sign between them, balancing it over the large windows that ran along the lower front wall to the double glass doors.

The sign read THE BOOK APOTHECARY. Underneath in smaller, fancy script letters: *We have the prescription for your reading addiction.*

Mary Katherine pulled on the reins. The buggy halted in the middle of the street. A strident horn

bellowed. She moved to the curb, ignoring the No
HITCHING NO PARKING sign.

A handwritten sign hung in the window that read
GRAND OPENING COMING SOON.

Dottie had pursued the dream without her.

The agonizing ache spread from the center of her
chest in all directions. Her head ached. Her fingernails
ached. Her toes ached. Drawing a single breath hurt.

The part of her that wanted to see this dream in-
carnate wrangled with the part that called it masochis-
tic. Mary Katherine hopped from the buggy. She wasn't
such a small person that she couldn't congratulate her
friend and wish her well.

Her hand felt slick on the door handle. Sweat
trickled down her temples despite the late October
breeze. She heaved a breath and entered.

Her silver hair in a straggly bun on the top of her
head, Dottie stood with her back to the door. As she
painted the far wall a pale eggshell blue, she sang along
to a country music song blaring from an old-fashioned
boombox radio nestled on a shelf next to a plastic bottle
of water covered with condensation. She wore a paint-
stained, long-sleeved white T-shirt, faded jeans, and
spattered tennis shoes that had once been white too.
Her voice soared with the music, hitting every note of a
song about giving the Tin Man a scarred heart. She had
a beautiful voice.

"Dottie?"

She plopped the roller in the flat pan and moved over
a pace.

"Dottie."

Still nothing. Mary Katherine flipped the radio switch. Dottie's voice petered out after a few seconds. She turned and smiled. "You're here."

"You didn't tell me."

"I didn't want you to think I was rubbing it in." She scratched her nose and left a blob of paint on its tip. "After I got the insurance money, I had to move quickly before Bob sold to someone else."

"I understand."

"I know you do." She turned and went back to painting. "I started ordering inventory yesterday. I missed you. You have such good taste. Your opinion means a lot to me."

"I'm sure you did fine without me. I don't know if ordering the books would be more fun or opening the boxes and putting them on the shelves."

"I like feeling them in my hands." Dottie laid the roller in the pan. She cocked her head from side to side to pop her neck and rubbed her right arm. "I ordered all the so-called Amish romances the tourists will love. You'd be amazed at how many there are." She gestured toward the front windows. "I'll have a whole section right by the door to catch their eye when they walk in."

Her own blue eyes were brilliant, her smile as wide as any since Walt's death. She was seeing it in her mind's eye. She padded in her paint-spattered sneakers to a spot farther to the east. "Here I'll have a section for herbal medicines, home health remedies, and gardening for my Plain friends." She swept her arms in a half circle. "Then we'll need a spot for story hour. You'll do *Noah's Ark* and *Jonah in the Belly of the Whale*. I'll do

Llama Llama Red Pajama and *What the Dinosaurs Did Last Night*."

"I'll do story hour?"

"Of course, my guest teller."

"You'll need a section for cookbooks."

Dottie swept back wisps of hair and left a blob of paint on her forehead. "Cookbooks. Of course. Amish cookbooks will be a big seller with the tourists."

"I was thinking of a cookbook for diabetics. Do you know if you have one at the library?"

"Why the sudden interest?"

"A friend."

"We do, I'm sure. But I'll order one for you." Dottie grabbed the water bottle and took a long swig. She set it down and wiped her mouth with her sleeve. "Cookbooks are meant to be used over and over. Do you like the paint?"

"I do."

"Good." Dottie smiled. "It makes me think of you."

"It does?"

"Your curiosity, your energy, everything about you is like sky. Endless and indefatigable. I never know what you'll come up with." Dottie pointed one finger at her and wiggled it. "What new project or idea or story. Being your friend makes my life fun and makes me better."

Mary Katherine opened her mouth. No words came out. She sank into the only chair in the room. A lawn chair with frayed woven strips for a seat that groaned under her weight. "I want this so much. It makes me ashamed how much I want it."

"There's no shame in having a dream."

"You see things differently than we do. We're to put others ahead of ourselves. God, then community, then self."

"I know. I hate it. Just kidding." Her expression dark, Dottie squatted. She pried open a can of paint and stirred it with a stick. "Do what you have to do, but don't kick yourself about it. You're only human."

"It's not just that." Mary Katherine studied her hands in her lap. "There's someone."

"Someone. A man. You didn't tell me." Cackling, Dottie dropped the stick and clapped. "Woo-hoo! Tell me. Tell all. Who is it?"

"Nothing to tell. He wants a fraa—a wife—who wants what he wants. Like all husbands do. He has something important in his life he needs help with. He thinks I want this more."

"You're not going to tell me who it is?"

"Nee."

"Is he right?"

Mary Katherine rose and went to the empty shelves covered with paint drop cloths. She touched the dusty canvas. "I thought I wanted this more, but I miss him when I don't see him every day. I miss everything about him. I think about him all the time. Like a lovesick girl. It's embarrassing. Shameful."

"I can't imagine feeling that for anyone but my Walt." Dottie's eyes reddened. She wiped at her nose with her sleeve and sniffed. "But there's nothing shameful about it. You've been alone a long time. I think Moses would approve."

Moses did approve. "If Walt told you he didn't want you to open a bookstore, would you set aside your dream?"

"He wouldn't do that, but if I thought he disapproved, I would think long and hard about it. I valued his opinion." Dottie leaned back and sat cross-legged, arms behind her. "If he had a dream that was really important to him, I'd support him all the way. Walt never liked being an accountant all that much. He wanted to be a teacher, but his dad was an accountant and he wanted Walt to join his business. So he did. He never complained, but numbers never lit him up like books do me. Life is short. You and I know that. We have to figure out what's important to us and the people we love. Then we must do that thing."

Dottie had come a long way in a short time. Much faster than Mary Katherine. The thought shamed her even more. "You're such a wise woman."

"I'm hanging by a thread. Every day I wonder if this will be the day the thread breaks and I fall."

"Neither one of us is falling." Mary Katherine knelt and hugged her. "We have the Lord and good friends."

"You'll get paint on you." Laughing, Dottie returned the hug. "Do you like the name? The Book Apothecary."

"I do."

"It's my prescription for healing me."

"I know."

"I don't know if it'll work, but at least I'm sleeping at night. I'm too exhausted not to."

"It's a start."

"My kids think I'm crazy."

"There's a lot of that going around."

They laughed together.

"It could be your prescription too."

"I'm fine." Knees cracking, back aching, Mary Katherine hopped to her feet. "When do the rest of the shelves get here?"

"Did you hear? Leo's making them for me."

"*Wunderbarr!*"

"I think so. We'll have an unpacking party when the books arrive."

"I should go." Mary Katherine picked up her bag and strode to the door. "I'm happy for you. You'll have your dream."

"I'd give it up faster than a flash of lightning if it meant getting Walt back." Sorrow swiped at her face, her smile gone. She gazed at something beyond Mary Katherine, beyond the walls of the store. "I miss him so much my teeth hurt. My fingernails hurt. My toes hurt. Everything in between hurts."

"I know."

"A bookstore is only a building. The love of a good man is everything."

Those words swirling around her so fast and hard she could barely see to navigate, Mary Katherine fled.

CHAPTER 32

A gunshot. Mary Katherine jerked straight up in bed. A gunshot echoed in that empty field half-way between sleep and wakefulness. The murky night quivered with the ensuing silence.

She closed her eyes and opened them. Her eyes adjusted to the dark. Her room was empty.

She had to think for a minute. Where was she? The dawdy haus. Yes, the dawdy haus outside Thomas's house. Her new home now that it was shipshape. The cough of a car engine that sputtered, then died. A backfire, not a gunshot.

Uneasiness wrapped itself around her chest and squeezed. Another burglary in the making? Brazen thieves ready to break in while she was home? While Thomas and Joanna slept in the big house. And their kinner. Fear mingled with uneasiness. If they broke into the big house, they might wake the kinner. They might come downstairs and find the burglars at work.

She didn't have Moses' shotgun anymore. Dylan kept it in the move. She threw off the sheets and hopped from the bed. She made quick work of her dress. Her heart pounded in her ears. Her fingers shook. Who were these people to prey on Plain folks who did nothing but mind their own business? They could have her stuff, all of it, but they might not understand that Plain people wouldn't fight them for those belongings.

The engine whirred and coughed again, a weak, sickly sound that quickly faded into nothingness.

The thieves should've chosen a better car.

Thieves in general weren't very smart or they wouldn't be stealing. They'd be earning an honest living.

Mary Katherine stomped into the kitchen and grabbed her broom. She lit the lantern she kept on the kitchen table. Her hands stopped shaking. The scent of phosphorus and kerosene must be what hell smelled like. Fueled by indignation that leaped like a gasoline-fueled fire, she marched to the front door and threw it open. One deep breath and she flung herself onto the porch. "Who's there?"

Her bare foot hit something small sitting directly in front of the door. She stumbled. Her arms flew out. The lantern slipped from her hand and fell into the yard. The sense that this had happened to her before galloped through her, borne on the chilly autumn wind. She summoned every ounce of strength to keep from falling.

Instead, she plopped facedown in the cold grass. Her nose stung. Her shoulder ached. *Please, Gott, don't let me start a fire.* She pushed back and managed to sit up on her knees. She grabbed the lantern and set it upright. The flame miraculously held steady.

It didn't matter. The headlights of a car blinded her. The engine whirred. It sounded cranky. It started, revved, died.

Leaves rustled in the breeze, sending a shiver through her. The headlights died. Blessed darkness.

A car door slammed.

The thief coming after her.

Mary Katherine felt around on the ground until her hand connected with the broom. Hauling herself to her feet, she brandished it at the dark. "Who is it and what do you want?"

"Why are you sweeping in the middle of the night, Miz Ropp?"

Disappointment at the familiar voice cascaded through Mary Katherine. "Tony? You're the thief?" Ezekiel trusted the boy, and he was a good judge of character. Tony had worked at the restaurant for two years. He was always polite and never shirked his duties. "How could you?"

He slammed to a halt just out of reach of her broom. "No, ma'am. No way."

"What are you doing here then?" She scooped up the lantern with her free hand and backed toward the porch. "Planning to rob me again? Making the rounds? Shame on you!"

"No, no, it's not like that at all." He moved toward her. "I'll show you."

Her hand tightened on the broom. "Stay back."

"Look on the porch. I was returning your stuff, not stealing it."

Mary Katherine risked a glance back. A tattered cardboard box lay on its side. The contents were strewn across the porch. She held the lantern up higher. Her enamel box, the chess pieces, and the mantel clock.

"Why would you steal from me and then return

my stuff?" She dropped the broom and sat, her legs suddenly weak. She settled the lantern next to her and picked up a black bishop carved from walnut. It felt solid and heavy in her hand. Moses' fingers had touched it many times over the years. A knot formed in her throat. She closed her eyes and breathed the night air. In and out.

She stared up at Tony in his ragged, long-sleeved Keith Urban T-shirt and faded jeans. "For jollies, on a whim, on a dare? Why?"

"I didn't steal from you. I promise." Tony tossed his long braid over his shoulder. His beseeching tone matched the look on his face. "I stole from someone else."

"Who? Why?"

"I can't tell you that." He edged toward his car, a dark-colored four-door that looked like it was held together by duct tape and chicken wire. "This stinks. The plan was to give your stuff back and get out of here. Nobody would know."

He kicked a tire with a scuffed Roper boot. "Stupid car. I just replaced the battery and put in a new starter. What is it now?"

"Why would you bring my things back? And how did you know where I live?"

Sighing, he hoisted himself onto the car's front end and propped his angular chin on his hands. "Because you were nice to Nicole. Because I listen. People talk at the restaurant. Your daughters. Your sons. Everyone. You moved from your house over here a couple of weeks ago. Besides, it's a small town. Everyone knows everyone's business."

How he knew didn't really matter. What mattered was the return of these stolen items. It didn't make sense. It was impossible to imagine Nicole sneaking into houses and stealing. Or tearing up the place like someone had done at Ezekiel's. "Did Nicole steal my stuff?"

"No. Seriously?" Even more adamant than before. "She's not like that. Nicole's cool. She's smart and works hard. She's going to college. She wouldn't do something stupid like this."

"Then what does my being nice to Nicole have to do with this stuff being taken?"

"I gave her a ride home from the restaurant last week. She was upset." Tony rubbed his eyes with both fists. He tapped his boot on the fender. "She told me some things. Things I promised not to repeat. But I didn't promise not to do anything about it. I decided to give some people a taste of their own medicine. That's all."

He decided to come to the aid of a girl he liked. A nice girl. A nice boy. Trying to do a nice thing. He needed to see that it was also important to do the right thing. "Would you like some hot chocolate?"

"I should go."

"I have peanut butter–chocolate chip cookies."

"I'm in."

After she had him settled at the kitchen table with his hot chocolate, complete with extra miniature marshmallows and two large cookies, Mary Katherine tried again. "Who's stealing from the Amish families and why?"

Tony's gaze bounced around the kitchen as if he might make a run for it. He took another large bite of cookie and chewed. Mary Katherine gave him her best you'd-better-tell-Mother-before-I-take-you-to-the-woodshed look. He squirmed and took a sip of the hot chocolate. "It's a game."

"I don't understand."

"The things they take are the prizes. The trophies. They have a trophy case, with the names and dates under the trophies. That's how I knew which things were yours."

"Who? Where?"

"I go to a really small school. I'm not a jock and I don't care about being popular, but I still have to get by for two more years before I can join the military. My life in this two-horse town is over if I snitch."

"Your parents taught you to be a good person, I can see that."

"They were migrant workers before we settled down here. They try to be, you know, worthy of the good things they get. That's how my mom says it. We should work hard and be good in exchange for what we've been given."

"Your mother is right. She taught you the difference between right and wrong."

"Yeah, sure."

"Do you think what these kids are doing is right?"

"No way."

"Is the way they're treating Nicole right?"

"No, hel—heck no."

"I understand you not being able to tell me who it is, but what if you told me where you found my things? The place where all the stolen stuff is? Just the place."

His forehead wrinkled in a frown, Tony gobbled the rest of his second cookie. He picked at the crumbs and tossed them in his mouth. He sipped his cocoa. He burped behind his hand, then wiped his mouth with his sleeve.

Mary Katherine waited, her own cup nestled tightly in hands that barely felt its heat as she anticipated his answer.

He rolled his eyes and sighed. "Are you gonna do something about these guys—people?"

"Yes. Maybe—probably not me personally. I'm not sure how, but yes, something will be done."

"I could tell you where, I guess. But it has to be like an anonymous tip. Like somebody left a note or called the sheriff or something like that."

For a second she feared the hooray had been said aloud. "I won't tell anyone it was you."

"I can even draw you a map." He grinned. "Even better, if I get my car started, I can show you."

CHAPTER 33

I f Thomas found out about this, Mary Katherine was
toast. History. Banished to the woodshed like a
naughty child for the rest of her life. Or called in for
counseling with Freeman again. A kneeling confession
before the church. What Ordnung rule was she breaking, exactly? She wasn't sure, but there had to be one
or even several. Was solving this mystery and stopping
the "game" that victimized her community wrong? Or
was it simply wrong for a Plain woman to get involved
instead of leaving it to the men?

It wasn't the stuff that was important, it was the idea
that making people uneasy and insecure in their own
homes was funny, somehow. The unintended conse-
quence was the testing of their faith. That God had this
under control. That He had a plan. That something
good would come from it. What it was, remained to be
seen. In time.

Surely.

Tony's car bumped, shook, and shimmied in the
deep ruts of the dirt road that led to William and Leah
Gingerich's farm and Ezekiel's dawdy haus. Tony's car
had obliged them by starting after a string of mutter-
ings from the boy that ranged from prayers to curses

followed by apologies. He had a mouth on him. His mother would have washed it out with soap. They hit another bump and Mary Katherine bounced. She grabbed the door handle.

More curses. Some in Spanish. More apologies. "Sorry. It needs a new suspension." Tony steered toward the middle of the road again. "It used to be my brother's car. He passed it down when he joined the Navy."

"That was nice of him."

"All the Lopezes go into the military. That's how we get an education and serve the country we adopted."

"Good for you."

"Yeah. Whatever. Nicole probably doesn't think so."

It didn't seem right to tell him about her conversation with Nicole only a few weeks earlier. Something about Mary Katherine seemed to invite confidences. Her grandma face? Or the lateness of the hour and the darkness. "Have you asked her?"

Tony snorted. "I haven't even asked her on a date."

"Does she know about what you did tonight?"

"No, and you can't tell her."

"Why?"

"I'm just the guy who buses dirty dishes at the Purple Martin." He shrugged bony shoulders. "She thinks I'm a loser."

She did not. Her questions the night Mary Katherine gave her a ride home made that obvious—to Mary Katherine. She bit her lip. "All hard work is honorable. I'm sure Nicole knows that. She let you give her a ride. She must think you're an okay guy."

"I don't know why girls make it so hard for guys to

tell. We're the ones who have to do the asking. They should give us hints."

"You should give Nicole a chance. Don't count yourself out without trying."

He pulled in front of Ezekiel's house and turned off the engine. "You think Mr. E. wants to go?"

"Yes. Go knock. When he comes to the door, tell him what you told me."

"Me?" Tony's voice ratcheted up two notches to a squeak. "I thought you were going to tell him."

"I can't. I'm a woman. I shouldn't be at his house in the middle of the night."

"This ain't the fifties." Tony looked genuinely confused. "Are you serious?"

Some might call it splitting hairs. Mary Katherine sat in a car driven by an Englisch teenager in the middle of the night. She likely couldn't make it much worse by knocking on Ezekiel's door. "Please."

"He's gonna be mad."

"Not at you."

"Fine." Tony shoved his door open and got out. Then he turned back and stuck his head through the open window. "If he shoots me, tell my mom I love her."

"Go."

. . .

Kerosene lamp in one hand, Ezekiel shuffled to the door. His heart hammered in his chest. Someone pounding on his door in the middle of the night would not bring good news. "I'm coming. Hold your horses!"

"Mr. E., it's me, Tony."

Ezekiel tugged the door open.

Tony Lopez stood on his porch, looking as if he expected a mountain of hurt to come tumbling down on him. "Hey."

Ezekiel rubbed his eyes to make sure he wasn't sleepwalking. His busboy was standing on his porch in the middle of the night. "Did something happen at the restaurant? What are you doing here?"

"Miz Ropp told me to come get you. She's waiting out in the car for you."

Ezekiel squinted. Maybe he should pinch himself to make sure he was awake. It had to be a dream. Mary Katherine would not get in a car with his busboy and drive to Ezekiel's house at . . . "What time is it?"

Tony glanced at the phone clutched in his hand. "One a.m."

At one in the morning. For a Plain woman, Mary Katherine had gumption. And then some. But she was also a mother and grandmother senior in age who knew what was expected of her. "Are you telling me Mary Kay is in your car right now?"

"Right now. Yes, sir."

"Don't sir me. Why is she in your car at my house at one o'clock in the morning?"

Tony whizzed through an explanation so bizarre Ezekiel considered the pinch again. "Now. She wants to go now?"

The boy nodded. He glanced over his shoulder. Ezekiel glanced with him. In the wavering lamplight, not much was visible. A beat-up old car on its last tire.

"She's pretty set on it." He paused, then shrugged. "Me too."

"Why is that?"

"I think there's a dog out there. I heard it bark. There was a padlock on the door. I didn't have any way to get it off. I saw lights up on the road so I didn't have time to look around anymore. I didn't want to get caught. We shouldn't leave a dog out there."

Sunny. "I'll get my clothes on."

Ezekiel whirled. He nearly ran into Burke, who stood in the hallway in a pair of blue flannel pajama pants and a white T-shirt. "What's going on?"

He explained. Burke rubbed his five o'clock shadow, then his eyes. "I'm right behind you."

"You don't have to go."

"Sunny's my dog too."

Fair enough. "Hurry up."

Five minutes later they were crammed into the backseat of Tony's ancient car with its peeling paint and nonexistent heater. Ezekiel laid the bolt cutters on the floor at his feet. He shivered and tugged his coat tighter across his belly.

Burke huddled next to him. His hands were stuffed in the pockets of a dark-green sweatshirt hoodie. "Whose property is it?"

"I don't know." Tony muttered something under his breath as the car's engine coughed and sputtered. A buggy would've been faster—and safer. "Some farmer."

"Is it Mark Meade's dad or Bobby Davidson's grandpa?" Those were the two Ezekiel knew were farmers. The rest lived in town. "How could they not know this was going on?"

The car jerked slightly to one side. Tony cursed. "Sorry. Nope. What makes you think that? It's some Amish dude."

Mary Katherine hadn't spoken since they left Ezekiel's house. Now she turned and craned her head toward the back. "I know I should've stayed home. I could've sent Tony to—"

"You couldn't stand it, knowing we were solving this mystery and having an adventure like the ones in your stories." Ezekiel smiled at her. He couldn't help it. Mary Katherine didn't have a proud bone in her body. She was humble. She accepted Moses' death as God's will. She even gave up her dream of owning a bookstore as God's will. But she didn't abide by wrongdoing that affected her family and her community. And she was stubborn. "If there is punishment to be had, I'll take it."

Burke's laugh turned into a cough. He put his hand to his mouth. Ezekiel glared at him.

Mary Katherine faced the passenger-side window. "If it comes to that, I'll take my own punishment."

"Punishment for what? You guys didn't do anything." Tony shook his head so hard his braid flopped. "You Plain folks are weird."

"That's a compliment, believe it or not." Ezekiel leaned against the torn vinyl seat and watched the dark night flash by. He couldn't make out any details. Life was like that sometimes. It flashed by so fast he couldn't recall how he'd gotten to this day, this moment. "If we find something, we'll have to tell Freeman."

"It will be necessary." Mary Katherine's tone was calm. "He'll know what to do next."

Regardless of the consequences. Ezekiel would like to spare her those consequences. Or face them with her.

The car shuddered, its frame shook, the motor revved. Tony cussed. This time louder.

Burke leaned forward and patted his shoulder. "You catch more flies with honey than vinegar, son."

"Don't give up on me now, baby, come on, girl." Tony patted the dash. "You're a peach, babe."

"My first car was an Impala, standard V-8, baby blue," Burke explained. "I called her baby too."

Ezekiel shook his head. "I guess I love my horses too, but I don't call them baby."

Tony made a sudden right turn off the highway onto a dirt road. Everyone heaved left and then straightened.

"Why did you turn here?" Mary Katherine echoed the question one second after Ezekiel voiced it.

"This is the way." Tony leaned forward, arms around the wheel as if peering beyond the headlights. "The turnoff is somewhere up ahead on the left."

Her eyebrows arched, Mary Katherine swiveled and looked back. Consternation ran rampant in her face.

Likely she could see it in Ezekiel's as well.

"What is it? Whose property is this?" Burke leaned toward his window and peered into the dark.

"Freeman's."

A few seconds later, Tony swerved again. They all heaved right and then straightened. They bounced along a dirt road with ruts so deep a wagon could disappear in them.

Another right turn onto a road—more of a narrow path. The route didn't lead to Freeman's house, for which Ezekiel gave thanks. The path ended. They drove through high grasses and wove between trees. The headlights bounced up and down in a crazy, dizzying pattern. "How did you ever find this?"

"I followed Ma—one of them out here. After . . . the person left, I snooped around and found Miz Ropp's stuff." Tony's voice was matter-of-fact. "Your stuff is there too, but I didn't have time to get it. I was sure Ma—he was coming back."

They rounded a curve, a second one, and finally came to a stop. "It's over that little rise there. I don't want to get too close in case someone is there." Tony turned off the engine and killed the lights. "I have a couple of flashlights. I keep an emergency kit in the trunk because this heap is always breaking down."

They climbed out and followed him up the slope. Ezekiel let Mary Katherine go first. Her breathing came light and fast. Her sneakers slipped in the loose dirt. She stumbled. He took the opportunity to grab her arm. "I've got you."

She looked back. Her expression was lost in the shadows of clouds rambling across the sky, capturing the moon, and then letting it escape. "Danki."

A smile chimed in the single word. She was getting her adventure. Crazy thing for a Plain woman of a certain age to want, but he understood—a little. Besides, if she wanted it, he wanted it for her. She wasn't getting her bookstore. She could use this in a story someday. A story he hoped to read.

At the top Tony hunkered down in the tall grass and pointed. "That's it."

It was the shambled remnants of a small, two-story stone house. The clouds scattered and the half moon shone down on it. Abandoned. Gray. Perfect in its isolation. Someone had boarded up the windows with plywood. The wood porch had disintegrated until only four steps a few feet from the sagging door were left.

"How far are we from Freeman's farmhouse?" Mary Katherine knelt next to Ezekiel. Her voice held trepidation. "Does he know he has outbuildings this far out, do you think?"

"A couple of miles. I reckon Freeman has been over every inch of this property since he bought it thirty years or more ago." Ezekiel swatted a swarm of gnats. "He may not have been out here recently, though, or even in the last few years. No reason. When they bought the land, they built a new house. They never lived in this one the Englischers used to live in. It was a mess even then."

"Which makes it perfect for a hideout for a bunch of kids. Who would look for them on an Amish man's property?" Burke lowered the flashlight he'd commandeered. "I don't see any cars. We need to get in there."

"What makes you think it's kids?" Tony's teeth chattered. The boy needed a jacket. "It could be druggies or a homeless guy."

"Stealing mantel clocks and chess pieces?" Mary

Katherine snorted, a most unwomanly sound. "And how would you and Nicole know about it?"

"Because your friends from school did this." Burke knelt next to Tony. He elbowed him. "Admit it. Your friends thought it would be fun to hang out and drink beer someplace where no one would think to look—an Amish farm."

"They're not my friends, and they never invited me to do anything." Tony groaned. He smacked his forehead with the palm of one hand. "They'll find out I told you, and I'll have to move."

"Why take things from Amish folks?" The images of Bobby, Mark, and the other boys hooting and hollering in his restaurant paraded in Ezekiel's mind. What would they want with his teakettle or pot holders? "Why not take something they could use?"

"It's a game. Like an initiation. Get in the house, grab something to prove you were there, then get out without getting caught." Tony heaved a sigh. "It's sick, but it's like a thrill for them. They don't do drugs and they don't have money, so they can't be seen with a new camera or an iPad. Their parents would be like, where did you get that? This is totally for kicks. Totally for the high they get from breaking in."

"Nicole will be proud of you for doing this." Mary Katherine squeezed his shoulder. "I reckon she'll even go out on a date with you."

"You think—?"

"Let's focus." Burke started down the hill. "Let's find Sunny and get out of here. We'll call the sheriff afterward."

Ezekiel went first. Single file they tromped through overgrown weeds and mud to the barn. Tony took the lead at the bottom. The door creaked and groaned, sounds far too loud in the night. Ezekiel took the flashlight from Tony. Its stream revealed a large open space that must've been the living room with the kitchen at the far end. Five or six folded camp chairs sat in a half circle around an empty fireplace that held the half-burned remnants of several logs. Plastic sports-drink bottles, pop cans, beer cans, beef jerky bags, and an assortment of other junk-food trash littered the floor. The place smelled of dust, mildew, and burnt wood.

To one side the squatters had fashioned makeshift shelves using half-rotted planks and five-pound coffee cans. Ezekiel rested the bolt cutters on his shoulder and stared. A copy of *Martyrs Mirror* was propped against the wall. He touched the cover. Probably a wedding gift. Precious to its owners although it had no value to the thieves, who wouldn't understand the significance of seventeen centuries of Christian martyrdom from the time of Christ to AD 1660. Next to it lay a child's faceless doll. Some little girl was missing her favorite toy. Then the faded tumbling blocks crib quilt—Bess's family heirloom. Mary Katherine scooped it up and hugged it to her chest.

"You probably shouldn't touch that." Burke spoke up. "All of this is evidence. We'll have to call the sheriff."

Her expression stubborn, Mary Katherine backed up a step. "This belongs to Bess. She'll give it to her firstborn daughter, who'll give it to her daughter."

"She'll get it back, I promise." Ezekiel gently tugged

the quilt from Mary Katherine's arms. "Dan will understand."

The thieves thought these small items with no material value would mean nothing. True material things were not to be hoarded or given undue importance, like idols, but they meant something to their owners. Next to a black Sunday hat on the bottom shelf lay his pot holders, the teakettle, and his calendar.

"It reminds me of a museum." Burke stood next to Ezekiel. His face was hidden in the shadows, but his disgusted tone said it all. "A shrine to their thievery prowess."

A soft whimper grew into a whine and then all-out barking. Ezekiel broke away from the display and strode toward the padlocked door on the other side of the fireplace. The others were right behind him.

"Sunny? Sunny!" He snapped the padlock on the first try. "We're getting you out."

Talking to a dog like he was a missing child. Ezekiel didn't care. Sunny didn't deserve to be kidnapped and held hostage by some ornery, selfish teenagers.

Burke jerked open the door. Sunny tore through and leaped straight into Ezekiel's arms, knocking him on his behind. "Whoa, hey, hey." The dog stood on Ezekiel's chest and lapped at his face, his woofs mingled with the rough wetness of his tongue. Slobber dripped on Ezekiel's face. "Okay, you mangy mutt, that's enough."

"He missed you." Mary Katherine patted Sunny's head and scratched behind his ears. The dog's tail thumped. He planted a slobbery kiss on her hand. "He misses everyone, it seems."

"Let's get out of here." Tony stuck his hand on the

black hat. "I'll get this stuff."

"No, no, don't touch it." Burke pulled Ezekiel to his feet. "We need to get Deputy Doolittle out here."

"Deputy Doolittle is already here."

Ezekiel turned.

Dan strode through the open door.

"So am I." A scowling Freeman brought up the rear.

CHAPTER 34

The ride in the back of the Daviess County Sheriff's Office cruiser was much smoother, even if it did smell of dirty dog. Mary Katherine sneaked a glance at Ezekiel. He had one hand on Sunny's back as he stared out the window. He hadn't said a word since giving Freeman and Deputy Rogers an explanation of their presence at the abandoned farmhouse. Deputy Rogers was still interviewing Tony when Freeman directed them to go home and get some sleep. Poor Tony. His plan to get out of this unscathed had been shot to smithereens. At least now the kids responsible would be properly punished.

Mary Katherine hadn't been able to read Freeman's expression. Did he understand why they'd come with Tony to find Sunny? Did he understand the urgency? Did he care? Freeman was a good man. Surely he understood. That didn't mean he would excuse her participation in the late-night escapade.

Sunny's happy panting on the seat next to her made it hard for Mary Katherine to regret it. She collapsed against the seat and let the rushing of the dark night air outside the car, the crackle of the radio, and the murmur of conversation between the deputy driving and Burke in the front seat calm her.

"You have a right to be angry with me." She ventured a small chuckle in Ezekiel's direction. "But I hope you'll forgive me."

"In the first place, I could never be angry with you." Ezekiel's voice was low. His head turned from the window. He glanced at the two men in the front seat. They were discussing trout fishing in the Ozarks. Ezekiel leaned over Sunny, who grinned up at him. "Life with you would always be interesting. In the second place, none of this is your fault. It is the fault of a bunch of misguided, spoiled kids who need a trip to the woodshed and a few nights in the county jail to give them a taste of what life behind bars would be like."

Life with her would always be interesting. Was that a good thing in a Plain wife? Probably not. "I should've told Tony to go to the sheriff. I should've told Thomas and let him handle it."

Freeman had said as much before he'd asked if the deputy could give them a ride home with stern instructions not to be late to church in the morning. Morning was only a few hours away. "We'll talk about this later," he'd said, his tone ominous.

"Would've, could've, should've." Ezekiel let go of Sunny. His hand captured hers. It was warm around her icy fingers. "Your heart is always in the right place. Freeman will remember that. I'll remind him."

She wrapped her other hand around his. "I don't know how you can justify my actions. I can't."

"You were concerned for your family. You stepped out in faith. You did what you thought was right."

All those things were true. But Plain women didn't go gallivanting about the countryside at night with Englischers and a widowed man. She wasn't in her rumspringa. She was a sixty-year-old widow with ten grown children. She knew better.

Freeman's son had seen lights at the old house earlier in the evening and told his father. He called Dan Rogers. They'd been watching the place, waiting. After interrogating Tony, Deputy Rogers had decided to continue to surveil—as he called it—the house until the true perpetrators—again his words—showed their faces. According to Tony, they always came there to party after games. The next one was in a few days.

Tony wasn't completely off the hook, but Deputy Rogers seemed to believe his story.

The car turned into the drive that led to her dawdy haus. Thomas's house was dark still. He didn't know of her escapade, but he would. Soon.

Ezekiel's hand tightened around hers. "I'll tell him I plan to be responsible for you."

"You'll what?"

"Here we are, Mrs. Ropp." Deputy Seth McKenzie peered at them with serious amber eyes in the rearview mirror. He'd removed his hat when he got in the car, revealing a massive mound of curly brown hair that added at least an inch to his skinny six-foot frame.

"Somebody—probably Deputy Rogers—will be by to take your statement tomorrow."

She'd already given her statement to Deputy Rogers and Freeman. "I have church in the morning."

"Understood."

Ezekiel still held her hand. She didn't want to let go either.

"Walk her to the door, man." Burke's voice held a note of laughter. He didn't turn around. The deputy's deep, hoarse chuckle followed. "Good grief."

"That's not necessary." She tugged her hand free and shoved her door open. "Thank you for the ride, Deputy. Good night, Burke."

Ezekiel met her on the other side. Together they walked up the steps. She put her hand on the doorknob and looked up at him. "I am sorry."

"I've been thinking."

"You have?"

"I've been thinking about how much I like to read."

Odd topic of conversation for the predawn hours after a night spent running after thieves and a beloved mutt. "You never mentioned that."

"With Burke around the house always reading, I caught the bug. I'm halfway through *The Adventures of Huckleberry Finn*. It's slow going. Sometimes I read it out loud to Sunny, before he went missing. It was Burke's idea—*Huckleberry Finn*, not the reading aloud."

What was he trying to tell her, and why now? She glanced over his shoulder. The deputy had turned the car around so it faced the road. A mournful Sunny stared out the back window at them, his tongue hang-ing out of his mouth. "I'm not a big fan of Mark Twain."

"I can see why."

"Why are we talking about this now?"

"If you want to have a bookstore, don't give up. Keep praying for Gott's will." His hands cupped her cheeks. He kissed her so quickly she didn't have a chance to kiss him back. "Don't worry about Freeman or Thomas. Or anyone. You want adventure. I'll give you adventure."

"I don't want adventure."

Not anymore. It only got people for whom she cared in trouble.

He stomped down the steps. "I lieb you, Mary Kay."

The words floated in the air, sweet as lilacs and roses.

"Wait. Ezekiel. Wait."

He slid into the car and it took off, spitting gravel and dust in the air.

"I lieb you too."

CHAPTER 35

If all else fails, bake. Ezekiel checked the timer on the oven where two deep-dish dutch apple pies baked. Ten more minutes. He cracked the door and inhaled the heavenly scent. Apple pie smelled like a content marriage. The thought made him smile. Whimsy for a Plain man. That's what Mary Katherine would call it. Whimsy. A feeling more like nostalgia for something vaguely missed befell him. He breathed it in, welcoming it, and went back to kneading the dough for a double batch of whole-wheat rolls.

The bell dinged. He glanced at the clock overhead. Too early for customers. It must be Esther or one of the waitstaff. He held his flour-covered hands up like a surgeon ready for the operating room and glanced out the double doors of the kitchen.

Burke and Carina stood in the foyer. Burke had his back to Ezekiel. Carina said something. Burke nodded. She held out her arms. Burke stepped into the hug. She laid her head on his chest and Burke's arms wrapped around her. They stayed that way, not speaking. Ezekiel turned away. A private moment in a very public place. None of his business, for sure. He went back to his task and laid the dough in a bowl and covered it with plastic wrap.

The bell dinged again. A few seconds later Burke pushed through the swinging doors. "Morning."

"You were out and about early today. Your shift doesn't start for hours."

His face etched with the same private-property-keep-out warning as usual, Burke slid off his fleece-lined, red-and-blue-plaid jacket and hung it from a hook on the far wall. "I have a hankering to make pumpkin pie."

"It's a little early for pumpkin pie. Thanksgiving is still three weeks away."

"Maybe I'm thankful now."

Ezekiel laughed. "Thankful for Carina?"

"Carina's headed home."

Ezekiel stuck a mixing bowl and utensils under a stream of hot water in the deep sink. He added a squirt of Palmolive and began to scrub. Tiny soap bubbles floated in the air, reminding him of Liliana. She loved bubbles. "You're not going with her?"

"I like it here." Burke washed his hands in the adjoining sink and dried off. "I like my job."

"But you like her too."

Burke grabbed a bag of sugar and a large can of pumpkin from the shelf. "I do. She'll be back. Now and then." Surprise mingled with something akin to fear in the man's tone. Like Ezekiel, he wanted more but feared the consequences of that want. The possibilities of loss and hurt and pain that came with any opening up to another human being. "That's enough for now. All I can handle for now."

Burke wasn't leaving. Relief flooded through Ezekiel, and with it the knowledge that his plan might also be God's plan. He might be on the right track. Without being selfish. His plan would be a balm to Burke's wounds as well as his own.

"By the way, I've found a little place here in town. I put down first and last month's rent. And a pet deposit. I'll be getting out of your hair."

"You can't have Sunny."

"I'll get my own dog."

Company on long, dark nights had been good. The smell of coffee perking before Ezekiel got out from under the covers had been nice. The companionable silences, nice. "Gut. That's gut."

"It's not much. A one-bedroom duplex with a little patch of yard and not a stick of furniture, but I figure it's time. I've worn out my welcome a long time ago."

"Your company was welcome. But a man needs his own place, I reckon. Yard sales are good for finding furniture. And the Goodwill. There's something else I want to talk to you about." Ezekiel stood by the table and watched the other man work. A thrill went through him like a kid about to win the fifty-yard dash. The unknown awaited him. Even at his age, a man could want that. A Plain man could need that. "It's about the restaurant."

Burke dumped the can's contents into a mixing bowl with a cup of sugar. He added two eggs. "Everything okay?"

"I believe it is. I hope so." He moved to the other side of the table so he could see Burke's face. "I have liked working here all these years. The Purple Martin Café has been my home since my wife died. It's been good for me and for my family."

Burke's gaze met Ezekiel's for a second. It held understanding and compassion. "The Purple Martin is a testament to your resilience."

Ezekiel didn't know exactly what that meant. "I want you to have it."

Burke's hands stilled. "Come again?"

"You plan to stay in Jamesport."

"As far as I know."

"You like food. You're a good cook. You're good with people. This is your new experience."

"You want me to manage your restaurant."

"I want you to own my restaurant."

"I don't have the money to buy a restaurant, even if I thought it was a good idea."

"I think you can afford the asking price. One dollar and the promise that you'll continue to make it a place families come because it feels like home."

His mouth open, eyes squinted, Burke shook his head. He glanced around as if seeing the kitchen in a strange, new light. "I can't pay you a dollar for this place. It's worth—"

"It's worth a million good memories, but working around food all day isn't good for my diabetes. I'm passing it on to you so you can make your own new memories."

"That's not why you're doing this, though, is it?"

"This place is perfect for you. You can feed people physically and spiritually. You could call it Pulpit and Pie."

"I would never change the name. This will always be the Purple Martin. Is this about Mary Katherine?"

The oven timer dinged. Ezekiel donned hot-pad gloves and slipped the pies from the oven. The crumbled tops of the dutch apple pies were golden brown. The scent of apple and cinnamon made his mouth water.

"Those look perfect. Nothing like making pie you can't eat."

"Kenneth will be glad you're staying. He's to have surgery after the first of the year. Your company will help him recover faster."

"That's another thing I'll miss about being out at your place. That and the fishing." Burke chuckled. "And your hot cocoa."

"Maybe he could help out around here. Learn to cook. Work the cash register when he gets a little older. His mudder worries about what he'll do as a Plain man unable to do hard manual labor."

"If his parents agree to it, I'd be honored to have him as my apprentice."

"I'm thinking about getting into the bookstore business."

Burke measured ginger and dumped it into the bowl, but his grin said he was listening.

"I talked to Freeman about it."

"I'd like to have been a fly on the wall for that discussion."

Freeman had been kind, if a little bemused by Ezekiel's plan. Others might see a grumpy, picky man, but Ezekiel saw through that to the compassionate heart that always longed to do the right thing in God's eyes. A bishop's job wasn't easy. "He's a good man. A wise man."

"Who sees right through you and your plan for going into the bookstore business, I'm sure."

"Can you keep a secret?"

Burke snorted. "I was a chaplain."

"I'm getting married."

Burke whooped. "Does she know that?"

"Not yet. I wanted to get things squared away first."

"Consider them squared."

"I've made all these plans and still . . ."

"She'll say yes."

Ezekiel wanted that assurance. "How do you know?"

"She risked getting in trouble to help you get your dog back."

"So she did. Still—"

"Don't be a wuss." Burke chortled. "She's worth it."

"A wuss? Plain men are not wusses."

"Cowards."

"Nee."

"Nee. I guess I'd better learn some more words from Kenneth if I'm going to stay around here."

"He'll be happy to know you're staying." Ezekiel removed his apron and tossed it in the laundry basket on the back wall. "Can you hold down the fort?"

"Absolutely." Burke looked around as if his new station in life had begun to sink in. "Are you headed out to Mary Kay's?"

"Nee, I need to stop by the bookstore first."

CHAPTER 36

Two blue jays flapped their wings and took off with pecans in their beaks. Mary Katherine apologized for interrupting their dinner as she climbed down from her buggy. Bess and Aidan's white A-frame house with its wraparound porch looked so fresh and white against the cloudy autumn sky. Like it had a fresh coat of paint. The flower beds were empty, but Bess had placed an arrangement of pumpkins and gourds by the front door along with a small chalkboard sign that read WELCOME, ALL WHO ENTER HERE. The sight made Mary Katherine smile for the first time in days.

Clutching her precious package in her arms, she trudged up the steps. She had plenty of time to visit now. A quiet life suited to a Plain widow woman. Freeman hadn't used those words when he pronounced her sentence—that's the way she thought of it—but that's what he meant. Taking care of the boplin, canning, gardening, and dispensing kisses to boo-boos. A sweet life. One she welcomed. Her grandchildren entertained her with their pretend play and funny stories. Just the day before she'd played hopscotch and jump rope—if holding the rope counted.

She climbed into bed too exhausted to write.

But not too exhausted to think. She didn't regret anything she'd done. She didn't regret making that trip.

Sunny was only a dog. The teakettle was only a teakettle. Bess's crib quilt was only a crib quilt.

But the look on Ezekiel's face when he saw Sunny bounding from behind that door had been priceless. She'd shared that moment with him. Ezekiel had lost so much. He didn't need another loss, even if it was only a dog.

"You want to share more with him."

We need to say good-bye, Moses.

"It's about time."

I'll always miss you.

"I wish you happiness, Fraa."

Sweet dreams, Mann.

She began to hum "How Great Thou Art," under her breath at first, then louder.

After a few bars, she stopped. The silence was replete with emptiness. Her new quiet life had grown quieter. It didn't help that she hadn't seen Ezekiel in two weeks. She hadn't been near the Purple Martin. She didn't dare. Freeman and the others were watching.

She hadn't gone to the bookstore either.

She missed Dottie. She missed Ezekiel. She missed the Combination Store and Jennie's chatter.

So be it. She had no one to blame but herself.

She tightened her shawl around her shoulders and paused. Despite the sun, the air had a distinct chill to it. She shivered and knocked.

A few minutes passed. She considered knocking again. The door opened. Barbara smiled out at her.

"What are you doing here?"

Barbara pushed open the screen door. "I could ask you the same question. I thought you were confined to the dawdy haus."

"Hardly. Visiting is allowed." She had plenty of time for visiting. "Where's Bess?"

"In here." Bess's voice floated through the open door. "Feeding the bopli. Come in, come in."

Doing as she was told, Mary Katherine followed her daughter into the living room. Material was spread across a table near the front window, and the treadle sewing machine held pale-green material in its teeth. "Getting some sewing done?"

"Among other things." Barbara's tone was airy. "Bess is showing me how to make her recipe for stuffed cabbage. It's one of Joseph's favorite dishes when the weather's cold."

"Gut for you. So things are going better then?" Mary Katherine plopped onto the sofa and undid her shawl. It was a cozy room with a cheerful fire roaring in the fireplace. "No more sugar in the spaghetti sauce?"

"I took your advice and slowed down." Barbara held out a plate of oatmeal-raisin cookies. "Have one. I made them. They have pecans in them that I picked from the trees in our front yard. Joseph ate four of them for supper last night."

She looked so proud and so happy. What a difference a few weeks made. Those adjustments to a new, married life could be made. Love smoothed the way. Perhaps this was something Mary Katherine could learn from her often wayward but always well-meaning daughter. Despite a dismal appetite that had nothing to do with a physical ailment, Mary Katherine accepted her offering. She laid the cookie on a napkin on the coffee table and picked up her bag. "It looks so gut. No wonder he ate four."

"Taste it, taste it!" Barbara's face creased in a frown. "How do you know if you don't try it? Are you afraid it's inedible?"

"Of course not." Mary Katherine took a cautious bite and chewed. Soft, chewy, sweet, a bit of crunch in the pecans, just the right consistency. "Yum. These are delicious."

"Told you!" Barbara crowed in triumph. "I also made a banana cream pie that was perfect, and I did laundry without turning the whites blue. Joseph hasn't complained once in three days."

Three days. A milestone in what would be a long marriage of fifty years or more, God willing. "Gut for you, Dochder. I'm so happy for you."

"You should try it. I know I had doubts about you marrying again, but now I know it's what everyone—even old women—should do. I know Ezekiel didn't just stop at the house that day to make sure the thieves didn't get you. He's courting you, isn't he? You should—"

"Whoa! Hush. Courting is private. If there is any courting going on, which I'm not saying there is. Or isn't." Mary Katherine shook her finger at Barbara. A daughter did not give her mother advice on courting. Even if she finally had it all figured out, while Mary Katherine did not. "I'm on my way to have a visit with

Samantha and Dylan's kinner, but I wanted to make a quick stop here first. I have something for you, Bess."

"For me?" Bess shifted Leyla to her shoulder and began to pat. A gusty burp followed. "Gut girl. Her—not you, Mary Kay."

The three of them laughed. "Deputy Rogers was kind enough to allow me to return it. He knows how much these simple things mean to us." She unwrapped the crib quilt and held it out. "You'll want this for Leyla."

Bess's eyes filled with tears. She shifted Leyla to the other side and held out her free hand. "You're so sweet to bring it to me. You didn't have to go out of your way."

"Jah, I did. I wanted you to have it as soon as possible." Mary Katherine's crib quilt had gone to her eldest daughter, just as Bess's would go to Leyla. "He also returned my missing items. Including pieces of Moses' chess set. It feels gut to have them back."

Especially now that she had sent Moses away. The wood felt warm to the touch, just as he had.

"Little bits of our past." Bess laid the quilt in her lap and wrapped Leyla in it. "She has no idea right now what it means, but someday she will."

"I wish I had a quilt to give my bopli." Barbara gazed wistfully at Leyla. "I can't wait to have a bopli who needs a quilt."

"We'll make one. We'll start your tradition." Bess smiled at her friend. "Choose a pattern and we'll start making it next week. You'll have it in time for Christmas."

"Maybe I'll be expecting by then."

"Barbara!"

Her daughter grinned a cheeky grin so familiar Mary Katherine had to smile back. "Is that stuffed cabbage I smell? It's making my mouth water."

"Ach, I better check on it." Barbara jolted to her feet and scurried from the room.

Mary Katherine leaned back on the sofa and blew out a huge sigh. "Danki for taking her under your wing."

"You did all the work, bringing her up." Bess chuckled. "She's a gut girl. She just needs a little polish. You have your hands full."

"So do you."

"What are friends for?" Bess kissed Leyla's soft blonde curls. "How are you?"

"Embarrassed. Ashamed. Defiant. If had to do the same thing over again, I would."

"I reckon Freeman knows that. Which is why he's keeping you at home."

"Wouldn't you have done the same?"

Bess shook her head. "I've asked myself that question, but a person never knows what they would do at any given moment until they're in that situation. What it does tell me, though, is that you trust Ezekiel with your life. That's something."

"It is something." What, Mary Katherine wasn't sure.

"Something to ponder. Is Thomas still mad?"

"Jah. All of my suhs are."

"It only means they care."

"I know. I better get going." She popped from the sofa and dropped a kiss on Bess's kapp. "Danki for being a gut friend."

"Same to you."

"Tell Barbara I'll see her Sunday. I think Joanna is inviting them over for supper."

"I'll tell her. We'll have a frolic in a few weeks. We can start making Christmas presents."

Mary Katherine wanted to stay, but instead, she said her final good-bye and headed out to the buggy. Half an hour later she pulled into the front yard that once belonged to her and Moses. She spent most of the drive talking to God, thanking Him for Bess and for Barbara's progress as wives. One less thing to worry about. Not worry. She didn't worry. Not much.

The pecan trees in her front yard—now Dylan's front yard—were loaded. Samantha should get the kids out there to pick them before the birds carried them off. The house looked as inviting as ever. A trampoline graced the spot next to the picnic table. Dylan had strung a tire swing from the biggest sycamore tree. A small pony cart was parked outside the corral. Children lived here again. It was a good thing. She would spend a lot of time here, now that she'd been forbidden from working in town.

She trudged up the steps. Samantha could use help today with laundry, cooking, yardwork, and the sewing, just as Joanna could. While she was here, Mary Katherine could pick up the last of her things for the dawdy haus. Not that she spent a lot of time there, mostly to sleep. She lingered on the porch. Should she knock or go straight in? It wasn't her house, but she was the grandmother.

The door opened. Samantha peered through the

screen door. "Mary Kay. You're here. Why didn't you come in?"

Mary Katherine smiled at the tiny, wren-like mother of four. "I was just thinking."

"I'll come out and think with you. It's a nice day for that, isn't it?" She let the screen door clunk behind her and settled on the porch steps. Mary Katherine plopped down next to her. Samantha gave her a one-armed hug. "You look pooped. Are Joanna's kinner running you ragged? Mine are looking forward to story time. Annabelle has a new story she wrote just for you. It has cows and ponies and a green cat in it. I made snickerdoodles special for your visit."

More cookies. A person could never get enough of homemade cookies. "It sounds wunderbarr. I can't wait to hear Annabelle's story."

"They're out digging up the last of the sweet potatoes for supper. They'll be in soon." Samantha wrapped her arms around her knees and raised her face to the sun. "Change is hard."

"My suhs are still so peeved at me."

"They'll get over it."

"I'm not sure Freeman will."

"I've only heard bits and pieces. Dylan won't talk about it. He gets this aggrieved look on his face and stomps around if I bring it up."

Mary Katherine told the story. When she got to the part about getting in Tony's car to drive to Ezekiel's house in the middle of the night, Samantha gasped and put a hand to her mouth.

"He's a teenager. I know him." Mary Katherine talked

faster. Laura and Jennie had had the same response. Joanna too. "He's worked with Ezekiel for years. It wasn't any different than hiring a driver. And my reason for going to Ezekiel's was a gut one."

"You should see your face." Chuckling, Samantha elbowed Mary Katherine's arm. "If you really thought everything you did was okay, you wouldn't feel so guilty. I don't think it's the ride with Tony that you feel guilty about, though."

"Would you have waited? Or sent Tony there on his own?"

"I'd have gone to Dylan. You could've gone to Thomas." Mary Katherine sighed. "Jah."

"But then you would've missed out on solving the mystery. And almost getting arrested."

"We didn't almost get arrested. Freeman knew kids had been trespassing on his property. He saw tire tracks. He heard Sunny barking. He called Deputy Rogers."

"Instead of investigating himself."

"Jah. He said it was the safest thing to do. What we should've done."

"The thought of talking to a sheriff's deputy makes me cringe." Samantha flapped her apron so it hid her pretty face for a second. "You're much braver than I am. I'm glad I have a mann to take care of these things. I'd rather be in the kitchen husking corn and snapping green beans."

"It wasn't brave. It was foolhardy. At least that is the way Thomas and the other kinner see it. And Freeman."

"When Moses was here, did you speak your piece in public?"

It was Mary Katherine's turn to raise her face to the sun and study the oak tree branches that dipped and waved in the breeze. "Nee. I didn't have to. He spoke for me."

"He was a gut, kind man. A good mann too."

"He was. He always asked my opinion. Many times he abided by it."

"And when he didn't, you knew why."

"Usually he was right. I never told him that." She wished she had. "He made me feel like a gut mudder and a gut fraa, even without saying the words. Sometimes he went another direction when I would've flapped around like a chicken with my head cut off."

"Dylan is the same. You raised gut suhs with your mann. Suhs and dochders. That's what we're called to do when we marry." Samantha flapped her hand to ward off a buzzing horsefly. "I learned that from my mudder and from you. It's what we do. I'm content."

Mary Katherine smiled at her daughter-in-law's simple but oh-so-wise words. Dylan had done well in choosing his wife. She raised the children and cared for her ailing parents without a single complaint. "Where are your mudder and daed?"

"My schweschder Patti has taken them to her house in Seymour for the week. That way her kinner get a chance to love on them too. We're all taking turns. Come have a snickerdoodle. They're still warm." Samantha stood. "I packed up the things you mentioned at church this morning. I'll have the kinner run the boxes out to the buggy while you have a cup of kaffi."

Coffee sounded good. Coffee and lots of sugar. Mary

Katherine hauled herself to her feet. Pain shot through her hip. She rubbed it. "Just a quick cup. I want to help the boplin with their sewing this afternoon. Before story hour."

"The boplin aren't boplin anymore."

Samantha patted her belly in an unconscious gesture that made Mary Katherine smile. Her heart danced in celebration, even as she held her tongue. Her daughter-in-law was in a family way. Another grandbaby on the way. *Number twenty-eight, Moses.*

No answer.

It was a habit she would break. She would get used to that silence. A feeling like nostalgia at a well-worn memory slipped through her, its fingers trailing across her heart, a soft touch. The acutely aching pain where her memories of Moses resided no longer hurt.

Samantha put her hand to her forehead and squinted against the sun. "Someone's coming. Looks like Laura. I'll pour kaffi for everyone and fix up a plate of cookies."

She went inside, leaving Mary Katherine to walk out to meet the buggy. Laura parked and eased from the buggy with the care of someone who didn't want to cause herself further pain. "Joanna said I'd find you here. How goes it?"

"Gut. Why were you looking for me?"

Laura tugged a cane from the buggy seat and started in the opposite direction. "Walk with me."

They settled into the slow pace of two friends who walked often together and knew each other's limits. Laura tugged her shawl over her chest with her free hand. "Winter is just around the corner."

"You didn't hunt me down to talk about the weather."

"I came to see if you'd figured things out."

"What things?"

"Mary Kay."

She kicked at a rock on the dirt road. "I know I stepped outside the boundaries. I goofed."

"*Goofed* is one word for it. The real question is why." Laura's tone was tart. "Have you figured out why you did it?"

"To have an adventure I could write about."

Laura laughed the raspy laugh of a woman who fought allergies on top of painful joints. She stopped in the middle of the road. Mary Katherine paused, waiting for Laura to catch her breath. "You asked."

"You know better."

Mary Katherine started walking again, her gaze on the tiny plumes of dust kicked up by her well-worn black sneakers. "If you know so much, you tell me why I did it."

"I want you to admit it. You know. I know you know."

This was a ridiculous conversation. Mary Katherine reversed course and headed across the field toward the vegetable garden where Annabelle, Mattie, Sean, and Karen grubbed in the garden. Mattie looked up, waved, and held up an enormous sweet potato. "Groossmammi, look, it's huge!"

"Indeed. I see a beautiful sweet potato pie in our future!" She cupped her hand over her forehead and squinted in the sun. The children had four five-gallon buckets full of sweet potatoes. A few eggplants and red beets lay in the grass next to the buckets. One last harvest before a November freeze in a week or two. "Good job."

"Stop stalling."

"When Tony told me Ezekiel's dog might be out there, I knew we had to go. I had to tell him."

"Why not tell Thomas?"

"Because it was Ezekiel."

"Jah."

Mary Katherine studied the puffy, dark clouds building on the horizon. They promised rain by nightfall. "And I . . . we . . . we're . . ."

"We're not teenagers on our rumspringa. Spit it out."

"I think we are—were—courting."

"You think."

"I'm pretty sure."

"A woman your age should know."

"It's been a hundred years since you courted. You're one to talk."

"I'm not the one banished from town." Laura flung her free hand in the air to punctuate her statement. "You gave up working at the store or the library or the restaurant because of this."

"I felt strongly."

"It's apparent he does too, so what was keeping you apart?"

"Dreams."

Laura cocked her head, her eyebrows raised. "Come again?"

"My pride. My arrogance. My independence. I wanted what I wanted. It wasn't what he wanted. He has a right to put his wants first." Mary Katherine drew a long breath, then another. Hurling accusations that boomeranged and had to be caught took a great deal of energy. "He's the man. I got wrapped up in wanting something I couldn't have more than what was truly important. Now it's too late."

"The bookstore."

"He wants a fraa who will work in the restaurant with him. Not a woman who has her nose in a book and her head in the clouds." She inhaled, the scent of thunderstorm and wet earth in her nostrils. "He's right to want that, and now I know I want to be his fraa more than I want a silly dream."

"Sounds like you learned your lesson."

"Too late."

"Or maybe not."

Sometimes Laura's cryptic responses irritated Mary Katherine's last nerve. She stifled the urge to shout. "What?"

"Have you considered that maybe Ezekiel learned something from your actions as well?"

Men didn't learn as fast as women. "I don't think so. I haven't seen hide nor hair of him since that day."

"Maybe you should give him a nudge."

"Being forward is what got me in trouble in the first place."

"If you're truly ready to move on with your life, it's simply a matter of going about it in the right way. The old way."

The old way. The smell of hay and kerosene and boy sweat welled up in her. Singings some forty years ago. The heat in the barn and the sweet taste and feel of cool water on a parched throat. The sidelong glances. The held notes of old German hymns and newer English songs. "I'm too old for singings."

Laura lifted her cane and made swirls as if writing in the air. "Didn't you and Moses ever exchange notes? I know Eli and I did."

The old way. A note. A writer should send a note. It made perfect sense. "You're a good friend, Laura. How will I get it to him, though?" More importantly, what would she say? "I'm banished."

"Jennie and I can have lunch at the Purple Martin tomorrow. We'll make Leo watch the store for an hour. It's gut for him." Laura's voice held glee. The woman was a born matchmaker. "I promise not to sneak a peek."

"Do you think? Really?"

"I think it's worth a try. Life is short, as you and I know."

So short.

"I'll borrow a pencil and paper from Samantha." Mary Katherine whirled, suddenly in a hurry to get to the house. "Come on, slowpoke, get a move on."

"Only you would call an old woman with a cane a slowpoke." Laura cackled. "Go on, don't worry about me. I'll get there eventually. Sometime next year."

Her laugh, like wrapping paper crumpling around a gift, floated behind Mary Katherine as she raced toward the house and toward hope.

CHAPTER 37

The aroma of birthday wafted through the dawdy haus. Mary Katherine snatched a dollop of chocolate frosting and popped it in her mouth. "Mmm. Yum." Amazing. Something so sweet could be made without sugar. Humming, she wiped her finger on her apron. If one of the kids had done that, she'd swat them with a wooden spoon. Sometimes frosting was made to be stolen.

She stood back and admired her work. Two dozen frosted chocolate cupcakes in neat rows in a plastic container that had a nice carry lid with a handle. The frosting wouldn't touch the lid and stick. Satisfied, she looked around. The kitchen, on the other hand, needed some work.

A rap on the door told her she'd run out of time. She smoothed her apron and then her kapp. She heaved a breath and the ache blossomed into a flower waiting for sun and water. It stretched toward an endless sky full of possibilities. She closed her eyes for a second. *Thank You, Gott.*

Another rap at the door, this one louder. She rushed toward the door, then slowed, determined to have this new beginning the right way. She opened the door and smiled.

Ezekiel grinned back. For a man who'd spent the day working in a restaurant, he looked fresh and clean. He must've changed his shirt and washed his face. He held a package wrapped in brown paper under one arm. "I got your note."

"Gut."

"Laura left it on the counter with the money for her meal. I felt like we were in school again."

"I'm blessed to have gut friends."

"We both are." He looked over her shoulder. "Are you coming out or am I coming in?"

"You're coming in." She stood back and inhaled his scent as he passed. Soap with a faint touch of smoked hickory.

"I wanted to give you something."

"But I wanted to give you something first." She darted into the living room and whirled. "Sit. Sit."

"It smells gut in here. Like chocolate." He sat in the rocking chair they'd brought from the old house. The one Moses used to sit in to listen to her stories. No ache. Only the light of Ezekiel's questioning smile. "It's not my birthday."

She held out the gift, wrapped in a brown paper bag she'd cut up. He took it and held out his. "I guess we had the same idea."

She set his aside. "You first. Hurry!"

"Fine. Give me a second. You're as bad as the kinner." His fingers seemed all thumbs as he tugged at the paper. He slid them under the tape and worked it off.

"Just tear it."

"You're worse than the kinner."

He held up the cookbook. "*Fix-It and Enjoy-It Diabetic Cookbook. Stove-top and Oven Recipes—for Everyone!* by Phyllis Good." His eyebrows lifted as he pushed his glasses up his nose and examined the text on the back. "'Recipes everyone will like, even if they don't have diabetes.' I didn't think it would be possible."

"It has five hundred recipes. And the ingredients aren't weird or fancy like some of those cookbooks. Jennie bought it at Dottie's store." Her voice didn't even quiver. No envy. No longing. Just pleasure for her friend who had her dream. "It's perfect for a restaurant owner who loves to cook and loves food, but also has diabetes. It has everything. Even desserts. Cookies."

He thumbed through the pages. "Cookies?"

"You should do a little research sometime. Artificial sweeteners that can be heated work really well." She popped from her chair. "I know it for a fact."

She rushed to the kitchen and returned with a plate holding two cupcakes. "I guess it is a bit like a birthday. A new way of life. A new way of looking at food. A new start."

"A new way of looking at people." He took the plate and set it next to the cookbook on the table that held her notebooks and pencils. He stood. "Especially people like you. You're kind to do this."

"I would do it for anyone I care about." Now her voice trembled. She wasn't afraid anymore. She was certain. She needed Ezekiel in her life. Dreams were dry crumbs in a person's mouth without the right person with whom to share them. She swallowed. She wanted his hands to touch her. She wanted his arms to hold her. She wanted him to tell her about his day and ask about hers in the cool dusk of evening at the supper table. "That's not exactly right. I mean it's right, but—"

"Open mine."

Her turn to be all thumbs. She ripped the paper off. "*Small Business for Dummies.*" Puzzled, she ran her fingers over the yellow-and-black cover. Confined to the country, she was the last person on earth to need this book. "Are you saying I'm a dummy?"

"Nee." His fingers touched her cheek. "But I do have something to tell you. To ask you."

"Don't you want to try the cupcake? It's sugar free." Her heart a painful drum in her chest, she brushed his hand away. "I have something to tell you too."

"Let's wait to have the cupcakes. They'll taste better when . . . when I know where I stand. May I go first?"

She wanted to know where he stood—they stood—too. "Jah."

"I'm retiring from the restaurant business."

"You're closing the restaurant?" She let the book fall into her lap. "Because of your kinner? Are they still pressuring you? You're not old. You like your work. It's gut work."

"I'm not closing it. I gave it to Burke."

The beauty of the idea sank in. "Are you sure?"

"He'll always be a chaplain. He's simply found a new mission field. I suggested he change the name to Pulpit and Pie, but he said it will always be the Purple Martin Café."

"You're not doing this for me, are you?" The question sounded so grandiose, so full of it, she gasped at her own audacity. "Forget that, I didn't mean—"

"Not for you, exactly. For my kinner and the little ones. For Kenneth. For the life that's left in me." He stepped into her space. "Life is work. Work is life. But we shouldn't use it to hide from people or because we're afraid of being hurt."

Mary Katherine studied the lines on his face. Laugh lines, hurt lines, loss lines. A road map of his life so far. Laugh lines should outrun the others. They should run in all directions. "What about Carina?"

"She's gone. Burke says she'll be back now and then. I hope for his sake she will." His hand gripped hers. "You said you had something to tell me."

It was hard to think with his fingers around her wrist and his future so wide open. "I don't know what to say now. I-I-I—"

He sat down and pulled her into his lap, his arms around her shoulders. "Breathe."

"You're not helping." He was so close and warm and alive. Her body turned into a waterfall. She heaved a breath and leaned her head on his shoulder. "What I have to say doesn't make sense now."

"Try me."

"I had it all planned out. I would cook in the restaurant. We could add some sugar-free pies and cakes and puddings to the menu. The cookbook has everything. There are lots of cookbooks too. Jennie looked them up for me at the library. The bookstore is going to carry some of them."

"The bookstore you wanted."

"Dottie's bookstore. I'm content with that. That's what I wanted to tell you. I don't need a bookstore. I don't need anything. Just you."

"It's funny. I came to tell you I don't need a restaurant. I don't need anything. Just you."

"Not funny. Perfect."

"I also came to tell you Freeman has given me permission to enter into business with Dottie."

The words fell into a heap at her feet, then rearranged themselves so she could comprehend them. "You're going into the book business?"

"I'm hoping *we're* going into the book business."

"What do you mean?"

"This is the way I explained it to Freeman. He would no longer have to concern himself with a certain widow. I would be responsible for her because she would be my fraa. We would work together with Dottie to make the store a success."

Breathing was no longer possible. The enormity of his plan, the enormity of his caring, the enormity of his willingness to embrace her wants, made it impossible for Mary Katherine to breathe, let alone talk.

She opened her mouth. No sound came out.

"Mary Katherine Ropp speechless. That has to be a first." He smiled, his eyebrows lifted in a question. "I hope it's a gut one."

Praying the tears would behave themselves, she nodded. She heaved a breath. *Get a grip, Mary Katherine.* She swallowed. "Dottie agreed?"

"Dottie is over the moon about it."

God's overwhelming grace swept over her. She managed a shaky smile. "I don't recall being asked to be anyone's fraa."

His arms tightened. His chin nuzzled her kapp. "How do you feel about a dawdy haus and kinner running everywhere and digging sweet potatoes in the fall and picking walnuts and reading me your stories on cool fall nights?"

She shifted so she could look directly into his eyes. "It sounds wunderbarr."

His face hovered over hers for a few seconds. Their lips met. The new silence in Mary Katherine's head filled with possibilities. Stories yet to be told. Giggles over silliness yet to be invented. Pies and chamomile tea with fresh lemon yet to be squeezed. Discussions of life's oddities yet to be wrangled.

"Are you sure you'll be happy?" He leaned back and stared into her face. "No voices in your head?"

"Only the one begging me to eat that chocolate cupcake."

He snatched one from the saucer and held it out to her.

"You first."

He took a big bite. His eyes rolled back. A hum like a cat's purr came from deep in his throat. Frosting decorated his lips and crumbs nestled in his beard. He chewed and grinned. "That is gut."

She returned the grin and dusted the crumbs from his beard. "I'm so glad you like it."

He offered the sad remains to her. She shook her head. "I want my own."

"Are you afraid of my germs?"

"Ha." She kissed him quick and hard square on the lips. "I don't think so."

He shifted so he could set his cupcake back on the plate and present her with the pristine, lovely one. She reached for it. At the last second he whipped it to his mouth and took another big bite.

Mary Katherine giggled and smacked his shoulder. "How could you?"

Frosting on his cheek now, he grinned as he chewed and swallowed. "I couldn't help myself. They are so gut."

She tucked his face between her hands and drew him in. "Life with you will be sweet." She kissed his lips and tasted chocolate, butter, and the joy of a new dream. His lips promised her a new story every day for the rest of her life. "I lieb you."

He smiled. "You'll marry me then?"

"I'm sitting on your lap, Ezekiel Miller."

"True. I lieb you too." He dropped a kiss on her forehead. "When?"

"Life is short."

"Then we'll talk to Solomon tomorrow."

Their new story, written in love and second chances, had begun.

EPILOGUE

S he might be wrinkled, gray, and a little stoop-
shouldered on the outside, but on the inside Mary
Katherine was twenty again. She'd done all this before. Yet it was new and special and like a wonderful
dream on this late November day. How could it not be
different? Her ten children and twenty-seven grandchildren sat—or wiggled—in the congregation that
filled Thomas's barn to the rafters. Her parents were
no longer with her. But they knew. Somehow, they
knew. Dottie sat on a bench next to Carina. Burke kept
Kenneth and Ezekiel's other grandsons company on
the men's side. Her friends and family joined together
to dedicate and celebrate a new beginning for Ezekiel
and her as a married couple.

Mary Katherine's insides quivered. Her legs trembled. *Please, Gott, don't let them collapse under me. Just
a few more minutes.* She clasped her hands in front of
her to keep her fingers from plucking at her apron.
Tears threatened. The faint scent of hay and manure
grounded her. Her legs steadied. She glanced at Ezekiel,
standing next to her with his sons, John and Andrew,
as his witnesses. His lips turned up ever so slightly. His

warm almond eyes behind dark-rimmed glasses encouraged her.

She focused on Freeman and his sonorous voice. Did she promise to take care of Ezekiel in sickness and in health as fitting a Christian wife? At their age, that was a given. And with Ezekiel's diabetes. She'd have to smack his hand if he tried to sneak a piece of the regular wedding cake. She'd made a sugar-free one especially for him. "Jah."

Did they promise to love and bear and be patient with each other and not separate from each other until dear God shall part them from each other through death? At twenty, that question had been so simple, so easy, because death had seemed a far, far speck in a distant future. At sixty, she'd shed any naïveté about the possibility—the near certainty—of the sudden cataclysmic void caused by the death of a loved one. A person could not love without risk. True love welcomed the risk. Better to risk it all than live with the deeper void of no love at all. "Jah."

The making of the vows ended. They returned to their seats. Blessings were offered. They knelt with the rest of the congregation and prayed.

It was over. And just beginning.

"Do you feel different?" Barbara beamed down at her. "How funny it feels to know I've been married longer than you have."

"Help an old woman up." Mary Katherine's insides had stopped quivering, but her hip and back hurt from sitting on the bench for the three-hour church service. "I still have more experience."

"Maybe so." Barbara grabbed Mary Katherine's arm and pulled her to her feet. She leaned closer. "But I reckon I still can do something you can't."

She glanced around, then patted her belly. Laughing, she scooted toward the door, dodging guests left and right. "I'm a server. I have to get inside before the tables fill up."

She took off before Mary Katherine could confirm. If Samantha carried number twenty-eight then Barbara's would be number twenty-nine. More joy. She listened for a split second. No voice in her head shared the happy news with Moses. He knew. He didn't need her updates. As Laura, Bess, Jennie, and the others descended on her with hugs, happy tears, and congratulations, she sought to find her new husband. Across the room Ezekiel was ten deep in men offering man-pats and similar words delivered in gruff voices. She smiled at him over Jennie's shoulder. He grinned and shrugged.

Two hundred-plus wedding guests, and what she really wanted was to take a walk at sunset with her new husband, Sunny running circles around them. Or to sit on the front porch, her sewing in her lap, and watch him peruse the newspaper for tidbits that made him laugh aloud and read them to her. She wanted to make coffee and argue with him about whether he was allowed a teaspoon of sugar in it.

He wasn't.

Until death do us part. She would take whatever time God gave them, but she would also take good care of Ezekiel. God expected that too.

"Come on, come on, let's get inside." Jennie tugged at her arm. "You have guests to greet."

"But—"

"To the eck, to the eck." Laura pushed from behind. "We have work to do."

"Is everything ready?"

"Don't you worry about a thing." Bess brought up the rear. "Your dochders learned well from you."

Five daughters. Five weddings. And helping the brides' families for her five sons. She could coordinate a wedding in her sleep. "Are you sure there are enough pies? We could send Angus to the bakery in town—"

"Hush." Laura pushed harder. They carried her along across the yard and into the house. The tables were decorated with white linen. Every place was set with a Styrofoam plate, silverware, and a glass. Dylan and Thomas's boys served as water porters and were busy filling glasses as guests swarmed the chairs. Mary, Ellen, Beulah, and Barbara marched through the aisles, carrying trays filled with roast-chicken casserole, mashed potatoes, rolls, fruit, Jell-O salad, coleslaw, pickled beets, and much more in their hands.

How many brides had their daughters organize their weddings? Their sons serve as ushers? It should be bittersweet, but it wasn't. It was lovely. Mary Katherine slipped into her seat at the corner wedding party table. Laura patted her shoulder. "I'll fix a plate for you."

"No hurry. I couldn't eat a thing."

"I could." Ezekiel loomed over her. "I'm starved. This marriage business is work."

A quiver of concern ran through Mary Katherine. It

had been a long morning. A long time since breakfast. "You need to eat."

"Here we go, mudder bird." He laughed and settled into the chair next to her. "I'm fine. I ate a gut breakfast. Leah was anxious this morning and fixed a huge spread. Eggs, bacon, toast, a small glass of juice. She even sent a peanut butter sandwich with me, just in case. No jam, in case you were wondering."

A good daughter. A good daughter-in-law.

Under the tablecloth Ezekiel's hand squeezed hers. Mary Katherine squeezed back as she studied his face. His eyes were clear. The laugh lines around his eyes and mouth were in full display. "How are you?"

"Eager to be alone with my fraa." He ducked his head. "Those are words I never expected to say again."

"I was just thinking the same thing. With my mann, I mean."

"Look at the happy married couple!" Dottie sailed toward them, both hands in the air, an enormous smile on her face. She'd donned a pink Western-style dress and brown cowboy boots for the occasion. Her rhinestone earrings sparkled. "Hugs, hugs, I need hugs."

Mary Katherine obliged. If Dottie felt any pangs of sadness on a day that surely reminded her of her loss, it didn't show in her expression. She radiated joy for a friend's good fortune. "Now you two take some time, honeymoon at Niagara Falls or someplace. I don't expect to see you at the bookstore this next week. I've got it covered."

They were still finding their way in this brand-new partnership. Mary Katherine more than Ezekiel, who still worked with Burke, teaching him the restaurant business. Every day was a blessing and an adventure. "Plain folks don't take honeymoons."

"No, but they take vacations. Take one. You two deserve it." She kissed Mary Katherine's cheek and trotted away. Her high Texas drawl floated over her shoulder. "I'm serious. If you show up at the store, I'm throwing you out with a swift kick in the seat of the pants."

No doubt she could.

In her wake appeared Burke, followed by Carina. She wore an emerald-green tea-length dress that made her tawny skin luminous. "Best wishes to the bride and groom." She held out a small brown paper–wrapped package. Burke, who'd chosen a black suit not so different from his Amish friends, did the same to Ezekiel. "Come on, open them. At the same time."

They obliged. Two quick rips and Mary Katherine held a book entitled *Don'ts for Wives, 1913*, by Blanche Ebbutt. Ezekiel's was identical, except for one word, *Don'ts for Husbands, 1913*.

"The advice is a hundred years old, but it's still good." Carina slipped her hand through the crook of Burke's arm. "It's really sweet too. They're reprints, of course."

"We figured you could use advice. You might have been married about seventy years between the two of you, but you're both out of practice." Burke's fingers slid between Carina's and their hands clasped. "Plus, you're both hardheaded and stubborn and set in your ways."

"Look who's talking." Carina's laugh was deep and contagious. "Mr. I-can't-visit-Virginia-I'm-too-busy."

"Sorry about that. He's a quick learner, but there's a lot to learn in the restaurant business." Ezekiel patted the book. "And thanks for this. It's very . . . thoughtful."

"Don't be sorry." Carina's laughter died. Sudden emotion touched her eyes. "Actually, I wanted to thank you for saving his life. You gave him something to live for."

"A person doesn't live for a restaurant." Ezekiel glanced at Mary Katherine. His smile held unspoken words. "Don't let him tell you otherwise. We'll train an assistant manager and Burke will have no excuses."

"It's not an excuse—"

"Hush." Carina put a finger to Burke's mouth. "Let's find our seats and let these two celebrate."

Still engaged in good-natured bickering, the two turned and disappeared into the milling crowd.

"What do you suppose is going on there?"

Ezekiel's gaze followed their friends. "Something good I hope. Something that can overcome distance and lingering despair."

Before Mary Katherine could respond, Nicole approached, Tony behind her. The girl had donned a simple blue dress that set off her beautiful peaches-and-cream complexion and deepened her gray eyes to pewter. It touched her knees and had long sleeves. Very modest. Tony looked like a scarecrow in an ill-fitting gray suit. He fidgeted with too-short sleeves but managed a grin. They were cute as could be. "Congrats, Mr. E., Mrs. M."

"You made it. We're so glad you could come." Mary Katherine hadn't been sure they would. That they were together was a perfect wedding gift. "Was it horrible sitting through three hours of talking in a language you don't understand?"

"We were late so we missed some of it. Tony's car wouldn't start. Again." Nicole pushed her hair from her face in a self-conscious gesture. "It was very interesting. Different. I would want flowers and a ring though. Definitely a ring."

Tony cleared his throat. "Yeah, like how do people know you're married to each other?"

"We know." Ezekiel shrugged and patted his chest. "In here. That's what counts."

"It's different." Tony's hand went to Nicole's elbow. Her cheeks turned a deep scarlet, but she didn't move away. Tony grinned. "This is like visiting a foreign country."

An Amish wedding or trying to figure out girls? He could be referring to both. "You should get something to eat." They were both beyond skinny. The mother in Mary Katherine wanted to fatten them up. "There's cake and pie and cookies."

"Did you hear about Bobby, Mark, Logan, and the other guys? Even Trevor got arrested." Tony's voice cracked in his excitement. "All they got was community service because you guys didn't press charges. I don't get that."

"We don't get involved in the legal system." Ezekiel didn't sound concerned over the leniency of the athletes' punishment. "The coach meted out his own punishment, with the sheriff's help. I reckon it's enough being seen picking up trash along the highway wearing those orange vests. Not to mention everyone knowing what they did. No need to have it on their records."

"No kidding." Nicole glanced at her phone. "My mother texts me every two seconds now. She's so sure I'll get into trouble just because they did."

"But you won't."

"Nope. It's not worth it." She turned to Tony. "Let's get cake. I want chocolate."

"I'll get it for you."

"You don't have to wait on me."

"You do enough waiting on people at the restaurant." Tony put his arm around her shoulders. The crowd swallowed them up.

"Now's our chance." Ezekiel jerked his head toward the door. "Let's go."

"We can't."

"Five minutes."

Mary Katherine looked around. Family and friends talking, laughing, hugging, enjoying the moment. It might work. "It's worth a try."

They slipped out the door, across the porch, and into the yard, without a single person questioning their headlong flight. "Hurry!" Ezekiel sounded breathless—from laughter.

They dodged behind the barn and halted, more because neither could breathe from laughing than because of exertion. A chilly wind blew through Mary Katherine's thin cotton dress. Clouds scudded across the sky and hid the sun. She shivered and wrapped her arms around her middle. "They'll realize we're gone in two seconds."

"So get over here." Ezekiel tugged her into his arms. The chill fled. "I've been thinking about this all morning."

"Ezekiel! You mean during those sacred vows, you were looking at my lips?"

"Nee, but right after the amen part."

Mary Katherine giggled and snuggled in his warm arms. "I feel . . . full of feelings."

"Young, old, certain, uncertain, foolish, wise, experienced, inexperienced."

"Exactly."

"I feel like Gott is so gut." His embrace tightened. "He's given me a gift."

His lips met hers in a kiss that left no question how he felt. Years of loneliness, years of determined acceptance of their lot in life, years of looking back for fear of what lay ahead, disappeared. Replaced by anticipation of time shared, of knowing they would face the future as one body knitted together by the vows they'd taken before God and family.

The kiss ended. Breathless, warm, her heart ricocheting against her rib cage, Mary Katherine stared up at her husband. "I lieb you, Mann."

"I lieb you, Fraa."

Never had those words, imbued with such hope and second chance, been sweeter.

"Mary Katherine! Ezekiel!" Kenneth's high, little boy voice carried on the stiff November breeze. "Laura says your food is getting cold."

"I think we've been found." Ezekiel's grip didn't

loosen. "The food may be getting cold, but I'm not." He kissed her again. A soft, lingering kiss full of promise.

As Kenneth's urgent voice moved closer, they drew apart and went to embrace their new life.

DISCUSSION QUESTIONS

1. Can you imagine yourself serving a meal to a man who broke into your house in the middle of the night? Why or why not? Do you think Mary Katherine, alone in the house with no phone, did the right thing?

2. Mary Katherine not only allows Burke to stay in her barn, she takes him to the Purple Martin Café to get him a job. What example does she set for Christians? Do her actions remind you of Jesus' treatment of the poor or lost? What does it mean to have a heart that breaks for those who are less fortunate?

3. Mary Katherine's son Thomas wants her to live with him so he can keep an eye on her and keep her safe. His desire to control her life comes from love. The Amish respect their elders and care for them without the aid of Medicare or nursing homes. How does Mary Katherine respond to his actions/attitude? How should she respond? How do we balance our desire to help people with respecting their desire to be independent?

4. Burke's daughter died of leukemia. His wife committed suicide. He is having trouble believing that God is good or can work for his good in "all things." Has there been an event in your life that shook your faith? Were you able to overcome your grief and anger to grow closer to God? How did you do it? If not, do Burke's words of wisdom resonate with you?

5. Barbara is having a hard time adjusting to married life. She comes home to her mother to escape. What do you think she should be doing?

6. Kenneth's friends include him in their play and games. How is that different from the way children with physical or mental disabilities are often treated in mainstream society? The Amish believe their "special" children are gifts from God. What can we learn from that attitude?

7. Burke blames himself for his wife's suicide. Have you ever blamed yourself for someone else's actions? With hindsight it's possible to know a great deal more than we do before something horrible happens. How do we reconcile our feelings with the reality that we are not in control and that God does have a plan, even when it doesn't seem possible?

8. Second Corinthians 1:3–5 says God is the God of all comfort. He comforts us in our times of grief and loss so we can provide that same comfort to others. Do you believe that the difficult times you have experienced are preparing you to minister to others in their time of need? Did your sorrow bring

you closer to God? How do you feel about having your character honed through painful experiences? What kind of person would you be if you never had difficult times?

9. Do you believe there's only one true love for you in this life? How do you feel about finding The One a second time? Is it possible? Why or why not?

10. Mary Katherine and Ezekiel were both willing to give up their dreams in order to be with the other person. They both took steps to help the other reach for those dreams. How do their acts of self-lessness make you feel? Could you or would you do the same in a similar circumstance?

ACKNOWLEDGMENTS

I have so much for which to be thankful. The support and kindness I receive from readers never ceases to amaze me. Your prayers for my writing and my health have given me great comfort as I continue on this journey. Thank you for reading my stories.

I'm thankful for my agent, Julie Gwinn. You made the transition to a new agent so much easier by your boundless enthusiasm and energy. Your kindness is deeply appreciated.

At the risk of sounding like a broken record (you remember what those are, right?), again I thank my editor Becky Monds for seeing the forest while I'm stuck in the middle of a bunch of trees. Your unerring sense of story never ceases to amaze me. I'm blessed to know you and to work with you. That also goes for the HarperCollins Christian Publishing team that works so hard to produce, promote, and sell these books.

My thanks to Julee Schwarzburg, my line editor for all my books with Zondervan. There's a certain rhythm a blessed writer is able to establish with editors who dig down into the nitty gritty of stories—to grammar, word repetition, number of children and grandchildren, whether a term is one word or two, whether a number is written out or appears as a numeral. I'm all over the place when it comes to style and consistency. I'm the most repetitious writer ever. I make the same mistakes over and over from book to book. And I'm having so much fun writing, I forget to pay attention to details. Which is why you are such a blessing, Julee. What's more, you are kind and gentle in your presentation of my waywardness. I've had snarky editors, and having someone make jokes at the expense of your baby is no fun. Thank you.

As always, I owe a debt of gratitude to my loving family, especially my husband, Tim, who puts up with me.

Thank You, Jesus, for placing all these people in my life. Every blessing comes from You. Thank You for the opportunity to write for You.

Read more Kelly Irvin in the Every Amish Season series!

Need something sweet?
Pick up *An Amish Picnic!*

*AVAILABLE IN PRINT, E-BOOK,
AND DOWNLOADABLE AUDIO*